Sign up for our newsletter to hear
about new and upcoming releases.

www.ylva-publishing.com

Other Books by A.L. Brooks

The Long Shot
Write Your Own Script
One Way or Another
Up on the Roof
Miles Apart
Dark Horse
The Club

Never Too Late for Heroes by A.L. Brooks
(The Superheroines Collection)

Dare
to
Love

A.L. Brooks

Acknowledgements

Thanks once again to the team at Ylva for all their work in bringing another novel of mine to life.

Big thanks to my wonderful beta readers, Katja, Erin, and Amy, and to Cari for the extra read-through at the end.

And an enormous thank-you, with a big bow on top, to my editor, the editor-in-chief herself, Sandra Gerth. Oh wow, did you ever push me on this one! But thank you so much for your guidance, your patience, and all the things you taught me throughout this process. I owe you so many ice creams…

Lastly, a few words for anyone who has picked up this book because they, too, are questioning their sexuality. Know that if and when you are ready, there is a wonderful community waiting to welcome you in. Follow your heart; you won't regret it.

Chapter I

"You want to do *what*?" The cappuccino in Carmen's hand wobbled precariously as Felicity's words sunk home.

"You heard me." Felicity sipped from her own coffee, then put her cup down on the table.

"And you're only just telling me now?"

"I've been thinking about it for a while." Felicity grinned. "I want one before it's too late."

"It appears our definitions of 'too late' are very different."

"Oh, sweetheart, don't be like that. *Loads* of people have them!"

"Yes, they do." Carmen held up a finger. "When they are much younger and their bodies don't have the—" She caught herself just as Felicity frowned.

"No." Felicity's eyes narrowed. "I don't think you want to finish that sentence."

Carmen shook her head. "You're right, I don't." She paused. "But... really?"

"Carmen, I love you, but sometimes you can be a complete stick-in-the-mud. I'm not ancient—I'm forty-four!"

"I know, and I didn't mean to imply you were ancient. But, well, isn't it a bit of a cliché? I mean, a middle-aged woman who's just divorced husband number two and—"

"*Middle-aged*?" Felicity screeched.

Several heads in the café turned.

Carmen's ire rose. She gave everyone a wave that she hoped suggested they could turn their attentions elsewhere and glared at her friend of over twenty years. "I apologise. But you do know what I mean."

Felicity huffed and sipped her drink once more. She blew out a loud breath as she lowered her cup. "I suppose so. But I'm still going to do it. You only live once."

"Well, that brings up yet another aspect to this. Isn't it awfully dangerous?"

Felicity snorted. "They use a needle, Carmen, not a carving knife."

Carmen rewarded her friend with a withering stare, which was blatantly ignored. "I know that, but don't you have to be concerned about the transmission of diseases if the needles aren't clean?"

"Of course—if you go to some backstreet, unlicensed hack. Funnily enough, I don't plan to do that."

"But how will you know if they're safe?"

"Carmen, please, give me some credit. I've researched! I know exactly where I'm going." Felicity cleared her throat. "The appointment is at eleven."

"Eleven? You mean *today?*" Carmen stared at her. "You didn't think to mention that when you invited me for coffee this morning?"

Felicity did have the grace to blush. "Well, yes, I may have left out that little titbit of information. But I want you with me! And I thought you might not come if I told you what was going on. Please, darling, I want to do this. And if nothing else, I'd value your opinion on the design."

"I… But… You…" Carmen stopped talking since she was clearly incapable of forming complete sentences.

Felicity leaned forward and patted her hand. "Close your mouth, darling, you look like a fish. And drink up; it's nearly time to go." Her eyes shone with excitement.

Carmen downed the last of her cappuccino, knowing there was no point in arguing any longer.

Ten minutes later, they stood outside the tattoo studio.

"Okay." Carmen turned to Felicity. "I'm only going to ask this one last time. Are you sure?"

"I am."

Carmen looked at the studio frontage and read aloud the name emblazoned on the window. "Phoenix Tattoos."

The banner was, she had to admit, artfully done, with a small image of a phoenix placed between the two words, which themselves were stylised flames in a wide range of oranges, reds, yellows, and gold. The window was tinted, so she couldn't see inside, but the exterior of the studio was spotlessly clean and the wood-framed door was polished to a beautiful shine.

Okay. Not a total cesspit, then. Maybe Felicity *had* researched properly.

Felicity let out a small squeak that Carmen hoped came from excitement. "Come on." She grasped Carmen's arm and pulled her up the step.

The inside of the studio was as surprising as the outside. The tattooist's chair sat towards the back of the room, centred on a shiny, cream-tiled floor and surrounded by stainless-steel counters. On top of those stood plastic boxes of all sizes, clearly labelled and organised into neat rows. Nothing was out of place, and everything looked immaculately clean. It was more like the kitchen of a fancy restaurant than how Carmen would ever have imagined a tattoo studio to be.

At the entrance was a small desk. To the right was a waiting area decorated with two large brown leather sofas which sat opposite each other on what looked like a real wood floor. A low table between the sofas held a selection of magazines and large folders. A water cooler took up one corner of the room and a machine for making hot drinks the other.

Wow. This looks nicer—and cleaner—than my doctor's waiting room. Carmen's preconceived notions about tattooists were diminishing by the second.

"Be with you in a second!" a velvety voice called from somewhere beyond the tattooist's chair.

A woman? The tattooist is a woman? Carmen sat on one of the sofas. *Well, why not? God, and you call yourself a feminist.* She shook her head at herself.

"Are you okay?" Felicity's brow was furrowed.

Carmen sucked in a breath. "I am. Just berating myself for walking in here with a bunch of preconceptions that I really should have known better about."

Felicity's smile was smug.

Carmen ignored her and reached for one of the folders on the table, intrigued as to what they contained. Her eyes widened as she flipped through the pages. Every page—or rather, plastic wallet—contained a beautifully drawn template for a tattoo design. There were mythical creatures, symbols, animals, plants, landscapes, cars, motorbikes, and every single one was drawn with an attention to detail that was incredible.

"Oh, wow." She'd come to a drawing of a phoenix, a copy of the bird that adorned the studio window. Up close like this, she could see the feathers and colours in all their glory; somehow the artist had even managed to capture the glint of triumph in the phoenix's eyes. "God, these are so good."

"Thanks."

Carmen snapped her head up; she hadn't heard the woman approach.

"Hello." The woman held out a hand. "I'm Ash."

Carmen stood and returned the handshake. "Hi, I'm Carmen."

"And I'm Felicity."

Felicity and Ash also shook hands, and Ash smiled. "Ah, you're my eleven o'clock."

Ash looked to be a few years younger than Carmen's forty-three, though it was difficult to tell—her skin was smooth and young-looking, but slight creases around her brown eyes told a different story. She was about the same height as Felicity, so perhaps 5'6". Her dark brown hair, shaved at the sides but left longer on top, flopped down to a loose, mind-of-its-own fringe. She wore a plain red T-shirt over black jeans. To Carmen's surprise, no tattoos adorned her arms. Another preconceived notion fled.

"That's me!" Felicity sounded like a giddy little girl. "How does this work?"

Ash gestured her back onto the sofa. "First, we have a chat about what you'd like." She sat next to Felicity, then looked across to Carmen. "Are you getting one too? I only have Felicity's name in the book, but—"

"No!" Carmen's response came a little too quickly, and she grinned sheepishly at Ash's raised eyebrows. "Sorry, I didn't mean that how it sounded." She exhaled. "I'm her moral support. As if she needs it."

Felicity snorted. "She's tagging along because I asked her to. I do actually value her opinion on the design."

"Okay, that's fine." Ash turned back to Felicity. "So you said when we spoke on the phone that you have a design in mind?"

Carmen liked Ash's voice—it was calm and gentle, but it was more than that. Her natural tone was easy on the ear, just a hint of her background— east London or maybe Essex, Carmen would guess—showing through. At the same time, it definitely didn't sound as if she was trying hard to cover up her roots. And while that meant her voice contrasted widely with both Carmen and Felicity's more upper-class accents, Ash didn't seem remotely bothered. *Nor should she be.* Carmen had lost count of the number of young actors, both male and female, she'd counselled over the last fifteen years for trying to hide where they were from with ridiculous put-on accents.

"I do." Felicity rummaged in her handbag and pulled out a folded piece of paper. "I was hoping for something like this." She pointed at all the folders on the table. "I know you have your own designs, and I hope it isn't too cheeky to turn up with my own, but—"

Ash held up a hand. "It is totally okay to turn up with your own. Those designs in the folders are there as inspiration, but I'm always excited when a customer knows exactly what they want. It sounded pretty simple when we spoke last week, but I just need to take a look at it to see if it's something that can be rendered by tattoo. Not everything can, okay?"

"I understand."

Felicity handed over the slip of paper.

Carmen watched as Ash unfolded it and studied it in silence. She seemed very serious about her work, and Carmen's respect for her climbed another notch.

"Okay, yes, this is definitely something I can do and in the timeframe we talked about. But first, some questions. Colour?"

"I'm happy with just black. I don't think it needs anything else."

Ash nodded slowly. "I think you're right, but I'd suggest adding a little grey shading here and here, just to emphasise it."

"Oh, that sounds good."

Carmen craned her neck to look at the picture. Although Felicity had briefly shown it to her in the café a few minutes earlier, she was intrigued by Ash's shading suggestion and how it would work.

Ash seemed to be aware of Carmen's movement; she twisted a little in her seat and turned the paper towards Carmen.

"Thanks," Carmen said, and Ash smiled.

Carmen stared at the picture, impressed once more with Felicity's choice. The piece of paper had been cut from a magazine and held a photoshopped black-and-white image of a small bird escaping a dark cage and heading up towards the sun above it.

With this second, longer viewing of the picture and with the knowledge of all that Felicity had gone through in the last few months, sudden realisation dawned. Carmen gazed into Felicity's eyes. "This...this is you, yes?"

Felicity, blinking rapidly, nodded.

"It's perfect." Carmen held out a hand, and Felicity took it. She squeezed it tightly for a moment before letting go.

"Okay," Ash continued after a second or two, clearly sensitive to the moment and earning yet more unspoken appreciation from Carmen. "Next question, where?"

Felicity sat upright and placed a hand on her left hip. "Here."

"Good, that area is a great choice. There's more fatty tissue there."

"I do hope you're not calling me fat." Felicity arched an eyebrow, but her eyes gave away her tease.

Ash's mouth quirked. "I would never." She tapped Felicity's leg. "It's just that you won't feel too much discomfort on a more, um, padded area."

Felicity looked relieved, and Carmen realised that for all her bluster, her friend was a little nervous.

"And finally, what size? Just like this"—Ash pointed at the picture—"or smaller? Bigger?"

"What do you think?"

Ash looked back at the picture for a few seconds. "I think this size is fine. Any smaller and I won't be able to get some of the detail in. And I don't think larger would have the same impact."

"Perfect."

"Ready to get started?"

For a moment, Felicity hesitated, then she straightened her shoulders and smiled broadly. "Hell, yes."

Ash chuckled and stood. "All right. Follow me. Want a drink of something? Tea? Coffee?"

"Just water would be good."

"I'll get that." Carmen stood, glad of an excuse to do something useful.

"That's great, thanks."

Ash smiled at her again, and Carmen noticed for the first time what an attractive face she had. It was striking, with a strong jawline and a slightly wide forehead. But her deep brown eyes and full lips softened those edges, and Carmen smiled as she wondered just how many admirers Ash had to beat off in any one day.

Would it be prejudicial of me to assume those admirers were mostly female?

It seemed obvious Ash was a lesbian or queer by some definition. Carmen could just imagine Maggie, her go-to person for knowledge of the queer world, tutting at her about judging based on stereotypes. She grinned as she headed over to the water cooler.

While Carmen poured out two cups of water, Ash directed Felicity into the chair. When Carmen joined them in the tiled part of the room, Felicity was reclined on her right side, her left hip upwards. Her skirt had been pulled down just far enough to expose the area that would be worked on.

"Are you sure I've left you enough room?" Felicity asked. "I can easily pull the skirt down further. I'm not shy about these things."

Carmen snorted. "That's true." She placed the water cups down on one of the counters.

"Shut up."

Ash chuckled. "Well, okay, a little further would be good. I have towels to cover anything else that's revealed, if you're uncomfortable."

"I'm fine." Felicity tugged the skirt down further over her hips.

"That's great, thanks." Ash moved Felicity's left arm back. "Let's just tuck that under there for now. If you get cramped or tired, just shout and we'll take a break, okay?"

"Okay. How long will it take?"

"It shouldn't take longer than the hour you've booked. We'll do thirty minutes first, unless you want to stop earlier, then have a break."

"Thanks."

Carmen watched in fascination as Ash pulled on latex gloves, then set up her equipment and prepared Felicity's skin for the tattoo. All the while she explained what she was doing and why. Everything was sterilised, and all of the inks and needles were in single-use packages.

"It's like going in for an operation." Carmen pointed at everything lined up on the table.

Ash nodded. "Exactly. I'm basically creating a small wound each time the needle enters her skin. So I need to take the same precautions anyone in the medical community would."

After completing her preparation, Ash reached for the tattoo machine, which looked like some kind of ray gun from a bad sci-fi TV show. She carried out a dry test with the gun on Felicity's skin, probably assessing how it would feel, before loading it up with the ink.

"Ready?" Ash asked.

Felicity nodded enthusiastically, and in the next moment the loud buzz of the machine filled the air.

"And remember, no matter how tempting it is, don't pick at the scabs!" Ash's face was stern.

Felicity saluted. "Understood!"

Carmen shook her head. "I'm sorry, normally she *is* a grown-up."

"Trust me, I've had worse." Ash threw them a sly grin. She showed them to the door. "Ladies, it's been a pleasure. Enjoy the rest of your day."

Carmen smiled up at her. "Thank you, Ash. This has been a wonderful education. I really admire the way you work." She meant every word—she couldn't remember the last time she'd watched someone at their work and been so impressed.

To her surprise, Ash blushed. Up until now, she'd seemed so laid-back and unflappable. "Thanks, that's…that's nice of you to say."

Felicity shook Ash's hand. "I second what she said. If I ever decide to get another one, I know where I'm coming."

Ash grinned. "I'd say there's a very good chance we'll meet again. They're addictive, you know."

"So I've heard."

Carmen stared at Felicity. That was Felicity's flirting voice; she'd know it anywhere. *What the…?*

Ash's grin widened, and she held open the door. "Bye. For now."

Felicity threw her a stunning smile, then sauntered from the shop.

Carmen stumbled after her. When the door closed behind them, she said, "What the hell was that?"

"What?" Felicity feigned innocence, swinging her handbag strap over her shoulder.

"Don't give me that butter-wouldn't-melt look. You were *flirting* with her!"

"Perhaps I was." Felicity laughed and looked up at the sky. "Gosh, what a glorious day!"

Clearly, she wasn't going to get anything more from Felicity on the subject, so Carmen dropped it. But it wasn't forgotten. Later, over lunch, she'd get to the bottom of this.

Felicity slipped her arm through Carmen's and tugged her down the street. "Come on. I'm starving. Let's go somewhere nice to celebrate. And I think we need champagne too!"

Carmen laughed. "All right, Ms 'I've got my first tattoo'. Let's celebrate."

Chapter 2

THE SMELL OF BURNT TOAST woke Ash on Sunday morning. Then swearing reached her ears from the kitchen area, and she chuckled. Her niece clearly hadn't yet mastered the art of making breakfast. Although her cursing was coming along nicely.

Ash pushed back the duvet and climbed out of bed. She dressed in casual clothes and made a quick trip to the bathroom. When she walked into the kitchen, Sophie was busy scraping the burnt bits off a slice of toast into the bin.

"Morning," Ash said.

Sophie spun round, eyes wide. Ash noted the dark circles beneath them and realised that wasn't the first time her niece had looked so ragged in the last few weeks. "S-Sorry, Auntie Ash. Did I wake you?"

"Not really. I was just dozing. Everything okay here?" She pointed at the toast.

Sophie blushed. "Um, no. Your toaster's a bit fancy, and I kind of didn't know what I was doing."

Laughing, Ash walked over, took the piece of toast from her hand, and launched it into the open bin. "Let's try this again. You sit at the breakfast bar, and I'll do the toast."

"Can I make you a cup of tea first?"

"That would be magic."

They set about their tasks in comfortable silence, moving with ease around each other.

"Jam?" Ash asked as she added two more slices of lightly browned toast to the pile on the plate.

"Got any Nutella?"

Ash laughed. "Definitely not. I'd weigh a ton if I had that in the house. It's jam or nothing."

Sophie sighed. "All right. Jam."

"Cool. It's in the fridge. Top shelf."

Sophie retrieved the jar of strawberry jam and brought it over to the breakfast bar. They munched the pile of toast Ash had made and sipped their tea.

"You look a bit tired. Didn't you sleep well on the sofa bed?" Ash asked after a while.

Her niece wouldn't meet her eye. "No, it was fine. What time are we going out?"

Well, that was a deflection if ever I heard one. But she'd cut Sophie some slack. She was fourteen, after all.

"Whenever you like. I need to shower first."

"Yeah, me too."

"Well, you go first, and I'll have another tea while I wait. I bet you take ages anyway."

Sophie stuck out her tongue but headed for the bathroom.

Ash's phone pinged, and she glanced at the screen. Another notification from the dating app. Online dating wasn't Ash's thing, but a woman she'd met at a party recently had insisted this app was different. She scrolled to it and opened the alert. Her heart lurched. *No way.* The woman looked so much like Vikki, Ash couldn't close the alert quick enough. Before she could overthink it, she deleted her profile and uninstalled the entire app. It wasn't as if she was in a hurry to date anyway—or lacking in offers. She smiled as she remembered the very flirtatious behaviour of that woman, Felicity, yesterday after her appointment. Clients often flirted with Ash; sometimes she was even tempted to follow up on it. But not with Felicity. Sure, she was definitely beautiful, but she'd worn just a bit too much make-up for Ash's liking. She'd actually found Felicity's friend Carmen far more attractive. Despite the posh accent, she had a more natural, wholesome look. More real.

Yes, but she is clearly straight. And we don't do straight women, do we?

She finished her tea, then retrieved her book from the bedroom and slouched on the sofa, reading. As expected, she had a decent amount of reading time as Sophie did indeed take an age. Eventually, however, Sophie appeared looking much fresher than she had earlier, wearing ripped jeans with a Princess Leia T-shirt, her long, blonde hair brushed and shiny.

"Finally." Ash rolled her eyes in an exaggerated fashion.

Sophie laughed as she flopped onto the sofa beside her. "What you reading?"

"Nothing you'd be interested in." Ash smirked. "It's a lesbian romance. All swooning femmes and tough butches."

To her surprise, her niece flushed bright red. Sophie had known Ash was gay since she was old enough to form words. It had never been an issue, and her reaction now was baffling.

Before Ash could say anything, Sophie leaped from the sofa.

"You okay?" Ash asked.

"Yep. Forgot my phone. Be back in a sec." She shot off in the direction of the bathroom.

Ash shook her head. As much as she and Sophie got on well, these past few months her niece had been a bit of a mystery. *Remember, she's fourteen. They're all like that at that age, aren't they?*

When Sophie returned to the living room, Ash headed off to the bathroom. To her pleasant surprise, she wasn't greeted by a room that looked as if a tornado had ripped through it. *Huh, so in that respect, she isn't like most fourteen-year-olds.* She showered, dressed, and styled her hair. As she exited the bathroom, Sophie was perched on the edge of the sofa, Ash's book in her hands.

"Hey, I'm not sure that's age-appropriate," Ash called. The novel contained some of the steamier sex scenes in her collection of lesbian romances.

Sophie jumped as if she'd been shot, and the book flew across the room to land with a loud *splat* on the floor beside the breakfast bar. She whirled round, her cheeks a vivid red.

"Hey." Ash walked over to her, hands held out. "It's okay. It's just, you know, got some adult content."

Sophie bit her bottom lip. "I...I know. I-I read some of it."

Oh crap.

"Er, right. Well, just don't tell your mum, okay? And, um, maybe stick to books more for your age."

A.L. Brooks

Sophie shuffled from foot to foot; her gaze darted to the book and back again. "What if…what if that's the kind of book I want to read?"

Her voice was so quiet, Ash had to strain to hear it. When the words registered, she nearly fell over from the shock. "I… What?" *Surely she doesn't mean what I think she means. Does she?*

Sophie was shaking.

Ash strode over and gently took hold of her shoulders. "Hey, are you okay?"

Her niece shook her head, and tears pooled in her eyes. "I need to tell you something."

"Okay. Want to sit down?" *I need to, even if you don't. I'm not sure I'm ready for this.*

Sophie nodded and practically collapsed onto the sofa.

Ash opened her arms, and her niece came willingly into a hug. She tucked her head under Ash's chin, and her tears dripped onto Ash's collarbone.

"Hey, come on. Whatever it is, you know you can tell me, okay?"

Sophie sniffed. "I know. You're the one person I can tell. But it's still hard to say it."

Ash waited her out, holding her close.

Sophie still shook but not as badly as before. "I…I think…" She wiped at her eyes. "No, I know it. I…I like…girls." She whispered the last word, but Ash heard it loud and clear.

Oh. My. God. was her first thought. Her second was: *Shit, Courtney's gonna go mental.* "You do?"

"Yeah." Sophie finally looked up at her. She was biting her bottom lip, her eyes wide, as if somehow expecting Ash to have a negative reaction to her announcement.

"Well, thank you for trusting me with that."

Sophie's smile was wobbly, but her eyes said it all; relief shone through them. "I-I've known for a while. I just, you know, wasn't sure."

"But now you are?"

"Yeah. Pretty much. I mean, there are some boys I still like. They're cute, I suppose. But it's… Girls are just different, you know? They…make me feel different."

"Well, you know I understand that."

13

Sophie spat out a laugh. "Yeah, well, that's why I'm telling you and not Mum."

Ash couldn't say a lot to that. "What about Trina, does she know?"

"No! Nobody else. Not yet." Sophie looked as if she'd rather jump into an ant nest than tell her best friend about her sexuality.

Trina definitely had her head screwed on right, and Ash wished Sophie would trust her. But maybe one day soon she would.

"Okay, fair enough."

Sophie hugged her closer. "Thanks. I knew you'd be okay with it."

"Of course."

And I am. But what the hell is going to happen when her mother finds out I knew long before she did?

Chapter 3

Sorry, something's come up. Friday instead? Dinner at Georgio's, 8pm? x

Gerald's last-minute cancellation would have annoyed Carmen if she was any kind of "normal" girlfriend. But their relationship had never been conventional, so it didn't surprise her when her main reaction was one of relief. Her day had been long—in fact, she was still at her desk, and it was past seven in the evening. Realising that she now didn't have to retouch her make-up, change her blouse, and slip into her going-out heels made her ridiculously happy. *Pyjamas and a glass of wine, here I come.* She fired off a quick text in return.

Fine by me. See you then x

Forty minutes later, she was home, a bottle of wine open, her business suit exchanged for soft yoga pants and a T-shirt.

She sank into the sofa and put her feet up on the coffee table. *Oh yes, that's better.* Her first sip of wine made her moan, the second elicited a sigh. *Much better.*

Her phone rang, and she groaned. *God, no, I'm done for the day!* She glanced at the caller display anyway, unable to break the ingrained habit despite her exhaustion. When she saw the name Tamsyn Harris, her mood lifted, and she quickly answered. "Hi, Tam!"

"Hello! Have I caught you at a bad time?"

"No, not at all. Just got home. I have my feet up and a glass of wine in my hand."

Tamsyn chuckled. "Sounds perfect." She cleared her throat. "So, um, Maggie and I were wondering if you were free to visit us tomorrow evening at any time."

Why did her star client, the winner of multiple acting awards and one of Britain's best-loved actresses, sound nervous? "You okay? You don't sound yourself."

"I'm fine. More than fine." She paused. "So, are you?"

"Am I what?"

"Free tomorrow evening."

"Oh! Sorry. Hang on, let me check." Carmen tapped into the calendar app on her phone. "Okay, my last meeting finishes at seven thirty. I'm bound to have a few more bits to do after that, so I could be at yours perhaps eight thirty."

"That's absolutely fine."

"Do I need to bring anything? Is this a work meeting?"

"No. God, no. We just… Well, there's something we need to tell you."

"Is everything really okay, Tamsyn? You're acting very odd."

Tamsyn laughed. "God, sorry. Yes, everything is fine. We'll explain when we see you, but honestly, it's nothing to worry about."

"Well, okay, then." Carmen was mystified, but she'd known Tamsyn long enough to trust her when she said everything was fine. "I'll see you tomorrow."

"I'm sorry I'm late," Carmen said as Tamsyn opened the door. "I don't know where the time went."

"Come on in." Tamsyn stepped aside to allow Carmen to enter the house. "And you're not that late. Don't worry." She led her through to the living room and motioned her into a seat on the sofa.

Carmen gratefully relaxed into it, and every muscle in her body sighed with relief. Another thirteen-hour day with no breaks. Had she eaten at all during the day? Probably. She wasn't hungry now, so that meant she must have found time for something.

"Maggie's out walking Gizmo before bedtime. She'll be back soon." Tamsyn moved to the centre of the room. "Sorry, when you were a little late, we couldn't wait as the poor little bugger would be holding on too long."

Carmen chuckled. "Look at you, Tamsyn Harris, all domestic and everything."

Tamsyn blushed to her roots. "Shut up."

"I'm only teasing. I think it's wonderful."

The sound of the front door opening reached Carmen's ears, and seconds later, Gizmo trotted into the room. He rushed straight up to her and leaned in for an ear rub.

"Well, hello there, young man. How were the streets tonight? Did you make sure we're all safe?" Carmen lavished some serious attention on the gorgeous little dog, and he lapped it up.

"He did," Maggie said as she entered the room.

Carmen extricated herself from Gizmo's attention and stood to give her a hug. "Hi."

"Hello, you. Long time, no see."

Carmen pulled back from the embrace. "I know, I'm sorry."

Maggie smiled, then turned to Tamsyn and gave her a lingering kiss.

After pulling back from their embrace, Tamsyn walked over to a small table on which stood a bottle of champagne in a cooler and three glasses. Carmen hadn't even noticed that so far. *Wow, my brain must be really fried to miss champagne right in front of me.*

"Are we celebrating something?" she asked. "Or is this just your regular Thursday night champagne?" She smirked when Tamsyn rolled her eyes.

"Ha ha." Tamsyn finished pouring the three glasses and handed one each to Maggie and Carmen. Tamsyn and Maggie shared a look that Carmen couldn't decipher as they took each other's hand.

"So, we asked you over because we have an announcement." Tamsyn paused and seemed to be collecting herself. Were those tears she blinked back?

Maggie leaned in to Tamsyn. "Want me to say it?"

Tamsyn visibly swallowed. "No, I can do it." She turned back to Carmen. "We're getting married!"

"Oh my God, that's fantastic!" Carmen rushed over to them both.

Mindful of their champagne, the three of them shared a clumsy hug.

"That's just the most wonderful news." Carmen was genuinely happy for them. Delighted, in fact. Their story was almost a fairy tale, and she couldn't have wished for a better ending for them both.

Once again she wondered just what she and Gerald were doing, playing at being in a relationship when it was nothing of the sort. It didn't help that everyone else she knew in her age bracket was either engaged or already married. She pulled away from the hug and ensured she had a smile on her face when she met their gazes. "So, when and where?"

"September 26th," Maggie said. "And at the cottage."

"Oh, I love that! It's perfect!"

"Will you come?" Tamsyn asked.

"Of course! Wouldn't miss this for the world." Carmen grinned. "Tamsyn Harris saying, 'I do', and to a *woman* at that. I assume you're not inviting the Daily Mail?"

"Ha bloody ha. No, we're not. In fact, none of the press are invited, and Tony's hiring a top-notch security firm to make sure no one attempts to trespass."

"Good!" She gazed at them. "God, I'm so pleased for you both!"

"Thank you." Maggie gave Carmen a warm smile. "And I'm glad you could pop over tonight. We wanted you to be one of the first to celebrate with us. After all, you played a major role in making sure this could come to pass."

"Oh, that was nothing. Well, nothing much once I'd got this one to admit she had a heart." Carmen thumbed in Tamsyn's direction.

"Whatever," the actress said.

Maggie chuckled.

Tamsyn raised her glass in a toast. "To Carmen. Friend first, agent second." Her brown eyes were filled with affection, and Carmen's cheeks heated. "I will be forever grateful for what you did two years ago, my friend. Thank you for teaching me that there was definitely more to life than a career and for helping me bring this amazing woman back into my life." Tamsyn turned her gaze to Maggie, who took her hand and brought it to her lips to kiss.

The depth of love between the two women was like a living, breathing entity holding space in the room, so palpable Carmen could almost reach out and touch it. She shivered as an intense wave of longing washed over her.

After a few moments, Tamsyn seemed to remember there was someone else in the room, her blush adorable as she looked back at Carmen. "Um, sorry. Where was I?"

"Thanking our friend." Maggie threw Carmen a warm smile.

"Oh yes." Tamsyn held out her glass, and Maggie followed suit.

Carmen clinked hers against theirs, and they drank.

After a couple of sips, which gave Carmen time to compose herself—her emotions were all over the place after what she'd just witnessed—she raised her glass. "To the greatest love story I ever heard. Long may it continue."

Tamsyn's eyebrows rose; Maggie let out a soft "oh, my," and Carmen smiled even as she still fought back mysterious tears that wanted to spill down her face.

She focused with all her might on tapping each of their glasses and sipping some more of the delicious vintage.

Tamsyn and Maggie stared at each other over the rims of their glasses, once again lost in their love. The purity of what they shared touched Carmen in so many unexpected ways, and she couldn't begin to fathom what was happening to her. She never felt things like this. For years now she'd been all business, focused on her career, not fussed about things like love and emotion. And yet what these two friends had together seemed to be releasing something in her she didn't know how to deal with: envy and longing. She was happy for them, of course, but a deep ache for what they had burned in her chest. Sadness filled her and set her tears free.

"Carmen!" Maggie set her glass down. "What's wrong?"

Carmen waved her off when she would have approached. "Nothing." She wiped at her eyes. "I'm just so happy for you both."

Neither of them looked convinced, but it seemed they respected her need to pretend that was the only reason for the tears.

Tamsyn motioned her towards the sofa again.

While their backs were turned, Carmen dabbed her eyes some more and swallowed down the rest of her emotions. *Shit, how embarrassing!*

"So, I assume work has been full on again?" Tamsyn asked once they were all seated.

Shooting her friend a grateful look for the change of topic, Carmen relaxed back into the sofa. "Yes! But all good. Well, mostly. I have one or two difficult clients, but nothing I can't handle."

"I bet." Maggie raised her glass in Carmen's direction.

"Ooooh, anything you can share?" Tamsyn asked.

"Absolutely not." Carmen gave her a smile. "But believe me when I say that I've spared the British public from a couple of TV disasters waiting to happen."

"Your country will never know how much it owes you."

"This is very true."

Now back on an even keel, Carmen opened up a little about her week. She would never name names; she always respected every celebrity's need for privacy, no matter how obnoxious or difficult she herself found them.

Tamsyn was on a long break before the wedding—and delighted about it. It was something that still took some getting used to for Carmen, given how much of a workaholic her biggest client had been for so many years.

"I still want you to let me know if any juicy new role for me comes across your desk," Tamsyn said. "But it needs to be *really* juicy to tear my attention away from the wedding planning."

Maggie patted Tamsyn's arm. "You'd think we were getting married in Westminster Abbey. It's a hundred people in our back garden."

Carmen laughed. "Yes, but she's won BAFTAs, don't you know? It has to be done *just right*."

"Do you two want me to leave the room so you can talk about me without the inconvenience of me being here?" Tamsyn said archly, but there was a smile in her eyes.

"Oh, no, where's the fun in that?" Maggie batted her eyelashes in feigned innocence.

Once again it struck Carmen how at ease Tamsyn and Maggie were together. The casual playing and teasing and all of it wrapped in a layer of warmth, love, and affection that was impossible to miss. *Have I ever had that? With Lewis, yes,* she mused, *but that was a long time ago.*

"Oh, and who will be your plus one?" Tamsyn asked. "Gerald, I presume?"

Carmen startled, then sipped her drink to give herself a moment to respond. "I suppose so. I mean, I would need to ask him, so as long as he doesn't have plans for that date already…"

Of course they would think she'd bring Gerald. Although their relationship was less than conventional, they *were* a couple in the eyes of everyone they knew. Tamsyn and Maggie had met him a couple of times, and they'd seemed to like him well enough. Yet somehow, the thought of taking him to something that special felt…off. As if it didn't quite fit the picture.

"Lovely," Tamsyn said, and for the first time in all the years Carmen had known her, she knew without a doubt that Tamsyn was one hundred per cent acting when she said it.

Chapter 4

"Hɪ." Cᴀʀᴍᴇɴ ᴅʀᴏᴘᴘᴇᴅ ᴀ ᴋɪss on Gerald's cheek before sliding into the seat opposite him. "I'm sorry I'm late."

He smiled good-naturedly, his blue eyes crinkling. "No worries."

He looked, as ever, very put-together this evening. His suit, one she didn't remember seeing before, was beautifully tailored, a dark charcoal grey that contrasted well with the pale blue shirt. She supposed he was handsome—other people had told her he was, but she'd been attracted to his calm and quietly amusing personality, not his looks. Certainly, he was easy on the eye, she thought as she found herself looking at him properly for the first time in months.

Their waitress definitely seemed to think so too. When he flashed her a wide smile, she fumbled handing him the menu.

"You look very nice." Gerald cast a quick look over Carmen's blouse. "I've always liked that colour on you."

The colour in question was a deep green, which Carmen knew did match well with her blonde hair. She'd made an extra effort tonight, having forced herself to go home first to change before dinner. It had been tight, time-wise, hence her being a little over ten minutes late for their date. But as ever, Gerald seemed to let such things wash over him, and his compliment made the effort worthwhile.

She nodded at him by way of thanks, but his gaze had already returned to the menu.

"I've been craving seafood all day," he said. "Care to share a platter with me?"

"Actually, I'd rather not. I've been really looking forward to having a steak."

He glanced up. A little twist to his mouth told her he was unhappy, but after a moment, he merely said, "Fine. I'll have the gambas. That should suffice."

There was something about the word *suffice* that lodged an uncomfortable sensation deep in Carmen's gut. He was compromising, which everyone needed to do now and then in any relationship. It shouldn't bother her because this was something they did quite often when they dined out or chose a movie to watch or a play to see. Somehow, this time, it didn't sit right with her. Not that she would change her mind about the seafood platter. But his use of the word *suffice* resonated with all the other thoughts she'd been having the last few days about their relationship.

And especially since she'd seen how connected Tamsyn and Maggie were.

"You're frowning," he said.

She blinked and realised her gaze had drifted. Once she focused on him again, she smiled brightly, determined to push her unsettling thoughts away. "Was I? No idea why." The lie slipped easily off her tongue but only added to her inner tension rather than helping to diminish it.

Dinner passed in an uncomfortable blur. Carmen was distracted by her thoughts and could only muster the bare minimum of conversation. Gerald seemed at a loss as to how to fix it.

But it's not his problem to fix. It's mine.

When they left the restaurant, Gerald held out his arm for her to hook hers through, and they strolled down the street in a silence she didn't find at all comfortable. Five minutes later, they reached the corner where they would have to make a decision as to whose home they were heading for.

I don't want to go home with him. Why?

She could blame tiredness, and it wouldn't be far from the truth. It had been one heck of a week again. She could also blame her period; it was due in a few days. But actually, she became hornier the closer her period got, so that couldn't be it. She pursed her lips and kept her head turned away from Gerald. She thought back on their evening, on how...bland...it had all been. There was never any drama or surprises with Gerald; she always got exactly what she expected from a night out with him.

"So, your place or mine?" Gerald gave her arm a slight tug to bring her round to face him.

"I…" She swallowed. "Do you mind if we just call it a night? I'm sorry, but I'm very tired."

Carmen surprised herself in finding the words, and it was obvious from the look that crossed Gerald's face that he was equally taken aback.

"Of course," he said, although another frown marred his handsome features. "Well, I'll walk you home anyway. It's getting late."

She wanted to say no to this too, wanting to just be by herself, but that would have seemed churlish. "Thank you, that would be lovely."

It took six or seven minutes to reach Carmen's house. Another walk completed in total—and awkward—silence. By the time they approached the last few yards, her stomach was in knots. It felt big, as if something fundamental was shifting between them. While one part of her wanted to let it run its course, the rest of her worried about what it all meant and where they would be when they said goodnight.

"Here you are, safe and sound." Gerald's voice sounded falsely amused, as if he had to make a big effort to sound casual.

Carmen breathed deeply before turning to him. "Thank you, I appreciate it."

He stepped closer and gave her a small smile. "Look, I'm not sure what's changed, but it's obvious something has. You haven't been you for a couple of weeks now."

Oh God. In all of her recent internalised wonderings, it had never occurred to her that he would be this astute. She stared at him. He was so nice. Why wasn't it enough?

"Is there someone else?"

"No! Definitely not. It's… I don't know." She sighed. "Somehow, lately, what we've got doesn't…" She shrugged. "I can't explain it."

"Perhaps I have become rather complacent? I have been busy, but maybe if I make a little more effort, could we—?"

"I don't think so," she said gently. "I think I would feel this way no matter what."

"And how *do* you feel?" His gaze bored into hers. "What exactly are you saying?"

An image of Tamsyn and Maggie popped into her head. Pieces of the puzzle clicked into place, and everything was clearer.

I don't have that. Not with him.

And I want it.

But not with him.

Her stomach calmed, and a strange sense of peace washed through her. "You're a wonderful man, Gerald. We've had a wonderful time. But I…I'm not in love with you, and I never will be. It isn't fair to either of us to keep doing what we're doing when I know that."

"I see." He took a step back and ran a hand through his hair. "Well, then I suppose that's it." He gave her a lopsided smile. "I've never known if what I felt for you was truly love. I'm not good with those sorts of feelings. But I do know that I'm very sad for this to be ending." He gave her a small smile. "But I thank you for the way you've handled it and for being so honest."

Somehow it didn't help that he was being so nice about it, and Carmen scolded herself for thinking it. Would it be better if he was shouting and angry? No, of course not.

"Thank you, for being so understanding." She raised up on her toes to kiss his cheek.

He said nothing, simply looked at her for a long moment, then turned and strode off down the street.

Carmen watched him go until he was out of sight. What the hell had she just done? She pulled her phone from her handbag. It was a little after nine but still early enough to call Felicity.

Her friend answered on the second ring. "Hello, darling, how are—?"

"I just ended it with Gerald."

There was a brief silence. "Flag a cab down; I'll get the wine open."

Carmen hung up and strode down the street to the junction with the main road. Within a minute she was in a cab on her way to Maida Vale. To her surprise, tears dripped from her eyes as she gazed out the cab window. They came from a mix of sadness at the parting with Gerald and gratitude for having a friend as reliable and supportive as Felicity. And, she had to admit, a touch of self-pity for being alone again, despite knowing that being with Gerald wasn't the answer.

Felicity let her into the house and gave her a hug. "Hmm, I see puffy eyes. Was it awful? Did he yell?"

"No, he was the perfect gentleman." Carmen followed Felicity as she led her through the house to the kitchen. "I have had a little cry, though. For all sorts of reasons."

Felicity pushed a box of tissues across the counter. "I cried buckets when Michael and I split up, even though I knew it was the right thing to do. Endings are always awful, no matter who decides to go."

"That is so true." Brief memories of Lewis leaving entered her mind, but she pushed them away. She was feeling raw enough as it was.

Felicity pulled a bottle of white wine from the fridge and held it up. "Yes?"

"Definitely."

Felicity poured them each a glass. They sat at the breakfast bar, its marble top illuminated by soft lights in the ceiling above them. They tapped glasses and took a sip or two.

"Did you and Gerald part on good terms?"

"We did. It seems he was more emotionally involved than I'd realised and was quite sad." Carmen ran her fingertips over the cool marble of the bar, her mind working hard to put all the pieces together to explain how she'd ended up where she was. "But I couldn't stay with him. I don't love him, and I don't think he loves me. Not really. Yes, we had a nice time together, but tonight I realised that just wasn't enough."

Felicity sipped her wine, then placed her glass down and laid her palms flat on the breakfast bar. "Good, I'm pleased for you."

"I'm sure you are. I know you never liked him."

"Actually, that's not true." Felicity's tone was sharp. "I think he's a very nice man, and God knows he's easy on the eye. I was simply never happy seeing you settle for someone who didn't fulfil you. Gerald was the latest in a long line of nice men, but not a man to set your world ablaze."

"Oh, come on. I could do a lot worse than Gerald." Carmen was surprised by her strong urge to defend him.

"Yes, you could." Felicity shook her head. "I'm not saying Gerald was awful. He's anything but. My concerns are more about you and what you seem to be willing to settle for in terms of a relationship. I think you've been selling yourself short for quite some time. I'm not sure why that is. You're a wonderful person, incredibly smart and driven; you're gorgeous for days and most definitely coming into your sexual prime"—Carmen's face burned—"and it's been difficult to see you in a relationship that lacked spark. You need to be with someone you can fully connect with. Gerald, lovely as he is, wasn't the one. And I think you deserve the one."

Carmen didn't know what to say. Felicity's words touched her, yet at the same time she struggled to accept them. "He was a great catch. I should have been happy."

Felicity shook her head once more. "He wasn't right for you; that's why it didn't feel right. No matter how compatible you looked on the surface, you weren't deep inside. Yes, I know, you felt you just wanted some casual company while you worked on building up the agency. Someone who would make no excessive demands on your time. I understand why that would be appealing—no pressure to commit, easy enough to change plans at a moment's notice." She paused, her gaze steady. "But remember how you felt about Lewis and what the two of you had?"

Carmen startled. Why did they have to talk about Lewis? Her hands trembled, and she covered the movement by picking up her wineglass. "Yes, I know. But that was because I was young and he was my first love and—"

"Age has nothing to do with it." Felicity waved a hand dismissively in Carmen's direction. "Lewis lit you up. You looked like you could take on the whole world when you were with him, and I don't mean because you were somehow an incomplete person when he wasn't around. I mean because he loved you for who you were and who you were yet to be. He'd stay up all night listening to you plan for the future and talking it all through with you. He'd drop anything to help you work on a project or proposal, and you'd do the same for him. You gave each other so much energy, so much support. And at the same time, you couldn't keep your hands off each other." She took a deep breath. "Answer me honestly, was that what you had with Gerald? Or any of the other men you've dated since Lewis?"

Carmen slumped in her seat. Felicity, as usual, was right. And now Carmen was coming to realise how much she'd missed having the kind of connection Felicity described. "No, I haven't."

To Carmen's surprise, Felicity didn't give her usual triumphant look at being proved right. Instead, she softened her posture and took Carmen's hand. "You need to be with a man just like Lewis again, someone who will actively support you every step of the way in whatever you want to do *and* make your toes tingle."

There was a wistfulness to Felicity's tone that gave Carmen pause. "I've…I've never heard you talk like that. Have you…? Didn't Michael do that for you? I never did understand why you two suddenly had so much trouble and ended up getting divorced. I mean, you said you just drifted but…"

Felicity blinked rapidly a few times. "He cheated on me," she whispered.

"*What?* How come I'm only just hearing about this now?"

Felicity's eyes glistened. "I was so embarrassed. She was his secretary, for God's sake. I never told a soul. I just couldn't face the looks I was going to get."

Carmen squeezed Felicity's hand. "Shit, I'm so sorry. And I'm sorry you didn't feel you could come to me with that. If I did anything to make you think that—"

"No! God, no. It was just… I couldn't bear talking about it, and I just wanted it all to go away." She sniffed delicately. "And yes, Michael did do all of those things for me that I wish for you, and that's what made it hurt even more." She swallowed. "I had it once, and it was wonderful. It turned sour for me, true, but I can't help it; I'm a hopeless romantic, and I still want all of that for you. He's out there somewhere. I'm sure of it."

By unspoken agreement they sat in silence then and finished their wine, holding hands across the breakfast bar.

Chapter 5

"Maybe you should take a break."

Monica's voice broke into Carmen's thoughts, startling her.

"What?"

Monica stood and walked across their shared office, her expression sympathetic. "I know from being cc'd on so many emails yesterday that you put in a full day on a weekend again, and you've been staring into space for at least ten minutes now."

"Have I?"

Shit, she'd had no idea. *How embarrassing—not exactly setting the best example to my assistant lately, am I?*

The good news was the weekend work had kept her mind off Gerald. The bad news was it meant all her thoughts about him and relationships in general had decided to revisit her brain just as she tried to sleep. She was exhausted.

"You have." Monica chuckled, and her long red curls bounced as her shoulders shook. "Maybe you need another coffee?"

"Probably. I'll just get Beverley to—"

"No, don't do that. Get out of here for a little while. You've got time—your next appointment isn't for another hour. Go to Alma's and get one of their amazing espressos."

Carmen exhaled a long breath. Yeah, maybe the walk to Alma's would be good. She laughed. "Oh, this wouldn't have anything to do with someone wanting a Portuguese custard tart by any chance, would it?"

Monica's wide-eyed look of feigned innocence merely made Carmen laugh harder.

"All right, all right. I'll go. You're right; I need some air."

"Is there…? Well, if it's work, you know I want to help in any way I can, right?"

"I do. But no, it's not work. Sorry, don't worry; I'm okay. Really."

To her credit, Monica didn't push any further. Instead she returned to her desk, opened the drawer, and pulled her purse out from its depths. "Here." She handed over a fiver. "Get me two, please."

Carmen ignored the proffered money. "My treat."

"But—"

"I insist. You've used your initiative this morning, and that needs rewarding."

"I have?"

"By insisting I get out of here. It's best for all of us if I shake off this mood." Carmen grinned at her, then retrieved her handbag. "I've got my mobile if anyone calls and—"

"Carmen, with all due respect, we can handle it until you're back."

Carmen rubbed her forehead. "Of course. Sorry." Sometimes it was hard to let go, even though she had recruited Monica for that very reason. "I'll be back in a while."

Monica threw her a wave, her attention already back on her own screen.

After letting her receptionist, Beverley, know where she was going—and obtaining an order for another custard tart—Carmen trotted down the four flights of stairs and out of the main door. The morning that greeted her was glorious, with warm sunshine and a blue sky dotted with small, fluffy white clouds.

Alma's was located a few blocks away, tucked down a side street. The walk lifted Carmen's spirits; the streets weren't too busy in the middle of a Monday morning, and the air was, for once in the centre of London, fresh and easy on the nose. She smiled to herself—she actually walked with a spring in her step. Who'd have thought, given how bleak she'd felt all weekend?

The café wasn't very busy when she arrived. An older couple sat at one table indoors, and outside two of the four smaller tables were occupied. She was about to step through the open front door when her eye was caught by the person at the table nearest the door. Was that…?

"Ash?" she tentatively asked.

The woman looked up, and a broad smile split her face. "Hey! Carmen, isn't it?"

"It is. Nice to see you again." Carmen didn't know why Ash was here, but it was rather lovely to see a vaguely familiar face out and about on her escape from the office. "You live around here?"

Ash laughed. "I wish! No, I heard this place had the best Portuguese custard tarts in town, and I made a long diversion on my way to work to find out if it was true." She pointed at a plate that looked as if it might have actually been licked clean. "It seems it is."

Carmen chuckled. "It really is. I haven't been here in a while, but I'll be leaving with a box of five."

Ash's eyebrows shot up.

"Not all for me!" Carmen hastily added. "Tempting as that might be."

Ash nodded. "I've had one, but I'm seriously considering having a second." She paused. "Hey, if you're not in a rush, do you maybe want to sit and eat one with me? I'll feel better if I'm not eating alone again." She grinned and spread her arms as if to show how perfectly suited the table was for two people rather than one.

The table she had chosen was directly in the warm sun, and Carmen had time, so why not? "That sounds great. If you're sure you don't mind."

"No, it would be good to have some company. Especially with someone who won't judge me for the second tart."

"Definitely no judgement here. Okay, give me a minute, I'll just order." Carmen walked into the café, paid for six of the pastries—two on a plate and four in a to-go box—and a double espresso, then returned to Ash with a large tray that held all the purchases. She placed it on the table before sitting and lifting the plate. "Here, one of these is yours."

"Wait, you didn't have to do that."

"I know, but..." Carmen shrugged. "At the risk of sounding overdramatic, it's good to be outside and spending time with another human being unrelated to my job, so think of this as my thanks for that."

"At least let me pay you for it." Ash reached into her pocket.

"Please, no. My treat."

Seeming to accept there was no point in arguing, Ash sat back. "Well, thank you. Next time will be on me."

"Sounds good."

Ash smiled at her, and once again Carmen was struck with how… *handsome* she was. It was a word she had always reserved for men up until now, but she realised how easily it applied to Ash. She wasn't wearing any make-up, and she didn't need it. Carmen loved Ash's fashion sense—today her T-shirt was bright yellow with a big red cartoon heart in the centre of her chest. And her hair looked amazing. She'd used some kind of product to slick her long fringe to the side. It totally worked.

"I like your hair today. I mean, I liked it the other day too," she added, "but this style looks just as good."

"Thanks. I like to mix it up."

"You're lucky." Carmen ruefully pointed at her own curly hair. "Really can't do a lot with this."

"I guess. But the curls totally suit you, so at least there's that."

"True! It would be a lot worse if this is what God gave me and it didn't suit me at all." Carmen laughed.

"Always be thankful for small mercies." Ash pulled her plate closer. "Something my gran used to say a lot."

"Wise woman."

"That she was." Ash picked up her pastry. "Cheers!"

Carmen picked up her own pastry, and they touched the edges in a pastry toast before each leaning in and taking a bite from their own.

"Oh God," Carmen mumbled around her mouthful.

"I know, right?"

Carmen swallowed. "How could I forget how good these are?"

They finished their treats in silence, but they shared smiles and chuckles as they did so. Carmen wondered why she felt so comfortable sitting here, stuffing a pastry in her mouth, with a woman she hardly knew.

"*So* good," Ash said when she'd finished. She licked a finger, pressed it against the remaining crumbs of the flaky pastry on her plate, and popped them in her mouth. The unselfconscious gesture was cute, and Carmen liked that Ash was comfortable in her own skin.

"This could become habit-forming." Carmen groaned and pushed her empty plate away, then downed the rest of her espresso.

"Well, I do owe you one, so you have to come back at least one more time."

"Bugger."

Ash laughed, the sound melodious, easy on Carmen's ears. Then Ash also pushed her plate away and sat back in her chair, her expression thoughtful.

"What?" Carmen asked.

"Well, I don't want to pry, but why did you need this escape so badly? You seemed…frazzled, when you first turned up."

Carmen leaned back and sighed. "I was. It's complicated."

"Ah."

"I know. God, what a cliché." Carmen looked away. There was no way she could share with Ash. She barely knew her and— "I split up with my partner on Friday night. He and I had been seeing each other for two years, casual but exclusive, and I just reached a point where I wondered why we were bothering."

The words left her mouth so quickly her brain couldn't catch up with the fact that she'd actually said them out loud. To an almost stranger. Her face heated.

"I'm sorry," Ash said.

Carmen picked at the crumbs on her plate. "You see, that's the thing. I should be, but I'm not. That probably sounds harsh, but I wasn't in love with him. I liked him. A lot. But that zing, that spark, it was never there. We had a good time, and he made it easy for me to fit the relationship around my work because he has a demanding job too. But it's like it was all surface. No depth. And for a long time I thought that was fine, but now I know it wasn't." She wasn't sure where all this openness with a relative stranger had come from. Normally, she kept such personal things close to her chest, only confiding in Felicity. Why had she found it so easy to say all of that to Ash?

Ash shrugged. "Then you've done the right thing. You should never stay with someone just because it's convenient, in my humble opinion. Feelings are important. They should always come first."

There was a bitter edge to her tone, and it didn't take a fancy education to know that Ash had been hurt by someone in her past.

"You're right. I've spent all weekend going over and over it in my head, wondering if I'd done the right thing, feeling guilty over hurting him. Now I do feel okay about what I did. Maybe I just needed a bit more time to come to terms with it all."

"Or the custard tarts have worked their magic." Ash smiled gently.

"Perhaps so." Carmen's laugh burst out of her.

Ash joined in her laughter, and God, it felt good to just sit in the sun and *laugh*.

A chime from her phone brought Carmen back down to earth. "Ugh. That's the fifteen-minute reminder for my next meeting. I have to get back." She stood, hooked her handbag over her shoulder, then picked up the box of pastries. She looked down at Ash, who smiled again, although not as brightly as before.

"This was lovely, Ash. I'm so glad I ran into you."

"Likewise." Ash withdrew a well-worn, brown leather wallet from the back pocket of her jeans. She opened it and pulled out a business card from one of the slots. "Here, take this. Call me when you want me to repay that pastry, okay?"

Carmen took the card. "I will. Bye."

"Bye."

Carmen walked down the street, careful to keep the pastry box steady, and puzzled over the sadness that overtook her as her distance from the café increased.

No, not from the café, she thought a moment later. *From Ash.*

How odd.

Chapter 6

Well, that was unexpected.

Ash grimaced as she walked to the studio. While it had been pleasant chatting with Carmen, even just for twenty minutes, the fact that her brain couldn't seem to rid itself of the image of Carmen laughing in the sunshine was not.

God, no, you idiot. No straight women. Remember last time? Ugh.

She unlocked the studio shutters, rolled them up, but then closed and locked the door behind her when she was inside. She didn't officially open for another half an hour and didn't need anyone interrupting her preparations.

A small stack of mail rested on the doormat, and she bent to pick it up. A glance told her most of it was junk—catalogues and flyers from suppliers she'd never use. She threw it onto the desk, then made her way to the small room at the back that doubled as her office and storeroom. Mondays were always stock-checking days, and within five minutes she had her tablet in her hand and cast an eye over every shelf.

By the time she'd finished that and placed the order, it was noon and time to open. When she flipped the sign to open and undid the latch, no one waited to enter, but she still got the same sense of satisfaction in the actions that she'd had from the first day she'd opened for business.

Her first client was at one thirty, so she cleaned up the waiting area and refreshed the magazines and artwork folders. Then she sat at one of the benches at the back and pulled out her sketchbook. She'd been reading a high fantasy novel on Sunday afternoon and had some ideas for sketches of the characters and creatures described in the book. Sketching always grounded her.

Fifteen minutes later, she threw her pencil onto the bench and folded her arms. *That* wasn't what she was supposed to have drawn. She glared at the small sketch, as if it were somehow directly to blame. What had started out as an idea to draw one of the heroines of the story had instead become a light sketch of Carmen. Even in black and white, it evoked memories of the sun in her blonde hair, those curls lifting gently in the warm breeze, her brown eyes changing in intensity depending on whether she was laughing or pondering the state of her relationship.

Yes, see, her relationship. She's straight! She's literally just finished seeing a guy she'd been dating for two years!

Ash stood and stretched and was beyond thankful when the front door opened. *Let's hope it's someone who can keep me chatting for a while, get my mind back in focus.*

Instead, Carmen's friend Felicity waited for her by the desk.

Ash almost groaned out loud. "Hey." She forced herself to sound cheery as she rounded the benches and joined Felicity in the front of the shop.

"Hello."

Felicity looked as if she were heading out somewhere important. She was dressed in a dark red trouser suit that Ash would bet had cost a fortune, a white shirt with the collars flipped up, and a Gucci handbag hung over one arm. Her make-up was impeccable, if a little too much again for Ash's tastes, but it highlighted her deep brown eyes wonderfully, and her shiny black hair framed the entire picture gloriously. "Do you have a minute?"

"I do. What's up?"

Felicity ducked her head, and pink tinged her cheeks. "Well, I'm probably worrying for nothing. I know you said it can sometimes take a while for the redness to go down, but..."

Hmm, nine days post-tattoo. Unless she's got super sensitive skin, which she didn't mention, the redness should have gone by now. "Want me to take a look?"

"Oh, yes, please!"

"Okay, come on through to the back." Ash walked to the back area. She motioned Felicity to stand by one of the counters, then pulled a pair of latex gloves out of their storage box.

"Can you pull your trousers down enough for me to see?"

"Of course." Felicity placed her handbag on the counter. She turned back and slowly—actually, the word *seductively* sprang to mind—opened her trousers and eased them past her hips.

The lacy underwear revealed by the action was, Ash had to admit, pretty sexy, but it wasn't the first time she'd seen a female client's underwear and it sure wouldn't be the last. She maintained her professionalism and waited patiently until Felicity's hands stopped moving.

Ash stepped closer. "May I?"

"Yes."

Did Felicity deliberately put that breathiness into her response?

Ash decided not to look at her. She had a sneaky suspicion what might be going on here and wasn't remotely interested in responding to it. Sure, Felicity was gorgeous, but she was almost over-the-top gorgeous, and that did nothing for Ash. Not like the understated beauty of someone like Carmen, for example.

Shit, stop that. Concentrate on your client.

Ash bent down, worried about what she might see, and inspected the tattoo and the area around it. There wasn't any redness at all, and her relief was soured by what she was now convinced Felicity was playing at. "There's nothing I'm seeing here that's giving me any cause for concern." She stood up straight and gave Felicity a friendly but professional smile. "You're doing fine."

"Oh, that's such a relief." Felicity placed a hand on Ash's arm. "Thank you."

Oh God, I think she's actually trying to bat her eyelashes at me. Ash eased away from Felicity's touch under the pretence of needing to ditch the gloves. Once she'd gained some distance, she said over her shoulder, "Happy to be of help. Give me a call if there's any more concerns."

When she turned back from the rubbish bin, Felicity had dressed again and stood with her arms folded across her chest, leaning against the counter. An enigmatic smile played around her lips. "Do I make you nervous, Ash?" She purred the question.

Ash barely resisted rolling her eyes. "Not at all." She shoved her hands into the pockets of her jeans. "Felicity, I'm flattered, really, but…no, thank you."

Felicity dropped her arms, and her cheeks took on their pink hue again. "Oh, dear. Was I that obvious?"

Ash shuffled on the spot. She just wanted Felicity to leave, not prolong this awkward conversation. "You kind of were. Sorry, I didn't mean to embarrass you."

"Oh, no, I rather think I've embarrassed myself." Felicity turned away and grabbed her handbag, hesitating a moment with one hand on the counter.

Ash gave her that space to compose herself.

Felicity turned back and walked the few paces across the room to Ash. "I'm sorry. I'm not sure what came over me. I mean, God, I've never dated a woman, never even *looked* before. I just…" She closed her eyes. "I think Carmen might be right. I think I am going through some sort of midlife crisis."

It should have angered her, the fact that a straight woman like Felicity thought Ash was easy pickings for a walk on the wild side. But Felicity's embarrassment and instant acknowledgement of the wrongness of her behaviour tempered any annoyance Ash might have felt.

Instead, Ash smiled at her. "I get it. I had mine a few years back. They're a bitch."

Felicity snorted, an indelicate sound that made her clap her hand over her mouth.

"Hey, you want a tea or coffee before you go? My next client isn't for a while. We can talk, if you want. If it helps?"

Felicity removed her hand, revealing a broad smile. "Bless you, but no, I'm fine." She inhaled deeply. "Again, I'm sorry for putting you in that ridiculous position. Honestly, I'm not normally like this."

Ash shrugged. "It's okay. It's… Well, look, it's pretty obvious something big and upsetting happened to you recently."

Felicity raised one eyebrow.

"The tattoo." Ash pointed at Felicity's hip. "I can tell a lot about people from the tattoos they choose. These things take time to get over. We all do some things that we think are out of character to get through them."

"This sounds like the voice of experience."

Ash grinned. "Possibly."

Felicity smiled again and looked far more relaxed than before. "Ash, thank you. I'm going to go and do some shopping. That always helps."

Laughing, Ash escorted her to the door. "You take care, Felicity. And I meant what I said. Call me if you have any more concerns about the tattoo. Don't be a stranger."

"I won't." Felicity briefly patted Ash's arm. "Thanks again."

She strode off down the street, Ash watching her go.

When she returned to the benches near the chair, her gaze fell on the open sketchbook. It was exactly where Felicity had deposited her handbag.

The sketchbook with the unmistakable drawing of Carmen on the page.

Ash hung her head. *God, please, don't let her have seen that.*

Saturday dawned gloriously sunny and warm, and Carmen was glad she could at least enjoy the morning having breakfast with Felicity before she had to sink herself into her work once more.

"More coffee?" Felicity held the pot out.

Carmen nodded. "Yes, please. And another of those chocolate croissants, if there's any left."

Felicity laughed, and after pouring them both coffee, she headed back to the kitchen.

When she returned with freshly warmed croissants, Carmen said, "As much as I'm enjoying this breakfast with you, you do know I don't need continual babysitting, yes?"

Felicity held up her hands. "Of course not. I'm just spending time with my darling friend. That's all."

Carmen rolled her eyes and sipped her coffee. "Of course. But seriously, I'm okay. I've done a lot of thinking this past week, and everything makes a lot more sense now." She smiled. "Actually, you know who helped me figure some of that out?"

"Who?"

"Ash. The tattooist."

Felicity inexplicably blushed. "Ash? Really?" She looked away and popped a piece of croissant in her mouth.

"You're blushing."

"No, I'm not. Anyway, you spoke with Ash?"

39

Carmen stared at her friend for a couple of moments. There was definitely something she needed to get to the bottom of here, but for now she'd continue her story. "Yes. It was the funniest coincidence. I bumped into her on Monday, and we had coffee together." Briefly, she told Felicity about their conversation. "It was so strange. I barely know the woman, and yet I felt so calm in her presence, and all these feelings and thoughts just tumbled out. And the strange thing was, I didn't feel embarrassed about it. It just seemed so natural to be talking to her about it. Isn't that odd?"

She didn't feel the need to share the other odd sensation she'd had, of feeling so lost when she walked away from Ash. *That* feeling she'd managed to push to the back of her mind all week, entirely unsure what it meant, if anything.

"Not at all," Felicity said hurriedly. She kept her gaze averted from Carmen's and shredded her croissant into tiny pieces.

"You're acting very strange. Even for you. What's going on?"

Felicity tutted. "What do you mean, 'even for you'?"

"Stop avoiding my questions."

Felicity shifted in her seat, then finally met Carmen's gaze. "All right, I'll tell you. But please promise not to laugh."

"I promise."

"Well, funnily enough, I, too, had an interaction with Ash on Monday. By the sounds of it, straight after your coffee with her."

"Oh?"

Felicity blushed again and placed both hands on her cheeks as if that would magic the heat away. "Oh God, I was such an idiot. I... After the tattoo appointment, I couldn't stop thinking about her. I've never pursued a woman before, although I have had my fair share of attention from them in the past," she said immodestly.

Carmen rolled her eyes, and Felicity scowled at her.

"Well, it's true! Anyway, there was something about her. So I, um, went back to the shop on Monday, and I may have, um, flirted rather badly with her, and she made it very clear she wasn't interested."

It took every ounce of strength Carmen had not to laugh, as promised. Her friend, propositioning a woman!

"I can see your lips twitching." Felicity frowned.

Carmen's lips ached from maintaining a straight line. "I'm trying, I really am."

"Don't bother. It was pathetic. Go ahead, laugh all you want."

Carmen shook her head. "No, I won't. But Jesus, what were you thinking?"

Felicity threw her hands up. "I don't know! She was cute and so very nice to us, and...I don't know. It just seemed like such a good idea for a while. I was intrigued. There's just... She has a presence, don't you think? And those eyes. My God."

"Are you seriously attracted to her?" And why did that thought make her stomach churn with something that felt remarkably like jealousy?

Felicity chewed on her bottom lip. "I'm not sure. Perhaps more attracted to the idea of doing something different, perhaps? I feel a little adrift, I suppose. I mean, look at me. I don't have a husband anymore, and my charity work only takes up a couple of days a week. I'm bored. I think I was looking for a little excitement to liven things up."

"Well, if I'm honest, then I'm glad Ash turned you down. She seems far too nice a person to just be someone's distraction."

"I know." Felicity looked contrite. "It was a temporary aberration. It won't happen again." She took a long drink from her coffee. "Besides, she was very nice about it, and we parted on good terms. I haven't, at least, damaged what little relationship I have with her."

"Good."

Now, if ever, would be a good time to talk about her own fascination with Ash, but somehow Carmen still wanted to keep that to herself. It was confusing, and part of her—a big part—thought it was ridiculous anyway. So, she changed the subject. "I forgot to tell you—Tamsyn and Maggie are getting married."

"Really? How lovely! Gosh, they kept that a tight secret. I've not heard a whisper."

"Yes, they're keeping it very quiet and small. I spoke to her PR manager Tony last week, and he said he was relieved they wanted it so low-key. He wasn't looking forward to handling all the fuss around a big wedding."

"I don't blame him!"

"So, I'm invited, and I'm allowed to bring a guest. Want to go?"

Felicity practically jumped up and down in her chair. "Oh God, I'd love to! When is it?"

"September 26th."

"This year?"

"Yes."

"Oh, bugger." Felicity slumped back. "I can't! I'm already booked on a trip to Italy with Cecilia that includes that weekend. Remember, she wanted to go away around the anniversary of Thomas's death and do something lovely to take her mind off it?"

"Oh, yes. I didn't realise it was that date, though."

"It's a shame. I'd love to go, but there's no way I'm letting Cecilia down."

"Of course not!" Carmen tapped her chin with one finger. "Maybe I'll ask Tristan."

Felicity laughed. "Tristan would *love* it. I can just picture him, mixing with all those celebrities."

"Hmm, perhaps my brother is *not* the best person to take along after all. He'd probably be fawning all over them."

Chuckling, Felicity nodded. "You can just go on your own, of course."

"I know." Somehow the thought filled her with sadness.

Felicity gave her a sympathetic smile. "Want a refill?"

Carmen glanced at the ornate clock on the wall. "I'd love to, but I can't. I really have to get some work done."

"You work too much." Felicity scowled at her. "Please promise me you'll do only the bare minimum this weekend."

"Yes, Mum."

Felicity huffed and stood. "Fine, don't listen to me."

Carmen laughed and pulled her friend into a hug. "Thank you for caring."

"Always, darling, you know that."

Chapter 7

ASH CAST A GLANCE AT her appointment book and confirmed that her next client wasn't until one o'clock. After that, it was full on until she closed at eight. It was a rare quiet Saturday morning, but she couldn't complain. It would mean she could treat herself to a proper lunch for once—albeit a takeaway from the fabulous Greek place down the road—and a slow read of the latest copy of *Wanderlust* magazine.

The door slammed open behind her, and she whirled around.

Standing in the doorway, her long, blonde hair a messy frame for her flushed face, was Sophie. "Thank God you're here." She stomped across the room.

"Sophie." Ash made her tone firm. "Door. And how many times have I told you not to slam it?"

Sophie stopped in her tracks. She seemed to deflate, her shoulders dropping along with her mouth. "Sorry." She returned to the door and carefully closed it. When she turned back to Ash, her face was pale, her lips a tight line. "Mum's just… Arghhhh!"

The cry of frustration could only mean one thing. Ash sighed. There went her quiet lunch. "Want some tea?"

"Yes. Please." Sophie threw herself onto one of the sofas, then sat up again to remove her baseball jacket. She struggled to get one arm out of the sleeve and mumbled and muttered to herself as she fought with it. Eventually, her arm broke free, and she hurled the jacket onto the opposite sofa.

"Perhaps you'd better take a few deep breaths before you wreck my studio." Ash folded her arms. "I'm here for you, you know that, but you have to treat my place with more respect."

Sophie looked as if she wanted to retort with something sharp but bit her lip at the last moment. She gazed up at Ash, her expression one of sincere remorse. "I'm sorry, Auntie Ash. I really am."

Ash breathed out slowly. "Okay, tea first, then you can tell me what's going on."

"Do you have any clients coming in? Sorry, I should have asked that first." Sophie's voice was subdued, and Ash turned back to her from the hot-drinks machine to answer.

"Luckily, no. I'm free for a couple of hours." She finished making Sophie's tea, carried it over to her, and set it down on the coffee table a good arm's length away. Just in case.

"Thank you."

"You're welcome." Ash took the seat next to Sophie.

They sat in silence for a minute or so, Sophie staring at the cup of tea, Ash patiently waiting her out.

"She's been going through my things," Sophie said eventually, her tone carrying anger even though it was quiet. "She...she found a journal I'd been keeping."

Oh shit. "When was this? This morning?"

Sophie looked up. "No, yesterday while I was at school." She rolled her eyes. "But of course she was at bingo last night so didn't get around to talking to me about it until this morning."

Ash grimaced. She could just imagine how that conversation had gone. Especially with Courtney no doubt nursing a hangover. If there was one thing for which her sister could be relied on, it was a Saturday morning hangover.

"Trina says it's my own fault for writing shit down." Sophie's head had dropped towards her chest. "That I should have written it on my laptop so Mum would never see it, but somehow it's not the same. I've always liked writing in a proper notebook." She looked back up. Her eyes had welled up with tears, and she brushed them away with a fierce hand.

"Yeah, I can relate to that. But wait, backtrack a moment. You told Trina? Does that mean she knows what's in the journal?"

Sophie's eyes went wide, and she paled even further. "Bloody hell, no! I'm not stupid."

Ash held out a hand. "Hey, I was just checking, okay? She's your best friend, and you know I thought she'd be very supportive if and when you ever decided to tell her."

"I know," Sophie whispered. "But I'm so scared. And now my bloody mum bloody knows, and it's *awful*." At that, she burst into the tears that had been threatening to break free for the last five minutes. She pressed her hands against her face and sobbed into them.

Ash wrapped her arms around her niece. She pulled Sophie close and stroked her hair, the way she'd done since Sophie had been a little girl. "Hey, shush now. Come on. It's going to be okay."

"No, it bloody isn't!" Sophie's voice was muffled against her shoulder. "She was so angry, Auntie Ash." She lifted her tear-streaked, blotchy face and stared at Ash. Her bottom lip trembled. "And God, she's really angry at you too."

I just bet she is. "Don't you worry about me. I can handle your mum." Ash grinned, and her reward was a faint smile.

"Yeah, I reckon you can." Sophie sniffed and huddled closer to Ash. She eased her slender arms around Ash's torso and held on tight.

Ash gave her a squeeze. "Do you want to tell me exactly what she said, or is it too painful?" She needed to know what she was up against so she could help Sophie through this.

Sophie sniffed again. "She…she said I was way too young to know that's how I felt. And that once I got a boyfriend, I'd be fine and forget about it all." She wiped at her eyes. "And she said it was all nonsense anyway, that I was just copying you because I'd…I'd always thought you were cooler than her and it was just hero worship gone wrong. She said…she said you'd always been a bad influence on me and this was the final straw." She started crying once more. "She said she'd stop you seeing me."

A range of emotions chased themselves through Ash—fear, anger, and sadness. Anger held the upper hand. "Huh, I'd like to see her try." She willed herself to calm down and stroked Sophie's hair again, the motion as soothing for her as it seemed to be for Sophie. "Look, she was just taken by surprise. I'm sure most of what she said she didn't mean." *I bloody hope so, anyway.* "I'll pop round tonight and talk to her."

"She's got the bingo gang round tonight for their stupid cheese-and-wine thing."

"All right, maybe not tonight. What about tomorrow?"

"She hasn't said she's doing anything, and I know she's not at work, so yeah, maybe." Sophie shut her eyes and shook her head. "I'm so not ready for this. I'm still working it all out myself."

"I know you are. And that's the main thing we need to get your mum to understand so that she can give you the space and time you need for it, yes?"

Sophie nodded against Ash's shoulder.

"I'll talk to her, I promise. But you should go home, you know."

Sophie sat up with a start. "And have her yell at me again?" Her bottom lip wobbled.

"She probably won't. She's got some thinking to do too." Ash sighed. "Look, you can stay here for a while, but promise me you'll go home later, yes?"

Sophie frowned but nodded. "Okay. Promise."

"Thank you. Does she know you're here now?"

"No. I told her I was going uptown to look in the shops. She didn't seem bothered."

Jesus, Courtney! She's your daughter, for crying out loud. "But you've got your phone with you, in case she calls?"

"Yes. But she won't."

There was no way Ash was going to agree with her niece out loud on that, even though she was one hundred per cent certain the youngster was right. "So." It was time to set the drama aside. "You hungry? I was going to get something from the Greek place and bring it back here. You in?"

Sophie lifted her head, and a smile broke out on her face that made Ash's heart clench. "Can we get them spano thingies?"

Ash chuckled. "Spanakopita?"

Sophie nodded enthusiastically.

"Definitely." Ash grinned. "Tons of them." After one last squeeze, she released her niece and stood. "Come on. They open in about twenty minutes. We'll get the first fresh batch straight out of the oven."

"Yes!" Sophie fist-pumped and leaped out of her seat.

Carmen eased her way past the group of people smoking outside the restaurant's main doors. As soon as fresh air hit her nostrils, she sucked it in with relief. Inside the private dining room it had been stuffy, and an atmosphere like that always played havoc with her sinuses. Her head ached, but not just from the sinus problem.

Once again she'd spent the best part of a Saturday evening being bored rigid at a client's celebration. This time it had been one of her classical actors, hosting a small gathering, as he called it, to mark his fortieth birthday. His idea of small differed from Carmen's: there had been fifty or so people crammed into a space probably only designed for forty at maximum. The noise level and all-round tedium of the conversations around her had wilted Carmen like a flower in a desert.

She stood for a moment on the pavement simply breathing. Sometimes, when she had to suffer such evenings, she wondered just why she did what she did.

I need a walk.

Not caring which way she headed, knowing she had her trusty Google maps app to rescue her if she got lost, she turned left, which seemed to lead her away from the strip of restaurants and bars and into an area a tad quieter. She looked around as she walked, not that familiar with this part of town. Somewhere behind her was Goodge Street station, and somewhere ahead, therefore, was Euston. *Maybe I'll head in roughly that direction and catch a cab from there.*

She turned the next corner, and her steps paused. She was at the top of the street where Ash's tattoo studio was located. *How funny.* She hadn't realised she was that close.

She wondered how Ash was. She'd thought about her a few times during the week and, of course, had discussed her over breakfast with Felicity. *I still can't believe Felicity went back to see Ash. How embarrassing!* Although, she had to admit, she could definitely understand Felicity's observation that Ash had a certain presence about her. For one moment she considered walking down to see if Ash was still at work but then shook off the thought. *Ridiculous idea.*

After crossing the street, she turned right and found herself in another busy road lined with pubs. However, now the noise didn't bother her so much, so she pushed on, sidestepping a big group of people outside one pub and—

"*Ooof!*"

Carmen walked into someone—or they walked into her—and bounced back off them. She swung both arms out to balance herself and with some windmilling managed to prevent tumbling onto her backside.

"Jesus, sorry!" a voice said.

She looked up—straight into the deep brown eyes of Ash.

"Carmen! Wow." Ash looked her up and down. "Are you okay? I didn't see you. I was too busy chatting and—"

"I'm fine." Carmen smiled at her; Ash looked mortified at having nearly sent her flying. "Nothing damaged."

"Thank God." Ash exhaled loudly.

Standing next to Ash was a tall, attractive woman, maybe in her early thirties, with short, bleached blonde hair and stunning blue eyes.

"Oh, hey, this is Hayley."

"Nice to meet you." Carmen shook hands with the woman.

"And you." Hayley smiled.

"You heading out or home?" Ash asked.

"Home. Just been to a client party a few streets that way." Carmen gestured over her shoulder. "You?"

"We're just off out."

They stared at each other for a few moments. Carmen couldn't help drinking in Ash's features; her hair, in particular, looked amazing, and her entire demeanour was relaxed and carefree. *Lucky her.*

Hayley tugged on Ash's arm and leaned in to whisper something in her ear.

"Oh, yeah. True," Ash said to her, then looked back at Carmen. "Sorry, we need to go."

"Oh, of course! Sorry." Carmen stepped back. "It was nice to see you again. And nice to meet you," she offered to Hayley.

"Same. Have a nice rest of the evening."

Carmen watched them go, her curiosity piqued. Was that Ash's partner? They weren't holding hands, but that didn't necessarily mean anything.

Many couples didn't, especially gay ones, even in these allegedly enlightened times. Somehow, though, she didn't think they were together, but she had no idea how she knew that.

She realised she'd been standing on the same spot for at least a minute, watching the two women, and gave herself a mental slap. *You're acting like a stalker. So Ash is out with someone tonight. So what?*

Walking on, she tried hard not to think about how Hayley had Ash's company all to herself for the evening. *Lucky her.*

Chapter 8

ASH SPENT THE TRAIN JOURNEY out to her sister's bracing herself for the reaction she might receive when she got there. She wasn't exactly looking forward to seeing Courtney, knowing it would probably involve a lot of harsh words and maybe some shouting.

She gazed out the window as the train neared Courtney's station. What a shitty weekend this was turning out to be. Her date with Hayley last night had been a waste of time, with each of them realising only an hour in that they had very little in common. Weirdly, bumping into Carmen had been one of the highlights of the night. *Strange how that happened.* She laughed softly to herself. *I'd have been better off taking her to that bar, not Hayley.* Carmen was easy to talk to and fun to spend time with. She wondered if she should give Carmen a call. They could be friends, couldn't they? Even if Ash did find her attractive, she could keep it under control. Couldn't she?

The walk from the station took only a couple of minutes, and she took a deep breath before ringing the doorbell.

"I told you, I don't want to talk to you." Courtney's greeting and the pissed-off look on her face was, unfortunately, just what Ash had expected.

"I know you did, but I'm here anyway." Ash shrugged. "So how about you invite me in for a cup of tea?"

Courtney scowled before walking away down the hallway—but she left the front door open.

Taking that as the best invitation she was going to get, Ash stepped into the house.

As usual, a myriad of smells assaulted her nose. Cigarette smoke was paramount—it seemed as if Courtney was back on them after trying to quit for about the fifth time. Bacon had been fried for breakfast, Ash would guess, and beneath that smell lurked the general odour of a house that wasn't properly looked after. Ash's sister had never been much of a fan of housework.

Ash peeked into the front room. Yep, all the windows shut tight even though it was a gorgeous day outside. She cast a glance over her shoulder. When she found herself unobserved, she ducked into the room and opened the top window a notch. She'd close it again before she left, but at least some air would circulate for however long she was in the house.

As she left the room, Sophie appeared on the stairs. Her eyes went wide when she saw Ash. "You came."

"Of course." Ash met her at the bottom of the stairs for a quick hug. "Said I would."

"Thanks."

"How's it been?"

By unspoken agreement they were keeping their voices low.

Sophie shrugged. "Okay, actually. She ignored me when I got home yesterday afternoon. I did my homework in my room, then listened to some music. Her friends came round, and after they'd gone, she asked if I was all right, then went to bed."

"So no more shouting?"

"No." Sophie frowned. "She kept looking at me kind of funny, though."

"Funny?"

"Yeah. Like she, I don't know, like she didn't know who I was."

Ash nodded. "She's found out something about you that's got her thinking, that's all." She patted Sophie's shoulder. "It'll be all right. Don't worry." *God, I hope I'm not making a false promise.*

"Okay." Sophie turned and went back up the stairs.

"Are you having this tea or what?" Courtney yelled from the kitchen.

With a heavy sigh, Ash made her way to the back of the house.

To Ash's surprise, the kitchen looked clean and tidy. Three empty wine bottles stood on the end of one counter, but other than that you'd never know Courtney had hosted her friends the night before. It even smelled a little fresher than the rest of the house; the back door had been propped open with a chair. Thankful for small mercies, she walked further into the room and helped herself to one of the chairs at the small table in the corner.

"Make yourself at home," Courtney said sarcastically. She grabbed two steaming mugs from next to the kettle, carried them to the table, and set them down before throwing herself into the chair opposite Ash's.

Courtney looked the same as always: a little rough around the edges. Her dyed blonde hair needed its roots doing, her eyes had dark smudges underneath, and her hoodie and sweatpants had definitely seen better days. "So, come to tell me how to raise my daughter, have you?"

Only just avoiding rolling her eyes, Ash shook her head. "Not at all."

"Well, what then? You're the one who's given her all these ideas, after all."

Ash held up her hands in a placating gesture. "Courtney, I haven't done anything like that, and you know it."

Courtney huffed and reached for her mug, her eyes averted, and everything in her body language told Ash she wasn't angry so much as confused.

"Look," Ash said softly. "I know this has probably surprised you, but—"

"Surprised?" Courtney glared at her. "Try really pissed me off."

"Why?"

"What?"

"Why has it pissed you off?"

Courtney opened her mouth to speak, then closed it again. After some moments, she tried again. "How can she know already? I...I don't understand."

"I know you don't." Ash kept her tone gentle. "But here's the thing. You don't have to."

"What the fuck does that mean?" Courtney's eyes blazed.

"It means you just need to support her."

"Support her? How? I don't want her to be...*that way.*"

It hurt, despite how at ease Ash was with her own sexuality and had been for years. She grabbed for her tea and swallowed a couple of mouthfuls. The pause helped to tamp down her anger. She knew it wouldn't help Sophie if she let it out, and she made sure she breathed deeply a couple of times before responding. "What *you* want isn't the issue here, Courtney. She's struggling with some pretty big things, and all she wants is some time and space to think about them." When Courtney made to interrupt, Ash held up a hand. "Listen, that's all she's doing at the moment, just thinking. You shouting at her isn't going to help, and if you're not careful, might just make it all worse. If she's gay"—Courtney glared at her again—"then that's what she is. Nothing you or I say will change that. Trust me, it doesn't work that way."

Ash leaned forward and made sure Courtney met her gaze. Okay, so maybe she *was* trying to teach Courtney how to raise her daughter. Tough. "The best thing you can do for her is just let her think it through, work out her true feelings. For all we know, it will pass. It might just be some crush on one girl, and in a year, two years, she's mad for some boy. We just don't know. And nor does she. So don't put any pressure on her to be one thing or another."

"But that's what you're doing!" Courtney hissed. "She said it in her diary! Said you were telling her it was okay if she was, you know, gay, like you, and to just accept it if she is. She's fourteen, Ash! She's too young."

Ash wasn't going to touch the whole "why did you even read her diary" conversation today—that would only end up with an even bigger shouting match. But when this storm had calmed, she'd be having that chat with Courtney about respecting her daughter's privacy.

"I was twelve when I knew, Courtney."

Courtney stared at her, and Ash returned the look with as much sympathy in her expression as she could manage. It wasn't her sister's fault she didn't understand.

"You have no idea how confusing it is at that age to know you are different but not know why. And when you know you can't talk to anyone about it, it's even worse." She could feel all her teenage anger reappearing and fought to keep her voice low and calm. "All I'm asking is that you don't do what Mum and Dad did to me. Don't try to make her something she's not, okay? Let her work this out. Please."

"I…I don't want her being unhappy." Courtney fiddled with the handle of her mug. "You're not exactly the best advert for it, are you, after what happened with Leesa and all them other women. And you don't have a girlfriend now, do you?"

Wow, that blow hit hard. Ash couldn't breathe for a moment, and her fists clenched and unclenched several times before she could speak.

"Yes, I've had a few relationships that have unfortunately all ended. Although some in better ways than others. That happens to straight people all the time too. And for what it's worth, I *am* actually a happy person. I don't need to be in a relationship to be happy. I've got a good life, and more importantly, I'm able to live that life as me, the *real* me." She stood, tired of the emotions raging through her body, of keeping her anger in check while she fought Sophie's battle.

From the scrunched look on Courtney's face, she'd maybe given her something to think about, at least. This was a first step, but maybe, just maybe, it would have some positive impact.

"Thanks for the tea. You know where I am if you want to talk about it. Any time, Courtney, I mean that. I love Sophie like she was my own, but I want to be there for both of you. You're my only sister. She's my only niece. You're both so important to me. Okay?"

Courtney pursed her lips but eventually nodded.

On legs that were strangely unsteady, Ash left the kitchen. At the last minute, before opening the front door, she remembered the window she had opened. As she stepped back towards the living room, Courtney's voice came from close behind.

"Don't worry, I'll shut it later."

Ash turned.

Courtney slouched against the wall of the hallway, turning a pack of cigarettes over and over in her hand. "I… Get home safe." She stared at Ash a moment longer, then turned away and walked back towards the kitchen.

Chapter 9

AFTER HER FIFTH CLIENT MEETING of the day, Carmen headed home on the first Thursday evening in July with weary steps. She'd no sooner opened the front door when her phone rang, of course. A glance at the caller display brought her some relief.

"Hey, Tristan."

"Hello. How are you?"

"Knackered." She placed her handbag on the hall table and kicked off her heels.

"You sound it. Are you still at work?"

"Just arrived home." She declined to mention that she would continue working even though she was now home. She'd had a gentle lecture from Beverley about working too much earlier that day, and one telling-off in a day was plenty; she didn't need one from her brother too.

"Okay, then I won't keep you from putting your feet up. I just wanted to check what time your train gets in on the twelfth."

Oh shit. "Ah, Tristan. Um." She sucked in a breath. "Here's the thing—"

"Oh, no, seriously? You're cancelling on us *again*?"

"I'm sorry. I genuinely intended to come that weekend, but then one of my clients got—"

"Well, I might have known it was your work."

He sounded angrier than she would have anticipated, and she stopped in the middle of the hallway so that she could concentrate on talking to him. "Tristan, I am so sorry. He's a very important client, a huge star in the making, and I've managed to set up a dinner with one of the top film producers in the US, who happens to be in London that weekend. This could get him—and me—some exceptional exposure. I'm so sorry, but I hadn't got round to putting our dates in my calendar, and I completely forgot I was already committed to you when I set up the meeting."

There was silence down the end of the line, and for a brief moment, she thought Tristan had hung up.

"I have always supported you in your work, you know that," he finally said. "But lately it seems that that's all you do, twenty-four seven. It isn't healthy."

"I know, it's…" She wasn't sure what to say. A part of her knew that she held on to her work too tightly, that she needed to let some of it go and trust Monica to do it instead. But she'd been a one-woman show for so long, that was easier said than done.

"Is everything…? Can I ask, is the business okay? Are you in trouble? Is that why you're working so many hours?"

Carmen snorted out a laugh. "God, no! The complete opposite. We're doing really well, and my client list is now overflowing. I mean, that's good, because clearly people trust me and my work speaks for itself, but…"

"Can you hire someone else to help out? Another Monica?"

"I might have to think about doing just that."

"And how does Gerald feel about this?" her brother asked. "He must hardly ever see you."

God, could this conversation get any worse? She nearly groaned out loud. "Ah, yes, about that…"

"What?"

"Um, well, I split up with him. About two weeks ago."

"Carmen! You're only just telling me this *now*?" Tristan sighed again. "I thought we had a better relationship than that." The softness of his tone hurt more than if he'd shouted. "I thought… Sorry, it's selfish of me, I know, but I really thought that would be the sort of thing you'd want to share with your little brother. Where have you gone? We never talk anymore. You just work; that's all. It makes me so sad."

She didn't have an answer to that, and it broke her heart. Why did she keep so much to herself? She had people who were there for her. Tristan and Felicity were both very good listeners, and Tamsyn and Maggie had become very good friends over the last couple of years.

"I'm sorry, Tristan." Tears welled up in her eyes. "God, I'm sorry. I'm so tired. I know it's self-inflicted, but I feel like I'm on some runaway train that I have to keep up with. I can't just stop, or I'll lose all the momentum I've built up the last few years." She tugged on a handful of her hair, the pain a small penance for the mix-up. "I'm so sorry for screwing up our weekend."

He exhaled slowly. "It's okay, but please don't do it again. And please look after yourself. You're worrying me."

"I know. I don't mean to."

"So, if I email you some new dates tonight, can we please, *please* make it a firm date this time?"

"Absolutely. I promise." She nodded firmly even though he couldn't see it.

"All right. Well, you get some rest. I love you."

"I love you too." She cleared her throat. "You're...you're a wonderful brother, and I'll try to be a better sister from now on."

"You're a fabulous sister." He chuckled. "Just not managing that whole work-life balance thing very well right now."

She managed a laugh, but it lacked conviction.

After wandering down to the kitchen, she sank onto a chair at her small dining table and rested her chin in her hands. Despite her tiredness, she was completely wired, as if she'd had far too much caffeine. Her heart beat way too fast, and her left foot tapped a staccato rhythm on the floor.

I need to calm down. I can't keep doing this to myself.

Her first thought was to call Felicity for a drink, but alcohol wasn't the answer.

Her second thought surprised her but had her quickly reaching for her phone again before she could out-think herself.

⁓

Thursday evenings were always busy. Ash had long ago stopped trying to figure out why and instead just went with the flow. Her final client was due in five minutes, a regular coming in for the next phase in a larger piece she was having created on her back.

She stretched a few times, using the chair as her barre. After each working session she needed to move her back muscles and flex her arms to keep everything loose. It was funny—in her former life, when she had worked for the investment bank, she'd never given stretching a minute's consideration. Yet she'd spent more time hunched over her desk there than she had over this chair. It never ceased to amaze her what people could become used to. Especially when they had no idea what a rut they'd got themselves into.

Her phone rang. "Phoenix Tattoos."

"Oh, um, hi. Ash, it's Carmen. From the—"

"Oh! Hey, Carmen. How are you?" Ash tried to pretend a little shiver did *not* run through her at the sound of Carmen's voice. *Down, girl.*

"Hi! I'm very well, thank you. And you?"

"Yeah, good."

"Is it okay to talk? Are you at work?"

"It's fine, yes," Ash answered. "And I sure am. I don't close until ten most Thursdays and Fridays."

"Ten?"

"I know, right? But it meets the demands of the market, so…"

"Hmm, yes, I know all about meeting those kinds of demands." Carmen sounded low.

While it was a lovely surprise to hear from her—Ash had, to be honest, thought she'd never see her again despite bumping into her that night nearly two weeks ago—it saddened Ash to hear her this way. "Are you really okay? You sound a little down."

"You're a very perceptive person." Carmen chuckled. "I'm a little frazzled, yes." She paused. "Look, I know this is very short notice, but I wondered if I could take you up on that offer to repay the Portuguese experience at Alma's tomorrow morning. I could do with a change of scenery and a break from my office, but if it's too—"

"Tomorrow morning would be great." Ash admonished her heart for beating just that little bit faster at the prospect of spending more time with the beautiful woman. *Straight beautiful woman, remember?* "How does eleven sound?"

The clacking of Carmen's keyboard reverberated through the phone. "Yes, I'll make that work. That's… Thanks, Ash, that's great."

"Hey, no problem. The weather's supposed to be great tomorrow. We can sit outside again, get you some more sunshine."

"That would be fabulous! I feel like I haven't seen daylight in days."

"Then we shall definitely do that."

The door opened, and Sonja, a tall woman with arms already covered in some stunning tattoos, walked in.

Ash acknowledged her with a quick wave. "I'll see you there, okay? Gotta go, my next client just walked in."

"Oh yes, of course. Great. See you tomorrow."

Sonja left at a quarter to ten, delighted with the progress on the huge stylistic mermaid they were creating on her back.

Ash loved working on the big pieces, watching them unfold over the course of a few sessions. And she loved it when a client was willing to put in that level of work and commitment to get the result they wanted. They'd agreed that two more sessions should do it, and those were already booked in Ash's calendar.

This tattoo, when completed, would definitely warrant a picture on the studio's wall. The best tattoos she'd finished took pride of place in her gallery, and Sonja was thrilled she'd make that coveted space.

Ash flipped the *closed* sign in the window and switched off the lights at the front of the studio. After cleaning up, she slipped her shirt on over her T-shirt, then set the alarm and rolled down the shutters. She fancied walking all the way home to Islington—it was a good couple of miles and would take her forty minutes or so, but it was such a beautiful evening it was worth it. She'd just hit the main road when her phone rang. Her caller display showed Courtney's name.

"Hey." Ash kept her tone bright despite her worry about what would have Courtney calling this relatively late.

"Hey."

"You okay?"

Courtney hesitated. "I'm... You know, I am trying."

Ash didn't need to ask what her sister was trying with. "I know you are. What's up?"

"She's put all these pictures up in her room!" Courtney's confused frustration came through loud and clear. "Of, you know, *women*."

Although tempted to laugh, Ash held back her mirth, doubting it would help matters at all. So now that Sophie's secret was out, she was letting it have some freedom. Good for her, no matter what Courtney thought. "Okay."

"*Okay*? Is that it?"

"Courtney, we talked about this last weekend. She's exploring. She's got some feelings, some of which she doesn't understand, but she's... It's like when you go to buy new clothes. You try things on, see what feels right, what looks right. She's doing the same thing but with feelings."

"So my house is one big changing room now, is it?"

"Courtney," Ash said gently.

"I know, I know." Courtney made a sound that was a cross between a groan and a growl.

She was quiet for a few moments, and Ash let her be. She weaved around some parked cars and ducked down a side street, away from the noisy main road. She'd taken this route once before, and although it would add a few minutes to the journey, it was worth it if she could concentrate better on helping her sister and her niece through this upheaval in their lives.

"You probably think I should find this easier because my sister's a lesbian, but it's different when it's your kid." All the fight had gone out of Courtney's voice.

"I get that."

"You're a grown-up," Courtney rushed on. "You're used to the world and how it can treat people. She's only fourteen. What's she gonna do when people start calling her dyke and muff diver and whatever else shitty things they'll yell at her at school?"

The fear in Courtney's voice made cold shivers run down Ash's spine. Yeah, she remembered all those insults. "Well, I guess that's a conversation you can have with her. Does her school have an anti-bullying policy in place that covers LGBTQ pupils? Does she know how to report it? Is she willing to? I mean, this is where you can really be her champion, let her know you're going to support her if that worst-case scenario comes about. I think that would mean a huge amount to her."

"Did...did Mum and Dad ever do that for you? You said something the other day, and... I think I was too young to see what was going on for you when you came out. I mean, you were nearly seventeen, I was twelve. Did they support you?"

Ash took a moment. She'd worked through her anger at her parents through her therapy and lost most of her bitterness about how they'd treated her. But it would be hard to talk to Courtney about a side of them her sister had never seen. She didn't want to darken Courtney's memories of them even as she wanted Courtney to learn from the mistakes they'd made. "No, I'm afraid they didn't. And they wanted to protect you, so all of our discussions on the matter took place when you weren't likely to hear them. Mum in particular was horrified at the thought that you'd find out."

Courtney gasped. "Shit, Ash, seriously? God, I'm sorry. I had no idea."

"I know you didn't. It's okay."

"Did…did it ever get any better? You know, before…"

Ash swallowed hard. Despite everything—the hurt her parents had caused her for so many years and the battle she'd gone through to become the person she wanted to be—she'd give anything to be able to talk to them again. About anything. "It got a little better, but I can't lie, it still wasn't brilliant by the time they died."

Courtney was silent for a moment. "I know someone at bingo. Rachelle. Her son's gay."

"Oh yeah?"

"I was thinking of talking to her. Maybe ask her some questions. You know, like how did she deal with it."

"I think that's a great idea." *As long as this Rachelle is okay with having a gay son. God, please let it be so.*

"Yeah, well, might help."

"I think it's great you're trying, Courtney. I really do."

"All right." Courtney's voice sounded a little gruff. "Hey, Sophie's just walked in. Do you want to say hi?"

"Sure! Put her on."

There was the rustling sound of the phone being handed over, and Sophie's muffled voice saying, "Thanks, Mum," before she said more clearly, "Hey, Auntie Ash!"

"Hey, you. How are you?"

"I'm good. I mean, I freaked Mum out with the pictures, but I think it's okay."

Ash was impressed her niece felt no need to lower her voice, even though Courtney must still have been within earshot. "Just out of interest, whose pictures did you put up?"

"Gal Gadot as Wonder Woman and Brie Larson as Captain Marvel."

"Oh, I see. Powerful superheroines do it for you, huh?" She kept her tone gentle and light so Sophie would know she was teasing.

"Shut *up*." Sophie huffed an exasperated breath down the line. "They're, you know, role models for what strong women can be."

"And they're also not exactly bad to look at."

"Maybe." Her niece's voice was quiet. "Is that...? Is it okay to think that?"

"Yes, Sophie, it is."

"Those arms," her niece whispered, and Ash found herself nodding.

"I hear you."

"Okay, this is too weird. I can't talk about this stuff with you anymore. It's...ew."

Ash laughed, then grimaced as she had to dodge around a cyclist who seemed hell-bent on running her down by going the wrong way up a one-way street. "If you can't talk to me, who can you talk to?"

"I guess. But it's just... Ugh, it's all so new, and saying some things out loud still seems like, you know, *huge*."

"I bet it does. Take your time. Set your own pace. No one gets to tell you how to do this, not even me who's done it before. But I'm here for you to talk to if you want to."

"Thanks, Auntie Ash. I...I really appreciate this."

"You're welcome." Ash glanced at her watch. "Hey, shouldn't you be in bed by now?"

"I'm fourteen, not four."

Ash smiled; she could imagine Sophie rolling her eyes.

"But," Sophie continued, "I am pretty tired, so I guess I'll say goodnight."

"All right. Sleep tight, monkey."

"Will you ever stop calling me that?"

"Do you really want me to?"

There was a slight pause before her niece said quietly, "No. I love it."

"Good. Talk to you soon, monkey."

Chapter 10

CARMEN STRODE DOWN THE STREET towards Alma's, enjoying the feel of the sunshine on her face. She hoped Ash had managed to snag them an outside table again—always assuming Ash had made it there first.

At the thought of Ash and their imminent meeting, Carmen once again wondered why it was the tattooist she'd called the evening before. *You barely know her. Why on earth was she the person you thought of seeing?*

She couldn't explain it. All she could remember was how calm and relaxed she felt around Ash. She wanted to feel that again, even for just half an hour. Derailing the weekend visiting Tristan and his partner in Paris had upset her. She'd worked late last night, of course, after talking to her brother and Ash, but it had been a struggle. Her mind had whirled with thoughts of Tristan, her career, and...Ash.

A shake of her head brought her back to the moment. She crossed the street and smiled widely; Ash sat at the same table as last time, waving at Carmen. She wore a dark blue, short-sleeved shirt, something loose and cool for the warmer July weather. It made her look even more the stereotypically butch lesbian, but it suited her. Carmen envied her relaxed look, given that she herself was dressed up to the nines, as always, in a skirt suit and high heels.

"Hi," Carmen said as she stepped nearer. "Good table."

Ash grinned. "Well, it seemed to work for us pretty well last time."

"Indeed." Carmen pulled out a chair and sat. "How are you?"

"I'm good. And you?"

"I'm... I've been better."

Hmm, interesting. She had been about to respond with a bland "I'm fine", but somehow the more honest answer had escaped her lips. What was it about Ash that lowered her emotional walls so easily? It was a tad unnerving. She slipped off her jacket and hung it on the back of the chair, using the time to compose herself. The warmth of the sun caressed her bare arms and soothed her.

Ash tilted her head. "Okay, before we go any further with this conversation, I think you need a custard tart and a coffee, yes?"

"You're a mind reader."

"It was an espresso, is that right?"

"A double, please."

Ash nodded and disappeared inside the shop.

Carmen sat back, letting the sun fall on her face. *God, I needed this.*

"Don't fall asleep on me," Ash said quietly, and Carmen snapped her eyes open.

"My God, I think I *did* just drift off there." *How embarrassing.* Carmen blinked a couple of times and sat up straighter.

"No worries." Ash's face was open and friendly. "You didn't drool, so you're good."

Laughing, Carmen rubbed lightly at her face just to verify the lack of drool. She sat up straighter to accept the coffee Ash passed to her. "Thank you. For the coffee and pastry. And for agreeing to meet with me."

Ash shrugged. "My pleasure. And to be honest, I'm never going to turn down an invite that involves custard tarts."

"Ah, so it wasn't my company that tempted you."

Ash took a big bite of her pastry and mumbled around it, "Nope, sorry to burst your bubble."

Carmen chuckled and reached for her own pastry.

They ate in a comfortable silence until the pastries had been demolished. Carmen downed her espresso in three mouthfuls and sighed happily as she placed the cup back on the table. "Exactly what I needed." She smiled at Ash. "Well, and the company too."

Ash dipped her head. "And you know I was only teasing just now."

"I thought so."

They smiled at each other.

Wow, her eyes are the deepest brown I think I've ever seen. Gorgeous.

"So." Ash drew the word out. "Want to tell me what made you need the emergency custard tart meeting?" She held up a hand before Carmen could respond. "And obviously, you don't have to. We can just sit here and enjoy the sunshine. Talk about the weather like normal Brits do."

It was so easy to relax when she was around Ash. "You're very good at this."

"What? Eating custard tarts?" Ash's eyes twinkled.

"No, you know what I mean. At making me feel at ease. It's…it's why I called you. Last night. I needed a dose of calm in my life, and I…I thought of you." Carmen swallowed. "Does that sound strange? Or stalker-ish?"

Ash laughed. "Definitely not that last thing you said." She seemed to think for a moment. "I suppose it's a little strange, given we don't know each other. But then, all friendships have to start somewhere, don't they? And I'm touched that you find me a calm influence." One side of her mouth turned up in a wry smile. "I've worked very hard to become that for myself, so it's kind of cool that it's rubbing off on other people too."

"How did you do it?" Carmen leaned forward so she wouldn't miss a word.

Ash's smile didn't waver. "Therapy."

"Really?"

"Mostly, yes." Ash paused. "Before I was a tattooist, I worked in investment banking for fifteen years. It wasn't a pretty place. But it took me a long time to figure that out and the damage it was doing to me. There was other stuff too." Her gaze drifted away, and she visibly swallowed.

Someone hurt her. Carmen thought about asking but feared it might be too invasive.

Ash briefly shook her head and turned her attention back to Carmen. "Anyway, I got out of banking and took a couple of years off. I spent a good portion of that seeing a therapist and some of it travelling around Australia and New Zealand. And the rest of it turning my love of drawing and sketching into something that could earn me some money. Something where I could be my own boss, control my own destiny, if you like."

"Good for you." Carmen didn't know why her throat had closed up a little. "I'm…I'm so impressed that you not only recognised what you needed but actually went out to attain it."

"To be honest, I had to." Ash's voice was quiet. "I couldn't have gone on the way I was without something serious happening."

Carmen swallowed. The idea that this strong, confident woman could have been brought so low as to consider harming herself made her shudder. "I understand."

Their gazes locked and held.

Ash cleared her throat. "So, the calmness you've seen in me comes from all of that. Of recognising where I was going wrong and fixing it and, as a result, being truly content with my life."

Carmen leaned back in her chair. "I can't imagine what that would feel like."

She was no longer surprised that such honest statements kept spouting from her mouth. Ash apparently had that effect on her, and it seemed stupid to resist.

"So, what gives with you? Why the frazzled-sounding Carmen on the phone last night?"

Carmen took a deep breath. "Well, basically, I'm letting my work rule my life. I know it, but I either don't know how to stop it or don't want to know."

"What do you do, workwise?"

"I'm a talent agent. You know what that is?" At Ash's brief nod, she continued. "I've become very successful in the last three years, after slogging quite hard to make a name for myself. Suddenly, it's all paid off, but there are consequences."

She told Ash all about the screw-up with Tristan, the workload, and her own bone-weary tiredness. "And on top of all that, as you know, I finished things with Gerald, which was the right thing to do, but it seems I've subconsciously used that as an excuse to work even harder."

"Kind of counterproductive?"

"I'm starting to think so. But you know what it's like when you're your own boss. Holidays are a distant dream, as is starting at nine and finishing at five."

Ash nodded slowly. "True. But is it just you in the agency, or do you have a team?"

"I have one assistant, Monica. I took her on about a year ago."

"So you do have someone who can help you. If you'd let her."

"And that's the crux, isn't it?" Carmen mused. "I guess I've become so used to being on my own and managing everything myself, I don't know how to let go some of the control."

"Do you trust Monica?"

"Oh, totally!"

"Well, as hard as it is, you probably do need to give her more to do."

Hmm, maybe Ash was right. If she gave more of her smaller clients to Monica to handle, she could go looking for some bigger fish.

"But." Ash raised one finger. "Not so that you can take on more to replace it."

Carmen's cheeks heated at being caught in exactly that thought. Ash was observant, apparently able to read Carmen even though they'd only spent a small amount of time together.

Carmen's phone rang, cutting into her thoughts. A glance at the caller display showed her the name of one of her C-grade celebrities, one who insisted on speaking to her every week. She groaned, but before she could swipe her screen to answer, Ash closed a warm hand over hers on the phone.

"Leave it." Ash's voice was quiet yet firm. "They can leave a message, which you can deal with later. This is your me time. Keep it."

Carmen stared into Ash's eyes, so brown they were almost black, and any protest she'd been about to make died on her lips. Instead, a slow smile formed, and a warmth that had nothing to do with the weight of Ash's hand on hers spread throughout her body.

Yes, this is *my me time. She's right.* She eased her hand out from under Ash's and hit the *decline* icon on the phone. "Thank you."

Ash still leaned far forward in her chair, her hand now on the table in front of Carmen, as if hovering to make sure Carmen had done what she'd wanted her to. "You're welcome." Ash dipped her head; her fringe flopped forward, and as she sat up, she swept it casually back. Everything she did seemed imbued with a calm strength that Carmen could only envy.

Ugh, when did I let myself start feeling this way? As if everything is unmanageable?

"I should get back." Carmen sighed and reached for her jacket.

Ash's smile dropped. "You sure?"

"I'm afraid so. But…" Carmen hesitated. Should she? They'd shared some important things today, things that friends would share. And she'd definitely like to hear more about Ash's travels, if nothing else.

Ash looked at her, one eyebrow raised in question.

"Well," Carmen plunged on. "The thing is, I've heard about this new gin bar opening over in Shoreditch, and I wondered if you'd like to meet me there one evening." A thought popped into her head. "Wait, do you even like gin?"

Ash smiled. "I do. And yes, I'd love to explore a new bar with you. That sounds cool."

"Wonderful. I expect weekends will be far too busy there for a few weeks as they're so new, but how about one weekday evening next week?"

"That sounds possible." Ash checked her phone. "I could get away on Tuesday at seven or Wednesday at eight."

Carmen picked up her phone, noting that there was indeed now a voicemail waiting for her. She scrolled to her calendar app. "Okay, Tuesday works!"

"You sound surprised." Ash chuckled.

"I am. I can't believe we didn't have to dance around our calendars for ages to find something that fits."

"Clearly, it was meant to be." Ash flushed pink to her roots. "Oh God, that sounded like some cheesy line, didn't it?"

"It's fine. I mean, it *was* cheesy, but it's fine."

"You know I'm a lesbian, right?" Ash asked, her expression serious.

Ash's confirmation of her sexuality wasn't necessary, but Carmen also didn't know why her skin tingled at the revelation. Carmen blinked at her. "Um, yes?"

"Okay. Good." Ash ran a hand over the back of her head. "I just wanted to make sure there was no misunderstanding going on. This"—she pointed between them—"is just a budding friendship. Nothing else, okay?"

Oh God, don't tell me she thinks I'm going to try what Felicity did? "I know. After all, I'm straight." *There, that's clear and should allay her fears.* "And you, um, you have a girlfriend, don't you?" Where had *that* question come from?

Ash frowned, then sat back, shaking her head. "You mean Hayley? No, no. We were on a date, but that didn't work out. No, I was more worried that you'd think I was, well, coming on to you. I wouldn't want you to get the wrong impression."

Ah. So Ash had been worried Carmen would misconstrue her intentions. How sweet. She didn't want to acknowledge the tiny voice somewhere in the back of her mind that said she was a little disappointed. Because that was ridiculous, wasn't it?

"Honestly, Ash, it's fine. I didn't think anything like that. I'm just enjoying spending time with you. And I want to hear more about your travels and how you became a tattooist."

The creases in Ash's forehead smoothed out. "Cool. I think a couple of gin cocktails could definitely be the means by which you get that information."

Carmen eased back in her seat, her shoulders losing their tension. "Excellent."

Ash grinned. "So, swing by the studio when you're done with work on Tuesday. We'll grab a cab from there, yes?"

"Perfect." Carmen pulled on her jacket and shoved her phone into her handbag. "This was lovely, Ash. Thank you."

"My pleasure."

They stood in the sunshine a moment longer, smiling at each other.

Carmen didn't want to go. She wanted to sit back down, order another coffee, and while away another couple of hours talking with this lovely person. Realising she was staring at Ash, she took a step back. "Right, well, I'll be off, then. I'll see you next week."

"Take care, Carmen." Ash's gaze held hers for another moment before she turned and walked away.

Carmen watched her go, aware that her pulse was back to racing and wondering why because she wasn't remotely stressed. Not now.

Chapter 11

CARMEN STOOD WITH HER HANDS on her hips, staring at the array of clothes presented to her by her open wardrobe. "This really shouldn't be this difficult," she muttered. "It's just a drink. With a friend. In a bar."

And the drink wasn't even until tomorrow night. Yet here she stood the night before, wondering what to wear. She tried to reason with herself that this was all so difficult because she had to dress in her usual style for work as she had two client meetings tomorrow. She'd either have to wear the same thing to the gin bar, which would probably leave her overdressed, or take something more casual to the office to change into for the evening. Somehow she knew that wasn't what was causing her indecision, but she couldn't put her finger on what exactly made it so tricky.

Her phone rang, and she smiled at the name shown on the caller display. "Hi, Tristan."

"Hi, big sister."

She groaned. "You always have to remind me I'm the oldest, don't you?"

"Of course! I'm the baby of the family and always will be."

"Whatever." She sat on the bed. "So, to what do I owe the honour of another call from you in less than a week?"

"Can't I just call and see how you are?"

"Yes, you can, but..."

He sighed audibly. "Okay, okay. Yes, I was worried, and yes, I am checking up on you."

"Oh." Now she felt awful. "I'm okay. Honestly."

"Are you at home? I mean, it's past eight, so—"

"I am! And no, I'm not working either."

"Very good. Do you even know what to do with yourself?"

"You're hilarious." She glanced again at the open wardrobe. "Actually, maybe you can help. I'm trying to pick out an outfit for tomorrow." She swung her legs round and stood. "I've got two client meetings tomorrow, so I need to be dressy for that, but then in the evening I'm meeting someone in a trendy new gin bar in Shoreditch."

"Hmm, that definitely sound like two different outfits."

"I know, but that's the trouble—I can't for the life of me decide what to wear in the evening."

"What's the name of this bar?"

"Sloe Down."

"As in s-l-o-w?"

She smiled. "No, s-l-o-e."

"Oh. Oh! I see. Clever." Tapping drifted through the phone. "Okay, *very* trendy judging from the opening night photos on Google. Hmm."

She waited. Tristan had always had a good eye for what suited her—he'd often been the person she took shopping in her late teens. Although he didn't know everything her wardrobe contained, he'd have a general idea that would be so much better than anything she'd come up with so far.

"Okay," he said finally. "I'm thinking some capri pants, but smart ones, if you have any, and some kind of off-the-shoulder top in a big, bold colour. You have amazing shoulders; you should show them off more often."

"Stop, you're making me blush." She stepped nearer the wardrobe. "Okay, I do have a dark blue pair of capris, and I usually wear them with a matching wedge-heeled sandal thingy."

"Sounds good so far."

She flicked through her tops. "Right, and as for the top, there is this, I suppose. Let me send you a picture." She flipped to the camera's phone, held up the top, a bright orange silky number with a wide neck that draped over her shoulders, in one hand and snapped the photo with the other.

A few seconds after she'd sent it, a long hum of approval came from her brother. "Definitely. That'll knock his socks off."

"It's not a he," Carmen said absently as she hung the top on a door handle and went in search of the sandals in the bottom of the wardrobe.

"Oh, sorry, I assumed when you said you were meeting someone, it was a date."

"No!" Carmen leaped up. Her head cracked on the shelf above the shoe rack, and she yelped. "Shit!"

"What did you do?" Tristan sounded alarmed.

Clutching her head, Carmen stumbled back to the bed. "Ouch. That's sore." She groaned. "I just forgot where my head was in relation to the shelf in the wardrobe."

"Poor you." Genuine sympathy imbued his tone.

"Thanks."

"So who are you meeting tomorrow, and why did you react so violently when I said I thought it was a date?"

Trust Tristan to have read *exactly* what had happened.

"I did nothing of the sort!" Did it sound as feeble to his ears as it did to her own? "I'm just meeting a friend. A new friend. Her name's Ash. She's a tattooist. And a lesbian."

Oh for the love of God, would her mouth *please* stop running away with itself?

There was a pause. "She's a...she's a tattooist?"

Although wondering why her brother had let her off easy, Carmen grabbed at her chance with both hands. "Yes! Remember Felicity decided to get one done to celebrate her divorce? Oh, and did I tell you she told me Michael cheated on her?"

"No! Oh God, poor Felicity."

"I know!"

And they were off, chatting about Felicity, the tattoo, and her cheating spouse. Everything else, especially Carmen's need to blurt out that she was going for a drink with a lesbian called Ash tomorrow evening, was all forgotten—or at least Carmen hoped so.

When they said their goodbyes, Carmen threw the phone onto the bed and began sorting out the rest of her clothes for the morning.

She'd just finished when her phone pinged with a text message.

And I obviously haven't forgotten about the lesbian you're seeing tomorrow night, but you'll tell me in your own good time, I know xxx

She groaned and flopped back down on the bed. What was her subconscious playing at? Why had her brain felt the need to inform her brother about Ash's sexual orientation? It wasn't remotely important to what tomorrow evening was about. Or even to what this new friendship meant. Not at all.

It would probably be better for herself, and Ash, if she actually believed that.

⁓⊷⊶⁓

When the door to the studio opened at a little after eleven on Tuesday, Ash looked up from her copy of *Lonely Planet* magazine. Her mouth dropped open as she took in who stood in her doorway, a large, tatty backpack held in front of him.

"No way." She grinned and tossed the magazine to one side.

"Yep, way." Damian grinned back just as widely, his always unruly, dark blonde hair even wilder than usual. He dumped the bag on the floor, opened his arms wide, and she practically ran into his hug.

"When did you get back?" she asked into his chest as he squeezed her and rocked her from side to side.

He released her and held her at arm's length. "This morning. You look fantastic!"

"Shut up."

He laughed. "You do! Don't argue with me; you know you'll lose."

Ash took a step back and looked him up and down. "You look like you haven't slept in about two weeks." She leaned back in and sniffed. "Or showered. Jesus, mate, where have you been?"

"Puh, I'm not that bad." He laughed, his incredibly white teeth—she never knew how he managed that given he spent half his life living out of a backpack—shining under the bright lights of the studio. "I did actually shower at Heathrow when I landed, so you can stop pretending I stink. Although you might be right about the not sleeping thing." He gestured to the couches. "Can I?"

"Yeah, of course!"

Damian shoved his bag into a corner near the front desk, then they flopped down next to each other on one of the couches.

He let out a long breath and slouched back into the leather. "Jeez, I'm done in. That was some trip."

73

"I lost track of you on Facebook after Mozambique. I mean, I knew you were safe because you kept sending me those random text messages, but I never quite figured out where you were."

He threw his head back and laughed. "Yeah, there's a reason for that. Got myself in a little bit of trouble in Zimbabwe and had to kinda go underground for a while until I could get across the border into Botswana." At Ash's sharp intake of breath, he raised a calming hand. "It's all good. I got in legit, and no one's any the wiser about Zimbabwe. It was all a stupid misunderstanding anyway." He rubbed a hand over his stubbly face. "If I'd known the policeman wanted that big a bribe, I'd have just paid it."

"Oh God, I don't want to know." Ash buried her head in her hands.

Typical Damian, skirting the edges of legality everywhere he went.

When she looked back up his blue eyes were, for once, serious. "Ash, I promise, I was safe. Don't worry."

Ash stared at him for a moment, but the truth was clearly written on his face. "Okay." She huffed out a breath. "You want a coffee?"

"I'd *love* one."

They chatted for about an hour, working their way through a couple of cups of coffee. Ash didn't have any appointments until two, and she was grateful for the sudden appearance of her friend. Not only to fill her time but also to take her mind off what she was doing that evening.

"So, wanna meet for some tea tonight?" Damian stretched his lanky body.

It had taken some time to get used to the Aussies insisting on calling the evening meal *tea*.

"Ah, sorry, I can't. I already have plans."

"Ooooh, hot date?"

"Shut up. No, just drinks with a friend."

"A *friend*?" He made air quotes around the word. "So, it isn't someone I know, then. Cos you'd have just told me their name, wouldn't you?"

God, he was like a dog with a bone when he thought he'd got a new bit of gossip to sniff out.

"She's a new friend. She's cool, works as a talent agent."

"Uh-huh." Even the way he made that sound told Ash he knew he wasn't getting the whole story.

"She's just a friend," Ash repeated, her tone firm.

"What's her name?"

"Carmen."

"Fancy."

"Whatever."

Damian laughed loudly again. "All right, Ms Secretive, I'll let you off right now. But tomorrow for food and I can grill you some more?"

Ash rolled her eyes. "Sure, sounds wonderful." She grinned when he waggled his eyebrows. "All right, all right. I finish tomorrow at eight thirty if I don't get a walk-in."

He stood and stretched. "Great. I'll come pick you up then." He ruffled her hair, a habit she knew *he* knew she hated. "Gotta get home and get some zeds."

She scowled at him as she rearranged her hair back into place. "I'll see you tomorrow."

He threw her a wave over his shoulder, bent to pick up his bag, and left.

Chapter 12

ASH LOUNGED ON THE COUCH, one leg crossed so its foot rested on her other knee, her arms outstretched across the back of the furniture.

It was five minutes after seven, and Carmen had messaged a few minutes ago to say she was on her way, apologising in advance for the fact that she'd be a few minutes late. Ash hadn't let it bother her; Carmen was ridiculously busy. Based on what Carmen had told her, it was a situation Ash thought Carmen should be doing something more serious to fix, but it wasn't her place to tell her new friend that. While she knew she had a tendency to try solving everyone else's problems, she wasn't going to do that with someone she barely knew. Especially not when their burgeoning friendship was still in its infancy. She'd almost overstepped when telling Carmen to ignore that call the last time they'd had coffee. She wouldn't make the same mistake again with someone she was only spending some casual time with.

She snorted softly to herself as Damian's teasing words came back to her about Carmen.

Sorry, mate, but I really am going to disappoint you on this one. Memories of the mess with Vikki played on her mind, and she told herself for the tenth time that day Carmen was and always should be in the friend zone.

A knock at the door pulled her from her thoughts. She stood and smiled widely as Carmen peeked through the window at her.

Ash swiftly crossed the shop and unlocked and opened the door. "Hey!"

"Hello. Sorry again that I'm late. But to be fair, it's a miracle I made it out this early."

"I bet." Ash grinned. "Want to come in for anything or just get going?"

"No, I'm good. Let's go."

"Cool, then just give me a sec to get my bag and lock up." Ash grabbed her messenger bag from the couch. She slung the strap over her shoulder, then walked around the studio flicking off the last of the lights. After the usual alarm, locks, and shutter routine, she turned to Carmen. "All set." She paused and allowed her brain to register Carmen and how she looked for the first time. "That colour looks amazing on you."

The orange top definitely did, somehow adding even more of a glow to Carmen's blonde curls.

"Oh." Carmen smiled shyly. "Thanks. I love your shirt. Very cool."

Ash grinned and looked down at her shirt. "It's great, isn't it?" The white shirt had a classic shape with a stiff collar and cuffs, which Ash always loved, but a variety of cacti dotted the cotton, each plant in garish colours. "I love wearing wild shirts. I make a point of collecting at least one from every place I visit."

She motioned to Carmen for them to start walking up the street towards the main road, where they'd have a better chance of flagging down a cab.

"And where does this one come from?" Carmen easily fell into step alongside Ash, although she was a little shorter, so had to look up to talk to her.

Ash realised that Carmen's outgoing personality and confidence had made her seem much taller in all their meetings so far. "This is from San Francisco. Found it in a flea market on a stall that specialised in second-hand clothes, but like, really good quality stuff, you know?"

"It looks it. So what other shirts like that do you have?"

They chatted about Ash's fashion tastes for the two or three minutes it took to find a cab. Once inside, they fell into a conversation about their respective working days while their driver weaved them expertly through the streets to Shoreditch.

"So was being a talent agent something you always wanted to do?" Ash asked as they exited the cab. She handed Carmen a tenner as contribution towards the fare but was waved off.

"I'll get this. You can get the first round." Carmen gave her a cheeky grin, then paid the cabby and thanked her before stepping back to face Ash.

"Hmm, okay, I guess that's fair."

"And no, in answer to your question," Carmen said as they walked up to the door of the bar. "Not remotely. I'll tell you all when I have a gin in my hand."

Ash held the door open. "Then after you." *You're acting like you're on a date. Stop it. She can open a door for herself.*

Sloe Down was built into a space that used to be a car repair garage. To suit its modern, funky vibe, the owners had left the original shuttered vehicle access doors in place at the front of the building. They entered the bar using the narrow pedestrian door to the left. Once inside, Ash glanced around appreciatively. The interior was industrial with more than a touch of comfort in the many sofas that were dotted all over the cavernous space. Clever use of large but soft lights hanging down from the high ceiling added to the relaxed atmosphere.

"Oh, this is fab!" Carmen gazed around the room.

"Isn't it? Great choice to come here."

"Good." Carmen smiled at her. "Shall we try to get to the bar?"

Ash looked over to where Carmen pointed and winced. The queue was long, but she shouldn't have been surprised since the bar was already trending on social media. She sucked in a breath. "Okay, I'm going in. What would you like?"

"I'd love a Negroni, please."

"Oooh, a classic." Ash nodded. "All right, if I'm not back in about fifteen minutes, send in the search party."

Carmen laughed. "I'll try to find us a spot to sit, okay?"

"Sure, I'll find you."

As it was, Ash had to admire the efficiency of the bar crew. They had a good system going of ordering at one end of the bar and obtaining drinks at the other. Within less than ten minutes, she weaved her way through the busy room, looking left and right for Carmen, until she spotted her waving from halfway up a spiral staircase towards the rear of the space.

"They have a terrace!" Carmen said when Ash joined her. "Do you mind?"

It was a warm, cloudless night, and Ash lit up at the thought of spending it outdoors. "God, no, not at all."

Ash handed Carmen her drink, and they stepped carefully up the curved, wrought-iron steps, arriving on a steel landing at the top. Two paces forward took them to an open doorway. Beyond was a terrace that ran the length of the building. It was decorated with a few potted plants and some basic outdoor tables, one of which Carmen swiftly snagged for them.

"Nice." Ash looked around as she sat. "I mean, it's London, so we won't see any stars when it gets dark later, but it's still cool to be sitting outside."

"Isn't it? I forget how cooped up I get in my office, so I don't know why I'm surprised I get so excited about outdoor eating and drinking."

Laughing, Ash raised her glass, and Carmen tapped hers against it. "Cheers," Ash said. "And thanks for the invite. I love discovering new places."

"Cheers. And me too."

They sipped slowly. Each let out appreciative moans as they replaced their glasses on the table's polished aluminium surface.

"What are you drinking?" Carmen looked quizzically at Ash's glass.

"Ah, I'm boring, I'm afraid. Plain old gin and tonic. Although I did go for Elephant Gin, as I've heard it's a little different."

"And?"

"And yes, it is. There's an unusual flavour in there I can't put my finger on. Want to try?"

Carmen tilted her head. "Sure you don't mind? I mean, I might have germs."

Ash grinned. "I've eaten street food in tiny villages all over the world. You know, the places you're never supposed to attempt if you're a westerner. I think I'm safe with you taking a little sip from my drink."

Carmen laughed and reached for Ash's glass. "Fair enough." She sipped, and Ash had to force herself not to watch Carmen's lips.

Humming, Carmen set the glass back down. "Yes, that is different, isn't it?" She laughed once more. "Oh, I so needed this, Ash. Thank you so much for accepting the invite."

"Hey, you're welcome." Ash was about to ask more, then stopped herself. *No, you're not her therapist, remember?*

"So, street food all over the world, huh?" Carmen leaned forward slightly in her seat. The shoulders of her top moved with the action and revealed more bare skin around her collarbone.

Ash admonished herself for noticing.

"You like travel, then?" Carmen continued.

Ash snorted. "Oh God, you could say that. It's my addiction."

"I can think of worse addictions to have."

"Now that's true."

"So, where have you been?" Carmen asked. "You mentioned Australia and New Zealand. They were first?"

"Yes, that's where I really got started. I mean, I'd done lots of the European cities, and with my job I'd been to the States a couple of times. But with the latter you never actually get to see the place you're visiting. Just your hotel, the office, and the airport."

Carmen nodded. "Yes, I know. I've been to L.A. so many times over the years and still couldn't tell you anything about it."

"Yeah, I get it. I think that's why the Australia trip has such good memories for me. It's the first trip I did where I got to fully explore the place, get an understanding for it, feel the culture."

"Tell me." Carmen settled back in her chair with her glass in her hand, her gaze focused on Ash.

Whenever Ash had tried talking to her sister or to her ex, Leesa, about her travels, their eyes had glazed over with boredom. Damian was the only one who understood her passion for it, but Carmen looked genuinely eager to hear all about it too.

"Do you remember I quit my job at the bank?" Ash asked.

Carmen nodded.

"Well that was the catalyst. For a lot of things, but travel was definitely one of them. I worked at the bank with an Aussie guy called Damian. We got on like a house on fire—in fact, he was the only one who kept me sane in the last couple of years there. Anyway, he suggested meeting me in Australia and we'd do a road trip. I ended up staying there for over three months."

"Wow!"

"Yep. It was so good. We saw so many places, met so many amazing people."

"Tell me," Carmen repeated quietly.

"Really?"

"Yes. Please. I'd love to hear about it. A road trip is something I have a dream of doing for myself." She chuckled. "In a convertible. Clichéd,

I know, but… One day." She pursed her lips. "So tell me what I've been missing."

When Ash finally noticed how dark the sky had become, she was stunned to realize she'd talked for nearly an hour. Her drink was long finished; Carmen had offered her another, but she'd declined and switched to water. Carmen had bought herself a second Negroni but also sipped at water too. She'd returned from the bar with a selection of nuts and crunchy snacks that they'd been nibbling on for the last ten minutes or so.

Carmen had asked insightful questions, appeared genuinely enraptured by some of the stories Ash had shared, and couldn't seem to get enough of hearing about the world and all the places she'd yet to see. Talking to Carmen was like talking to her own younger self, the person she had been fifteen years ago, when she had started to earn the serious money at the bank and the world opened up to her.

"So where's next?" Carmen asked.

Ash grinned, her excitement instant. "Three weeks in South Africa next month. I'm heading to Kruger National Park for a self-drive safari, and I cannot wait."

"Okay, I'm not jealous. Not at all." Carmen grimaced, but her eyes sparkled. "God, that sounds amazing!"

"I know. I've been planning it for months, and I can't believe it's less than four weeks away."

"So what happens to the studio while you're gone?"

Ash shrugged. "It's closed. I never book clients in August—lots of people are on holiday themselves, so I decided early on to take that month off every year. So far it's worked brilliantly."

"God, I can't imagine closing my entire business for a whole month!" Carmen shook her head.

"When was the last time you took a proper holiday? From your reactions to my tales, I get the impression it's been a while."

Carmen huffed out a breath. "Yes, it has. I think I mentioned how hard I've worked to build up my agency, to get the kind of reputation I have now. Well, of course, that's come at a price." She gave a rueful smile. "My brother lives in Paris, and he keeps inviting me over to stay for at least a weekend. I can't even find time to do that." She absently stroked the pale skin of one of her forearms as she spoke.

Watching Carmen's fingers move made Ash wonder how they would feel touching her skin. Stroking her, teasing her. *Whoa.* Ash reached for her water and took a long gulp. "So how did you get into this line of work? And is it what you were always going to do? I mean, if I'm prying, then say so, but it just… Well, it seems to me that your work doesn't make you very happy at the moment and stops you doing other things you'd really like to do, so…"

Carmen's shoulders slumped. She drained the last of her Negroni. "Once I got started in this industry, I loved it. I loved how every day threw up something different. I loved how many interesting people I met. When I took the step to branch out and start my own agency, I was so excited about what I could do. Scared, yes, but I had confidence in myself because I knew I was right where I was supposed to be."

"That's so cool. Not many people have that luxury. They end up in jobs that just bring in the money, not jobs that challenge them or satisfy them."

"Exactly. I saw it happen to so many of my peers from university. I knew I was lucky, and I've counted my blessings ever since. So it doesn't sit well with me that I'm so unsatisfied now."

"Is it really dissatisfaction, or are you simply tired?"

"That's the sixty-four-million-dollar question, isn't it? And the trouble is, these days I'm too tired to even begin to figure out the answer."

"And is work one of the reasons why your last relationship didn't work out?"

"Not directly." Carmen pushed her empty glass around. "I don't think relationships are really my thing. Work is what I'm good at." She looked thoughtful for a moment. "I've only ever had one serious relationship in my life, with a guy called Lewis in my early twenties. God, I loved him to distraction."

"What happened?"

"Lewis was always deeply invested in the well-being of others. He wasn't religious, but helping others was almost like a calling for him. We met at uni, in a walking group, and we fell hard and fast. But within a year of him leaving—he was a year ahead of me—we knew we had to make some big decisions. He was applying for jobs with refugee agencies and charities that would take him far from home for months at a time. I knew it was what he really wanted, so I didn't want to stand in his way."

"And he left?"

"He did." Carmen shook her head. "It was awful. We were both heartbroken. But although it took me a while to get over him, I don't regret what happened. He would write to me, still does occasionally, and the sheer joy that came off the page was wonderful to experience."

"Ugh, that's kind of sad but great."

"It is, isn't it?" Carmen hesitated, looking across the table at Ash. "What about you? Any great loves in your past?"

Ash wondered how to word her response. "Um, two, I suppose. Although one wasn't even a relationship. My last serious girlfriend, Leesa, I was with for about two years. We split up soon after I left the bank when I discovered she was only after my money."

"No! Seriously?"

Ash nodded. "Yes. When I announced I was leaving and likely to set up a tattoo studio in the future, she freaked out. Turns out she'd got quite used to the money I earned, the posh dinners we could have, the luxury weekends away in the countryside."

"Oh, Ash, that's awful!"

"Yeah, it hurt; I can't lie."

"I'm scared to ask how the other one ended."

"Other one?"

"You said you'd had two great loves, but that the other one wasn't even—"

"Oh. Yeah." Ash huffed out a breath. "That one's more difficult to talk about."

"Oh. Well, another time, maybe."

Now Ash felt guilty for holding back. "Okay, short version. We worked together. She was engaged to a guy, but she and I got…close. Nothing in particular happened, but I fell for her, big-time. Then she married him anyway. It was pretty messy." *And that's an understatement.*

"Oh."

Ash stood up; she needed to get away from this conversation. "Want another drink?"

"Love one." Carmen rifled in her handbag and pulled a twenty from her purse. "My turn to pay though."

Ash grinned. "No problem."

"Wait, you went on a walk in an area known to have rhinos, and the advice you were given if you saw one was to climb up the nearest tree?" Carmen put down her drink and stared at Ash.

Ash laughed and shook her head. "Look, you make it sound worse than it was. Honestly, it was fine. There were two guards, both armed. The walk was properly certified, and I'm pretty sure the guy was joking with the tree-climbing advice."

Carmen didn't know whether to be envious of Ash's devil-may-care attitude or alarmed by it. Ash was so many things Carmen wasn't—brave, carefree, relaxed. She could admit to herself that she might have a little bit of a hero-worship crush thing going on right now.

Listening to Ash talk was as intoxicating as watching the way she used her hands to emphasise her words and the way her entire face lit up whenever she shared a particularly happy memory. Carmen had even managed to forget about her phone all evening. Usually the thing was practically glued to her left hand, but there was something about being in Ash's presence that made it easy to want to forget her work for a couple of hours.

"Hey, I've been meaning to ask," Ash said. "What's the origin of your name? I mean, Carmen isn't exactly a classic English name."

Carmen chuckled. "No, it isn't. When she was younger, my mother loved going to the theatre and the opera. And her favourite opera is *Carmen*, so…"

"Really? That's kind of out there, isn't it? I mean, it's not quite how I imagine upper-class people naming their kids. Aren't they all named after their great-grandmother or great-grandfather or something?"

"Normally, yes." Carmen laughed. "It was so surprising she went through with it. She's such a traditionalist about most other things. She followed that up with Tristan for my brother, from *Tristan and Isolde*, her second-favourite opera."

"Even fancier."

"He loves it. Thinks it only adds to his natural sophistication." Carmen winked.

"Okay, I like the sound of him already."

Carmen nodded. "He's a great brother." She sipped some more water. "So why tattoos?"

"Always been fascinated by them, ever since I was a kid. My dad had been in the merchant navy when he was younger, and his arms were covered in them. He'd tell me all the places he'd been and where he'd had each tattoo done, and I always thought it would be cool to get some of my own. Then, the more I got interested in art at school, the more I thought about possibly joining the two things up."

"But you didn't? Well, not right away."

A frown marred Ash's features. "Yeah. Parental pressure when you're sixteen and you've left school with only a couple of O levels to your name means finding a job, any job, to bring in some money." She paused. "I was luckier than some. My mum cleaned houses for some pretty well-off people. One woman was some high-ranking manager at a bank and got chatting to her cleaning lady, my mum, one day, and heard all about me, the sixteen-year-old daughter who was smart and polite. I don't know if she did it because she genuinely believed in giving someone a chance or if she just thought it would make her look good in the eyes of her other posh friends, but she pulled some strings and got me a clerical job. It was nothing much, but..." She shrugged. "I *am* smart. I proved myself worth much more within a few months, and within a few years I was working in trading."

Carmen could have been mildly insulted by Ash's words about a rich person wanting to look good to their friends. But she knew many of her mother's close circle only gave money to those in need for that exact reason. That and for the tax benefits. Equally, Ash's story conjured up discomfort for the privileged life Carmen had been born into, where financial worries were non-existent. Carmen's life through school and university had been easy in that respect, in comparison to Ash's. It made her even more admiring of the woman who sat opposite her.

"Your mum sounds lovely, talking about you like that to her clients."

Ash's eyes shadowed. "She had her moments, yes."

The air between them was suddenly a tad uncomfortable.

"Sorry, Ash. Now it seems I've hit a nerve. I'm—"

Ash raised a hand. "No, it's okay. My parents died in a car crash about twelve years ago. We weren't close when they died, despite what my mum had done for me at sixteen." She rubbed at the back of her neck. "They were homophobic. Really didn't handle me coming out to them very well when I was going on seventeen." Ash's troubled eyes betrayed her calm demeanour.

Carmen wanted to touch Ash's arm or hand or do something that would show her concern for what had clearly been a hard time in Ash's life. But they weren't at that point yet in this friendship, were they? "Oh, I'm so sorry." Carmen took a deep breath. "My brother is gay, and my mother is… She's never fully accepted it. His boyfriend, for example, has never been invited to Christmas lunch, even though Tristan's been with him for over six years now. I know her actions haven't affected me directly, but I can at least empathise somewhat."

"Is your brother okay?"

"He is, actually. He's very happy with his life. It took him a while to get there, given the way she reacted when he first told her. But she has calmed down since then, and apart from Christmas, it's generally okay. I think he knows she does love him, even if she doesn't understand him. My father is better about it—he's always been the one with the live-and-let-live attitude. Even so, he hardly ever asks about Tristan's life other than his work. I know Tristan puts on a brave face, but it hurts him."

"Isn't that funny? It was my dad who was better about it than my mum too. When I was thinking about telling them, I always assumed she, being such a nurturing woman, would be okay with it. But she really wasn't."

The pain in Ash's eyes pushed Carmen's earlier reticence into the shadows. She placed her hand on Ash's forearm. Their gazes locked, and there was gratitude for Carmen's action in Ash's expression. There was something else too. Carmen couldn't name it, but it left her feeling a tad breathless. "I'm sorry you went through that. And I admire you for being the strong person you are now, despite all that."

"Thank you." Ash exhaled and rolled her shoulders.

The action pulled her arm away from Carmen's touch, and the loss she felt seemed out of proportion to the moment.

"God, families," Ash murmured, her gaze still holding Carmen's.

Carmen nodded. She was strangely warmed by this odd connection they'd found between their histories.

Ash sat up straight. "Enough of that. Let's go back to talking about near misses with rhinos." She grinned.

Carmen glanced at her watch, and her heart sank. It was past ten already. How had they spent three hours together, and it felt like only thirty minutes? "Ugh, I'm sorry, but I ought to go. I've got another early start and—"

"It's okay." Ash nodded in understanding. "I hadn't realised it had got that late, actually."

"Me neither. I…I've really enjoyed this evening, but it's flown by."

"And we never even got to the part about the crocodile in the campsite in northern Australia."

Carmen gasped and shuddered. "Perhaps I don't need to hear that one." She shook her head. "I'm beginning to think you've got a bit of a death wish."

Ash laughed. "I don't actually go looking for these adventures, you know. They just kind of happen."

"Hmm, well, remind me never to go on holiday with you." Carmen startled as she realised how forward that might sound, but Ash's warm smile kept her from trying to take the words back. She grinned sheepishly instead and reached for her handbag. "Okay, I'm going to go in search of a cab."

"I'll keep you company until you find one. I'm going to walk home."

"You sure? Will it be safe?"

"I'll be fine. I only take the main roads, and it's not that far. But thanks for your concern."

"Okay, I believe you. But would you text me when you're home?"

Ash's smile was even warmer than a moment ago. "I will."

They walked close together, not quite touching. Even so, Carmen could feel the warmth of Ash's arm near hers. It comforted her, but she couldn't for the life of her figure out why. *It's because we've formed a connection this evening.* The shared interest in travel, the fact that they'd both had homophobic parents—those were the sorts of things people bonded over, weren't they?

People buzzed around them on the busy street, but within seconds Ash spotted a cab with its light on and waved it down.

"Thanks, Ash. And I don't just mean for the cab. This was a wonderful evening."

"Wasn't it? I love meeting new people, hearing their stories. And we barely touched on yours—you let me talk far too much."

"But your stories are far more interesting than mine."

"I somehow doubt that." Ash looked at Carmen with such a depth of interest, it stole her breath.

The cab pulled up.

"Well, this is me." Carmen looked at the cab, then back at Ash, who stood with her hands in the pockets of her jeans. Her pose was confident and strong, her shirt fitting her body like a glove, her face open and welcoming. She looked… Carmen struggled with breath once more as the word *gorgeous* ran through her mind.

"I hope you get a decent sleep tonight," Ash said quietly. "And, well, give me a call if you want to meet up anytime, okay?"

Carmen nodded, not sure what she'd say if she tried to form words. *What the hell is happening to me?* She stepped into the cab, pulled the door shut, and threw Ash a weak smile as the driver pulled them away from the kerb.

Chapter 13

WHEN DAMIAN WALKED INTO THE studio on Wednesday at a quarter to eight, Ash grinned at him. "Well, you look tons better."

"Whatever." He wandered over to the couches and threw himself onto one.

Ash chuckled, then turned back to her client, a woman called Julia, who'd just had a green sea turtle tattooed on her right thigh. The turtle joined the numerous other sea creatures Ash had been inking onto Julia's leg for the last two years; she now had an almost complete coral reef scene stretching from her ankle to her groin. Ash finished taping the cling film over the site. "All done."

"Beautiful. Thanks, Ash." Julia settled up, and they said their goodbyes.

"Okay, give me ten minutes to clean up, and then we can go," Ash called to Damian as she began collecting up used ink bottles, tissues, and other detritus.

"No worries. Hey, fancy Thai tonight? I haven't had a decent Thai in weeks."

"Sure. You choose where. I'm easy."

"Cool."

Fifteen minutes later, they were on their way to Tottenham Court Road or rather to one of the side streets leading off it towards the university district. Somehow Damian always knew the best—and out of the way—places to eat in whatever city he happened to be in.

They caught up as they strolled along, Damian filling her in on some more details about the mix-up in Zimbabwe, but mostly talking about Botswana and what a fantastic place it had been.

"You need to add it to your list," he said as they crossed behind a line of stuck traffic, horns blaring and music pumping all around them.

"Yeah, it sounds like it."

They arrived at the restaurant, and the waiter led them to a small table along the far wall, where they wedged in between a group of four young women on one side and two earnest-looking men on the other. All their neighbours had textbooks spread out between them.

The waiter handed them worn menus and took their beer order before scurrying off.

Damian opened his menu, ran a finger down page three, then slammed his menu shut. "Sorted."

"Seriously? I haven't even looked yet."

He laughed. "I always know what I want and just needed to check they hadn't scrubbed it off the menu."

Ash shook her head. She turned her attention back to her menu and concentrated on making her own choice. It was a good menu, lots of things she recognised and some she didn't, which meant she had to pick something from the latter category. "Chicken peanut massaman for me."

"Oh, good choice." Damian nodded sagely. "I'm having sour soup. The name does not do it justice, trust me."

"I believe you." Ash grinned. "But I'll need a taste, just to be certain."

They ordered, and while they waited for their food, Damian told her his plans for the next few months. Then he gave her a wicked grin.

"So, how was your not-date last night?"

Ash had done well not dwelling on it since she and Carmen said goodbye the night before. She'd thrown herself into work at the studio today, even doing extra cleaning and sorting of stock to keep herself busy and her mind *not* on Carmen. But of course, it was too much to hope that Damian had forgotten all about her evening out. "It was a nice evening, but with a bit of a strange ending." She shook her head. "She's a nice person. Runs her own business and she's interesting and smart. We shared some personal stuff that showed we have more in common than I would have thought, given how obviously different our upbringings are. She's posh, but not in an arsehole way, you know? Anyway, it was good spending time with her and getting to know someone new."

"But...?"

"But I definitely felt like I'd said or done something wrong at the very end of the night, as we were saying goodbye, because she kind of blew me off. Didn't really say goodbye, and when I did as she asked and texted her to say I'd got home, I just got an 'okay, good' back, but nothing else."

"But this is just friendship, right? You're not pining after this woman, are you?" Damian, for once, looked serious, a rare frown on his face.

It was tempting to lie, but this was Damian. He knew more about her than anyone else. She'd been sharing everything with him since the Australia trip, and she couldn't stop now. "I'm…confused," she said eventually.

"Ah."

"I know." She slumped in her chair.

Damian cleared his throat. "I rarely tell you what to do, right?"

She nodded, wary of what was coming next.

"And I know you've shared a lot with me over the years, and I know there's stuff you haven't, and that's cool." He pulled at the label of his beer bottle, leaving small flakes of paper in a pile on the table.

Ash had never seen him so nervous. What was going on?

"Well," he continued, "I guess I'm worried. After the way you just talked about this Carmen chick, I'm… Well, I'm worried she's going to be another Vikki." He winced as he said the name, as if expecting an outburst.

Ah. Ash sat back. She wasn't angry. Actually, she was pretty touched. "She's not going to be another Vikki. Seriously, I'm just friends with Carmen." She held up a hand when he made to interrupt. "Yes, she is attractive and fun to be with. I'm not an idiot; I can see that. But I'm not the person I was when we knew Vikki. I've learned a lot since then, and it's all good. You don't have to worry, okay?"

Damian leaned forward and rested his elbows on the table. He stared intently at her for a few moments. "All right, then. Good." He sat back and swigged from his beer. "And at least now I know I definitely did the right thing."

"What right thing?"

Damian squirmed in his seat. "Shit, didn't mean to say that." He rubbed at his stubbly chin. "Ugh, I probably should have told you this back then, but I didn't want to stir up old wounds."

He was talking in bloody riddles, and it was annoying the crap out of her. "What are you talking about?"

Damian puffed out a long breath. "I got a call from Vikki, a few years ago now. She and Dave were getting divorced. She wanted to know if I knew where you were as she'd lost touch. It sounded off. Not sure why, but it just did. So I kinda lied and said I wasn't in touch with you anymore but agreed to meet her for a drink, for old times' sake. After three large glasses of wine she was hammered, and it all came spilling out."

"What did?"

He ran a hand over his face. "Ugh, how much she missed you. How much she regretted marrying Dave and hurting you."

"She really said that?" Ash didn't know what to do with this knowledge. It was the last thing she ever expected to hear.

"Yeah, she did." Damian snorted. "I never put them together. I mean, she was all bubbly, fun, and sexy for fucking days, and he was…" He shook his head. "A wet mop. Anyway, look, you can tell me I was wrong, but you were going through the shit with Leesa at the time, so that's why I told her I didn't know where you were. Well, that and I remember how fucked-up she made you feel after all that went down."

Ash held up a hand. "No, no, that's fine. Thank you. You're right; there's no way I would have wanted to get back in touch with her. It would have been…" She shook her head. "No, too messy."

The news that Vikki and Dave had divorced didn't surprise her in the slightest. She actually felt bad for both of them. But she had zero regrets about Damian acting as her shield; Vikki was all in the past, and that's where she would stay.

"Phew." Damian threw her a weak smile. "Hey, I'm sorry I compared the situation with Carmen to that. I just got worried you were getting all silly again."

"Nope. Silliness is not going to happen. Trust me." She smiled at him and reached for her beer. Somewhere in the back of her mind, a little voice was asking if she was one hundred per cent sure there was nothing to worry about. Because it was far too easy to think about Carmen and to look forward to when she might see her again.

Chapter 14

"Carmen? *Carmen!*"

Carmen blinked a couple of times, and Felicity's face came into focus once more. "Sorry, what was that?"

Felicity held up a Hermès scarf and raised her eyebrows. "I asked if you thought this suited me?"

Carmen glanced once at the scarf, its silk printed in dark blues and greens, and nodded. "Totally." She had no idea how long she'd drifted off—she hadn't even known they were looking at scarves.

They were in Harvey Nichols, finding Felicity a new ensemble for a charity dinner she was hosting in a couple of weeks at the Savoy. It was Thursday evening, only two days after Carmen had spent the evening with Ash at Sloe Down, but it seemed much longer.

Yes, probably because for some reason that's all you've been able to think about.

Her work had suffered. Her sleep had been sporadic at best. A few times she'd caught Monica and Beverley exchanging puzzled or worried looks.

And she'd spent nearly an hour with Felicity already this evening and somehow still hadn't mentioned to her best friend that she'd had a night out with Ash and that her response to it confused the hell out of her.

She couldn't get Ash out of her mind. With no trouble at all she could conjure up that image of her standing on the kerb, hands in her pockets, looking so relaxed and…gorgeous.

There was that word again.

Felicity stepped closer, her face only inches away. "Have you been abducted by aliens?"

"What?" Carmen stared at her.

"It's the only explanation I have." Felicity shrugged, her forehead creased. "It looks like you, and the voice is yours, but you're rather like a shell of yourself." She laid a hand on Carmen's arm. "Are you all right, darling?"

"I think I'm attracted to a woman."

Good God, what *was* this lately with her just blurting things out with zero censorship?

Felicity opened her mouth, then closed it again. She dropped the scarf on the table next to them, grabbed Carmen by the wrist, and pulled. Felicity had always been freakishly strong, and Carmen's feet moved before she could think to resist.

"Wh-what are you doing?"

"We need to sit down for this."

Felicity led her to the lifts, and when one arrived, she pulled her in and pressed the button for the top floor.

Three minutes later, they were perched on two stools at the Fifth Floor Bar, glasses of champagne in front of them. Enticing scents from the food people ate around them reached Carmen's nose, but her stomach recoiled; her nerves were too taut to contemplate eating. The bar was busy, and a loud hum of conversation and clinking glasses filled the air.

"Felicity, you didn't need to—"

"On the contrary." Felicity lifted her drink. "I think I did." She held out her glass.

Carmen raised hers, and they tapped.

"So," Felicity said after a moment. "Would you care to explain what you blurted out downstairs?" She arched one eyebrow. "And don't try to tell me it was nothing. You haven't been *you* ever since you split up with Gerald. Well, before then, actually. And now you tell me you're attracted to a *woman?*"

Carmen could pretend. Say it was merely her work and that everything would be all right once she got on top of that again. But that would be a big lie, and she and Felicity had a better friendship than that. "I think... Something is happening to me, and I don't..." *God, how do I even explain this? I barely understand it myself.*

Felicity, to her credit, kept quiet.

Carmen reached for her hand and held it tight. She needed an anchor, the holdfast of her friend's strength and love while her emotions spun in free fall. "I honestly don't know how to say it. It's absurd. Completely absurd."

Felicity's eyes widened, and her hand beneath Carmen's tensed. "Oh. Oh, Carmen, I'm sorry. Look, you know I love you, I do, but I don't *love* you. You understand? I mean, obviously I'm awfully flattered, but—"

What the—? Realisation dawned. "*No!*"

Heads turned from all around the semicircle of the bar.

Carmen sucked in a breath and lowered her voice. "God, no, that's not what this is."

"Oh! Oh God." Felicity blushed a deep red. "I'm so sorry, darling. I thought… God, never mind." She reached for her champagne and took a gulp.

Carmen leaned her chin in her hand. "It's okay. I'm not exactly being clear, am I?"

"No, you're not. Honestly, what is going on?"

"Ash."

Felicity frowned. "Ash?"

"Yes, Ash." Carmen swallowed. "I, um, seem to be… I'm really attracted to her."

Okay, well, it was out there now. Actually, saying the words out loud for the first time was good. She'd expected internal panic and the cold finger of fear to trace down her spine, but no, apart from a rapidly beating heart at sharing such a monumental thing, it was fine.

Hmm, okay.

She braced herself for Felicity's response, unable to look at her, focusing instead on the rise of the bubbles in her champagne glass.

"You? To Ash?" The lines on Felicity's forehead deepened. "You mean…?" She waved a hand in the air. "No, sorry, you need to explain."

Carmen sighed. "Well, that's the tricky part. I can't really explain it. Not even to myself. I mean, I'm straight. I'm forty-three years old, and I've always been straight. So why do I keep thinking about her?"

"I'm baffled, darling. I mean, you barely know her. Oh God, you're going through some sort of midlife crisis, aren't you? Don't make a fool of yourself, darling. Not like I did." She flushed.

"No, it's not that." Carmen could understand why Felicity would think so, but she was insulted nonetheless. "These are genuine feelings, not something silly and throwaway."

Felicity folded her arms. "You shared a pastry one morning a couple of weeks ago. How can that make you think—"

Guilt rushed through Carmen. She held up a hand. "Um, not quite."

"What?"

"I have actually seen her a couple more times since then."

Felicity's eyebrows shot up. "And you're only telling me this now?" She threw her hands up. "Why am I not up to date?"

She looked genuinely hurt, and it clutched at Carmen. "God, I'm sorry. I honestly never meant to keep it from you, but it got very confusing and…" She paused as the reason became crystal clear. "I think I didn't want to talk about it because if I kept it inside, it would just go away."

"Only it hasn't?" Felicity's voice was gentle.

Carmen shook her head.

"Well." Felicity nudged Carmen's glass towards her. "Then I think we're going to need another one of these while you fill me in."

"Thank you." Carmen took Felicity's hand and squeezed it.

"Of course, sweetheart. Did you honestly think I'd run away screaming if you told me about your secret sapphic tendencies?"

Carmen laughed and shook her head. Warmth spread through her chest, and her heart rate slowed back towards a normal pace. "No, I didn't. But thank you."

They drained their glasses, and Felicity signalled for another round. "So start at the beginning, please."

Over the second glass, Carmen slowly filled in the gaps. It helped to talk it through, of course, even if the entire concept still took some getting used to.

"Okay," Felicity said once Carmen stopped talking. "It does sound as if you two have shared some good and important time together. But," she held up a finger, "are you sure it's an attraction? As in, this is someone you would actively want to date? And then kiss and eventually go to bed with? Because that's a big step to consider, don't you think?"

At the word kiss, a strange sensation of butterflies and tension flooded Carmen's stomach. Thoughts she'd tried so hard to shy away from over the last two days invaded her brain: Ash's mouth, with those full lips, on hers. Ash's arms wrapped around her, pulling her closer. Her hands in Ash's hair, deepening the kiss…

The butterflies and delicious tension in her belly flew south. *Oh God.* She placed a hand on her cheek. The heat there was intense.

Felicity grinned. "Ah, I see."

Carmen fumbled for her glass and downed the contents in one.

Felicity laughed, then stopped, a hand clutched to her chest. "Wait! I just remembered something. That disastrous day I went to her studio to, um, you know…" Her cheeks pinked once more.

"I remember." Carmen wondered why a feeling distinctly similar to jealousy now roiled in her stomach.

"Well, there was a sketchbook open on the counter. She's very talented. Beautiful use of shading. Anyway, there was a sketch of you in there!"

"Wh-what?" Carmen's heart skipped a beat. "Surely not. That's…that's ridiculous." *How did it get so warm in here all of a sudden?* "Why would Ash have a sketch of me?"

Felicity tilted her head and smiled wickedly. "Ah, yes, why indeed?"

Carmen sat back. Ash had sketched her? The thought made her glow. Then she sobered. *Don't get carried away. She probably sketches everyone she meets.* The idea that Ash had drawn her for any other reason was preposterous, no matter what Felicity seemed to be inferring. Wasn't it?

Ash wasn't good with early mornings. Getting into town for nine on a Friday where she had back-to-back appointments from noon until late in the evening wasn't her favourite way to start the day. But she had no one else to blame but herself—she'd realised the night before that her last tetanus vaccination had been years ago. After finding out her GP was fully booked for the next two weeks, she'd instead made her way to a travel clinic near Marylebone High Street and waited in line for a booster jab.

As she left the clinic, the morning sun hit her fully in the face, and she couldn't help smiling. Yes, the early start had been a pain, but now she was ready for her big trip.

Okay, that's all great, but now I need coffee.

Across the street from where she stood was a genuine Italian espresso bar, and she eagerly trotted over the road towards it. Inside, the smell of roasted coffee beans hit her nose, and her tired nerves stood to attention.

"What can I get you?" the woman behind the counter asked.

"Double espresso, please." Why not? She'd need all the help she could get for the rest of the day.

"Good choice," a soft voice said behind her.

Ash whipped round to find Carmen behind her, a half smile on her face. It was such a shock to see her there, out of context, as it were. And especially after Tuesday evening had ended so strangely. Ash had pondered calling Carmen a couple of times since then, but something had held her back.

"Carmen! Hey. What a nice surprise." She willed herself not to gawk; Carmen looked amazing today in a silky, pale green dress that just about reached her knees. *She always looks like a million bucks.*

"My office is just around the corner." Carmen thumbed behind her. "What brings you to this part of town?"

"My own stupidity." Ash laughed at Carmen's bemused expression. "Realised I needed a tetanus booster."

"Ah, for the big trip. The travel clinic over the road?"

"Exactly. Didn't take too long." Ash turned to the barista to pay for her coffee, then swung back to Carmen as a thought hit her. "Can I get you a coffee?" *Friends do that, right? I'm not overstepping by offering.*

Carmen's face lit up, and her smile this time was breathtaking. "I would love a coffee, thank you."

Ash added a second double espresso to her order. She tried hard not to read too much into the fact that she already knew what Carmen's preferred coffee choice was. Not daring to meet Carmen's eye, she instead handed over a ten-pound note to the barista. "Bad day already?" she said to Carmen over her shoulder.

"Oh, no, not really. Just a long week."

"And we did stay out late on a school night on Tuesday, didn't we?" *Okay, stop that. That was your flirting voice. What were you saying to Damian only two bloody nights ago? Just friends. Just friends.*

One corner of Carmen's mouth quirked up. "Indeed. Are you in a rush to get to the studio? I have a little while until my next meeting. Want to sit and drink our coffees here?" There was a slight tremor in her voice.

Ash could swear Carmen was nervous. But why would that be? "Sure." The word was out before she could stop it, but friends did coffee all the time so where was the harm?

"Great. I'll grab us that table by the window."

"Perfect." *Yep, totally. Nice little romantic corner just made for two. What am I doing?*

By the time she'd waited for the coffees to be made, she'd managed to calm her breathing a little. She carried the small cups over and put them carefully down on the table. She pulled out the chair opposite Carmen and squeezed into the small space between it and the table.

"It's rather cosy back here, isn't it?" Carmen frowned. "Sorry."

"It's fine. So, how's life in the talent world?"

Carmen waved a hand. "The same. How about the tattoo world?"

Ash grinned. "Also the same. Have you had any time off this week, other than Tuesday evening?"

A delicate blush stole across Carmen's cheeks, and her gaze darted away. "I saw Felicity last night. We went shopping."

Why was she blushing? What exactly had they gone shopping for? Ash nearly choked on the images her mind conjured. "Nice." She managed to keep her tone even, thankfully.

Carmen's sudden laugh startled Ash. "You sound as excited as if I'd said I'd been to the dentist."

Ash held open her arms. "Yeah, well, shopping is not my favourite sport."

"I would never have guessed." Carmen's mouth twitched. "But wait a minute, you love shopping for your colourful shirts."

"That's different. That's always on holiday. Everyone knows holiday shopping isn't the same."

When Carmen laughed like that, with her entire face lit up and her head thrown back, Ash's brain and libido short-circuited. *God, she's beautiful.*

"I suppose that's true, yes." Carmen sipped her coffee. "So, um, any plans for the weekend? Other than working, obviously."

"I'm out to dinner tomorrow night after work. A late supper over in Shoreditch. Then Sunday will be my lazy day—reading, lounging around, eating pizza."

"Oh, that sounds blissful. One day I might have one of those again." Carmen gave a lopsided grin. "Maybe when I retire."

Ash tapped her chin. "Maybe you should aim for one a little earlier than that."

Carmen shrugged, then finished her coffee. Her phone, which was on the table next to her cup, buzzed. She glanced down at it and audibly sighed. "And that's my cue to leave. It's always me who ends our dates, isn't it?" She blanched and closed her eyes. "Sorry, wrong choice of word. I didn't mean—"

Ash held up both hands. "I got what you meant. No worries."

Carmen stood and picked up her handbag. "Sorry, I need to go." Her face was now a deep shade of pink.

"Hey, are you okay? You seem a little…" Ash cast around for the right word. "Um, unsettled?"

Carmen's blush spread to her neck, and her gaze darted away. "I'm fine. Honestly. Definitely fine. I'll, um, call you. We'll do Alma's again, yes?"

Taken aback at Carmen's almost sprint for the door, Ash barely had time to nod before she was gone, the bell above the door clanging.

Ash slumped back in her chair. What the hell was *that* about?

Chapter 15

"Thank you for coming over." Carmen motioned Maggie into the house. "And thank you for working with my ridiculous timetable." Her voice was at a higher pitch than normal, and she inwardly admonished herself to remain calm.

It was past ten on Monday night. Not exactly the most sociable of times for a visit, but Maggie hadn't hesitated to agree when Carmen had called. It had finally dawned on Carmen late on Sunday that either Maggie or Tamsyn would be perfect to talk to about the situation with Ash, given they both knew exactly what it was like to be attracted to women. Tamsyn was out of town so Maggie was the lucky winner.

Despite the late hour Maggie, as always, looked fresh and relaxed. Her hair was pinned up in a loose ponytail, and she wore jeans and a white T-shirt.

"No problem." Maggie squeezed Carmen's arm. "Come on, Giz, in."

The dog trotted into the house and waited patiently for Carmen to ruffle his ears and scratch under his chin.

"I could have left him at home, even though Tamsyn's away, but I know you love him, so…"

"Oh yes, it's fine to bring him. And I do love him." *And he helps to soothe my nerves.* Her hands had lost some of their tremble as she petted the small dog. She straightened and smiled at Maggie. "Thank you."

They walked through to the living room. Gizmo immediately flopped onto the floor beside the armchair, a place he always gravitated to whenever he visited.

Maggie sat on the sofa.

"Can I get you something to drink?" Carmen asked. It was polite, of course, but it would also delay her a little longer. Her heart raced at the prospect of what she needed to say.

"Do you have any camomile tea?"

"Coming right up."

Deciding tea was probably the best idea for herself too, given the late hour and her all-over-the-place emotions, Carmen made a pot and carried it and two mugs on a tray back to the living room.

Maggie flicked through one of the trashy entertainment magazines that Carmen kept on the coffee table. "Do you actually read these?"

Carmen laughed. "Not read, no. But I need to keep up with what everyone has been seen doing. I've got entertainment news feeds on my laptop every morning too. It's pretty tedious."

"I bet!"

Carmen sat beside Maggie, the nerves still churning in her stomach. She reached over to the tea pot and poured before passing one mug to Maggie and leaving the other on the tray for herself.

"Thanks." Maggie raised her mug in salute.

"No problem."

Silence followed. Carmen knew she had to start the conversation, but had no idea how to do so.

"Carmen, are you okay?"

Carmen followed the line of Maggie's gaze. Her hands clenched at the hem of her skirt. She had such a tight hold on the material her knuckles were white. She let go of her skirt with a loud exhale. "God, not really, no."

"It's not... You're not ill, are you?"

Carmen met Maggie's concerned gaze. "No, nothing like that. Don't worry." She ran a hand through her curls, then sat up a little straighter. *Come on, you've told Felicity. Just spit it out.* That was the whole point of asking Maggie over, after all. "Okay. Here's the thing. I'm attracted to a woman, and I don't know what to do about it."

Maggie shifted in her seat and folded her hands together in her lap. "Wow. That's so far removed from what I expected from this late-night chat." She smiled. "And now I need to know more. Details, please."

Carmen reached for her tea, her hand trembling. After a couple of fortifying sips, she told Maggie all about Ash.

Maggie listened without interrupting, occasionally nodding and smiling but otherwise allowing Carmen to relate the tale at her own pace. "Well, she certainly sounds lovely," she said once Carmen had finished her story. "And it does sound like she's had quite the effect on you."

"You don't think it's a bit odd? Me having an attraction to a woman this late in life? Don't most people realise they're gay or bi or whatever when they're much younger?"

"Sexuality doesn't come with a timetable." Maggie tilted her head. "Just because the likes of me and Tamsyn realised ours thirty years ago is irrelevant." Her eyes narrowed. "And just because you are attracted to Ash doesn't mean you have to slap a new label on yourself that quickly if it doesn't make you comfortable."

"Okay." Carmen exhaled and eased back in her seat.

Maggie put her tea mug down. "There are many people who discover much later in life that they're attracted to someone of the same sex. Funnily enough, I read a couple of articles about this recently. Women who had always been with men, but then in their late thirties, early forties, and even later, they find themselves attracted to a woman." She paused. "For some it's hard to face up to. But just because we're not teenagers anymore doesn't mean we can't go through big changes in our lives and our relationships with others. Sexuality is an evolving concept for many women." She shrugged. "So you're not alone, if that's any consolation."

Carmen swallowed. Hearing that did make a huge difference. "It is. Thanks."

"I can send you links to these articles. It might help."

"Yes, please." Carmen took a deep breath. "So, um, what do I do about it all? About how I feel about her."

Maggie twisted in her seat to face Carmen. "Look, don't take this the wrong way, okay?"

Carmen's shoulders tensed. "Say whatever you need to, please. I'll take all the advice or thoughts I can get."

"Okay. Well, if your attraction is purely physical and you just want a quick roll in the hay to see what it's like, then you need to make that crystal clear to her. And if she's up for it, she'll—"

"No!" Carmen said the word so loudly Gizmo leaped up from his slumber and stood in full alert mode, looking out for danger. She reached over to him and rubbed his head. "Sorry, little guy. Didn't mean to startle you."

The dog huffed, snuffled at her fingers, then lay down.

When Carmen turned back to Maggie, there was a wry grin on her friend's face. "Okay, so it's emphatically more than a one-night-stand thing, yes?" Maggie asked.

Carmen's face warmed, and she nodded. "If I tell you sex is the last thing on my mind, I don't mean that to sound like I'm not physically attracted to her. Because I am." Her face burned hotter. "But right now it's more about just wanting to be with her. I mean, spend time with her. Not anything else. Not yet." Her cheeks were burning now.

Maggie patted her hand. "I knew what you meant."

Carmen exhaled, trying to calm her swirling thoughts. "I can't get her out of my head. How interesting she is. How when I'm with her, I feel so relaxed and happy. I know I could talk about anything with her and she'd never judge, even if she disagreed. I know that she's interested in my life and who I am as a person, not my status or what I can do for her career."

Maggie smiled. "Then you got it bad."

"I think I have," Carmen whispered. She placed her hands on her warm cheeks. "It's all a little overwhelming."

Maggie sat quietly beside her, simply giving her time.

"Thank you. For listening and for advising and..." Carmen's throat closed up, and no more words would come.

"You're welcome. Hey, come here." Maggie held out her arms.

Carmen slipped into the hug.

Maggie held her close, rocking her gently.

Carmen didn't cry, even though she thought tears were close, but simply allowed herself to be comforted.

"It's a big thing, this discovery," Maggie said into her hair, "and there's no rush to do anything about it, okay?"

Carmen nodded and pulled away slightly so that she could look at Maggie. "I know. I've managed to work myself into a bit of a state the last few days. First, to accept that's how I feel about her, and second, to wonder what to do about it all. The number of times I've just sat at my desk and stared off into space is embarrassing. God knows what Monica and Beverley must think."

"Oh yeah, tell me about it. My God, the first time I realised I was attracted to women, I thought I must be wearing some enormous neon sign that announced it to the whole world every time I left the house. It feels like it's so big it can't possibly be kept inside."

"It really does." Carmen sat back and shook out her arms and shoulders. "God, I don't think I realised how much tension I've been carrying around since I blurted it out to Felicity on Thursday."

"How did she take it?"

"Oh, she was fine, of course. Well, once we got past the awkward moment of her thinking *she* was the object of my affections."

Maggie guffawed. "Oh my God, I would have paid good money to see that unfold."

"It was pretty priceless, yes." Carmen chuckled. "Thankfully, she wasn't offended when she discovered she was out of the picture."

Maggie grinned.

"Then bumping into Ash again on Friday had me all twitchy. I couldn't relax around her, just knowing I knew this big thing about myself now. I dread to think what she thought of me." Carmen cringed.

"I doubt she noticed. You're hyperaware of everything to do with her because it's all so new to you and seems so enormous."

"I suppose so." Carmen licked her lips. "She, um, messaged me later that day. To ask how I was. I'm ashamed to say I haven't replied yet."

"But why not?"

"I honestly didn't know what to say. I could hardly tell her the truth, and answering with a bland 'I'm fine' seemed ridiculous given the circumstances."

"I kind of understand, but leaving her hanging like that…"

"I know." Carmen sighed, then squared her shoulders. "Should I tell her how I feel about her?" It was the paramount question in her mind and had been all weekend.

"Do you have any inkling at all if she's attracted to you?"

"Not really, no. She's done a sketch of me, Felicity said. But I'd guess she sketches a lot of people." Carmen rubbed at her chin as she thought back on all of her interactions with Ash. "There has been a couple of… looks, I suppose you'd call them, and they did make me wonder, but…" She huffed out a breath. "I feel like my usual gift for spotting if someone is interested in me has gone all wonky now I'm using it in a situation with a woman, not a man."

"I understand." Maggie tapped her chin with one fingertip. "For starters I guess all you can do is keep seeing her, keep checking in with your feelings. And see if you pick up any hint of the attraction being reciprocated."

"She did tell me she only wanted to be friends." Carmen tried not to let her sadness about that colour her tone.

Maggie's eyebrows rose. "She did? In what context?"

Carmen told her about the awkward conversation at Alma's.

"Hmm. Strange." Maggie's gaze drifted. "I suppose she may have said that because she *is* attracted to you but didn't want her attraction to get in the way of what she thought was only ever going to be friendship. Because she assumes you're straight and therefore nothing else is possible. Sort of nipping it all in the bud before it gets away from her. Or she's not attracted to you, and friendship is really all she's after. In which case, I'm sorry, but there's not a lot you can do about that."

Carmen's mood fell. "Maybe I shouldn't bother. If nothing else, I don't want her thinking I'm only doing what Felicity did. Maybe it would be easier if I just walked away now."

"Don't be daft." Maggie poked her in the arm. "Come on. It's just an unknown quantity right now. There's no harm in seeing her a few more times and figuring some things out."

Carmen's heart thudded. "It's all a bit scary."

Maggie's smile was sympathetic. "I know. It *is* scary. But sometimes it's the scary things in life that get us what we want."

Chapter 16

"Oh, I'm so glad you talked to Maggie last night!" Felicity's voice was filled with excitement.

Carmen wedged the phone under her chin and began tidying her desk. For once she was leaving work at a reasonable time and didn't want anything getting in the way of her escape. "I know. She really put my mind at ease. Not that you didn't, but—"

"I understand; don't worry. So," Felicity continued, "what happens next?"

Carmen's stomach completed a full roll. "Well, as soon as I get home, I am going to pluck up the courage to call her again. Ash, I mean."

"Hurrah! This is *so* exciting."

"Why do I get the feeling you're living vicariously through me at the moment?"

"Because I am. God knows there's no one with any potential on my horizon." Felicity laughed. "So, sorry, darling, but you're going to have to keep me entertained."

They'd known each other long enough for Carmen to know that Felicity was only teasing. "All right, I'll see what I can do." Carmen rolled her eyes. "Right, I'm going now. If I don't just get home and do this, I probably never will."

"Good for you. Let me know how it goes, okay?"

"I will." She finished packing up her desk and locked up the office behind her. Her heart raced all the way home, and a multitude of what-ifs spun round her mind. *What if she's just not interested in me? What if she doesn't answer? What if she's got herself a girlfriend in the last week or so?*

By the time she reached her street, she was practically hyperventilating and willed herself to take a few deep breaths.

For God's sake, you're forty-three years old! You sound like a bloody teenager. Get a grip.

Earlier in the day, when Monica had been out to lunch, Carmen had read the articles Maggie had sent her. It had been comforting to read about other women her age who had been through the same extraordinary realisation. And interesting that it was usually triggered by meeting someone amazing. Sometimes the feelings weren't reciprocated, and the women had to deal with rejection while still working their way through understanding their new identity. For others, the object of their attraction became their long-time partner.

Would that happen to us? If I ever found the courage to act on this, would Ash be interested?

Carmen opened her front door, her breathing still laboured. This was worse than ending things with Gerald. *God, was that only a month ago?* She walked through the house to her office and deposited her laptop, then took a deep breath.

Yes, ending things with Gerald *was* only a month ago. So although her newly admitted attraction for Ash was strong, it had developed quickly and therefore needed to be treated with a little caution. *This could just be some rebound thing. Maggie was right—I need to see Ash a few more times and test what I'm feeling. There is no need to rush anything.*

With her breathing and pulse closer to normal levels, she took the time to change out of her office clothes and into some loose cotton shorts and a sleeveless T-shirt. It was a warm evening so she threw open the doors that led from the living room to the garden. With a glass of iced water in one hand and her phone in the other, she stepped out onto the small terrace and sat at the wrought-iron table.

After taking one last deep breath, she dialled Ash's number.

Ash closed the door to the studio and flipped the sign to *closed*. It wasn't quite eight in the evening, her official closing time, but she was done. It had been a long day—seven appointments, two of which had been nearly two hours each.

Her phone trilled from where she'd left it at the front desk, but by the time she got there, the caller had rung off. When she picked up the phone and saw who the missed call was from, her heart pounded.

Carmen.

Given the silence from her in the last week or so, Ash had pretty much given up on hearing from her again. She still didn't know why Carmen hadn't replied to her text message, but she wasn't going to push. If Carmen didn't feel the need to respond, that was her right, no matter how much it hurt. Ash flopped down in the chair behind the desk.

A moment later, her phone beeped with the notification of a voicemail.

Do I really want to listen to that? Now's my chance to back away from whatever this is and save the risk of feeling more for her than I should. Before she could out-think herself, she listened to the message Carmen had left.

"Hi, Ash, it's Carmen. I hope you're well. I'm sorry I haven't been in touch for a while. I did get your message, but life, um, got in the way. So, I-I was wondering if you'd like to meet for coffee again one morning. Or catch up for a drink after work sometime. Whatever, you know, works best for you. Bye."

Carmen's voice trembled for the duration of the message. Why would that be? Ash's urge to talk to Carmen, to comfort her and find out what was troubling her, warred with her own sense of self-preservation when it came to this attractive—and straight—woman. It would be far too easy to get close to Carmen, and that could only lead to trouble. Except, Ash was wiser from her experience with Vikki, so surely that would keep any untoward feelings in check, right?

Okay, one last chance to walk away. Ignore Carmen's message and cut her out of your life.

No. I can do this. She's a great person to hang out with, and it doesn't have to mean anything more than that. I can do this.

Carmen answered on the third ring. "Ash! Hi!"

"Hi there. How are you?"

"Oh, I'm fine. And you?" Carmen's voice croaked.

"All good."

"You listened to my message?"

"I did." Ash didn't plan to play hardball, but she was hoping to pull a little more out of Carmen with her short answers. If nothing else, some hint as to what had led to the non-communication would be good to hear.

"Again, I'm so sorry for not contacting you earlier than now. Things have been a tad difficult."

Ash's armour cracked. "Are you really okay?"

"I am. I promise." Carmen's voice strengthened. "So what do you think about meeting up?"

Carmen almost sounded convincing with her answer, but Ash was well aware of the diversionary follow-up. She'd let it slide for now. It was obvious Carmen wanted them to meet up, and she'd focus on that positive element. She opened the calendar on her laptop. "Coffee or a drink sounds great, but I'm pretty booked up for the rest of this week. How about Saturday?"

"Ah, sorry, no can do. I have dinner with some clients on Saturday."

"Monday?" Ash scrolled through the calendar. "My last client comes in at six, and we should be done by around seven thirty. Want to meet me here at the studio again, and we can go on from there?"

"That sounds great!" There was a catch in Carmen's voice that Ash couldn't interpret.

"Great. I'll see you then." After hanging up, Ash tapped the phone against her chin while her mind whirled. *Is this a mistake? The last thing you need is another hot-and-cold friendship with a straight woman you find attractive.* If Carmen was going to give her the runaround with a big push-pull thing, Ash would have to stop it in its tracks. And quickly. But equally, if she had any suspicion she herself was feeling more than she should, she would back away just as fast. She would know the signs, and she'd be able to act before it got out of hand.

So she'd give them this chance to see how things were between them and then take it from there. It didn't have to mean anything more than that. At all.

She could just imagine Damian rolling his eyes at her.

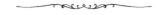

Carmen sprayed some perfume on her wrists, then tugged her dress down. She took one step back from the mirror. *Yes, that will do.*

The dinner tonight was hugely important for Matthew Hemmings's burgeoning acting career. At the moment he was in the lower ranks of B-list British actors, but with the right exposure, the right deals, the right contacts, he could hit the A-list very quickly. She needed to bring her best game tonight to get him the big step forward he deserved. All her experience, honed over the last fifteen years of running her own agency, would come into play.

It was such a pity that she couldn't find an ounce of motivation to make all that effort tonight.

Oh God. She breathed deeply, one hand pressed against her roiling stomach. *What is wrong with me?*

She'd been fine in the office the night before, fine-tuning her strategy and the plans she'd been thinking about for weeks now. The producer they would meet tonight was big-time Hollywood. Major blockbusters littered the man's resume, and Carmen knew exactly what to say and how to say it to get Matthew through that door. But when her alarm had failed to go off this morning and she'd slept through until eleven, her first waking thought hadn't been panic about the hours she'd missed. Instead she'd relished the feel of the cotton sheets on her naked skin and luxuriated in the sheer joy of having slept for ten blissful, uninterrupted hours.

She should have cared about how much work she could have completed between eight—her normal waking hour on a Saturday—and eleven. But no, she'd simply strolled downstairs at a languid pace and put the coffee machine on. She'd taken a large steaming mug of coffee out to the terrace and—almost beyond belief—read the newspaper for an hour. It was as if she'd been body-snatched. The part of her brain that would normally scream at her to keep going, get back on that treadmill and work, work, work had been silent.

Come on. This is what you do. It's what you love, remember? The thrill of pushing someone up the ladder—and of earning herself a nice rate of return in the process—had propelled her on for so many years now, she was at a loss to figure out why it had deserted her tonight, of all nights.

Her phone chimed, and her stomach flipped once more; her taxi was outside.

Well, I can't delay any further.

She walked downstairs, picked up her handbag, and left the house.

Carmen felt as if she were on a knife-edge: one wrong word, one tiny slip in concentration and she could blow this entire thing. Although it had taken every iota of energy and professionalism she possessed, the evening had progressed well so far. Matthew and Ivan, the producer, seemed to get on famously, and Carmen knew they were almost there.

As the two men chatted about a play they both admired, her mind drifted to her…date?…with Ash on Monday. *Is it a date? I mean, there will be drinks, probably, but friends drink together, don't they?*

"Wouldn't you agree, Carmen?" Ivan asked.

Um, what? Shit, what did he just ask? Praying her face didn't colour, Carmen cleared her throat. "I'm sorry, I missed that?"

Ivan tilted his head. "You seem a little distracted. Is everything okay?" A small frown settled in the centre of his forehead.

Scrabbling for a good response, she picked up her napkin and fanned herself. "I'm actually feeling a little light-headed. It's rather close in here, don't you think?"

Ivan narrowed his eyes.

She rushed on. "I'm sorry, let me just go throw some water on my face. I'll be right back." She stood without waiting for an answer, gave Matthew what she hoped was an encouraging smile, and walked as quickly as she could towards the ladies' room.

Once inside she did take the time to splash a little cold water on her face, if only to remove the blush colouring her cheeks.

Good God, how embarrassing! She never lost concentration like this. Never.

Am I starting my menopause? Jesus, I am so not ready for that.

After drying her hands and face, she gave herself another couple of minutes of simply standing, breathing deeply, to calm down. When she returned to the table, Ivan and Matthew were still chatting.

"Everything okay?" Ivan asked.

"All good, thankfully. Sorry about that. It's been a long week." She threw him her most dazzling smile.

He nodded. "It's no problem. But I think we're all done here, yes? I have another appointment I need to get to, so…"

Carmen settled the bill, and the three parted company outside the restaurant. Once Ivan had left in one taxi and Matthew in another, she stood on the pavement and inhaled a long breath.

Okay, somehow I pulled that off.

Just.

She rolled her neck a couple of times. *God, I'm shattered.*

As she climbed into a taxi a couple of minutes later, her phone chimed. She pulled it from her bag, and a smile split her face.

I hope your work evening is nearly done and you're on your way home. Just wanted to check we were still on for Monday evening? I've heard about a new wine bar a couple of minutes from the studio that's supposed to be kind of funky. Want to try?

God, now even a simple text message from Ash could calm her soul. It was ridiculous but lovely, all at the same time.

A funky wine bar sounds perfect. See you then!

The thrill that shivered down her body was completely out of proportion to the situation.

Wasn't it?

Chapter 17

"So, MONKEY, WHAT DO YOU want?" Ash looked across the rough-hewn table at her niece. They were in the beer garden of Courtney's local pub, The Fisherman, and were lucky to have snagged a table on such a warm Sunday.

Sophie ran a finger down the menu.

"Yeah, come on, Soph, make a decision." Courtney rolled her eyes.

Ash tilted her head, wondering what was going on. There was a tension to Courtney that she couldn't read.

"Give me a minute." Sophie glared at her mum, then returned to her perusal of the menu. She chewed on a strand of hair, and Ash had to laugh as both she and Courtney reached across to pull the hair from her mouth. It was a habit they'd been trying to break Sophie from for years now. Clearly, they'd got nowhere.

Sophie huffed at them but did as she was told. "All right. The chicken burger."

"Finally!" Courtney stood.

Ash handed her a twenty. "This should be enough, right?"

Courtney frowned before leaning in close to Ash. "I don't need your money, you know?"

Ash sighed. "I just want to treat you both. That's all. I'm not trying to offend. I know you can afford this. But coming out for lunch was my suggestion so I'd like to pay. Okay?"

It took a moment, but eventually Courtney nodded, took the money, and headed inside the pub to order their meals.

Ash understood where Courtney's reluctance came from. Her sister had worked hard to turn her life around, especially since Sophie's father, a guy Courtney met on a trip to Corfu, had buggered off when Sophie was three. Ash knew her sister would be offended by the thought of any charity, regardless of who it came from.

"So, how's things?" she asked Sophie.

Sophie shrugged. "Okay."

"Just okay?"

The teenager shrugged again. She picked up her phone and started tapping on the screen.

"Sophie?"

Sighing, Sophie put down the phone. "Auntie Ash, it's fine." She looked away. "I've kind of got bigger things on my mind than Mum and her problems, you know?"

"Oh? Anything you want to talk about?"

Sophie looked back at Ash. "No. I... No." She nibbled a fingernail.

"You're not having any trouble from anyone at school, are you? Comments or—"

"No!" Sophie stared at Ash. "No one knows anything so no one can say anything. It's just..." She looked around, then lowered her voice. "I...I like someone, okay? And I know I should be able to talk to you about it, but I can't. It's... I can't."

Ash's heart lurched. "Okay." She held her hands up. "I'll say no more. But you know where I am, okay? Any time."

Sophie pushed out her bottom lip but nodded a moment later.

"All right, food'll be about twenty minutes." Courtney appeared beside them and sat heavily in her seat next to Sophie. She reached for her beer and took a long drink. "Mm, that's better." She smacked her lips.

Sophie rolled her eyes.

Ash smiled and took a sip from her Coke. "So, how's work?" she asked Courtney.

Her sister glanced over Ash's shoulder, her gaze wandering. "It's fine. Nothing changes, but that suits me."

"Think you'll get a crack at being manager one day?"

Courtney focused back on Ash. "Not at that store. Brian's been there ten years already, and he's quite happy to stay until he gets his pension.

Nah, if I get a chance it will be at another store. Then I'll have to see how far away it is and whether it's worth the extra travel." Her gaze drifted once more, beyond Ash, and her face lit up. She stood and waved at someone. "Hey, Hels! Over here!"

Ash swivelled in her seat.

Approaching their table was a woman about Courtney's age, maybe a little older, with dyed red hair and wearing a tight, white skirt and even tighter, pink top. She had a large glass of white wine in one hand, and loping along behind her was a teenage boy. He looked to be about sixteen and was tall, dark-haired, and dressed in skinny black jeans and a grey T-shirt.

Courtney and the woman hugged exuberantly.

The boy scuffed at the ground while casting furtive glances in Sophie's direction.

Ash turned in her seat. Her niece was engrossed in her phone and completely oblivious to his presence. Ash wanted to laugh but held it back.

"This is my friend Helen, from bingo. This is my sister, Ash." Courtney pointed. "And this is my Sophie."

Sophie looked up, her eyes wide. "H-hello."

"Hey, nice to meet you Helen." Ash nodded at the new arrival.

"And you! But call me Hels, everyone does." Helen tugged on the boy's arm and pulled him nearer. "And this is my Ryan."

"Sophie, say hello to Ryan." Courtney's voice was overly sweet.

Ash took in her sister's excited demeanour. Then she looked at Sophie— who now wore a frown—before transferring her attention to Helen and Ryan.

And then it clicked.

Oh for fuck's sake, Courtney. Surely not. Ash only just held back a groan.

"All right?" Sophie offered the ubiquitous teenager greeting.

"All right." Ryan's response was mumbled, his head down, looking at his own feet.

"Why don't you sit here, Ryan?" Courtney pointed to her vacated seat next to Sophie. "And us adults will sit over here." She walked round the table to sit next to Ash, with Helen sitting on Ash's other side.

Ash stared at her sister. "What are you doing?"

"I'm not doing anything." Courtney smiled and reached for her beer.

Before Ash could respond, Sophie narrowed her eyes and said, "Mum, can I talk to you for a sec?"

"What's up, love?" Courtney shifted in her seat.

Sophie's frown deepened. "In private."

In awe of her niece's composure, Ash watched as Courtney made a big show of getting up and walking away from their table to where Sophie now stood about three yards away.

At first their conversation was muted, even though Sophie gesticulated expansively. That lasted all of a minute before their voices rose, and everyone around them became privy to their argument.

"How dare you? I can't believe you did this!" Sophie threw her hands wide. "God, it's bad enough you read my bloody diary, and now this? Even if I wanted a boyfriend, I can find one myself, you know? I don't need you interfering in any of this. Any of it, you get me?"

The last few words were shouted, and all heads in the vicinity turned to watch the show.

"Keep your voice down!" Courtney spat.

"No, I won't! I want everyone to hear this. I want them all to know what a bitch you are!" Sophie was crying now, and Ash suspected it was from a combination of frustration and hurt.

Her heart broke for her niece.

"You had no right to read my diary." Sophie wiped at her eyes. "No right at all. And now you have, you think this is the way to deal with what you read in there? What bloody century are we living in? What, you want an arranged marriage for me now or something?"

"Sophie." Courtney's voice was tight with warning. "This isn't the place to—"

"I don't want to hear it!" Sophie held up a hand in her mum's face. "I'm sick of you. I'm going home." She stomped to the table, swept up her phone and rammed it in her jeans pocket, then strode off towards the gate that led out of the pub garden.

"What the fuck are you lot looking at?" Courtney shouted at the pub's customers.

Ash didn't hear any of the responses; she was out of her seat and racing after Sophie.

Ash slowly closed the door to Sophie's bedroom, thankful that at last her niece was asleep. Her tears had fallen long and hard, but at least she had accepted Ash's comfort. She'd held Sophie until she was spent, then encouraged her to lie down. She knew Sophie probably wouldn't sleep for long—if nothing else, hunger at her missed lunch would wake her in less than an hour—but she needed a few minutes of calm.

Jesus, Courtney, Ash thought. *Could you have fucked this up any worse? And where the fuck are you?*

The sound of a key turning in the front door had Ash striding across the small landing and running down the stairs.

Courtney walked into the house and held up a hand when Ash made to speak. "Don't. I don't need a fucking lecture on how to raise my own kid."

"Actually, I think that's *exactly* what you need." Ash's body flashed hot, then cold; she clenched her hands at her sides to stop herself from grabbing her sister and giving her a bloody good shaking.

Courtney pushed past her and marched off towards the kitchen.

Ash followed and shut the kitchen door behind them.

"I don't want to hear it." Courtney's back was to Ash. "It's bad enough I probably can't go back to The Fisherman for about a year after all that."

"Are you kidding me? *That's* your biggest worry?" Ash folded her arms across her chest. "What about Sophie? Her feelings? Why is this all about you?"

Courtney turned to Ash, a snarl on her face. "You don't have any idea about raising a kid, so you don't get to tell me what it is I'm doing wrong!"

"Well, given you can't figure it out yourself, I think someone ought to spell it out for you." Ash stepped closer to her sister and stood in front of her, hands on her hips. "How on earth did you think setting her up with one of your mates' sons was going to 'fix' her, huh? When are you going to realise that she doesn't need 'fixing'? She just needs some time and support to work this all out for herself." Courtney made to move away, but Ash caught her arm. "You keep going like this, and you're going to lose her. She won't want anything to do with you. Is that really what you want? All because you can't handle the thought that she might, and I repeat, *might*, turn out to be gay?"

Courtney's expression was haunted. She swallowed a couple of times before speaking. "I was trying to help. You don't understand. You never will." She wrenched herself out from Ash's grip. "Now get out of my house."

"Courtney—"

"I said get out! I've had enough of you sticking your nose in my business. Go on, fuck off!"

Ash's blood boiled, but she knew it was pointless to carry on the argument. Courtney was in self-righteous mode, and experience told Ash she needed time to get past that. Admittedly, this time it worried Ash more than before; she'd never seen her sister so wound up.

Should I go? Or should I stay for Sophie?

Ash met Courtney's gaze and held it. "What are you going to do?"

Courtney's eyebrows rose. "For fuck's sake, I'm not going to harm my own kid. Jesus, what do you think I am?"

She looked genuinely horrified, and Ash's fears abated. "Fine. Then I'll go. She's upstairs asleep, by the way. Thanks for asking."

To her credit, Courtney blushed. "Okay."

"Figure this out, Courtney. Before it's too late."

Courtney stared at her for a moment, then turned away.

Chapter 18

CARMEN WAS A BAG OF nerves as she turned into the street where Ash's studio was located. She'd decided to walk from the office in the vain hope the evening air would calm her. Her plan had failed. The nearer she got to the studio and to seeing Ash again, the more her anxiety rose.

She was half an hour early, and she hoped Ash wouldn't mind. In order to take her mind off the evening ahead, Carmen had ploughed through her work like a woman possessed and unfortunately finished by six thirty. It was now just before seven, and the studio was only a minute or so away.

When she reached the door, she breathed deeply a couple of times, then pushed it open.

A girl, possibly no more than fifteen years old, with long, blonde hair, sat at the front desk. "Hello," she said. "Can I help you?"

"Hi, um, my name's Carmen. I'm here to meet Ash." Carmen looked towards the back of the room.

Ash had her back to her as she worked on someone lying on their front in the levelled-out chair. The buzz of the tattoo gun filled the air.

The girl ran a fingertip down the length of the appointment book. "Sorry, I don't see you in here."

"Oh! No, sorry. Not an appointment. I'm a...friend."

The girl frowned. "Okay, just a sec."

Before Carmen could tell her not to interrupt Ash while she was working, the teenager quickly made her way to the back.

As the girl stepped into Ash's line of sight and spoke to her, Ash lifted the gun away from the client's skin, whipped round, and smiled warmly at Carmen. Then she turned back to her client and said something. She received a nod and laid the gun down on the work table. Moments later she strode across the studio towards Carmen, and any nonchalance Carmen may have hoped to muster deserted her.

Ash looked *so* good. Her jeans hung low on her hips, and the blue, sleeveless T-shirt wasn't quite long enough to cover the short strip of flat, tanned abdomen that peeked out from above the waistband of the jeans. The T-shirt fitted like a second skin to Ash's body, emphasising her toned biceps and full breasts.

Carmen blinked as her gaze locked on Ash's chest. *Okay, she has breasts. So do you. Stop staring!*

"Hey! You're nice and early." Ash's hair was swept back again, a look that Carmen was coming to realise was her favourite.

"I…I'm sorry. I got finished early and—"

Ash held up a hand. "Hey, it's no problem. Not at all. I've got about another twenty minutes with my client, and then I'm done. You okay to sit here and wait?"

"Absolutely." Carmen willed her heart to slow and her eyes not to stare quite so hard at the vision before her.

"Cool. Let me introduce you to Sophie." Ash beckoned the girl over. "Sophie, this is my friend Carmen. Carmen, this is my niece, Sophie."

"Hello." Carmen was thankful for the diversion, if only to pull her gaze away from Ash's body. *What the hell is wrong with you?*

"Hi." Sophie seemed a little shy, but she smiled.

"Sophie's on school holidays, so I've hired her to help me out for a couple of weeks."

"Good move." Carmen grinned.

"I think so." Ash gave her niece a one-armed hug before stepping back. "Okay, I'll be with you soon."

"Can I get you a drink?" Sophie asked once Ash had walked away.

"That would be great. But just some water, please." *And I'll take a large fan if you have one.*

Sophie gave her another shy smile and walked over to the water cooler.

Carmen followed her and sat on one of the leather sofas. When Sophie returned with the water, Carmen thanked her and took a sip.

"So are you, like, my auntie's girlfriend?"

Carmen choked on the mouthful of water and, to her horror, spat half of it back out and over the front of her dress. *Hells bloody bells!*

"Hang on, I'll get a napkin!" Sophie shot off and returned a few moments later with a bunch of paper napkins in her hand.

"Thank you." Carmen dabbed at the water on her dress. All the while her face burned. *God, how embarrassing!*

"Did it go down the wrong way?"

Carmen looked up. The willowy girl looked genuinely concerned. "Yes, it must have. Thanks for the napkins."

"No problem." Sophie sat next to Carmen. She crossed her long, jeans-clad legs and pushed her hair out of her face before resting her hands in her lap. "So, are you?"

"I'm sorry, what?"

"Are you Auntie Ash's girlfriend?"

More composed to handle the question at the second time of asking, Carmen managed a smile. "No, I'm not. We're just friends."

"Oh." Sophie sighed. "I wish she'd get another girlfriend." She glanced over her shoulder as if to check her aunt couldn't hear her. "I think she deserves one. She's great."

Carmen tried not to show her alarm at Sophie's open discussion of her aunt's love life. "She is."

"How do you know each other?"

"We met here, actually. My best friend had a tattoo done, and I came along to watch."

"Cool. What tattoo did she get? And where?"

Carmen pointed at her hip. "Here. It's black and white, and it shows a bird escaping from a cage."

"Does it mean something?"

"It does. She recently got divorced." Carmen shrugged. "I suppose like many people who get tattoos, she wanted something to commemorate her new life starting."

"Makes sense."

"Would you ever get one?" Somehow it was easy to talk to Sophie.

"I'm not sure. I love watching her work, and I think it's awesome how she creates the designs, but..." She grinned. "I'm not sure about the pain. I don't think I'd like that bit."

Carmen laughed. "I think I agree with you. Besides, you're still young; you've got plenty of time to decide."

"That's true. And I'm not sure school would like it. Or my mum." She rolled her eyes.

"Mums aren't supposed to approve of anything, are they? Isn't that in the contract?"

Sophie laughed. "Hah, that's a good one." The phone rang, and she stood. "I should get back to work. Don't want the boss to sack me."

"Absolutely not. Although I'd put in a good word for you."

"Sweet." Sophie hurried back to the front desk and picked up the phone.

Carmen exhaled slowly. *Okay, so the niece is lovely, and Ash does not seem to have a girlfriend. Apart from spitting water all over myself, the evening is going well so far.*

Her phone buzzed in her bag, which lay alongside her thigh. She fished it out and smiled ruefully at the message from Tamsyn she'd just received.

Wait, I go away for a few days, and you turn all sapphic on me? I can't believe I missed your big news! Call me when you get a chance x

Carmen had told Maggie it was okay to share her revelation. She hoped Tamsyn wasn't too upset at being left out—she had been Carmen's friend for longer than Maggie after all. But the tone of the text message seemed to suggest she was taking it well.

I will. Hopefully I didn't shock you too much. It was great being able to talk to Maggie. And it will be good to talk to you about it too.

She didn't have to wait long for a reply.

What are you doing tomorrow?

Carmen laughed.

Nothing. I'll come to yours as soon as I've finished work.

Perfect! Xx

She had just slipped the phone back in her bag—after remembering to put it on silent mode—when Ash walked over.

"All done." She smiled widely.

Carmen stood. "What were you working on?"

"Just finished a piece that's taken a few sessions to do. A mermaid, on her back." Ash pointed at the woman who chatted to Sophie at the front desk. "Here, take a look." Ash pulled her phone from her pocket, swiped a couple of times, and held up a picture for Carmen.

The mermaid was huge, covering the woman's back from waist to shoulder. The design was stunning; blues and greens mingled with silvery scales, and bright red hair tumbled over the mermaid's shoulders to fall just short of her voluptuous breasts. They looked so realistic Carmen almost thought she could reach out and pinch one of the nipples. *Good God, what is it with you and breasts today?*

"It's amazing." Her voice came out as a weak croak. She cleared her throat. "Such fantastic colours." *Yes, focus on the colours.*

"Thanks. The client's very happy, and that's the main thing." Ash motioned for Carmen to walk with her over to the desk.

Sophie locked the door behind the departing client, then turned the sign to *closed*. "Finished!"

Ash laughed. "Yep, all done." She turned to Carmen. "We just need to clean up, and then if you don't mind, we need to escort this one to the Tube so she can get home."

"I don't mind at all." *Maybe having a teenaged chaperone will stop me from making a fool of myself. For a little while at least.* "Can I do anything to help with the clean-up?"

"Nah, we've got it covered. Haven't we, monkey?"

Sophie scowled at Ash. "Auntie Ash! Not in public."

Laughing, Ash walked off to the back of the shop.

Carmen waited by the desk for the few minutes it took the pair of them to get the studio tidy and swept. Ash and Sophie each retrieved a bag from somewhere and met her at the front door.

The walk to Tottenham Court Road station was fun. Sophie and Ash obviously had a wonderful rapport and connection. Carmen noticed that Ash treated Sophie like an adult, never talking to her in a condescending tone and happily covering serious subjects as well as frivolous.

"So what do you do, Carmen?" Sophie asked as they waited at a crossing. "I mean, where do you work?"

"I'm an agent. For actors and actresses, mostly for TV, but I have a few clients who are in films too."

"Cool!" Sophie's eyes were wide. "Are they all, like, really famous?"

Carmen chuckled. "Some of them, yes. Most of them you might recognise in the soaps or some of the crime dramas that are around."

"Who's the most famous?" Sophie turned to walk backwards as they crossed, her attention totally focused on Carmen.

Ash hovered protectively nearby, seemingly ready to grab her niece if she tripped.

Sweet. They reached the far side and turned into a side street.

As it was public knowledge who Carmen represented, she didn't mind sharing the name, especially with Ash's delightful niece. "My top client is Tamsyn Harris."

Ash and Sophie stopped walking in unison and stared at her.

"T-Tamsyn Harris?" Ash's eyes bulged.

Carmen grinned. "Are you a fan?"

Ash pulled at an imaginary too-tight collar and feigned fanning her face. "Just a bit."

"She's amazing!" Sophie said in an awed whisper.

"Oh, yeah." Ash's expression had turned dreamy.

Ash's niece dramatically rolled her eyes and tapped her aunt's arm. "Stop drooling."

"Like you aren't too." Ash winked.

Sophie gasped. Her gaze darted between Ash and Carmen.

Ash reached out to her niece, her hand trembling. "Sophie. Shit, I'm sorry, I…"

Sophie looked skyward, then shook her head. "It's okay. It's…" She huffed out a breath.

Carmen wasn't sure what was going on but knew it didn't concern her. She took a step back.

"No, it's okay." Sophie gently pulled her back in. "I don't mind you knowing. Although Auntie Ash could have been a bit more subtle about it."

Ash looked mortified. "Sophie, really, I didn't mean it to come out like that." She rubbed at the back of her neck. "I've just got so used to being so open with you about it, I forgot where we were and who we were with. It won't happen again, I promise."

Sophie slipped her arms around Ash's waist and hugged her. "It's all right."

Ash held her tight, her eyes closed.

Carmen's throat constricted. The love these two shared for each other was incredible to witness.

Sophie let go of her aunt and looked sheepishly over at Carmen. "Sorry, too much drama. We can go now."

Carmen smiled. "You take your time. You're obviously sharing something important, so…" She shrugged.

"Yeah, I guess it is." Sophie scuffed at the ground with her sneakers. She looked back up at Carmen. "I'm working through some stuff. About my sexuality." Her face was bright pink, but she held her head up high. "And Auntie Ash is being a massive support." She smiled. "Even if she does have a big mouth sometimes."

Oh, wow. Carmen's heart lurched. *How can a teenager seem so calm about this when I'm freaking out?* "I'm sure she is," Carmen managed to squeeze out. "She's good at that."

Ash blushed.

"And I'm in awe of you, Sophie, for being so confident. And about being okay to tell me. Thank you."

"No worries." Sophie's phone pinged, and she pulled it from her pocket. She groaned. "That's Mum. Wants to know how long I'm going to be." She looked over at Ash. "God knows what she'll be like with me after all that stupid crap yesterday, but I guess I'd better get going."

Ash grimaced. "I know. You can message me anytime, yeah?"

Sophie nodded.

"All right, then let's get you on that train."

They walked the remaining couple of minutes in an easy silence and said goodbye to Sophie in the large entranceway to the station. Thankfully it was after the worst of rush hour, so although busy, it wasn't too crowded with people.

To Carmen's surprise, Sophie gave her a quick hug as well as Ash. "It was nice meeting you."

"The pleasure was all mine, Sophie. Have a safe trip home."

"I will. And yes," Sophie said as Ash opened her mouth, "I'll be careful, *and* I'll message as soon as I've met Mum."

Ash grinned. Once Sophie was out of sight, she turned to Carmen. "Thank you so much. For all of that."

"Oh, no problem. She's a wonderful young woman."

"She really is." Ash bowed her head. "She's going through some crap right now, and I feel awful for outing her like that."

"She forgave you. And you didn't do it with any malice."

"I know. But still…" Ash exhaled. "Come on. Let's go get that glass of wine, yes?"

Carmen's heart rate picked up. "Sure, I'd love to."

Chapter 19

IT TOOK THEM ONLY A few minutes to backtrack a little towards the studio and reach the wine bar about three streets away.

Ash's mind whirled the whole way. *God, how could I have let slip what Sophie is going through? Jesus. It's bad enough her mum's making it difficult for her without me making it worse.*

She was grateful, however, that Sophie had remained relatively unruffled—and also that Carmen had made it all seem so everyday. *Thank God she didn't express anything but support for Sophie too.* She couldn't have imagined Carmen doing anything else, though. If there was one thing Carmen seemed okay with, it was everyone being who they were, with no judgement from her on whatever that was.

"Will Sophie be okay? I mean, with me knowing about what she's dealing with at the moment?"

Ash smiled. "She will. I'm so proud of her for the way she's handling the whole thing."

"She seems so level-headed."

"She is. It's amazing. Her mum—my sister, Courtney—has her ups and downs, and she's not taking it very well right now. But Sophie's just standing up for herself at every turn. Don't get me wrong; she's had some moments with it, both in coming to terms with it herself and about what other people might think, especially at school."

For a moment, Carmen blanched, then composed her features. It was so quick, Ash almost missed it, but before she could question the reaction, Carmen asked, "And her mum's struggling?"

Ash's chuckle lacked mirth. "Oh yeah." She told Carmen about the disaster the day before.

"Oh my God, how embarrassing! For everyone. What on earth was your sister thinking?" Carmen stopped walking. "Sorry, that was rather presumptuous of me. I don't have any right to go around criticising your family or—"

Ash laughed and shook her head. "Oh no, be my guest. I'm pretty sure you'd be a lot nicer about her than I'm feeling right now."

Carmen nodded. "Okay."

They continued walking.

"It must be so hard for Sophie."

"God, thank you. That means a lot, that your first thought in all of this was for Sophie."

"Well, of course. I remember my brother coming out. I know my mother is much better about it now, but it was a pretty hard time for him to begin with."

Ash glowed with the warmth of Carmen's words and, in fact, Carmen's whole demeanour this evening. Apart from that one moment, she seemed self-assured, calm, and free of whatever had troubled her the previous week. Ash wouldn't push, but if the conversation led to a point where she could ask, she'd do it. A friend would, right?

They reached the bar a minute later.

"Now, I only read about this place, and it sounded interesting. I don't know anyone who's been." Ash held open the door for Carmen. "So if it's awful, we don't have to stay, okay?"

Carmen smiled and walked past her.

A hint of her perfume teased at Ash's nostrils, and she admonished her libido when it perked up in response. *Not thinking about her that way, remember?* But that had been hard to fight ever since Carmen had appeared at the studio earlier, looking incredible in a burnt orange dress that highlighted every curve of her body. Inwardly, Ash groaned. *Am I getting close to that point where I should be worried about how I feel?*

"It'll be fine, don't worry," Carmen said over her shoulder as she stepped into the dim space.

Easy for you to say. Oh, wait, she means the bar.

129

The bar was old-fashioned, with dark wood walls and floor, and rickety tables dotted around the small space. However, the wine list was impressive, as were the prices, which were significantly less than Ash would ever have believed for a central London bar that sold wines from all around the world.

"I love this place!" Carmen gazed around. "I feel like I've stepped back in time."

Ash smiled. "Yep. I was worried that was a bad thing, but actually, this is kind of cool."

They chose a glass of white each. Carmen opted for a full-bodied Chardonnay, which didn't surprise Ash at all. Something told her Carmen would always order the boldest dish on any menu, wanting to challenge herself at every opportunity. Ash ordered a Pinot Blanc, something she'd had a couple of times in restaurants but rarely found on offer in bars.

"So," Ash said once they'd clinked glasses and taken their first sips, "how have you been?"

Carmen's free hand fluttered on the table. "Good. Very good." Her voice sounded overly cheery.

Ash tilted her head. "Really?"

Carmen seemed to crumple before her. She slumped back in her chair and shook her head. "No, actually. But I hate that every time I see you, I'm complaining about my job. My work, which I created for myself! I don't have any right to moan about it."

"Ah." Ash smiled. "Okay, so now I know that work hasn't been so great again, but we can leave it at that. Talk about something else."

"Yes, please!" Carmen drank from her wine again. "Your trip! It's only a couple of weeks away now, isn't it?"

"Eleven days. But who's counting, right?" It was hard not to get excited. Kruger had been on her wish list for years. "Everything's organised. Especially now I've had that jab. All I have to do is turn up."

"So what's the plan? Wait." Carmen's face scrunched into a frown. "*Is* there a plan? Or are you one of those scary, fly-by-the-seat-of-your-pants travellers?"

Ash's face warmed. "Um, yes, there's a plan. If my friend Damian was here, he'd be laughing his head off right now. Wait, I'll show you." She pulled her laptop from her backpack and opened it. The spreadsheet was already open, of course, so she turned the screen to allow Carmen to see it.

Carmen leaned in, bringing her head close to Ash's. There was that tease of perfume again, and the warmth from Carmen's bare arms crept across the space between them to drape itself over Ash's skin. Goose bumps erupted on the back of her neck.

"What am I looking at?" Carmen asked, but she wasn't looking at the spreadsheet. Instead her brown eyes, a couple of shades lighter than Ash's own, gazed at Ash. Carmen swept that gaze downward, raking over Ash's face, stopping at her mouth before flicking back up again to meet Ash's eyes. Carmen wet her lips.

Ash's goose bumps shot across her whole body. *Jesus, when did it get so hot in here?*

Carmen sat back quickly and cleared her throat. "I mean, I can see that it has lots of information on it, but how does it work?" Her gaze now was anywhere but on Ash, her cheeks flushed.

What the hell's going on?

"Ash?"

Ash sat upright, pushing thoughts of how kissable Carmen's lips had looked just now far, far from her mind. "Sorry, um… Yes, this is my famous travel spreadsheet." Why was her voice so hoarse? She coughed and tried again. "Damian laughs at me, but it's the only way I know how to plan these big trips."

"So how does it work?" Carmen, too, seemed to be having trouble talking in a clear voice.

They simultaneously reached for their glasses and each took a gulp.

"Well, it's got all the info I need for each destination in one place." Slowly, Ash took Carmen through her spreadsheet, thankful for the distraction it offered from whatever had happened a few moments ago. As she talked Carmen through all the sheets, she wondered just how nerdy she came across to her new friend.

Carmen, whether out of politeness or not, seemed to take it in her stride, however. "No, I can definitely see why this would be useful. And I can also see why Damian teases you." She leaned in again. "It is a tad nerdy."

Ash laughed. "Okay, okay. I can't deny it. I'm a travel nerd and proud of it."

Carmen raised her glass. "To your amazing trip!"

Ash tapped her glass to Carmen's, and they drank once more. They were back in the friend zone, that heated moment behind them. That had to be better, right?

"Talking of trips." Ash set down her glass. "Have you rearranged to visit your brother in Paris?"

"Yes!" Carmen punched the air with her fist. "I have written it in the calendar this time *and* booked the train already."

"Well done." Ash gave her a mini round of applause. "I bet he's pleased."

"He is. It'll be five months since I've seen him by the time I get there. I'm going next month. I was lucky to get the tickets, actually." She winced. "I had to book first class, to be honest. It was the only thing on offer this relatively late."

Ash shrugged. "Hey, you do what it takes, right? Nothing wrong with first class." Was Carmen embarrassed by spending that kind of money?

"I suppose." Carmen sipped from her drink again and tapped the table. "I'm always nervous talking about money. So many people in my life have resented what I have."

Ash wasn't sure what to say. Years ago, before she had started to make progress at the bank, she probably would have been one of the people scorning Carmen for her privileged position. However, she knew from first-hand experience that having a lot of money didn't mean life was all rosy. Far from it, sometimes.

"Sorry, I've made you uncomfortable, haven't I?" Carmen stared at her across the small table. "You probably think I've got no right to complain, given my background. Born into money, everything so easy from the get-go." The bitterness in her tone was unmistakable.

"Actually, not at all. Sure, you probably had a lot of things growing up that I didn't. And I bet you found it easy to get into university and buy your first home and all those things." Ash held up a hand when Carmen would have interrupted. "But I know from earning a high income myself in the past that being rich is not all it's cracked up to be. I always thought it would be, and I worked my arse off for years to attain a level that I thought would bring me true happiness. And then I realised that was a pile of shit. That money isn't everything." She locked gazes with Carmen. "You've come from a privileged background, and yes, that has helped you get where you are. But unless someone like me has walked in your shoes, we have no right to make any assumptions about how easy and good your life has been because of it."

"Thank you." Carmen's eyes were misty. "For what it's worth, I turned my back on my family's money and status the minute I turned eighteen. Everything I've done since then I've done on my own. I never once tapped into the funds that could be available to me. It was important to me to be my own person." She took a sip of her wine, looking more composed. "But I know despite that, some people will never look past my accent and the assumptions it will cause them to make." She smiled wanly. "I'm glad you're not one of them."

Ash nodded. "I'm not. Of course, if you were a stuck-up bitch about it all, then it would be a different matter."

Carmen threw her head back and laughed.

They stayed for a second glass and left the bar shortly after nine. Carmen was surprised she'd talked about her background so much—Ash now knew all about just how well-off Carmen's family was. She hadn't flinched as such, but her eyes had widened considerably when she'd heard there was an actual family estate.

"Cab or Tube?" Ash asked as they stepped out onto the street.

"Cab, I think." Carmen checked her phone. Six emails and two missed calls. *Ugh.* "I ought to deal with a few things before I get to bed."

"You can tell me it's none of my business, but are you going to slow down any time soon?"

Carmen sighed. "You know what it's like running your own business. I can't afford to slack, or the whole thing could fall to pieces. It's my reputation that's built this agency, much like it's yours that keeps that studio going."

"I'm not suggesting slacking." Ash pursed her lips. "Please don't take this the wrong way, but the last few times I've seen you, you've looked so tired. I'd like to think we're friends now, and as a friend, I'm telling you I'm concerned."

Friends? Yes, they were that. *But is that all she sees me as?* Carmen knew they'd had that moment in the bar, their heads pressed close together over the laptop. It had been more tempting than Carmen would ever have realised to lean in and kiss Ash. She'd held back—just—determined not to rush anything or risk embarrassing herself or Ash. But she also knew that being with Ash made her feel good, and so did Ash's concern for her well-being.

"I understand. You're not the only one expressing concerns." Carmen smiled ruefully.

"Felicity?"

"Yes. And my brother and Tamsyn too." Carmen pushed her handbag up into her shoulder. "She's been with me from the beginning and seen it all happen, and yes, she's worried too." A yawn threatened to escape, as if to emphasise the subject of their discussion. "I know you're all correct, but I honestly don't know what to do about it."

Ash placed a hand on Carmen's arm.

Carmen's breath caught. She almost didn't hear Ash's next words.

"Look, I'm unfortunately pretty busy before my trip, but afterwards, do you want to spend some time brainstorming? Maybe we can come up with a new way forward for you?"

Carmen blinked and worked hard to focus on Ash's words, rather than her touch. She wanted to take Ash's hand in her own. Feel their fingers entwine, know what it felt like to hold a woman's hand. Ash's hand.

"Carmen? You okay?"

"Yes. Yes, of course. Sorry." She pulled gently away from Ash's touch. "This was lovely. Thank you."

"It was. I'm...I'm really glad you called again." Ash looked as if she wanted to say more, then stopped.

"Me too." *What was she going to say?*

"So," Ash said brightly, almost *too* brightly. "Shall we try and do something before I head off? Perhaps coffee and a certain type of pastry one morning?"

"Sounds great." Carmen looked round for a cab. "I should go."

Ash smiled. "Okay. I'm going to head that way." She pointed behind them. "Bye."

"Bye."

Carmen watched her go, watched the way she walked, with her hands in her pockets, her stride long for someone not that tall. She walked with a grace that was almost cat-like. Mesmerising.

At the corner Ash looked back. When their gazes met, she stopped and tilted her head, a quizzical look on her face. Her long fringe framed one side of her face; the setting sun highlighted the other side.

God. She's beautiful.

Part of Carmen wanted to head towards Ash, run into her arms, and tell her all the thoughts she'd been having. The other part of her wanted to get away as fast as she could.

The latter won.

She threw Ash a quick wave, then spun around and walked in the other direction. Her pulse beat in her head as she increased the distance between them.

The first test of her feelings since admitting she was attracted to Ash had resulted in a highly positive result: definitely still attracted.

The trouble was, she didn't know if that was a good thing or bad.

Chapter 20

"Did you have a nice time last night?" Sophie asked as she twirled on the desk chair.

Ash's heart skipped a beat. "Yeah, it was good."

More than good.

Last night had told Ash so many things, not only about Carmen but also about Ash's feelings towards her. Ash honestly thought she could talk to Carmen about anything with zero fear. She'd never had that with Leesa. And not with Vikki either. *I'm getting close to that imaginary line, aren't I?* The one she'd imposed on herself, the emotional checkpoint that was supposed to stop her getting too caught up in spending time with this beautiful and interesting woman.

The trouble was, they connected so well, in so many ways. Despite their different backgrounds, they had a lot in common. Carmen was easy to talk to, about a variety of topics, and Ash had never felt the need to scramble around for a subject. But that moment after they said goodbye, when Carmen had been watching Ash, what the hell did that mean? Was Carmen into her? Was she not so straight after all? Or was she, just like Vikki, toying with the idea of being with a woman, playing Ash along, willing to hurt Ash to satisfy her curiosity? Somehow Carmen seemed too nice to play such games, and Ash almost felt guilty for suspecting her of being anything but nice.

She pulled her sketchbook from the back of the bench. There was a two-hour lull between appointments. Sketching would take her mind off things, as always. She opened the book and nearly groaned aloud. Facing her, almost accusingly, was the rough pencil sketch she'd made of Carmen a few weeks ago.

I didn't do her justice.

The sketch was good; she knew that. But it hadn't captured everything that made Carmen so beautiful. The representation of Carmen's eyes lacked their true depth, the passion that had flared in them when their heads were bowed so close together over the table. The way Ash had drawn her hair lacked the bounce and play of the curls whenever Carmen laughed. The neck…God, the neck that made Ash think all sorts of erotic things that she had no right thinking about a woman who was supposed to be a platonic friend. No, the drawing did not show any of that.

She closed the book and sighed.

"Are you okay, Auntie Ash?"

Ash looked up, realising her head had been in her hands. "I'm all right, monkey. Just a little tired."

Sophie snorted. "Did you have too much to drink last night?"

"No, I did not." Ash gave her a mock glare. "Just got some stuff on my mind; that's all. Hey, you want to get some food?"

"Yes! I'm starving." Sophie leaped out of her seat. "But I can go get it, if you like?"

"Sure." Ash pulled her wallet from her back pocket.

"No, wait. Can I treat you?" Sophie shuffled from foot to foot. "I kind of want to say thank you. You know, for everything."

Ash was touched. "Aw, you don't have to do that. You're saving up for that new iPad, aren't you?"

"Yeah, I am. But I really want to do this."

Ash dropped her wallet back on the bench. "Then be my guest." She smiled at Sophie. "I'll have the special salad from the Greek place, please."

"Cool."

Ash watched her go, marvelling at how grown-up she seemed to be all of a sudden. She'd be fifteen in a couple of months, yet she seemed to have matured way beyond that already, especially since confiding in Ash about her feelings for girls. If only Courtney could see that, instead of treating her like a child still. Ash swivelled in her seat.

Maybe that was the problem. In Courtney's eyes, Sophie *was* probably still her little girl, the one who ran around the garden with her Barbie dolls and wanted cuddles every five minutes. *Maybe I should take that into account the next time I speak to my sister. Try and help her to see what an amazing young woman Sophie has become.* If Carmen, a virtual stranger, could see it, then maybe that was the one thing Courtney needed a push with.

Carmen.

Jesus, what am I going to do about that?

"Come on in," Tamsyn said as she opened the door.

Carmen gave her a smile, stepped into the house, and they shared a quick hug.

Gizmo ran up to greet her, his tongue lolling.

Then Maggie appeared and gave her a longer hug.

Carmen's emotions threatened to spill over once more. *What is it about being in this house with these three that keeps doing this to me?*

"So, tell me quickly what you'd like to drink, and then we can get to the juicy stuff." Tamsyn waggled her eyebrows.

"Have some sensitivity, won't you?" Maggie slugged her in the arm. "Give the woman a minute to breathe."

Tamsyn stuck out her tongue at her fiancée, then turned back to Carmen. "So, are you ready yet?"

Carmen laughed. "Get me a gin, and then you can hear it all."

"You're too soft on her," Maggie said, but she smiled.

"Probably. But I can't afford to lose my top client, so..." Carmen shrugged, and Maggie laughed.

They sat in the living room, on the huge sectional sofa, with Gizmo stretched out on the floor in front of them.

Tamsyn curled her legs up under her and turned to face Carmen. "So, how was last night? You were seeing her again, weren't you?"

Carmen nodded. "We went to a wine bar." She told them everything about the evening up to the highly charged moment over the laptop. At this point she faltered, her cheeks burning.

"What? Why are you bright red all of a sudden?" Tamsyn kept her tone soft.

Carmen rubbed at her face. Damn her pale complexion. "Um, well, then..." She sighed. Why was this so hard to say out loud? *Come on. They're both lesbians. It's not like they don't know what it's like to feel this way.* "Okay, here goes." She breathed in. "We had to lean in quite near to each other to be able to look at the screen. And, well, our heads got quite close, and I could smell whatever perfume or cologne she wears, and her eyes were intensely focused on me, and all sorts of ludicrous things started happening to me, and… My God, I wanted to kiss her so badly."

"Oh, wow," Maggie whispered. "I've got goose bumps!"

"Me too." Tamsyn stared at Carmen. "Did you?"

Carmen shook her head. "No. I chickened out. Besides, I have no idea if she feels anything for me. I think ambushing a woman with a kiss in the middle of a wine bar wouldn't have been the best idea."

Tamsyn snorted.

"But, do you think she wanted you to? Or that she wanted to kiss you?" Maggie asked.

"I…I have no idea. I mean, she was looking as intently at me as I was at her, but why would she think I'd want to kiss her? She thinks I'm straight." Carmen hung her head in her hands. This was just impossible.

"So what happens now?" Tamsyn's tone was gentle, all hints of her earlier teasing now departed.

"I have no idea." Carmen slumped back in her chair. "There was a moment, right at the end of the evening. She'd walked away after we said goodbye, and I couldn't help watching her go. She turned and caught me watching, and I wanted to run over to her, but…"

"You backed away?" Maggie finished.

Carmen nodded. "I was so torn. Part of me wanted to just blurt it all out."

"But the rest of you was scared?" Tamsyn asked.

"Yes."

"Oh, honey, don't worry. We totally get that. Me especially." Tamsyn smiled ruefully.

Carmen gave her a wan smile in return. "Yes, I suppose you do."

"But look what happened to me in the end." Tamsyn took hold of Maggie's hand and gave her partner a look filled with love. "I got through it, and I've never been happier."

"Sweet talker," Maggie muttered but blew Tamsyn a kiss when she looked affronted.

"True." Carmen snorted softly. "God, talk about the tables being turned. Back then, I talked you into following your heart, and now here I am receiving the same from you."

"What goes around comes around." Tamsyn smirked.

"You know, I never told you this." Carmen turned to Maggie. "You know she made me read your book, the one based on the time you two had spent together in Norfolk?"

Maggie nodded, looking curious.

"Well, um, it touched me. I remember thinking how wonderful it would be to find someone who made me feel that way. I never imagined in a million years that person could be a woman. It's...it's made me think if, subconsciously, after reading your book, I started to wonder if I was barking up the wrong tree with men."

"Maybe you did." Maggie shrugged. "But you did meet Gerald soon after, and you were, mostly, pretty comfortable in your relationship with him."

"Yes, I was." Carmen sighed. "But now I know comfortable isn't really what I want. Maybe it is like many of the women in those articles said. Sometimes it just takes the right person to come along and show you what you really want. And sometimes that person happens to be a woman."

"So, what are you going to do about *your* woman?" Tamsyn asked.

"For a start, I think I'm going to have to stop running away." Carmen's throat tightened. "I've never done anything so terrifying in my life, but...I cannot stop thinking about her. About being with her. I woke up this morning wondering if that was too soon to ask her out for coffee again. Is that silly?"

Maggie shook her head, her smile warm. "No, it isn't. It's wonderful."

"Only if she feels the same way."

"Which she might."

Carmen thought back once more to that charged moment she and Ash had shared. That look in Ash's eyes. The slight flush on her cheeks. Yes, maybe Ash did feel something. A shiver of excitement ran through Carmen. If Ash did feel something for her, then yes, it could be wonderful.

Chapter 21

"CARMEN, HERE'S THOSE CONTRACTS YOU need for Friday."

Monica handed her the stack of papers, and Carmen took them even though Monica's words had barely registered. *What's happening Friday? God, I'm losing it.*

"Thanks." She managed to give Monica a small smile.

Come on, this is ridiculous! It's just one text message asking someone you like if they'd be interested in meeting for coffee this week.

She'd never had this much trouble asking out a man. Why should it be any different with a woman?

Because somehow all *of this feels different because Ash is a woman.*

She put the contracts on her desk and sat back down in her chair.

Monica left the office, and Carmen exhaled a long, slow breath. This was her chance, a few minutes of peace. She picked up her phone and opened the messaging app.

Hi! It was great to see you the other night. Hope you got home okay—

She tapped the delete key multiple times. *You know she got home okay; she texted you to say so! She'll think you're an idiot if you ask again. Okay, try again.*

Hi! It was great to see you the other night. I was thinking of making some time in my calendar tomorrow morning (Thursday) for coffee and a certain pastry. Care to join me?

Okay, how did that sound? Too flirty? Not flirty enough? Was she even supposed to be flirting with a woman who just wanted to be friends? Carmen groaned. She negotiated actors' career-changing contracts with less concern. Before she could change her mind, she hit the send button and leaned back in her chair.

When the reply pinged less than two minutes later, she nearly fell off the chair in her haste to pick up the phone from her desk.

Love to! Eleven work for you?

Carmen scanned her calendar. She had a one-to-one with Monica at ten thirty, but that could easily be moved to the afternoon. Other than that she was free all morning, for once. *It's a sign.*

Perfect, see you then xx

It wasn't until about thirty seconds after she'd sent it that she realised she'd ended the message with the two kisses. Her head hit the desk with a loud thud.

"You got our favourite spot," Carmen said as she approached.

Ash grinned. "I did. Had to shove some old guy out of the way to make it happen, but, hey, what can you do?" She shrugged, then smiled when Carmen laughed. God, she loved it when Carmen laughed like that. As if she didn't have a care in the world.

"Did you order?" Carmen asked.

"No, I waited for you."

"Thank you."

They stared at each other for a moment. Once again there was that charge in the air between them.

Stop it! You're near the line, remember? Ash didn't want to reach the line, didn't want to have to pull back from seeing Carmen because she couldn't trust her libido—or heart. But everything she'd told herself over the last couple of days since their wine bar date—about stepping back and remembering to stop herself from feeling things she shouldn't—had flown out the window the minute Carmen arrived. And it wasn't just Carmen's beauty that turned Ash's mind to mush. It was the thought of spending time with her again. Of talking to her, asking about her day, delving a little deeper into what made Carmen who she was.

Ash coughed and stood. "Your usual?"

Carmen nodded; her gaze, which had until that moment been locked on Ash's eyes, flicked away. "Perfect, thanks."

Ash hurried into the café, her heart racing. She ordered their coffees and two of the custard tarts but took a moment to breathe before she returned to their table. After setting down their drinks and plates, she pulled out her chair and finally looked at Carmen once more.

"So, how's Sophie?" Carmen reached for her coffee.

"She's great. Although there's not a lot for her to do in the studio, she never complains of being bored. Mind you, partly that's because she's glued to her phone when it's quiet."

"Of course! That's how teenagers spend their days, isn't it? How old is she?"

"She'll be fifteen in October."

"Gosh, she seems so much more grown-up than that!"

"I know. I was only thinking that the other day."

"You love her very much, don't you?"

Ash smiled. "I do. And it's not just because she's my only niece or nephew. She's just an amazing kid."

"I think it's wonderful that you're supporting her. Given that her mum isn't doing so well with it, it's great that Sophie has someone she can talk to."

"Yeah. It's causing some friction between me and Courtney, but I'm sure we'll work that out. And it never occurred to me not to support Sophie. Even in this day and age, it's tough to come out. Especially when you've realised that young."

Carmen choked a little on her coffee and placed the cup back on the table. She coughed a few times but waved away Ash's offer to get her a glass of water. "Sorry, went down the wrong way." Carmen blushed and looked away.

"Have some custard tart. They fix anything."

Carmen looked back at her and smiled. "I'm sure they do."

And there it was again. That…sizzle between them.

It's there, isn't it? I'm not just imagining it. She couldn't help herself; the awareness excited her. *Oh crap, now what do I do?*

The sound of a phone ringing broke into their strained silence, the first truly awkward moment they'd shared since they met.

Ash's relief nearly had her slumping in her chair.

"Sorry." Carmen dropped her untouched pastry on its plate before fishing her phone from her handbag and answering it. "Yes, I'm just out at Alma's. No, that's tomorrow. What? *Today?* Oh my God." She ran her free hand through her curls. "Okay, I can be back in ten minutes. Stall her, okay? Tell her I'm stuck in traffic on the way back from another meeting. Thank you, Monica. You're a star."

Carmen hung up and shoved the phone back into her bag. She jumped up. "I'm so sorry. I've apparently messed up my calendar. I have to get back."

Ash stood too, worry for Carmen running like ice in her veins.

Carmen looked panicked. Distraught, almost. "This has never happened to me." She stepped back from the table. Her hands twisted at the strap of her handbag. "I never miss meetings. Never!"

"Hey." Ash laid a hand on Carmen's arm. "It's fine. Go. You've got this, okay?"

Carmen nodded, but her gaze was distant, her posture ramrod straight. "Thanks." She whirled around and strode off.

Ash allowed herself one minute to watch that determined stride, then tore her gaze away from Carmen's legs. If she was honest with herself, she had no small measure of relief at the abrupt ending to their time together. *And now I probably won't see her before I go away, because she's bound to throw herself into her work again to make up for whatever this mistake is.* She ran her hand through her hair. Maybe that wasn't such a bad thing. A few weeks apart would give Ash plenty of time to get her head back on straight. She almost groaned aloud at her inadvertent pun.

Carmen broke her vow with reference to always taking the stairs and rushed down the corridor towards the lift. This was an emergency, after all. The thing seemed to take an age to reach the top floor. All the while her left foot tapped out an erratic rhythm as her heart pounded far too fast.

How did I screw this up?

Her calendar app stated quite clearly that this meeting was booked for eleven the following day. She scrolled through her deleted emails to find the chain that had set up the appointment.

Her heart sunk. There it was, in black and white: meeting with Emma Francis, agreed for eleven, Thursday, 23rd July.

Which had been fifteen minutes ago.

How did I put that in the wrong bloody day?

She swore under her breath. Hopefully, Monica's story about traffic would hold water, and her potential client, a promising young actress currently appearing in a minor role in a West End play, would be gracious enough to accept Carmen's apologies.

My mind's just not on the game these days. Not with everything that's happening with Ash.

She shook her head as she exited the lift and scurried into the reception area. *Now is not the time to dwell on that—focus!*

Beverley gave her a rueful smile as Carmen walked quickly by.

"Does she have a drink?" Carmen threw over her shoulder.

"She does. She's fine, Carmen. Don't worry."

Carmen dashed into the office, threw her handbag onto her desk, then grabbed her laptop.

"Need a coffee?" Monica asked from behind her.

Carmen whirled around. She hadn't even seen her assistant standing in the centre of the office, such was her haste to gather herself together. "No, I'm fine. Just some water, please."

Monica nodded, her eyes narrowed in her quizzical exploration of Carmen's face. She opened her mouth, seemed to think better of it, and turned away to the water cooler.

With the glass of water in one hand, her laptop in the other, Carmen took a deep breath and straightened her shoulders. *You've got this. Focus.* She strode out of the office to the small conference room.

When she opened the door, Emma Francis, a stunning blonde with elfin features, smiled at her from across the table.

"Emma." Carmen held out her hand. "Carmen Lyttleton. It's wonderful to meet you."

Carmen flopped down onto her sofa and let out an extended breath. *Jesus, what a day.*

Thankfully, the meeting with Emma had gone well, despite its shaky start. But the tension of the morning, of having to abandon Ash in the middle of their coffee date, and the embarrassment Carmen had experienced when seeing the puzzled look on Monica's face had left Carmen worn out.

She pulled her phone out of her handbag. The text message from Ash, sent at a little after eleven thirty that morning, was still unread. Carmen had been wary of opening it. She knew it was ridiculous; absolutely none of this was Ash's fault. It was all Carmen's own doing, her own confusion over what she was feeling for Ash. But somehow it was easier to ignore Ash than face up to her own culpability.

Come on. You're a grown-up. Don't be unfair to the woman. She could almost hear Felicity scolding her.

The text message was everything that made Ash so attractive.

Hey, I hope you made it back okay for the meeting. I'm sure you wowed them! Remember, it's the weekend soon. Take some time to chill. And as soon as you want to buy me another pastry, you know where I am. Although I did eat yours after you left, so maybe that means I owe you?! Ha ha! Speak soon. Ash x

"My life would be so much easier if you weren't so bloody nice," Carmen said aloud as she stared at the phone's screen.

She threw the phone onto the sofa and laid her head back against the cushions. *What am I going to do?* Everything seemed to be getting into such a mess. Her work was clearly suffering, yet so were her heart and mind. What was happening to her with regards to Ash was a big thing. Huge. Surely she should devote proper attention to it. Discovering that something as intrinsic as her sexuality seemed to have changed wasn't an everyday occurrence, after all.

But if I do spend more time working that out, how do I keep up the concentration required to maintain and grow my business?

A low groan escaped her throat. This was impossible. She picked up the phone once more. Her upbringing and her sense of ethics dictated that she should at least respond to Ash. But what to say when all she wanted to do was run away and hope these feelings would disappear?

She sighed. *No, I don't want them to disappear. I like how I feel when I'm with her.* And she liked how excited she was, deep down, at the prospect of being with someone again. She hadn't felt that way in a long time. What did it matter that the object of her affections was another woman?

Slowly, she tapped out her reply.

Everything was fine. Sorry again for sprinting off. I don't blame you for eating my pastry. I would have done the same! Not sure if we'll find time to meet before you head off, but let's see how things go.

She sent the message before she could change anything. She knew it wasn't the most encouraging of replies, but right now all she could think was that she needed some time. Proper thinking time, to figure out what was going on with her emotions.

Maybe it's a good thing she's away soon. Maybe some time apart will show me if this is real or not.

Chapter 22

FRIDAY DAWNED SUNNY AND RIDICULOUSLY hot—it was already beyond warm at nine in the morning and sticky by ten. Ash was thankful she'd installed air conditioning in the studio as she made her way there.

To her surprise, Sophie was already outside the studio when she arrived. "Hey. Have you been here long?"

Sophie shook her head. "Not really. Mum had a call asking her to go in a bit early, so I decided I might as well get going too."

Ash opened up the studio and motioned Sophie inside. "So, had breakfast?"

"Yeah, I'm good." Sophie made them both tea, and they got on with setting up for the day.

"So how are things at home? You mentioned yesterday that your mum might be calming down a bit?" Ash asked as they sat on one of the leather sofas. Her first client was due in ten minutes.

"Yeah, kind of. Like, she asked me if I was doing okay and if there was anything I wanted to talk to her about. It was...okay."

"And did you? Talk to her?"

Sophie blushed. "No. I mean, I guess I'd like to, but..."

"Still awkward?"

"Yeah, totally." Sophie fiddled with the mid-thigh rip in her long denim shorts. She dipped her head. "When...when you first liked someone, you know, a girl, did you ever think they might like you back but then think you were imagining it?"

Ash's breath caught. *Huh, yeah, and not just when it was the first time I liked a girl. Thanks, universe.* This *conversation, right now?* She swallowed before responding. "Um, yeah, that happened to me."

Sophie glanced up, then down again. "And, um, what did you do?"

"I...I told her I liked her. Eventually."

"And did she like you?" Sophie's voice was small.

Ash wrapped one arm around her niece's shoulders.

"Or was it a disaster?" Sophie looked quickly at her, wide-eyed, then ducked her head again.

"No. I was lucky. Although she didn't like me that way, she never told anyone what I'd said. I guess that's why I liked her so much in the first place. She was a good person." *Just like Carmen.* Ash shook the thought off. *This is about Sophie. Focus on her, not your own drama.*

"I think I would die if I told K—her and she didn't like me back."

Ash smiled and kissed the top of Sophie's head. "You wouldn't die. But yeah, it would be hard. I get that."

"I don't know what to do." Sophie looked up at last, and her teeth worried at her bottom lip. "I like her so much. I see girls and boys walking around town, holding hands and kissing down at the park, and I..." Her blush deepened. "I really want that too. With her," she whispered.

Ash's heart lurched. "Honestly, I don't know what to advise. A part of me wants you to just go for it—ask her if she'd like to go out and see how it goes. But a big part of me doesn't want you to get hurt. I'd hate to tell you to do it and then we find out she's a nasty bitch who tells the whole school."

Sophie shook her head. "I don't think she's nasty. She never seems to gossip or take the piss out of anyone. She's pretty quiet."

"What's her name?"

Sophie hesitated and went back to picking at the hole in her jeans. "Keisha. We have French together."

"Do you sit next to her?"

Sophie's mouth fell open, and she leaned away from Ash. "No! I couldn't do that."

Ash nudged her with her shoulder. "Maybe that would be a start, once school starts up again. You could at least talk to her some more, right?"

Sophie blinked a couple of times. "Um, yeah, I guess I could do that."

The door opened, and a tall woman walked in.

"Sorry, time to go to work." Ash stood. "But we can talk more later, okay?"

"Yes. Thanks, Auntie Ash."

Ash's mind was busy with a whirl of thoughts as she walked over to her client. Sophie working her way through all that she was feeling but not shying away from any of it. Whether Courtney would ever come to accept Sophie for who she was or might be. Carmen and whatever the hell it was that was going on there.

Ash hadn't done anything about contacting Carmen since their aborted meeting yesterday. The message she'd got from Carmen late last night had seemed a little cold. As if Carmen was distancing herself. *And maybe that's a good thing.* She smiled at her client and motioned her towards the chair, every action on autopilot as her brain still churned. No, Carmen distancing herself didn't feel good. It left an emptiness in Ash that she didn't want to acknowledge. Because if she did, she'd have to admit that her feelings for Carmen were already running deeper than she would want.

"You okay?" Ash asked Sophie when her niece flopped onto the sofa beside her three hours later.

Sophie shrugged. "Suppose so."

"What does that mean?"

Sophie turned to look at her. Her eyes were a little wild. "I'm thinking about telling Trina."

Ash swallowed before responding. "But that's good, right?"

"I hope so," Sophie mumbled.

"You've known each other since you were little. I'm convinced she's going to be cool with this. Really." Ash patted Sophie's arm.

"I hope so."

Sensing there was no point in pushing this tense subject, Ash stood. "Tea?"

"Yes, please."

Sophie's phone rang as Ash made their tea. Ash tried hard not to listen in.

"No, it's just… Well, I just wanted to talk to you. I'm at the studio now, but I'll be home later tonight." A pause. "Well, yeah, it is pretty important." A longer pause. "Yeah? That…that would be cool. Okay. Bye."

Ash carried over their mugs of tea. "Everything okay?"

"Yeah. Yeah, it's… She's coming here. Like, now. She's in town to return some shoes she bought on Saturday." Sophie's eyes looked even wilder than five minutes before.

"That's great." Ash glanced at her watch. "I've got my next client in ten minutes but even if I'm working, feel free to talk with Trina here, or you can go somewhere else. I honestly don't mind, okay?"

Sophie nodded, her hands twisting the bottom of her T-shirt. "Okay. Thanks."

The client arrived, and she got him settled in the chair. This was an easy piece: a string of barbed wire encircling his bicep. She got started, settling herself into that calming zone where it was just her, the tattoo gun, and the ink following the lines she'd laid out. At some point through the work, the front door opened and closed. After reaching a convenient pause in her work, she flicked a glance over her shoulder.

Sophie and her friend Trina sat with their heads together on the sofa. Although still looking worried, Sophie *was* talking. And Trina was listening.

God, I hope I've read Trina right all this time. Ash turned back to her client.

Half an hour later, the piece was done. After wrapping the arm and giving the client the usual spiel about aftercare, Ash showed him to the front desk.

She risked another glance at the two young women as the guy fished his wallet out of his pocket. To her utter relief, they sat close together, laughing.

The client left, and Ash strolled as casually as she could manage over to the sofa. "Hi, Trina."

Trina looked up. "Hey, Ash. All right?"

"Yeah, I'm good." Ash looked across at Sophie. "Okay?"

Sophie's smile was so wide she looked like a cartoon character. "Totally cool." She grabbed her friend's hand and squeezed.

Trina rolled her eyes. "Of course it's okay!"

Ash gave her a quick nod. "Thanks. It's never easy, you know."

Trina's expression turned serious. "I get that. But, you know, Sophie's my bestie. There's nothing she could tell me that would make me forget that." She turned to Sophie and grinned. "Well, unless she told me she was in love with that arsehole Justin Bieber. Then we'd have a big problem."

Sophie laughed. "I think you're safe." She looked up at Ash. "Thanks for telling me to tell her. I know I took a bit of time, but you were right. I feel so much better for just getting it out there."

"I'm pleased." Ash hugged her. "Listen, why don't you two take off? Go grab a McDonald's or something?" She pulled a twenty from her wallet and handed it to Sophie.

"Really?" Sophie's whole face lit up.

Laughing, Ash stepped away from the sofa. "Yes, really. Go on, have some fun."

"Cool. Thanks, Ash." Trina beamed at her.

The girls left, and the studio fell silent. She had a twenty-minute gap until her next client, so she made herself a tea and sat on the sofa, gazing unseeing out of the big window. The late-afternoon sun cast a soft golden glow onto the wings of the phoenix painted on the glass. Every time she looked at the image, her pride at what she'd achieved and at how she'd turned her life around swelled. She'd worked hard, not only on her business but also on figuring herself out, and her emotional strength these days was a huge source of satisfaction.

Her mind returned to her earlier troubling thoughts of Carmen and where her feelings were leading her. *She's straight,* her protective inner voice said, trying to stop the internal conversation in its tracks.

Ash sighed. Yes, Carmen was straight, and even if she was curious about what being with a woman was like, Ash's past made her immediately want to back away from what that could lead to. But Carmen was also beautiful, intelligent, amusing, and driven to succeed, something that Ash always admired in a woman. Something else she admired was a woman who remained kind alongside that drive, and Carmen was all that.

So what were her options? Stop seeing Carmen? That thought just made Ash feel sad. So keep seeing her, but always with the awareness of the dangerous line she was walking between friendship and wanting something more. She'd be able to control that, wouldn't she? After all, what happened with Vikki was lesson enough. *You're a strong person now, and you haven't run from anything in years. You can handle this if you keep your wits about you.*

Pep talk complete, Ash finished her tea and walked to the counter near the chair. Her sketchbook was wedged behind a box of disposable gloves, and she tugged it out. Determined, she ripped out the page containing the sketch of Carmen and crumpled it up into a ball.

Chapter 23

"ANNABELLA, I THINK I'M GOING to have to say no to that idea." Carmen leaned her chin on her hand, the phone pressed to her ear, and barely managed to bite back an exasperated sigh. *And it's only Monday morning. God help me.*

Across the room, Monica caught her eye and smiled knowingly.

Carmen had to look away to avoid laughing.

"But everyone is going on that show and doing something outrageous," Annabella Mitchell whined in her ear.

Carmen was thankful that the technology of phones prevented her from reaching into the receiver and slapping the woman. "I know, and I know it's very popular. But honestly, you're not hearing what I am from the best directors and producers in the business about the people who are going on it. I'll be frank: they're not impressed. It's seen as, well, you know, cheap. And tacky. And we're trying to do better for you than that, aren't we?"

Annabella sighed.

"And while I'm sure your, um, sex toy collection *is* impressive"—across the room Monica snorted, but Carmen didn't dare meet her eye—"I honestly think you need to consider the long game here. Five minutes on the front pages next week isn't going to be worth anything the week after if no one will work with you."

"Ugh, I suppose you're right."

"You know I am. Have I ever steered you wrong before?"

"No, I suppose not."

God, it was like talking to a six-year-old, not a woman in her mid-thirties who'd been the darling of Britain's top-rated soap for the last eight years. Clients like this made Carmen wonder why she'd ever wanted to work in this business.

"So you carry on as you are and leave me to work my magic, yes? I've got a couple of good leads I'm following, and I'm sure I can get you something worthwhile very soon."

Another big sigh. "Okay, Carmen. Thanks, darling, you're the best."

I know, Carmen thought as she hung up, just before she laid her head down on the desk.

Monica's laughter spilled out as if expelled from a cannon, and Carmen shot upright again.

"Sex toy collection?" Monica spluttered.

"Don't." Carmen held up a hand. "She wanted to show the whole lot off on that reality show, *My Secret Passion*. Some friend of hers thought it would be good for her image. Make her seem more interesting."

Monica laughed so hard she clutched at her side with one hand while the other gripped her desk to presumably stop herself falling off her chair.

Carmen shook out her shoulders. "God, I don't even know why I still represent her. Maybe I can pass her off at her next contract renewal."

Monica nodded a couple of times. "Maybe you should. I mean, come on; she's not exactly in the same league as most of your other clients."

"True. I suppose I felt a kind of obligation—she was one of my first when I branched out, and she stuck with me when people didn't really know who I was."

"I know. But that's also true for Tamsyn Harris, and she and Annabella are definitely not in the same league." Monica hesitated, then leaned forward. "Look, I know I've only been here a year, so if this is out of line, tell me."

Carmen said nothing, wondering where this was going.

"Well, it just seems to me that you might not realise what your own reputation is now. I mean, when I tell people in our world I work for you, they're impressed. Like, *seriously* impressed. I'm just wondering if you need to focus on the more elite clients and move the company in that direction." Monica blushed but sat up straighter in her chair. "It's…it's just that if you only had people like Tamsyn on the books, you could be just as successful but maybe not have to work so hard, and your image would be better as a result. Quality not quantity, you know?"

"I can't just drop the clients I don't like." Carmen scowled. "What kind of message would that send to anyone who wants to work with me?"

Monica squared her shoulders. "I don't mean that." She stood and walked over to Carmen's desk. "Keeping people like Annabella might be doing you more damage than good. And it's not about liking her. It's about her talent and her potential. She has very little of the former and therefore next to nothing of the latter." She folded her arms across her chest. "Compare her to Daisy Menon. She's a bitch; neither of us like her, but she's a brilliant actress and is going to be winning awards soon. She's worth keeping, not the likes of Annabella. I'm sorry if I'm out of line, but I think you need to look at this. If for no other reason than you're working yourself into the ground."

Carmen stared at her. Since when did Monica get to tell her how to run her own business? The business she knew better than the back of her hand?

"I'll take a coffee if you're making one," she said, forcing her tone to be polite.

Monica's mouth pressed into a tight line. Then she spun on her heel and marched out of the office.

Carmen watched her go, her anger simmering. It wasn't Monica's job to tell her what to do. She was merely here to assist. To take the pressure off Carmen's workload and—

She slumped back in her chair. Yes, that was exactly what Monica was here for, to take the pressure off. *And she's just suggested a way that could happen, and I treated her like dirt.*

Carmen dropped her head into her hands and groaned softly. How to be a class A bitch in one easy lesson. *Nice going, Carmen.*

Monica was right. Carmen did have an awful lot of what she called small potato clients. The ones she'd held on to because of loyalty, even though they had considerably less talent than her top clients. How far did loyalty go? And how come she hadn't seen this? Carmen answered herself in the next moment: because she had been far too immersed in the business of building the company up to take the time to step outside and see where it was going.

Monica walked back into the room, two steaming mugs in her hands. Wordlessly, she placed Carmen's on her desk and turned away.

"Monica," Carmen said quietly.

After a moment's hesitation, Monica turned back. Her face was set in a hard mask. "Yes?"

"I'm sorry. That was out of line."

Monica's entire posture relaxed. "I'm sorry if I—"

Carmen held up a hand. "No. You, my young Jedi, are brilliant."

"I-I am?" Monica's coffee wobbled in her hand.

"You are. Everything you said was exactly what I needed to hear. Thank you."

Monica beamed at Carmen. "You're welcome." She cleared her throat. "We've...we've been so worried."

"We?"

"Beverley and me. We love working here, but we hate seeing you so run-down and stressed."

"Well." Carmen reached for her coffee. "Let's see if we can do something about that, yes?"

Monica nodded and turned back to her own desk. A moment later the sound of her tapping vigorously against her keyboard filled the office.

The message from Ash pinged on Carmen's phone a couple of hours later, and her heart missed a beat when she saw it.

Hey, how are you? I go away at the end of the week and wondered if you'd like to meet before I go? I'm free each morning until 11:30, but only have tomorrow evening free after eight. Every other night I'm working till ten! Let me know if anything works for you

Thankful she was currently alone in the office, she allowed herself a small smile. It was great to hear from Ash, even though Carmen had almost convinced herself over the weekend that stepping back was the right idea. Except that, every night, when she'd finally turned her phone off and settled in to try to sleep, her mind had inevitably turned to Ash. Thoughts of what might be, if she only had the courage to ask for it, taunted her.

Ash by her side, making her laugh, grounding her.

Ash holding her, kissing her, and touch—

She sat bolt upright. Nope, not going there. Not in the office.

It shocked her, how far her fantasies were taking her. Sure, she'd fantasised about her boyfriends in the past, but doing so about a woman was a whole new ball game. Her face heated as she recalled locating that copy of Maggie's book on her Kindle and flicking through to all of the sex scenes. It had been far too easy to picture herself and Ash in the positions described.

And if she ever wanted the chance to find out how it would feel in reality, she knew what she had to do. Even if the thought scared her witless.

She breathed out slowly. For starters, she could make sure she had time to see Ash this week, before she went away. If she held back much longer, Ash probably wouldn't contact her again. There were only so many times a person could be ignored before they gave up. And Ash was too good a person for Carmen to treat her that way.

No, she had to see her.

She flipped to the calendar on her laptop and scanned the week ahead, then picked up her phone.

Hi! Thank you for getting in touch. Sorry again for Friday. Hope you had a good weekend. How about meeting on Wednesday? I'm free from 10:30 to 11:30, if that works? And yes, I have checked my calendar this time! Would be great to see you.

The reply came about half an hour later, just as she grabbed her purse to head out and buy some lunch.

10:30 Wednesday is perfect. See you at our usual spot.

Chapter 24

CARMEN HADN'T SLEPT WELL TUESDAY night, but that wasn't a surprise. Nor did it surprise her that her stomach was in knots as she walked along the street leading to Alma's. It was a hot day, and she was glad she'd worn a sleeveless silk blouse paired with linen trousers. *The last thing I need is to turn up sweating like I've run a marathon.*

Now only a block or so away, her heart decided to join her stomach in its cartwheel routine. Her pulse rate jumped to a level that couldn't be healthy. She breathed deeply and slowly to try to restore some semblance of calm.

She crossed the last junction and looked towards the café.

Ash waited for her at their usual table. She threw Carmen a beautiful smile, and Carmen's steps faltered. *My God, how does she do this to me?*

Eventually reaching the table, Carmen pulled out a chair and gratefully sank into it. "Hi."

"Hey. How are you?"

"I'm actually very well." Carmen grinned as Ash clutched both hands to her chest. "I know, I know. But I have good news about my workload, you'll be pleased to hear. No more complaining from me!"

"I'm pleased. About the workload, I mean. I would never suggest you've been complaining." Ash faked an innocent look, but her eyes twinkled.

"Ha ha." Carmen willed her heart to slow. Ash looked adorable, and it was making her tongue-tied. "How's life at the studio? And how's Sophie?"

"How about we get some coffee, and then I can fill you in?"

"Oh! Yes, of course. Sorry." Carmen smiled sheepishly. She stood just as Ash did.

"No, I've got this." Ash waved Carmen back into her seat.

"You sure?"

"I am. I did eat your last pastry, after all."

She winked, and Carmen's insides fluttered for an entirely different reason than nerves.

When Ash returned a few minutes later, a tray in her hands, Carmen had just about talked herself into a more normal state of pulse and breathing. It hadn't been easy.

Ash passed her a coffee and a plate with a pastry, laid her own on the table, then headed back inside the café to return the tray. Once she'd sat down again, she leaned forward. "So, in answer to your questions, the studio is great. Really busy this week, which I love. And Sophie is brilliant. She came out to her best friend, Trina, and it went very well."

"Oh, that's wonderful!"

"It is. I never doubted Trina, but it's always so hard to know how anyone is going to react when it comes down to it."

Carmen shivered, despite the warm weather. *Yes, I think Sophie and I have a lot in common these days.* So far, having only told Felicity, Tamsyn, and Maggie about her attraction for the woman sitting opposite her, she knew she'd been fortunate to have such good reactions from them all. How would she feel if it had gone differently? If she had a Courtney in her life? *Well, actually you do—there's still Mother to think about.* But maybe not in this decade.

"Are you okay?"

Carmen's gaze drifted back to focus on Ash. "Sorry, what?"

"You zoned out there. Is everything okay?"

Her cheeks burning, Carmen reached for her coffee to give herself a moment. "Oh, yes, fine. Just a few things on my mind, but all good. Trust me."

"Okay." Ash drank her own coffee, then took a big bite out of her pastry.

"So, are you all set for Friday? Packed already?" *Yes, let's talk about something other than people's sexualities and coming-out processes.*

"Not quite packed, but there are piles of clothes and stuff everywhere in the flat." Ash laughed. "I like to lay it all out beforehand, then do a final inventory to make sure I've got everything. It'll all get packed up tomorrow night."

"It's so exciting. And I'm so jealous!"

"I can always try to squeeze you into one of my suitcases." Ash tapped her chin, her eyes sparkling.

Oh God, don't tempt me. Carmen's knees shook at the thought of being alone with Ash for three whole weeks. Fearing she was blushing profusely again, she attempted a chuckle, which came out more like a choking sound. She covered that—she hoped—by eating the last of her pastry.

"I'll miss these when I'm gone." Ash gestured with her last morsel of pastry before popping it into her mouth.

"We'll have to meet up as soon as you're back so you can get your fix." Thankfully, her voice sounded close to normal.

Ash nodded. "I like that plan." Her smile was warm and genuine, and Carmen melted all over again.

This is getting out of control. A small part of her was tempted to just tell Ash how she felt, to hell with the consequences. The rest of her thought she was mad to even consider it. But wouldn't it be better to just get it out there? At least know where she stood? All the worrying about it and the tension that filled her body every time they met was wearing her out. With sudden clarity she realised she couldn't go on like this. She was bold and brave with her work. Now maybe it was time to be the same with her heart. *Okay, but I can't just blurt it out. Maybe I could lead the conversation into how much I'll miss her when she's away and—*

"Look, I'm sorry, but I really have to go." Ash's mouth turned down, and she shook her head. "I'd love to sit here longer and hear more about what the next few weeks will bring for you, but I've got so much to get through before Friday."

God, I can't launch into it now, can I? Bugger. "Oh, okay. I understand." Carmen gathered up her handbag and stood, grateful her shaky legs didn't give way. She inhaled deeply. *When she gets back from her trip. I'll tell her then.*

"I'll walk you to the corner." Ash gestured up the road.

They fell easily into step, and despite Ash's genuine need to get back to the studio, she kept her pace slow. She'd meant what she'd said—she didn't want to walk away. Not yet. Something was troubling Carmen; that much was obvious. And irrespective of that, once again Ash found herself just wanting to talk to Carmen, to listen to whatever she had to say about whatever subject they happened upon. *I'm going to miss her while I'm away.* The thought was bittersweet.

"Will you let me know you got there okay?" Carmen asked quietly. Her cheeks, once again, sported a deep shade of pink.

The request warmed Ash in a way that nevertheless made alarm bells ring in every corner of her brain. "Of course, if you like."

"And maybe let me know if you see anything amazing?"

"Like, maybe, some giraffes?" She remembered Carmen saying they were her favourite African animals.

Carmen grinned. "Exactly."

"I'm sure I can do that too."

They reached the corner where they would part ways.

"So, here we are." Ash groaned inwardly at the inanity of what she'd said, as if Carmen wouldn't know exactly where they were.

"Yes." Carmen inhaled deeply, then, to Ash's surprise, held out her arms.

Ash moved on autopilot, before her brain could kick in and warn her why accepting a parting hug from Carmen would be a very bad idea.

Too late. Carmen wrapped her arms around Ash's shoulders, and her body pressed close. Not inappropriately close, only as far as a hug between friends would go when they wouldn't see each other for a few weeks. But still, every nerve ending in Ash's body leaped to attention and demanded that she step closer, just a little closer, and—

Carmen let out a moan as Ash's arms tightened around her.

Shivers spiralled down Ash's spine, and she closed her eyes as Carmen pressed her cheek to hers. There was warmth everywhere and softness and curves, and Ash knew this was dangerous. Oh so dangerous. She began to pull back, but Carmen's grip tightened.

"Ash." Carmen's voice was a whisper against Ash's cheek. "I...I think I need to tell you something."

Ash tried to pull away once more, but Carmen wouldn't let her.

Instead, she turned her face upwards to meet Ash's gaze. "I'm…" She wet her lips. "I'm very attracted to you." Her voice was husky, her cheeks flushed.

Ash's heart thumped, missed a beat or two, as elation at Carmen's words soared through her. Then her fear took hold and shattered that elation. Memories of the heartbreak with Vikki roared into her mind with a vengeance.

"Ash?" Carmen was shaking.

Or is that me?

"I…" Ash hesitated. *What the hell do I say?*

Carmen gazed up at her. "Is there…? Do you feel the same way?" She visibly swallowed. "Ash? Say something. Please?"

Ash held up a hand. "Wait. Please, just…wait." Her mind whirled. Carmen's proximity, the feel of her in Ash's arms, was overwhelming. And terrifying. *This is too much. I can't do this again. Especially with Carmen, who already gets me in ways Vikki never did and therefore has the potential to cause me even more heartache.* Some risks just weren't worth taking. Her heart raced, and her palms were damp. She knew what she had to do.

It took more emotional effort than Ash would have imagined, but she lifted her arms away from Carmen's body and eased gently out of her hold. She made sure to meet Carmen's gaze when she spoke and chose her words carefully. "Thank you for telling me. I know that must have been hard for you. And I don't want to negate anything you just said or how you think you feel, but I just want to be friends. That's all." *Yes, keep saying it, and maybe one day you'll believe it yourself,* said a small voice in the back of her mind.

Carmen seemed to shrink in on herself and backed away so rapidly she nearly slipped off the kerb. "Oh. Right. Of course." She passed a hand over the front of her face. "Um, okay. I'd better get going and—"

"Carmen, I'm sorry." Ash stepped forward and reached out to help Carmen keep her balance.

"No, it's all right." Carmen's gaze darted everywhere but on Ash. "I…I never should have said anything. I'm so sorry."

Ash made to move even closer, but Carmen held out both hands, as if to put up some kind of force field in front of her.

"No, please. It's okay." Carmen paused and looked skywards for a moment. "I suppose it's a good thing that you'll be away now. Give me time to get over the embarrassment." Her voice was so quiet on those last few words, Ash strained to hear her.

Ash ached to pull Carmen back into her arms, to somehow make this all okay. Like tell her how she really felt, but her fear and panic were too strong. "Please don't be embarrassed. And honestly, I meant what I said. I'd still like to be friends." *How do I sound so calm when I'm anything but?*

"Friends." Carmen's voice was low and a little wobbly. She shifted her handbag higher up her shoulder and took two big steps back. "Listen, you have a great time away, and, um, I'll perhaps give you a call sometime when you're back."

Despite her resolve, despite knowing she was definitely doing the right thing, the safe thing, Ash's heart sank. There was hurt written all over Carmen's face and deep sadness in her eyes. The idea that this might be the last time they saw each other sat heavily on Ash's soul.

Carmen, her eyes wet, threw Ash one last weak smile before she turned and walked away.

Chapter 25

AT A LITTLE AFTER NINE on Tuesday evening, Carmen's doorbell rang, startling her so hard she dropped the spoonful of tea she'd been preparing to put in the teapot. Tea leaves scattered all over the counter and floor. She was already feeling beyond low, and the sight of the mess brought tears to her eyes.

The doorbell rang again. She walked to the front door and peered through the security peephole.

Felicity's face appeared in the lens.

Carmen scowled. *I might have known.* Sighing, she opened the door.

Felicity looked her up and down. "You're okay, then?" Her voice held a hint of steel, and shame hit Carmen instantly.

"I'm sorry." She stepped back and ushered Felicity into the house.

"There had better be a bloody good explanation for ignoring me for days and putting me on the verge of calling all the hospitals within a ten-mile radius to see if you'd been in a bloody accident!"

Carmen rubbed a hand across her forehead. "Come in. I'll pour you a gin and tell you everything."

Felicity's intense gaze softened. "Sweetheart, what's happened?"

"Come on." Carmen walked back to the kitchen and headed to the end of the counter, where she kept her alcohol.

To her credit, Felicity kept quiet as Carmen mixed their drinks. She took a seat at the breakfast bar and murmured her thanks when Carmen handed her drink over.

Carmen took a couple of fortifying sips of her own gin and tonic, then leaned against the breakfast bar opposite Felicity. "Last week I met up with

Ash for one last coffee before she went away. I'm still not entirely sure how it happened, what triggered me to do it, but I ended up telling her how I feel about her."

Felicity's mouth opened, yet no sound appeared.

Carmen's smile was wry. "Yes, exactly. And, of course, she doesn't feel the same way and just wants us to remain friends, so I'm all shades of mortified now."

"And that's why you've been hiding from me since then?"

Carmen nodded. "I didn't want to talk about it."

"I suppose you've been working all this time too?"

"Of course. It's my go-to when everything else turns to crap."

"That explains the huge bags under your eyes. Oh, I am *so* sorry this happened." Felicity patted Carmen's free hand. "But you don't need to be embarrassed. Surely, she was nice about it, wasn't she? I can't imagine her being anything else."

"Oh yes, she was. Perfectly lovely." She sipped her drink. "And I know on one level that I don't have anything to be embarrassed about. People do this all the time, don't they?" At Felicity's nod she continued. "But it's more than the embarrassment. I...I honestly don't know what to do. I miss her. And I'm quite sure she doesn't miss me the same way, and that hurts. More than I care to admit, actually."

"I don't mean to sound trite, but it will pass. It always does. I mean, yes, the way you spoke about Ash, it was obvious you felt quite a bit for her. More than you've had for anyone since Lewis, it seems, but it's not like you were actually involved, was it?"

"I know, I know. And yes, missing her is a complete waste of my energy, given she doesn't want me."

Felicity frowned. "Is that actually what she said?"

"Huh?"

"Did she actually say she didn't want you? Didn't share the same feelings?" Felicity's gaze was back to intense, and it was a tad intimidating.

Carmen cast her mind back to that awful couple of minutes in the sun the previous Wednesday. "Well, no, not in so many words. I told her that I was attracted to her, and she said she just wanted us to be friends."

"Ah-ha!" Felicity's eyes gleamed with triumph.

Carmen stared at her. "What?"

"Darling, do you remember I found that sketch of you she'd done, when I, um, paid her that visit?"

"Yes." Carmen drew the word out. "But what does—?"

"I think that means she does find you attractive."

"Maybe she thinks I'm nice to look at. But that's very different from actually being attracted to someone or wanting to date them, isn't it?"

"I suppose so." Felicity tapped one fingertip against her chin. "But you said yourself there have been some looks, some moments, between the two of you, in many of your meetings. Don't you think that might mean it's more than her finding you beautiful?"

Carmen sighed. "Even if it does, she's said she's not interested, so it's a moot point."

Felicity leaned forward and pressed a fingertip into the marble top of the breakfast bar as if to emphasise her point. "She didn't say that. She didn't say, 'I don't feel the same way', or 'Sorry, but you're not my type'. If someone told me they were attracted to me and I didn't feel the same way, I'd come right out and say so."

"Hmm, but that's you. And we know you're always more, um, outspoken than a lot of people."

Felicity snorted. "Perhaps. But I stand by what I said. I think there's something else going on here. God knows what, though. Have you heard from her since she arrived in South Africa?"

"Um, yes, I have. She messaged to say she'd landed okay and then again yesterday to say she was all settled in Kruger."

They'd been sweet messages, chatty and friendly. However, both had stung just a little as memories of the woman who had sent them swamped Carmen and left her feeling helpless in the face of her emotions. She'd only answered the first one, with a simple "Glad to hear it!" She needed much more time before she could engage in the kind of banter Ash seemed to be looking for.

Felicity's grin was wide. "I don't think you should give up hope on this just yet, darling. I think you might be in her thoughts just as much as she is in yours. There might yet be something here."

Carmen wanted to believe in Felicity's optimism, but all her mind could focus on was the memory of Ash looking like a startled rabbit ready to bolt as soon as Carmen's confession had registered.

"I'm not so sure about that," she whispered.

Ash lifted her binoculars once more. The viewpoint above the river here at Olifants Camp was sensational.

Below her, a group of three giraffes were drinking from the water. With their front legs splayed wide, they looked like giant tripods. *God, Carmen would love this.* Ash quickly snapped a couple of photos on her phone. Melancholy seeped into her bones.

It was a gorgeous day. The air was filled with birdsong and the sounds of insects. She'd spent the entire morning at the viewpoint, taking some time to just breathe it all in. After driving for a week around Kruger, stopping at one camp after another, she'd deliberately planned to have a few days at this one stop so that she could relax a little. She should be feeling happy, and on one level she was because Kruger was everything she'd hoped it would be. But…

She couldn't stop thinking about Carmen and how everything had gone so wrong ten days ago. And she also couldn't help thinking about how wonderful it would be to share something this beautiful with her. She could picture Carmen sitting beside her, her eyes wide in delight at the scene before them.

And every night, even though she was desperate for sleep, her mind insisted on letting her imagine holding Carmen, their heads touching, talking quietly about what they'd done that day and where they might go the next day.

Why did I turn her away? She'd been second-guessing herself every day since she'd walked away from Carmen that Wednesday morning. She had no recollection of what she did in the studio on the Thursday. *Jesus, I hope I set the bloody alarm.*

Carmen was pretty much everything Ash would look for in a partner. Not only that, holding her for those brief moments had been one of the most arousing experiences of Ash's life. And also one of the scariest. When Carmen had been in her arms, all she could remember was holding Vikki that way. *And look how that turned out.* A sour taste filled Ash's mouth. She stood and paced around the lookout, which she thankfully had to herself at the moment.

"I definitely did the right thing," she said out loud, standing with her hands on her hips, gazing down to the river below. "I know I did."

Except...somehow her mind wouldn't quite let her believe it. *Carmen looked so upset when I backed off.* If it really was just a curiosity thing, as Felicity's had been, would she have looked so hurt? Or maybe that had been the embarrassment. She probably just felt it a little stronger than Felicity did. *God knows I'd feel it that much if I'd done that to someone.*

Later, as she picked at her lunch in the camp's restaurant, she used their Wi-Fi to catch up on messages and Facebook. There were no texts from Carmen, which didn't surprise her, even though it stung just a little.

A message from Damian cheered her up, asking how the trip was going and if she'd be able to visit the couple of great viewing spots he'd recommended. He'd told her about them before she left, but in all the rush to get ready and the drama with Carmen, she hadn't written them down. She tapped out a reply to thank him for reminding her. He was online, and the three little winking dots told her he was replying.

No worries. How are ya?

I'm good, she lied. *Having a great time.* Also a lie.

Cool! Beers when you get back. We haven't caught up in ages, mate!

Maybe by the time she got back to the UK, she'd have figured out how to deal with everything related to Carmen. Because Damian was like a bloodhound when he got even a hint of trouble brewing, and she'd never get away with such lies face to face.

Sounds great!

What was one more lie added to the list?

Chapter 26

TRISTAN LOOKED AS DAPPER AS ever, even in shorts and a short-sleeved shirt, when Carmen spotted him waiting for her at Gare du Nord. It was nearly ten o'clock at night, but he looked fresh and rested, his dark blonde hair, curly like her own, longer than she remembered. They hugged for several moments, and she berated herself yet again for not making time for her brother.

"Jesus, you look exhausted!" Tristan held her at arm's length.

"Thanks." The response lacked the bite she was aiming for; she didn't have the energy.

He cupped her cheek. "Okay, whatever is going on, you can tell me over the champagne waiting for us back at the apartment."

"Fair enough." She looked around. "No Jean-Pierre?"

"He's at home, preparing a few late-night snacks for us." He slipped his arm through hers, grabbed her small roller case with his other hand, and led her towards the Métro.

The journey was quick and easy. Tristan and his partner now lived in a two-bedroom apartment in a fantastic old building a few streets away from Le Jardin du Luxembourg, south of the Seine. It was her first visit here, and as they climbed the ornate marble staircase up to the third floor, Carmen admired the beautiful building. Once again she found herself inordinately proud of what her brother had achieved.

As they stepped through the front door, Jean-Pierre rushed out of the kitchen. He also wore shorts but with a plain white T-shirt. His beard was, as ever, immaculately trimmed and his dark brown hair swept back from his head in a graceful wave. "You are here!" He pulled her into a warm hug, then kissed her cheeks. "At last." He smirked as he stepped back.

"I know, I know." Carmen held up her hands. "But better late than never."

"*Très vrai.*" He smiled and motioned for her to follow him to the living area, where the coffee table was covered with delicious-looking plates of savoury pastries, cheese, and crudités.

Within minutes Carmen had her shoes kicked off, a glass of champagne in her hand, and two handsome men sitting beside her with deep frowns on their faces.

"You look so down." Jean-Pierre took her free hand and held it lightly. "What's wrong?"

There was no point in trying to pretend she was all right—she'd seen herself in the mirror that morning and knew how big the bags were under her eyes, how wan her skin looked. And that was after she'd put concealer on.

"I'm not sure where to start." She leaned back against the sofa and took a quick sip of her champagne.

"Is it work?" Tristan asked.

"Partly." She blew out a breath. "Yes, that's definitely playing its part. I'm working on a new business model, and the transition phase is a little tricky. I'm letting go of about twenty clients, and some of them are not going to be happy about it. So I've been meeting with my lawyer to make sure everything is above board and there can be no comeback."

"While I'm not unhappy to hear you're reducing your workload, please tell me dropping these clients will actually achieve that? You're not going to replace them with twenty more, are you?"

"No, I'm not. I promise. The idea is to take them out of the equation so that I can then focus on the key clients. Maybe take on one or two more of those to compensate for the loss, but definitely no wholesale replacement."

"Thank God." Tristan squeezed her forearm. "The last two years it's been hard to watch from afar as you've run yourself into the ground."

"I love what I do. So of course I was going to work hard at it. But yes," she said when he made to interrupt, "even I can now accept it was getting a little out of hand."

Her brother grinned and raised his glass. "Here's to a new Carmen, one who can actually have a social life. Or maybe even a little romance." He waggled his eyebrows.

Carmen's long sigh caused the amused look to slide off his face. "Maybe not that last part," she said softly, annoyed to feel tears welling.

"What?"

"I'm having a little disaster in that area at the moment. I think it's safe to say that romance will be the furthest thing from my mind for the foreseeable future."

"Who is he?" Tristan narrowed his eyes. "Want me to track him down and have the 'don't you dare hurt my sister' talk?"

She tried to laugh, but it didn't get very far. "Her name is Ash, and no. But thanks anyway."

Tristan's eyes bulged. "*Her*? Wait a minute, that tattooist?"

Carmen took a fortifying sip of champagne before answering. "Yes. Her. Top this up, and I'll tell you all."

Tristan nearly fell over his own feet in his rush to get to the bottle on the table.

Over the next hour—and into a second bottle of champagne—Carmen told them everything.

"And you never had any attraction for women before? At all?" Tristan asked.

"Not at all." She shrugged. "I don't begin to understand this, but I know I'm not alone. Those articles Maggie sent me made that perfectly clear."

"And is it just her? What I mean is, if this really is over before it started with Ash, do you think you would continue dating women?"

Carmen's mind whirled. "I honestly don't know. I haven't thought that far ahead. I've been so wrapped up in her and what I hoped we could have." She paused, opening her mind to the question. "I don't think I can discount it. Now I've met a woman like her, one who does make me feel all the things I feel, then quite possibly I will continue dating women. Or at least have that as an option. Does that make me bi? I don't know." She shook her head. "All I know is I can't think beyond her right now. It's all still too raw. She's who I wanted, and it can't happen. So I need to regroup, concentrate on work again for a little while to keep me occupied, and then we'll see."

"And you are sure she's not interested in you?" Jean-Pierre asked.

"As sure as I can be. Mostly." She groaned. "I don't know. Felicity is convinced Ash feels something."

"Ash could just be scared." Jean-Pierre's kind hazel eyes held her startled gaze. "I have a theory that might explain her reaction, her words. It happened to me, and I know many other gay people who have experienced the same thing so…" He rubbed his fingers across his chin. "Perhaps someone used her as a little, um, experiment in the past."

"Experiment?" Carmen frowned. "To satisfy some curiosity, you mean?"

"Exactly." Tristan sat forward. "I've had that too." He turned to Jean-Pierre. "How come we never talked about this before?"

Jean-Pierre laughed. "We probably wanted to forget it all."

"That's true."

"Wait, you've both had men initiate something with you just because they were curious?"

"Oh yes." Tristan rolled his eyes. "Mine was a colleague, about ten years ago. Took me out to dinner, ordered champagne, the whole works. I honestly thought I'd found my dream man. And then he hit me with the sucker punch. 'I'm married, but I've always wondered…'." He shuddered. "Ugh, gross."

"Oh my God." Carmen stared at them both. "That's what Ash thinks I'm doing?"

Jean-Pierre held up one finger. "Maybe. It is only a theory."

"Well, if she thinks that about me, no wonder she ran a mile." Her understanding rapidly gave way to anger. "Wait a minute. She thinks that *I* would do that? How dare she?"

Jean-Pierre smiled gently at her. "Don't take it personally. It's not about you. It's the situation; I'm sure. She would be nervous of anyone who she thought was straight suddenly announcing they find her attractive. If that is the reason she's stepped back, I mean no disrespect, but I can understand her caution."

Carmen rubbed at her face, her tiredness now exacerbated by the three—or was it four?—glasses of champagne she'd had. "But if that is what's going on with her, is there anything I can do to allay her fears? I mean, she's said no to anything more than friendship, and surely I have to respect that."

"Yes, of course," Tristan said. "But is there any harm in starting that conversation? Not to press her into something she doesn't want, but simply to understand her? I mean, if you want to maintain a friendship with her, wouldn't you like to know who she is and how she thinks?"

"True." *But can I make a friendship work when I have all these feelings for her? How do I shut those down?* Not to mention how hard it would be for her to hope for more and then be hurt again.

"Maybe she also needs to hear more from you about how you feel. About how this isn't a need to have one night and that's it. Maybe she needs to know that you have real feelings for her." Jean-Pierre pulled her into a one-armed hug. "Because you do, don't you?"

"Yes," she whispered. "But having already put myself out there and been rebuffed, I have to be honest and say that the thought of telling her any more is terrifying. At this point, I'm not even sure if I want to get in contact with her at all. I don't know what I'd say to her, how I'd be able to relax with her after my big revelation."

"Please don't run away from this," Tristan said quietly. "I haven't met many of your partners, but I know I've never seen you so lit up about someone as this. Something other than work has grabbed at your heart, and I for one am delighted to see it."

It was true, but she shrank away from the implications. Life was so much simpler when work ruled her heart, not her relationships. Work never left her unable to concentrate or sleep. She'd thrown herself into her career tenfold once Lewis left. She'd never blamed him for following his calling—in a way, they were like peas in a pod when it came to their passion for their work, even though his involved working with refugees in far-flung corners of the world. But was that why she'd never properly committed to any of her subsequent relationships? Had she been scared to feel too much for someone in case they, too, left?

Given how she felt right now, grieving and hurting even though she and Ash had never even got started, maybe that fear was fully justified.

Chapter 27

THE WEEK AFTER HER TRIP to Paris kept Carmen busy and distracted during the days and able to spend a lot of time—too much?—thinking during the evenings. However, she was grateful for the space afforded her because she had to process all that she was feeling and all that Felicity and Tristan had said to her.

She knew the easiest thing to do would be to stop seeing Ash. Then she wouldn't have to deal face to face with the aftermath of confessing her attraction. Nor would either of them have to figure out how to navigate their friendship with that confession hanging over them. But that would mean losing her friendship and support, things that Carmen had come to treasure so highly.

After messaging Carmen that first day or so of her trip, Ash had remained silent in the face of Carmen's non-response. It didn't upset Carmen; rather, it made her grateful, and she would have messaged to say thanks if it wasn't for the fact that she didn't want to get into a chatting situation.

But now it was Thursday, the night before Ash returned to the UK, and Carmen was still undecided about what to do. She stirred her camomile tea. Had Ash had a good trip? What animals had she seen? Carmen chuckled. Had she had any misadventures with rogue beasts? Despite everything, she was itching to hear Ash talk about Kruger and her experiences there. The memory of them sitting in the gin bar, Ash excitedly talking about all she was planning, resurfaced. It warmed Carmen, and a smile tugged at the corners of her mouth.

She sipped her tea, then sat back in her chair. *And I want to see her.* Her heart thudded. If she wanted to meet with Ash, to talk about the trip as friends would, then she needed to treat the occasion as just that: a meeting between friends. Nothing else. No matter what anyone else might think about Ash and her motivations or feelings, she had told Carmen they would just be friends. It was that or nothing, and Carmen knew without a doubt she didn't want nothing.

She inhaled and let the breath out slowly. "Okay," she said aloud into the quietness of her kitchen. "Friends it is."

———

Ash had just walked through her front door on Friday morning, lugging her heavy case behind her, when her phone chimed with a new text message. Assuming it was either Damian or Sophie welcoming her back, she didn't bother to read it until she'd unpacked. When she did finally scroll open her phone's screen and saw that the message was from Carmen, she flopped onto the sofa.

She had returned to the UK assuming their friendship was over. So many times she'd wanted to message, to ask if Carmen was okay, but if she had and she'd received nothing in return, she would have felt even worse. So she'd kept her distance and crossed her fingers that somehow they could resurrect their friendship.

Hi. I hope you had a good trip. I'd love to hear all about it! Any chance you're free to grab a coffee on Sunday? Maybe at Alma's?

Ash put the phone down on the coffee table, wanting some time to think the request through. Certainly, there was nothing in it to suggest Carmen was being anything but casual. *Okay, well, you wanted to be friends, and she's holding out an olive branch that might lead to that.* It should have been a relief, so why was disappointment her overriding emotion? She picked up her phone once more.

Hi! Just got back. Trip was brilliant. Coffee on Sunday sounds good. What time is best for you? I'm free all day.

They swapped two quick messages, agreeing on eleven. When nothing else came back from her final text, Ash left the phone on the sofa and headed for the shower, trying hard to ignore the annoying little jolt of excitement stirring in her stomach at the thought of seeing Carmen again.

———

Ash arrived at Alma's just before eleven on Sunday and grabbed the last table outside. To her surprise, Alma's ran table service and a full lunch menu on the weekends. Maybe they could have a meal after their coffees. Assuming Carmen had time—or the inclination. After ordering a coffee and a glass of water from the waitress, Ash sat back and let the morning sun bathe her face.

Carmen appeared a couple of minutes later, looking incredible in a light blue, sleeveless summer dress and low sandals. A pair of sunglasses was pushed up into her hair, the blonde curls bobbing as she walked. She was beautiful, and she took Ash's breath away.

"Hi," Carmen said quietly when she reached the table.

"Hey. It's really good to see you." And it was. Too good.

Carmen pulled out the remaining chair and sat. "How are you?" Her smile was wide and confident, her entire demeanour poised and controlled.

Ash had to admit she was surprised, given how their last interaction had ended. *Wait, you're disappointed she seems perfectly okay with everything between you? Did you think she'd be pining? Get over yourself.*

"I'm good, thanks," Ash said. "And you?"

"Great. Really good."

Jesus, any minute now one of us is going to say, "Nice weather, isn't it?" Could this be any more awkward? Before Ash could come up with a better line of conversation, the waitress appeared and took Carmen's coffee order.

"Want a pastry too?" Ash looked across at Carmen with a small smile.

"Why not? It would be rather silly to come here and not have one."

The light-hearted comment seemed to break some of the tension. Ash's shoulders relaxed, and she grinned. "Well, obviously."

The waitress reappeared with their pastries, and they ate in a silence that was much more comfortable than Ash might have anticipated. She snuck a few glances at Carmen and once again was struck by how at ease she seemed this morning. There was no indication of embarrassment over what had been said the last time they were together. *So maybe it was just a silly crush thing, like Felicity's was, and she's over it.* And that was good, right? The kernel of disappointment lingering in her stomach said otherwise, and it annoyed her.

"So," Ash said after she'd eaten about half her pastry. "How was Paris?"

Carmen took a sip of her coffee. "It was lovely. They're doing very well for themselves." Her gaze flicked away, but her smile didn't waver.

"Great."

"And work is very good. Important stuff happening this week that has me all fired up."

Ah, so perhaps that was also it, maybe even the main reason for the put-together Carmen. "That sounds good. What's happening?"

"Well, firstly, I'm in love with my job again, which feels wonderful. And secondly, wait for it—I'm cutting my client list!"

"No!" Ash shook her head, then listened, a smile on her face, as Carmen launched into an enthusiastic explanation of how she was going to turn her business model upside down. There was a fire in Carmen's eyes she hadn't seen before. Ruefully, she acknowledged that she was a little jealous Carmen's job seemed to have taken up all her thoughts once more.

They finished their pastries and pushed their plates to the side.

"So," Carmen said. "Tell me about it. Which animals, how many, where, how. All of it!"

Ash laughed; Carmen's enthusiasm was infectious. She pulled out her phone and opened the album of photos she'd taken, then launched into the first story of her time away. As she related her tales, Carmen often chimed in with good questions or excited exclamations. She was adorable to observe when she was animated about something, and Ash's emotions were all over the place by the time they reached the final photo. *You wanted this, remember? You wanted your friend back, with no other nonsense in the way.* And here she was, in all her glory, but Jesus, did she have to be so bloody attractive?

"I'm so jealous." Carmen smiled. "This trip looked fantastic. I have to do something like that one day."

"Ah, you will, I'm sure. Get yourself a boyfriend who likes to travel." Ash winked.

Carmen sat back in her seat. "Um, yes." She paused. "Or a girlfriend. Who knows?"

Girlfriend? What the—?

"What?" Carmen asked, eyes narrowed. "You look like I just shot you."

Ash ran her hand across the back of her neck, not quite sure how to phrase what she wanted to say next. "I guess I'm just a bit... Well, girlfriend?"

Carmen opened her mouth, then closed it again. She drummed the tabletop with her fingers. "It's possible. I mean, not right now. I, um, need a little time. But in the future, why not?"

"Time?" Ash's brain was working overtime to make sense of what Carmen was saying, but nothing was slotting into the right places.

Carmen blinked and shifted in her seat. "Well, yes. I'm still working on moving past what I feel." She blushed and looked away.

Ash's stomach roiled as if she'd just completed a full loop on a rollercoaster. "What you feel?"

Carmen turned back to face her. "Yes." She huffed out a breath. "Don't make me spell it out. Being rejected once was bad enough."

"I didn't realise." Ash's voice just made it past her tight throat. Carmen seemed to be saying that her feelings for Ash ran deeper than Ash had dared to believe—or accept. She didn't know what to do with this. Even if Carmen felt more than a crush or infatuation, that still left Ash facing the prospect of risking her own feelings in a way she'd sworn not to do again.

Carmen barked out a hollow laugh. "I thought I'd made it pretty clear before you went away." She leaned forward slightly. "Did you think I was just like Felicity?"

Guilt and confusion coursed through Ash. "Yeah, actually."

Carmen closed her eyes and took a few deep breaths before again meeting Ash's gaze. "I'm not curious," she said quietly, her cheeks flushed. "Not just having some fleeting thought about what it might be like. It's all about you, Ash. I love spending time with you. I love talking and laughing with you. I also find you incredibly sexy, and when I'm not with you, I can't stop thinking about you."

"I think about you a lot, too." Wait, where had that come from? Panic surged through Ash. "I mean, I enjoy spending time with you. As a friend. Maybe that's what's confusing you, having a lesbian as a friend." Ash attempted a smile, but it barely lifted the corners of her mouth.

Carmen glared at her. "I've been friends with a few lesbians for years now, and not once have I felt for them what I feel for you. And just because I haven't felt this way about a woman before doesn't mean my feelings now, for you, are superficial, or aren't valid. As much as Sophie is experiencing something new, so am I. Why aren't you treating my feelings the same way you are hers? Are the rules different for a fourteen-year-old discovering her sexuality compared to a forty-three-year-old?"

Ash swallowed hard. She didn't want to put down Carmen's feelings, but she also needed to protect herself. "No, of course not. I'm sorry. Truly. I should never have joked about this."

Carmen's posture eased somewhat.

"But the thing is," Ash continued, needing to explain, if she could, why Carmen's words made her so hesitant, "because this is all so new for you, there's no guarantee that this is what you'll want longer-term. Yes, your feelings are real now; I'm not saying they're not. It's more about how permanent or not this change for you might be."

Carmen twisted her napkin in her hands. "Nobody can guarantee anything. I know that. And I know how nervous that is probably making you, but—"

"Hi, I'm sorry to interrupt." Their waitress stood next to the table. "But I've just realised this table is reserved for someone for lunch. I'm really sorry, but I need to clear it and ask you to move." She placed their bill down on the table.

Ash couldn't tell which of them was more relieved by the waitress's words, her or Carmen.

They stood, and each laid some money on top of the bill, then stepped away with the waitress's words of gratitude following them to the street. A few paces away from the café, by unspoken agreement, they stopped and faced each other.

"I'd better get home," Carmen said, not meeting Ash's eye. Her face was pink, and her shoulders slumped.

Ash wanted to tell her it would all be okay, but that was something she couldn't promise. As much as she was drawn to Carmen, her fear of getting hurt was simply too strong to throw caution to the wind and say, "Sure, let's go for it, see where it leads us." Even as a large part of her ached to do just that. "Okay. Which way do you go? Can I walk you?"

"I'll head in the direction of the Tube. If I happen to see a cab en route, I'll grab it." Carmen finally met her eye. "If you want to walk with me, that's fine." She didn't sound convinced.

Ash blew out a breath. "Thanks."

They walked in a strained silence. Carmen led them around a corner and into a much quieter side street.

"What will you do with the rest of your day?" Ash asked.

"A little work. Some gardening." Carmen threw her a glance. "That's my stress reliever."

"Sounds good. Look, I really am sorry. You've just really taken me by surprise with all this."

"I didn't mean to make you uncomfortable. With all the things I said." Carmen gave her half a smile. "But I did need to make you understand."

"I know. I get that."

Carmen looked as if she wanted to say something else, but then turned away again, her expression closed off, her head bowed.

Ash wanted to break the silence, to find a way for them to part today on better terms, but had no idea how to achieve that. *I need to explain to her how I feel, but how will she understand that yes, I am attracted to her, but no, I don't want to get involved with her?* Ash didn't even believe herself; how could she expect Carmen to?

They reached a junction with a side street. Cars were parked close to or haphazardly half on, half off the pavement.

Carmen, seemingly still wrapped up in her own thoughts, twisted to sidle through a small gap between two cars.

"Wait!" Ash jumped off the pavement, grabbed Carmen's arm, and yanked her back just as a motorbike roared past the spot Carmen would have walked into.

Carmen landed heavily against Ash, her arms automatically reaching out to arrest her progress. Her hands landed on Ash's waist; her chest was pressed close to Ash's.

"Oh my God!" Carmen gasped for breath. "That was close. Thank you."

Ash's heart thumped. "You're...you're welcome."

Carmen was so warm in Ash's arms. So soft and so close. Her breath, tinted with a hint of the coffee they'd drunk, washed over Ash's lips, and something throbbed low in Ash's belly.

"Ash?" Carmen almost breathed the word.

Ash stared at Carmen's mouth, at the way her lips parted under Ash's gaze, her tongue gently licking the plump pinkness of her lips. Ash groaned and dipped her head.

At the first touch of their lips, Carmen tensed; in the next moment, she melted. And then she kissed her back in ways that made Ash's knees go weak and the rest of her body turn to jelly.

Ash gently explored the soft mouth beneath hers, her arms tightening around Carmen with every second that passed. The kiss was good. Unbelievably good. And when Carmen moaned, sweetly, softly, Ash couldn't help licking delicately across Carmen's top lip, asking the question that was answered a millisecond later.

Carmen's tongue tentatively met hers, and Ash's world tilted beneath her feet.

She ran her hands up Carmen's back and into her hair, tugging her even closer, deepening the kiss with each tongue stroke. Her body was on fire, yet she was shivering. It had been a while since she had last been kissed, but she wasn't sure she'd ever been kissed like this. Every cell in her body cried out in pleasure; her nipples hardened, and between her thighs wetness formed as her clit pulsed.

She had no idea how long they kissed. They never fully pulled back, but every now and then one of them eased back to take a breath, turn her head the other way, then resume the pleasure-filled exploration.

Finally, reluctantly, as her brain began to override her libido, Ash lifted her head and broke the kiss. Breathing heavily, she looked down at Carmen in a daze.

"W-what was that?" Carmen asked, her voice husky. "I thought you…" She licked her lips again, and Ash trembled. "Why did you kiss me?"

"I-I don't know. I couldn't help it. You…" She took a step back but still kept a hold of Carmen, reluctant to lose contact with her warmth. "Sorry, I shouldn't have; that was—"

Carmen's finger on her lips stopped the rest of her apology. "Shush. I'm not sorry. Not at all. I'm just a tad confused." Her smile was wan.

"You and me both."

"Should we talk about this?"

"I don't know." Ash finally released Carmen and stepped back, her motion stopped by her heel hitting the kerb behind her.

"Actually." Carmen raised a hand. "Let's not. Let's just leave this where it is. Let me go home with a smile on my face, okay?"

Ash couldn't help laughing. "Yeah, okay. Understood."

Carmen exhaled slowly and looked left and right before crossing the road.

Ash followed, her mind in a tailspin, her body still thrumming.

They walked in silence, but this time it wasn't uncomfortable. At the next corner they reached the main road, and Carmen gestured to her right. "The Tube is that way, but I can see a cab approaching. I'm going to grab that, okay?"

"Sure."

Carmen gave her a half smile before turning to flag the cab down. When she turned back, her smile was stronger, more confident. "Bye," she said as she opened the cab door.

Ash watched the taxi drive off, her mind still not quite caught up with the fact that she had kissed Carmen—and that Carmen had kissed her back in a way that made Ash want to do it all over again. And again and again…

Chapter 28

CARMEN'S HANDS TREMBLED AS SHE searched her handbag for her phone. Her skin was still on fire from the kiss, even though it had been at least thirty minutes since she had been in Ash's arms.

She kissed me.

She still couldn't quite believe it. Not after how difficult their conversation at Alma's had been. Nor could she believe how incredible it had been to be kissed by a woman. By Ash. Soft, yet powerful. Hungry, yet tender. She shivered at the memories; she had not wanted that kiss to end. With Ash's arms around her, her body pressed close enough to feel her breasts against Carmen's own, she'd wondered if her knees would give way. She'd also wondered just where that level of passion could lead, but when Ash had pulled away, her eyes a little wild with fear, Carmen had somehow known that it was the right move to keep it light, to back away and call it a day. Jean-Pierre's words came back to her, and now, after that kiss, she began to believe that maybe he and Felicity were right about Ash and how she felt about her.

Finally, her fingers closed on the phone, and she pulled it from the depths of the bag. Ignoring the notification that she had eight new emails awaiting her attention, she called up Felicity's contact details and pressed the *call* icon.

"Hi, darling, how are—?"

"She kissed me!"

"*What?*"

"She. Kissed. Me."

"Ash, I take it? I mean, just to be clear that's—"

"Yes, Ash! Bloody hell, who else do you think it would be?"

Felicity guffawed. "Well, a few days ago you were all, 'I'm okay; I'll get past it; she doesn't want me, and that's okay'. So forgive me for checking."

"Okay, fair enough." Carmen dumped her handbag and walked into the living room. Her pulse raced and her knees wobbled, so she needed to sit.

"You need to start at the beginning." Felicity sounded exasperated. "How did you go from where you were before she went away to her kissing you today?"

Carmen relayed in detail how the kiss started and how it had seemed to go on for hours, and yet seemed to be over far too quickly. She was only marginally embarrassed at sharing the knowledge of the intimacy with her friend.

"Oh my word." Felicity inhaled sharply. "I've got goose bumps."

"You should try it from my side," Carmen said without thinking.

Felicity barked out a wicked laugh that made Carmen flush.

"So what happens now?" Felicity asked. "Are you an item? What does this mean?"

And just like that, Carmen's mood deflated. "I have no earthly idea." She rubbed at her forehead, where a deep frown had instantly appeared.

"Well, at the risk of sounding smug, it does seem I may have been right about her reciprocating the attraction, hmm?"

"Maybe."

Felicity snorted. "And if I am right, then I think there's still a good chance you and Ash can work this out. No one kisses someone like that unless there are some kind of feelings involved, do they?" Her voice was quiet. "Believe me, I'm not trying to get your hopes up unnecessarily, but…"

"I know. And yes, I want to believe that's true." Carmen sighed. "I'm happy that she and I didn't dissect it afterwards. But I suppose we need to, don't we?"

"You probably do. And soon. Before too many doubts creep in. For each of you. I know you. You'll throw yourself back into your job in a heartbeat if you think things are too difficult with Ash."

"Sometimes I hate that you know me so well."

Felicity chuckled. "Sorry, sweetheart. That's what over twenty years of friendship will do."

"I know. And I'm only joking. I'm so thankful I have you to talk to. I couldn't do this without you."

"Oh, pish." The emotion in Felicity's tone belied her throwaway words. She cleared her throat. "And I want regular reports, madam. None of this keeping me in the dark for days on end."

"We really need to get you a date."

"God, no. Living vicariously through you is much more fun."

Carmen leaned her head in her hands and sighed.

Ash awoke on Monday morning with her eyes full of sleepy dust and her head muzzy. Her night had been crap, to say the least. For starters, getting to sleep had been troublesome as her brain insisted on replaying the kiss, from the delicious start to the reluctant finish, on a continuous loop.

Why did I kiss her? Why did I just confuse things even further?

She hauled herself out of bed and jumped straight in the shower, hoping the cool water would wake her. Or knock some sense into her. As she soaped her body, memories of Carmen's hands gripping her waist assaulted her. Carmen had kissed her as if she couldn't get enough. The heat between them had been intense, and it scorched her body even now.

Ash moaned and for a moment seriously considered doing something about the arousal that flared anew at the memories. Then she stopped her wandering fingers. It didn't seem right somehow.

I can't offer her anything, despite that kiss. Well, not a relationship, anyway. She finished washing and turned off the shower. Maybe it would be okay, though. Ash was a lot wiser after surviving Vikki. She was going into this with her eyes wide open. *Maybe Carmen and I won't last long, but we can enjoy it while we have it.* It didn't need to get serious. No investment of her heart, which she could surely keep locked away tightly. Perfectly doable.

Feeling much better, both from the shower and the processing, Ash dressed and had a cup of tea. She'd just finished planning what she needed to do in the studio to get it ready for reopening on Friday, when her phone pinged with a text from Sophie.

Mum says she'll b home by 6 tomorrow but if u want 2 come early that's ok 2 xx

Ash pinged off a quick *ok* in response and put the phone back down. She and Sophie had messaged a few times while she was away, so Ash knew all was still okay for her niece with her situation at home. She and Courtney were, in Sophie's amusing words, circling each other like two lions forced to share the same cage. So the invite from Courtney, sent via text message on Sunday evening, to have dinner with the two of them on Tuesday had been a pleasant surprise. Was it a good sign? Was Courtney thawing a little?

God, I hope so.

Thankful for the distraction and suddenly realising what the time was, Ash puffed out a breath and stood. She was meeting Damian for brunch, and it was time to go. She gathered up her keys and wallet and left the flat. Talking with Damian all about Kruger and his plans for his next trip was exactly what she needed to take her mind off everything else.

Damian was waiting for her in their favourite greasy spoon café on Essex Road and already had a large mug of tea waiting for her. "You look tired, mate. Bad night?"

Crap, I was hoping it wasn't that obvious. "Yeah, probably the heat."

"It wasn't *that* warm last night."

"Ah, but you're an Aussie, so you're used to it being hot. Us Brits wilt as soon as the temperature gets high enough to not need a jumper."

He laughed. "Yeah, that's true. So, what are you having? The usual?"

"You bet."

Damian stepped up to the counter and ordered their food—full English each, with extra toast—and returned to the table with the cutlery and paper napkins.

They passed an easy hour talking about the sights she'd seen, ordering second mugs of tea, and taking their time. Damian wasn't working until he started a contract in Edinburgh the following week, and she could go to the studio any time as it was still officially closed.

"Hey, what happened with that chick you met?" Damian asked after downing the last of his tea.

"Hayley?"

He blinked at her. "Who's Hayley? No, I mean the posh one with the fancy name. Carmen?"

"Nothing happened." The words left her in a rush, and she couldn't meet his gaze. An instant later, she knew she was busted.

Damian sat back and folded his arms across his chest. "What have you done?"

She glared at him, her defensiveness on the rise. "What do you mean? I haven't done anything."

"Nah, you're hiding something. Oh jeez, you didn't sleep with her, did you?"

"No!"

"But you want to."

Her life would be so much easier if he couldn't read her like a bloody book. She huffed out a breath, knowing there was no use in pretending any longer. "I kissed her. Yesterday."

"Oh for fuck's sake." He ran a hand through his hair. "I thought you said there wasn't going to be anything silly going on. I thought you said she wouldn't become another Vikki. I mean, this Carmen chick is straight, right? And what did you say about straight women?"

"That I'd never get involved with one again." She mumbled the words into her chest, her head hung low in defeat.

"Exactly! Look, I'm not trying to tell you how to run your life, but you *did* make me promise, way back when, to tell you if I ever thought you were doing something dumb again, right?"

"I did."

"And here we are." His voice was gruff.

"I know."

"So?"

She looked up at him, saw the concern etched across his face. "This is a little different, I think. She said she has feelings for me, that it's not just some straight woman curiosity thing."

"And you believe her?"

"Yeah, actually, I do."

He watched her for a moment, his teeth worrying at his bottom lip. "Watch out for yourself, all right? You were a mess after Vikki. I'd hate to see you that way again."

"You're not the only one," she muttered and reached for the remains of her tea.

Chapter 29

ASH LOCKED UP THE STUDIO at three on Tuesday, pleased with her progress. Since yesterday she'd managed a deep clean of the entire studio, sorted out the stock room, and completed the two small repairs she'd needed to make to the front desk and one of the sofas. She'd also managed—mostly—not to think about what was or wasn't happening between her and Carmen.

Now it was time to catch up with her sister. She was surprised to find she was nervous, but they hadn't exactly left things in a good place the last time they'd seen each other. *God, I hope we're not at each other's throats again.* She smiled ruefully. *If nothing else, clashing heads with Courtney will at least keep Carmen off my mind.*

The train journey was uneventful, and at four thirty she rang their doorbell.

Sophie answered quickly and threw her arms around Ash for a long hug. "I'm so glad you're back! I mean, I'm glad you had a good holiday, but I missed you."

Ash squeezed her niece. "I know what you mean. It's good to see you." She stepped back. "You look really chilled."

"I am!" Sophie pulled Ash into the house and shut the door. "Mum's had some kind of personality transplant this weekend. She's been amazing!"

"She has?" Ash followed Sophie through to the kitchen, which was cleaner and tidier than she'd ever seen it, and out to the garden.

Sophie led her to the small plastic table and chairs that sat under a bright orange umbrella. On the table stood a bottle of supermarket lemonade and some glasses.

"Wow, this looks nice," Ash said as she sat.

Sophie flushed and bit her bottom lip. "Well, I wanted to give you a proper welcome back. And, you know, just do something nice for you."

Ash swallowed. "Aw, that's sweet of you. Thanks."

"So, lemonade?"

"Yes, please!"

Sophie poured them each a glass and sat next to Ash.

"So, backtrack. Your mum?"

"Yes! I honestly don't know what's going on with her, but yesterday she told me if I wanted to put up some more posters, I could. Of anyone I liked. Actually, what she said was, 'If there's any other women you want to put on your wall, go for it.'"

Ash tilted her head. "Seriously?"

"I know, right?"

"Wow."

"Exactly."

They sipped their drinks for a few moments. Ash tried to process what she'd just heard. It sounded as if Courtney was well on her way to accepting Sophie's sexuality, but where had this epiphany of Courtney's come from? And more importantly, would it last?

"Oh, and she's told me she wants some time with just you tonight, so I'm being sent to my room after dinner." Sophie pouted.

"Right. Well, I doubt we'll talk the whole night, so I'm pretty sure you'll see me again after your mum and me chat, okay? And besides, us two are here now, aren't we?"

Sophie immediately perked up. "Yeah, cool. Okay, tell me everything about the trip. And show me your photos!"

It was a few minutes after six when Courtney came home.

"Hey." Courtney stood framed by the kitchen doorway. "All right?" Dark circles shadowed her eyes.

"Yeah. You look tired." Ash had never seen her sister look so drained.

"Yeah." Courtney's smile was weak. "Busy day. Got two new members of staff, and they're useless. No idea why Brian hired them." She grunted and turned back to the kitchen. "I'm opening some wine. Want one?" she called over her shoulder.

"Sure."

Ash and Sophie exchanged a look.

Sophie fiddled with her glass of lemonade. "She wasn't that grumpy when she left this morning."

"Yeah, some days work can do that to you." Ash stood. "You stay here; I'll go talk to her."

Sophie nodded and immediately pulled Ash's iPad across the table and began flicking through the photos again.

Ash made some noise as she entered the kitchen, not wanting to startle her sister.

Courtney turned to face her, an open bottle of white wine in her hand. "White okay?"

"Totally." Ash stuck her hands in her pockets and leaned casually against the doorway. "You okay?"

Her sister let out a loud breath. "Yeah, sorry. Just been one of those days." She poured out two glasses of wine and handed one to Ash. "I'll shake it off in a minute. Probably after a bit of this." She raised her glass and threw Ash a much warmer, more relaxed smile.

"Cheers." Ash raised her glass and took a sip. It was cheap stuff, but she knew after a few more mouthfuls, she wouldn't care.

Courtney took a couple of large swallows, then set her glass back down. "Let me go change, freshen up, and then we can make dinner, yeah?"

"Sounds good to me."

Ash didn't want to push her sister, but she couldn't wait to find out what was going on. Courtney looked as if she had a lot to say; there was something in the way she'd looked at Ash over the top of her wine glass. And somehow Ash got the sense that it wasn't going to be some big rant at Ash again.

Sophie was right; something had definitely changed.

Oh well, I guess I'll find out after dinner.

The three of them prepared the meal together, and it was more fun than Ash would have anticipated. By the time they started, Courtney seemed to have shaken off her day, and the three of them laughed and teased their way through putting together burgers and a large salad. Ash couldn't remember the last time she and her sister had been so at ease.

They took the food out to the garden, and Sophie topped up her lemonade while Ash poured more wine for herself and Courtney.

"Cheers." Sophie raised her glass.

Ash and Courtney clinked theirs against hers, and they all took a quick sip before tucking into the food.

Later, once the plates were cleared away, Courtney looked across the table at Sophie and gave her a quick nod.

Sophie pushed back her chair and left the garden without a word.

"So." Courtney poured the last of the wine into their glasses. "I wanted to talk to you about some things."

"Yeah?" Ash kept her voice even, despite the nerves that jangled in her stomach.

Her sister looked away even as she drummed a rhythm on the table. "Yeah. About Sophie and about what's been going on."

"Okay."

Courtney turned back to face her. "I'm sorry for all that crap I threw at you. And I'm sorry for not being more supportive of Sophie the last few weeks."

"You don't really need to say sorry to me." Ash paused, wondering if her next question would be well received or not. "Does she know you're sorry?"

Courtney sighed. "No, that's next on my list. I wanted to talk to you first, though. I need to get it out so that when I talk to her, I can do it more calmly." Her fingertips tapped gently against the tabletop. "I just got scared, you know? She's growing up so fast, and this just seemed like one thing too many for her to deal with." She twisted in her chair. "I know I said some horrible things last time we spoke, and I know I've done some crap things to her. I'll try to make it up to her. And you. I promise."

Ash leaned forward. "You seem different. Has something happened?"

"Yeah, kind of." Courtney finished the last of her wine. "I finally got off my arse and spoke to Rachelle from bingo. Remember? The one I said had a gay son?"

Ash nodded.

"Yeah, well, should have done that weeks ago. Saw her Saturday night, and fuck, did she give me some lessons."

"Really?" Ash's hopes soared.

"Yeah. I mean, she said all the things you said, but somehow hearing it from her, from someone I didn't know that well, made it sink in. She was like me when her boy told her he was gay. Wouldn't have it, tried to talk him out of it. Tried to change him. Then…" Her voice caught. "One day, he tried to kill himself. Left her a note saying he couldn't bear it if she couldn't love him anymore. Luckily, she'd felt sick that day and left work early. Came home and found him in time." She sniffed.

Ash's stomach roiled. *Poor kid. And poor mother.*

Courtney's tears spilled over.

Ash quickly grabbed a tissue from her back pocket and handed it over.

"Thanks. And she told me, she'd never realised what her words were doing. How much damage they were causing to this boy who was her pride and joy." She sobbed, the tears now pouring down her face. "And…and I can't…do that…to Sophie. She's my everything. I…can't…lose her."

Ash left her chair and wrapped her sister in her arms, smoothing her hair with one hand as she rubbed gentle circles on her back with the other. "You won't lose her, you hear? Not now."

Sophie appeared in Ash's line of sight, standing in the kitchen doorway, her eyes wide, her mouth open. "I…I just came back for my lemonade. I wasn't listening, honest."

Courtney swivelled in Ash's arms. "Oh, love, it's okay. Come here." She pulled back from Ash's arms slightly so that she could hold out a hand.

Sophie rushed over and fell to her knees next to her mum's chair. Her eyes were wet and filled with fear. "Are you okay? Is everything all right?"

Courtney pulled Sophie close, wrapping the three of them into a tight embrace. "Yeah, I'm okay. And you, my lovely girl, are more than okay. You're bloody brilliant, you hear?" She kissed the top of Sophie's head. "Just exactly the way you are."

Ash gave up trying to hold back her own tears and let them fall freely as the three of them pressed their heads together and clung to each other.

Chapter 30

CARMEN PACED THE TICKET HALL of Mornington Crescent station. It was a little before one on Sunday afternoon, and she'd been here for fifteen minutes already. She hadn't planned on being that early, but somehow her nerves had got the better of her, and she'd left the house just to have something to do.

What if she's changed her mind?

After making the arrangement to meet, they hadn't messaged again. Carmen knew why *she* hadn't—a mix of fear along with a determination not to overplay this. Despite initiating the kiss the previous Sunday, Ash had acted like a spooked horse afterwards. So it hadn't surprised Carmen not to hear much from her the rest of the week. Except now she couldn't help wondering if Ash would even turn up.

She exhaled a long breath and turned to face the front of the ticket hall. Her next breath caught in her throat. A pulse pounded solidly in her neck, and her skin flashed hot and cold.

Ash stood in the entranceway to the station, perhaps eight feet away, and she looked unbelievable. Again.

How was she supposed to act all casual when Ash looked like this? The blue shorts showed off toned legs with a hint of tan. The tight T-shirt, white with three dark brown feathers across the chest, emphasised the swell of Ash's breasts and the play of muscles in her arms.

Breathe. Breathe.

"Hi." Carmen found her voice and took a couple of steps closer. *Do I hug her? Do I—?*

When Ash stepped forward, Carmen's internal monologue ended abruptly. Ash slipped one arm around her back while the other hand landed on Carmen's waist.

"Hey," Ash whispered near her ear.

Carmen shivered and ached to press closer to Ash's firm body. Before she could move, however, Ash pulled back.

Her gaze flitted from side to side, and she shuffled her feet, her hands now tucked deep into her pockets.

Spooked herself again, I'm guessing. Something is definitely holding her back. Carmen was almost elated by the thought. *She wants me. She just isn't sure she should act on it.*

"How are you?" Ash asked, now looking a little more relaxed.

"I'm good. And you?"

"Yeah, really good." Ash stumbled as someone bumped her from behind.

"Sorry!" the young man said and hurried on.

Ash looked around. "It's a bit busy in here. Shall we move?"

"Sure."

Ash led Carmen out of the station and turned right before crossing the road. "Had a good week?"

"Very good! Finally sent out the termination letters to the first clients I'm dropping, after approval from the lawyer."

"Were you scared?"

It was so like Ash to see right to the big issue around the announcement. *She's so good at reading what's important to me.*

"Terrified." Carmen threw her a glance. The warm yet concerned expression on Ash's face made her feel hot and cold all over once more. "But by last night we'd only had one awful reply. So I suppose that's not too bad."

"One out of twenty? I'd take those odds." Ash grinned.

"Yes, you're right. I suppose I would have preferred not to upset anybody."

"I understand." Ash's tone was gentle. "But you also have to look out for you and your business. Don't worry; you've done the right thing in my opinion."

"Thanks. That means a lot." And it did. It was wonderful how, despite the strange limbo status they seemed to be in regarding any romantic involvement between them, Ash was still so supportive of Carmen and what was going on in her life.

They zigzagged through the streets towards and around Regent's Park and reached the brasserie a few minutes later. It was tucked into a secluded corner next to one of the bridges spanning the canal. Part of a warehouse that had been converted into various small shops and workshops, it had a Bohemian feel, with mismatched chairs and tables.

The waiter greeted them and led them to a small terrace on the first floor.

"What a great place!" Carmen gazed around as she took her seat. "I love the vibe."

"Yeah, and the food's good too. It's not all window dressing."

They ordered drinks, something non-alcoholic for each of them. Carmen couldn't speak for Ash, but she was already buzzing enough from being with her once more. By the time the waiter had returned with their drinks, they'd chosen their food.

"Lamb chops for me." Carmen's stomach growled at the prospect.

"Chicken for me." Ash sat back in her chair and sipped her drink. While her body seemed relaxed, her gaze darted left and right, and her hand trembled when she replaced her drink on the table.

Was she nervous or scared? Or both? *And what can I do about that?* She decided to start things slow. "So, how has your week been?" Carmen reached for her own drink.

"Great. I had dinner with Courtney and Sophie on Tuesday." Ash leaned in, her expression serious. "She's had a complete turnaround as far as Sophie is concerned, and everything between them now is really good. I'm so relieved."

"Oh, that *is* good news. Thank God."

Ash blew out a breath. "Yeah. I saw Sophie on Friday when I reopened the studio. She was pretty much bouncing off the walls with happiness at how different her mum is now. I'm so proud of my sister for pulling it together."

Their meals were delivered, and they began to eat, commenting on the dishes and letting each other sample from their plates. As they ate, they chatted about what each of them had planned for the week ahead. Ash seemed to relax within minutes, and by the time they'd diverted into a lively discussion about the latest scandal to hit the government and swapped recommendations for films they'd recently loved, Carmen was as light as a feather and daring to hope their future was a little more assured.

After the waiter had cleared their plates and they'd ordered coffee, Carmen inhaled a deep breath. *Okay, let's get this out there—I'm tired of dancing around it.* "So how are *you*? And I don't mean your business or your family. I mean you in reference to the elephant in the room from last Sunday."

Ash startled. She gave Carmen a wry smile that slowly widened into something warmer and almost conspiratorial, sending a roll of excitement through Carmen's body. "Ah, yes. Last Sunday. You mean, when I pounced on you, right?"

Carmen chuckled even as her skin heated. "Yes, the pouncing. That's exactly what I mean."

Ash shifted in her seat. "I didn't plan that."

"I guessed as much."

"I just… You looked and felt so good, I couldn't seem to stop myself."

"I didn't want you to stop." Carmen's voice was low and husky, and she shocked herself with the desire it portrayed.

Ash visibly swallowed before steepling her fingers and propping her chin on them. "I'm not looking for anything serious. I have some concerns about getting involved with someone who's only just exploring what being attracted to a woman could mean. But…"

Carmen's heart pounded. "But?"

Ash met her gaze and held it, and the heat there made Carmen feel as if her very bones were melting. "But we seem to have something between us, so maybe we could have some fun exploring that."

Ash waited, holding her breath. She hadn't intended to offer anything to Carmen, never mind something that sounded like a friends-with-benefits arrangement. But Jesus, Carmen looked amazing today, wearing a sleeveless dress that showed off every delicious inch of her collarbone and shoulders, and it was playing havoc with Ash's libido—and her common sense.

"Oh." Carmen's previously warm gaze turned a little colder. She swirled her drink as she maintained eye contact. "Those concerns you mention are to do with that brief story you shared with me once? The woman who was engaged to a man and married him anyway?"

Ash licked her lips. "Yes. As I said, it was a mess. I don't have any desire to repeat it." At Carmen's frown, she hurried on. "I know, that sounds like I'm already passing a judgement on you based entirely on the behaviour of someone you don't know. But she hurt me badly, and I'm cautious as a result."

Carmen didn't immediately respond. She nibbled at her bottom lip in a way that was far too distracting. "I think I can respect that. And yes, you're right; I am only starting to explore what this means. Plus, of course, I have my business to focus on. So maybe you're right. Something fun and casual could be just what we both need." Her words were light, but there was an edge to them that left them lacking in conviction.

Ash's stomach tightened. *Is she sure this is what she wants? Am I?* "Really?"

Carmen's smile was dazzling. "Yes. Why not?" This time she sounded completely convinced.

So why not indeed? They knew what the ground rules were. They were consenting adults. So why were Ash's palms damp? And why did she feel so empty?

They drank their coffees in silence, simply looking at each other. Carmen appeared to be deeply in thought, but at the same time, her gaze pulled Ash in. *I'm scared of letting myself get drawn too close to her, and yet I can't seem to stop myself from wanting her anyway.*

When the waiter brought the bill, they split it, then walked out of the brasserie onto the path that ran parallel to the canal.

"Take a walk with me?" Ash gestured to the path. "Unless you have to be somewhere."

"I think a walk would be lovely." Carmen surprised Ash by linking their arms.

Their gazes locked, and the heat between them rose in an instant. There had been a hint of it as they drank their coffees. But this, now, moved them from a quiet sizzle up to a definite simmer, one touch or a look away from a full explosion. Ash could feel it in every nerve ending, every inch of skin. Her gaze dropped to Carmen's mouth.

Carmen licked her lips, the tip of her tongue sliding slowly between them, and a throbbing began between Ash's thighs that nearly made her moan out loud. They might be considering whatever it was between them as only casual, but it was obvious it wouldn't be lacking in power.

The intensity of the situation was almost too much. Needing a moment to collect herself, Ash turned and gently tugged Carmen into a slow walking pace.

They strolled on for a few minutes in silence. It was a beautiful afternoon, the sun hot but nicely dappled by the trees lining the canal. Many people, often in couples themselves, were enjoying the same walk. *Wait, we're not a couple. Not really. Are we?* Ash's confusion mounted. *What are we doing? And why am I trying to pretend it's not affecting me?*

Carmen's arm, wrapped up in hers, was warm and soft. Their paces matched, and occasionally their thighs brushed, only adding to the tension in Ash's body. Carmen's perfume, floral but not in an overpowering way, came to Ash's nose on the soft summer breeze and teased her. Carmen's eyes, when they met hers, were a deeper colour, her pupils dilated, and of course there were her lips: soft, plump, and *so* kissable.

They came upon a quieter stretch of path, where the trees hung low over the edge of the water, and Ash couldn't stand it any longer. She tugged Carmen to a halt under the draping branches of a huge weeping willow that hid them from the rest of the world and stepped in close.

Carmen gasped but didn't resist when Ash pulled her into her embrace.

God, it felt so good to hold her again. Every curve on Carmen's body moulded itself to Ash's more solid frame, and her softness set every inch of Ash's skin on fire.

Carmen wrapped her arms tightly around Ash's back and lifted her chin, her gaze now so dark it took Ash's breath away. Before Ash could say anything, check if Carmen was okay with whatever this was, Carmen pressed upwards and kissed her.

It was better than she'd been remembering. So much better. There was more heat, more thrilling sensations coursing deep into her core. Carmen seemed to want to possess Ash, deepening the kiss with penetrating tongue strokes. She moved one hand from Ash's back into her hair, stroking gently at the shaved area at the back of her neck.

Goose bumps broke out all along Ash's arms. She fought to take some control over the situation—for crying out loud, she was the one with all the experience—but somehow her body wouldn't respond, needing instead just to be taken. Consumed. Carmen was running this show, there was no doubt about it, and it was all kinds of exciting to let her do so.

When they broke for air some minutes later, they stood gazing into each other's eyes, their chests heaving.

"Is it me, or are we rather good at that?" Carmen asked quietly. "And I'm asking seriously. I obviously don't have any experience of kissing a woman, and I just wondered." She flushed sweetly, and Ash ran her thumb over one pink cheek.

"No, trust me, you don't need to worry. You, we, *are* very good at that."

Carmen smiled, and her eyes twinkled. "I'm glad to hear it." She tugged Ash back in. "So let's do a little more of it, hmm?"

Chapter 31

WEDNESDAY WAS A CHAOTIC DAY of meetings, phone calls, and emails, but Carmen didn't mind—anything to make the day pass quickly and keep her occupied. Otherwise she would have spent hours gazing into space, thinking about Ash. She spent every moment when she wasn't working thinking about Ash.

Yes, but does she think about me? She seems pretty okay with us as we are. Casual.

Her mood dimmed, and she stood up quickly, not wanting to follow that last train of thought to its conclusion. The ringing of her phone was a welcome distraction—until she saw the name on the caller display. Her heart skipped a beat.

"Hi, Ash."

"Hey." Ash's melodious voice sent a delicious shiver down Carmen's body. "Still at work?"

"How did you know?"

"Lucky guess."

Carmen smiled. "Are you in between clients?"

"Well, not exactly. My last client just cancelled."

"Oh, that's a shame."

"Actually, I'm pleased." Ash paused. "It means I have the rest of the evening free. Don't suppose you could get away and maybe meet for a drink?"

There was something in her tone that Carmen couldn't quite decipher, but whatever it was made her stomach perform a slow but not unpleasant roll.

We saw each other last night, and now she wants to see me again.

That didn't sound that casual. *And I don't want it to be.* She sat up straighter in her chair as the implications of that worked their way into her brain. She'd been trying to deny it, but there was no escaping it. No dressing it up as this laidback thing they both wanted. *I don't. I want more. But what if she doesn't?* "I think that sounds like a wonderful idea."

They quickly made a plan to meet at a bar roughly halfway between their workplaces and hung up.

Carmen stared at her phone for a few minutes afterwards, her mind whirling. They'd said casual, but tonight would be the third time they'd seen each other in the last week. Was Ash trying to tell her she wanted something more? Or was it only Carmen who wanted to fall deeper into what they had together?

They had one glass of wine each in the bar before the noise of a large party two tables over became too much.

"I don't have the patience for that anymore," Carmen said as they left the bar. "Must be my age."

Ash laughed. "Well, I'm younger than you, and I hate it too, so…"

Carmen smiled at her, then a small frown marred her forehead. "Ugh, I should probably get home. I have another busy day tomorrow. Walk me to the ring road again?"

"I'd love to."

They fell into an easy pace alongside each other. When Carmen tentatively entwined her fingers with hers, Ash wasn't remotely surprised—or displeased. She wondered, for the hundredth time since Sunday, how something that they'd said would be a little bit of fun already felt like so much more than that. Rather than think that through, she simply held Carmen's hand a little more tightly, revelling in the touch.

A minute or so later, they came across a small park area and, without a word being spoken between them, diverted into it. It wasn't much more than a football-field-sized patch of grass edged with trees, but a few people were out enjoying it on this late summer evening.

Carmen slowed their pace, and Ash had no issue with her wanting to extend their time together.

"So, here's a question I've been meaning to ask for a while." Carmen met Ash's gaze. "You don't seem to have any tattoos yourself, yet you talked about how your father had many and you'd always wanted one."

"That's because the tattoo I have isn't visible." Ash pointed at her back.

"Oh! And what is it?"

"It's a phoenix. The same design as the logo for the studio."

"Why a phoenix?"

Ash pondered, just for a moment, making up something trite, brushing it off. But she couldn't do that, not to Carmen. Somehow being honest with her was the only possible path. "It might sound a bit out there, but in that last year at the bank, I knew I was falling into a bad place, and even though it took me a while to pull myself back up, I knew deep down, long before that, that I needed to. I think, when I went looking for this tattoo, I was subconsciously telling myself I'd rise again. That I'd get that new life I didn't know I was looking for."

The memories of that time were still painful for her, but she had no qualms about sharing a hint of it with Carmen. She'd had no problem sharing anything with her the past few days, and it worried her a little. Sharing had made her feel warm, comfortable, and a whole host of other things she shouldn't be feeling with someone she wasn't supposed to be getting serious about.

"Hey," Carmen whispered, and the next thing Ash knew, Carmen's arms were around her, holding her gently yet firmly, her hands making soothing circles on her back. "It's okay."

"Wh-what is?" God it felt so good to be held like this. Protected. Cared for.

"Whatever it is that made you suddenly look so sad." Carmen brought one hand up to Ash's face and placed it on her cheek. "One day, if you want to, I would like to hear all about that time in your life. But only if you want to. I will understand if you want to forget it."

"I'd like you to know." Ash's voice croaked. "I...I know I could trust you with it. That you wouldn't judge. But not now."

"No, not now."

"Thanks," Ash said softly. "It's been a long time since someone held me like this."

"Then I'm glad it's me who is here doing this now."

Ash raised her head, and Carmen eased her hand away from her face so they could look at each other. They were only a couple of inches apart. And there it was again, that intensity. Only this time it wasn't purely desire that weaved its way between them. There was something else here too. Something so palpable Carmen thought it might be possible to touch it in the air around them. Something that went far beyond physical attraction.

Ash's gaze locked on hers, and what Carmen saw there nearly had her gasping out loud. *Does she even realise how she looks at me?*

Ash blinked and wet her lips. "Carmen, I…" She shuddered in Carmen's arms. "I don't know what's happening." She exhaled and looked skywards, the golden pink light of the setting sun illuminating her worried features. "That's not true. I know, but I…I don't know what to do with it."

"You're scared." Carmen kept her voice low, non-accusatory.

"Yes."

"This is real for me." Carmen reached up once more to cup Ash's face. She ran her fingertips lightly over the smooth skin of her cheek before dragging her thumb over Ash's full lips. "This isn't a game. I'm not fooling around with you to satisfy some idle curiosity. I promise."

"So much of me wants to believe you." Ash dropped her gaze and pursed her lips. "But there's a part of me still so scared of what happened once before."

"I understand. Or at least I think I do. I'm a little scared myself. The last time I let myself feel this way about someone, he had to leave me."

Ash flinched at the male pronoun.

"I have dated men, Ash. I'm not going to apologise for that."

"No!" Ash's gaze was back on Carmen's, her eyes wide. "You don't have to." She tensed in Carmen's arms but didn't pull away, much to Carmen's relief. "This is my problem. My thing I have to get past. I'm sorry; I shouldn't have reacted that way."

"It's okay. From what little you've told me, it's understandable. But I'm not her. Please remember that." Carmen held Ash's gaze, hoping by will alone she could convince Ash she could be trusted.

"I will." Ash blinked a couple of times, and her posture relaxed once more. "So, um, what now?"

Carmen gave her a gentle smile. "You're asking me? I'm the inexperienced one here."

Ash chuckled. "I don't know about that. You seem to be handling things far better than I am." She ran her fingertips along Carmen's jawline. "Okay, here's what I think. If we're going to do this, as in, stop pretending this is just some fun, casual thing and recognise it might be more than that, then I, um, would like to do it properly."

"Properly?"

"Exclusive. Monogamous. If there's an us, I want a proper us."

"Oh God, absolutely." Carmen's entire body thrummed at the thought of being considered part of an *us* with this extraordinary woman. "I only want you. Just you." Her voice was husky and low.

Ash moaned, low and quiet, but it sounded like a rumble of thunder in Carmen's ears.

Carmen leaned up and did what she'd been wanting to do, deep down, ever since they said hello at the bar earlier.

Soft. *Dear God, so soft.* Ash's lips were like silk beneath hers. Everything inside Carmen seemed to take a seismic shift sideways as their lips pressed together. This kiss was different from all the others they'd shared. There was an emotional level to it, one Ash seemed to reciprocate in equal measure. Those emotions imbued the kiss with something that made Carmen's heart lurch in excited anticipation of what they could become.

She lost herself once more in the feel of Ash in her arms, Ash's mouth moving gently against hers, Ash's heat permeating every inch of her where their bodies joined.

Carmen shifted closer. Her entire body tingled as their kiss deepened. Her mind emptied; she was nothing now but touch and emotion.

Ash moved a hand into her hair, bringing her closer yet. Her tongue gently swiped across Carmen's bottom lip, and, with a small groan born of hunger and an incredible need, Carmen parted her lips and let her in.

When their tongues touched, every sensation increased tenfold. Her body was equal parts liquid heat and fierce shivers. Carmen sank into the kiss, tasting Ash, revelling in the velvet texture of her tongue, the incredible arousal her touch stirred.

Finally, they came up for air. They held their foreheads together, their breathing heavy in the still air.

"That just keeps getting better and better," Carmen whispered.

Ash merely nodded and dipped her head once more.

Chapter 32

CARMEN'S HEART LEAPED WHEN SHE saw Ash waiting for her at Tottenham Court Road station on Sunday evening. She wore a short-sleeved, plain white shirt over tight-fitting black jeans with black boots. Her long fringe had been boosted with some kind of product and was a sexy, messy tumble swept to one side of her head.

Good God. Carmen clutched for breath. *She's stunning. And she's my date.* Carmen stepped off the top of the escalator and walked over to meet her.

Ash's gaze raked down Carmen's body and back up again, and the action sent a thrill coursing through her. The little black dress was one of her favourites, and she'd hoped Ash would appreciate it.

"Jesus," Ash said as Carmen reached her. "You look incredible." She leaned forward and dropped a sweetly soft kiss on Carmen's cheek.

"Thank you." Carmen couldn't help it; she needed to touch. She ran her fingers lightly over Ash's bare forearm. "So do you. Those jeans look like they were tailor-made for you."

Ash placed one hand on Carmen's waist and tugged her a little closer. "That dress looks like it was painted on. It's beyond sexy."

Carmen flushed, but not from embarrassment. She tilted her head, and their gazes locked. Every time they met, the heat level between them seemed to rise just a little more. It was intoxicating.

"Later." Ash lifted her other hand to tenderly stroke Carmen's cheek.

"Are you reading my mind now?"

Ash nodded slowly and grinned. "Let's just say your eyes are very expressive."

Chuckling ruefully, Carmen stepped back.

"So where are you taking me?" Ash bounced on her toes. That and her excited grin made her seem about eight years old.

Carmen laughed. "I told you, it's a surprise. Are you always this impatient?"

"Sometimes." Ash waggled her eyebrows. "But it's more like, once I know someone has a surprise for me, I *have* to know what it is. I drove my parents up the wall at Christmas when I was little."

"I can imagine." Carmen slipped her arm through Ash's. "Come on. I won't keep you waiting any longer."

They headed out of the station, and Carmen led them through the streets into the heart of Bloomsbury. Soon they stood outside the entrance to a private art gallery.

"Ta-da!" Carmen threw her arms open.

Ash looked at the entrance, then her gaze travelled over the front window. *Africa Inspirations* was written in black and gold lettering across the expanse of glass, and Carmen saw the moment it clicked in Ash's brain.

"You've brought me to an exhibition of African art?"

"I have. I assumed you'd like it."

"Oh, wow! This is awesome." Ash kissed her cheek. "That's… God, that's so thoughtful. You're amazing."

Carmen looked into Ash's eyes, and her stomach flipped over several times. Ash's expression was full of awe, but also warmth and appreciation and…tenderness.

"You're welcome." She smiled and took a step back. "Come on. Let's go in."

The exhibition was so good Ash knew she'd have to go round twice to make sure she'd appreciated it all. She still couldn't believe Carmen had arranged to get them an invite to this exclusive premiere, but it was more than that—Carmen had taken Ash's interests into account and designed an evening entirely for her enjoyment. It made Ash feel about ten feet tall.

Carmen appeared at her side, carrying two fresh glasses of champagne. She handed one to Ash, and they tapped glasses before sipping. "They're beautiful, aren't they?" Carmen nodded in the general direction of the paintings.

"They are. This is a wonderful exhibition."

Carmen opened her mouth to speak, but a new voice to Ash's left cut her off.

"Carmen! I thought that was you."

Ash noted the slight shift in Carmen's expression but couldn't quite read what it meant. It was almost panic, but undercut with something else.

"Frederick." Carmen's smile seemed forced. "How lovely to see you."

Ash turned to see who had approached. The man was perhaps in his mid-fifties, with greying hair and a red-veined face that suggested he drank a lot of alcohol. He wore an expensive-looking suit, and a Rolex hung loosely on his left wrist. He almost smelled of money, and Ash was reminded of all the overpaid wankers who'd run the investment bank division she'd worked for. She only just held back a grimace.

"How are you?" Frederick asked of Carmen, although he flicked a glance to Ash and back again.

"I'm good. And you?"

"Oh, fine, just fine." He looked at Ash once again, then said to Carmen, "I saw Gerald yesterday for lunch."

Carmen looked completely unperturbed by the comment. "How is he?"

"He's well. I still can't believe you two aren't together anymore. You were such a great couple."

His almost snivelling tone set Ash's teeth on edge. This guy was a creep.

He gave Ash another look, longer this time, and she found herself torn. Surely Carmen should introduce her, even if the guy was an arsehole? But she hadn't, so did that mean she didn't want him to know who Ash was? *Do I offer a handshake or what?*

While Ash pondered the options, Frederick turned back at Carmen. "So, how's business?"

Their stilted conversation batted back and forth, interspersed with yet more looks from Frederick in her direction. Meanwhile, Ash's anxiety—and, she had to be honest, annoyance—over just why Carmen hadn't bothered with introductions climbed.

"Well," Carmen said eventually, "if you'll excuse us?" Without waiting for a response, she lightly touched Ash's arm and led her away from him.

Ash followed her to the far end of the gallery, breathing evenly to ensure she didn't say something too biting once she did have Carmen's attention.

"I'm very sorry." Carmen put her glass down on a small table and turned to face Ash. "I know that was rude of me, to not introduce you."

Ash placed her glass next to Carmen's. "I don't know about rude, but it was pretty awkward."

Carmen winced.

"Why didn't you?"

"Frederick is…" Carmen huffed out a breath and ran one hand through her curls. "He's an ass. He and my ex, Gerald, worked together for many years. I've met him a few times and never trusted him. I have a feeling if I'd been dating anyone but Gerald, Frederick would have attempted something with me."

"Well, he sounds nice. But that still doesn't really explain why you pretended I wasn't even there." Okay, maybe that came out a *little* harsher than she'd intended.

Carmen flushed a deep pink. "I'm sorry. I panicked. The last thing I wanted to do was give him any reason to be on even worse behaviour, so I decided not to introduce you. You know, as my partner. I…I'm not sure we're even calling each other that, and I can only imagine what he would have done with that titbit of information if I'd offered it." She shook her head. "I could have just introduced you as a friend and left it at that, but I didn't want *you* being insulted. So, I…I did nothing. I screwed up, and I'm sorry."

"So it was all about him being a wanker? It wasn't anything to do with being embarrassed to have a female partner?" She had to know and sooner rather than later. No matter how good things had been between them the last couple of days, so far they'd not been seen together as a couple by anyone Carmen knew.

"Absolutely not!" Carmen took a step back and lowered her voice. "You…you think I'd think that?"

She looked horrified, and it made Ash's stomach clench. "I'm sorry. I know that sounded bad. But you're so new at all of this, and *we're* so new. I guess I need to remember that and not jump to any conclusions when situations like this crop up."

"It would help, yes." There was a hint of acid in Carmen's tone Ash had never heard before.

Ash stepped in close and took Carmen's hand. "I'm sorry. I didn't mean to hurt you. I could have maybe phrased it differently but I had to be honest with you about how it made me feel."

Carmen exhaled and squeezed Ash's fingers. "You're right. We do have to be honest with each other." She pursed her lips. "It's a bit of a minefield, isn't it? I mean, all this getting to know someone properly. Not being casual." She gave a wry smile.

Ash laughed and stepped even closer. "It is. But I'm up for it, if you are?"

"Definitely." Carmen's voice was husky, and Ash's skin tingled.

"Want to call it a night?"

Carmen glanced around the room. "I don't necessarily want to stay here now." She turned back to Ash. "But it's not even eight o'clock. I know it's Sunday and we both have to work tomorrow, but I don't want the evening to end."

"Well, let's get out of here and find somewhere to sit. Maybe have a glass of wine, a little bite to eat?"

"Sounds lovely."

Ash leaned in, emboldened by the warm smile Carmen sent her way, the kind of smile that lit her up from the inside out. "And maybe we can have another slow walk somewhere quiet. *Really* slow."

Carmen's eyes smouldered, and Ash's temperature rocketed.

At just after eight on Tuesday night, Carmen pushed open the door of Ash's studio.

Ash stood from her seat at the desk. "Hey. This is a nice surprise."

"Hi. I, um, just thought I'd pop in and say hello." Carmen's face was warm. Such impromptu gestures were not her style at all. At least not when she'd been dating Gerald or any of her boyfriends in the last ten years or so. But she hadn't been able to get Ash out of her mind after their Sunday art gallery date. Not after the words they'd spoken and the new level of understanding they had. And the kisses. Oh God, the kisses. Carmen didn't think she'd ever felt so much from kissing a person. Not even Lewis. When she was wrapped up in Ash's arms, with Ash's mouth making wondrous things happen to Carmen's senses, time seemed to stop. The bench they'd found in the corner of a square near the British Museum had become their enclave, and if it hadn't been for the hardness of the seat, Carmen could have stayed in Ash's arms for hours. As it was, she'd gone home aching, aroused, and barely able to remember how to get her key in her front door.

"You can pop in any time." Ash walked around the desk.

Carmen couldn't find words. Ash looked so good, so tempting in a sleeveless, black T-shirt that showed off her glorious arms and those tight, black jeans that always held Carmen's attention.

"You okay?" Ash stopped and stared at her.

Carmen nodded, then moved. In two paces she was face to face with Ash, her hands on Ash's waist. The small gasp Ash gave as Carmen pressed their lips together, hard, was one of the best sounds Carmen had ever heard. She pulled Ash closer and kissed her with everything she had, feeling the strength of her everywhere they touched.

Ash's arms quickly enveloped her, and she returned Carmen's kiss with a fervour that made Carmen shiver. When Ash's tongue dived deep into Carmen's mouth, her arousal leaped into fifth gear. Possibly even sixth.

Carmen moaned into Ash's mouth, sweeping her tongue against Ash's. Moments—minutes? hours?—later, she pulled back slightly so she could nibble Ash's bottom lip.

Ash broke the kiss first, breathing hard. "Jesus, what a way to say hello."

"I just… I couldn't help it. You're so…" Carmen swallowed. "You're so sexy." In a small part of her brain, telling another woman she was sexy sounded odd. But the rest of her stood up and shouted, *Hell, yes!*

"Honey, you beat me by a country mile in the sexy stakes." Ash gave her a lopsided grin. "Not that I'm sorry you're here, but how come you are?"

Carmen's face heated. "Couldn't stop thinking about you."

Ash gazed at her for a few moments, then cleared her throat. "Want to sit, or is this a flying visit?"

"Sitting is good." *Before my knees give way.* Arousal still burned brightly within.

They snuggled up together on the sofa.

"How was your day?" Ash trailed one fingertip into Carmen's hair and twisted a curl around before letting it fall and repeating the gesture.

The motion sent delicious tremors down Carmen's back.

"I'm good. Today was busy but okay. My favourite client came in, but all we talked about was you."

"Huh?" Ash looked adorably confused.

"Tamsyn Harris." Carmen smiled as Ash's eyebrows shot up.

"It's going to take some getting used to, you knowing her as well as you do."

The idea popped into Carmen's head and out of her mouth a millisecond later. "Well, you could get to know her too. And Maggie. Soon, if you like. How would you like to be my plus one at their wedding?"

"Are you serious?"

"I am." She hadn't thought about it in advance, and now that it was out there she should have been nervous. There'd be plenty of people from her world at the wedding, and turning up with Ash on her arm would be a rather large statement. But the more time they were together, the more Carmen knew this was something special, something to be proud of, and she shouldn't be scared of showing it.

"When is it?"

"Well, I suppose that might be the only problem. It's on a Saturday, the 26th of this month."

Ash rubbed at her chin with her thumb, then stood. She retrieved her mobile from the desk, sat back down, and scrolled a couple of times. "I might be able to make it work. I've got three clients booked in that day, but they're all regulars, so if I call them tomorrow, maybe that's early enough to be able to switch them around. Perhaps even to the Sunday."

"Ah, the wedding is in Norfolk. It would be, well, a whole weekend away."

Ash grinned. "A whole weekend with you? Even better. Okay, I am definitely going to try to make this work somehow. How soon do you need to know?"

"There's no rush. If I'm not going with you, I'm going on my own. Tamsyn's booked out so many hotel rooms in the local area, one more room being required isn't a show-stopper." Carmen paused. Fierce heat rose up her neck to her face. "Um, I mean, assuming we'll be in separate rooms. I…I don't know what your thoughts are on that."

Ash shifted in her seat and rubbed at the back of her neck. She looked as red as Carmen felt. "Yeah, um, I don't know. Maybe separate rooms would be a good idea. I mean it's up to you. I want you. I guess that's obvious."

Her wry grin tugged at Carmen's heart as her words made Carmen's libido leap to attention.

"But I know this is all new for you, and I'm totally okay with you setting the pace." Ash held her hand.

Part of me wants to rush that pace. Right now. Carmen's cheeks burned even hotter. But the rest of her was still a nervous wreck at the thought of actually getting naked with another woman that way. *One day I do need to get over this, but not right now.* "I think, um, two rooms is probably for the best."

"Well, all right, then." Ash cleared her throat. "I have to say, this is pretty amazing. A whole weekend together." She nudged Carmen. "And trust me when I say, that's the best part about it. Sure, I want to meet your friends, and I know one of them is a world-famous actress and all that. But it's the chance to spend such quality time with you that's got me all excited. Just so you know."

"God, could you get any more adorable?" Carmen was thankful they were past the awkwardness over the hotel rooms.

"I'm adorable?" Ash's smile lit up the room. "Seriously?"

Carmen rolled her eyes. "Yes, you are, but don't go getting all big-headed on me."

Ash laughed and pulled Carmen into her arms. "I'll try not to. Now, it's been"—she looked at her watch—"at least ten minutes since I last kissed you. That's way too long."

The kiss she gave Carmen then would keep her awake, Carmen knew, for quite some time later that night.

Chapter 33

On Thursday, Carmen worked non-stop from eight in the morning. She'd promised herself she'd finish by seven, if at all possible; she and Ash had a late dinner date at nine, and she wanted to be able to go home and change before then. But the pile of work on her desk and in her in-box laughed at the idea of her finishing so early. *Okay, maybe eight and I don't go home and change. I'm pretty sure I have a spare blouse in the cupboard.*

These few weeks of transition between the old business model and the new were naturally going to be like this, but she couldn't wait for it all to be over. Despite a few unhappy customers, she still thought it had been the right move to streamline the client list.

And maybe when the dust has finally settled, Ash and I could book ourselves a couple of days away somewhere. The thought gave her a thrill. Yes, they'd be spending a short weekend together soon, but that was all about Tamsyn and Maggie's wedding. A couple of days of just her and Ash, now that was another story. *Maybe during the week so she doesn't lose her Friday and Saturday business.* She knew by now that Mondays and Tuesdays were Ash's quietest days. So yes, maybe head out of town early on a Monday, find some nice, cosy cottage to hole up in. Real fire, good food and wine, comfy bed…

Her cheeks blazed, and she jolted so hard her wireless mouse flew across the desk and very nearly ended up on the floor. Lately, thoughts of getting more physical with Ash had taken up residence in her brain on a regular basis. She just wished they wouldn't do so when she was at work.

"You okay?" Monica asked.

Carmen looked up, hoping her face would reveal nothing of her thoughts. "All good. Just had one of those twitches. You know, someone walking over your grave."

"Ugh, I hate those!"

Carmen made to say more, but a loud voice from the reception area turned her head in that direction.

"*I don't care if she's busy, she can see me now!*"

"Uh-oh." Monica rose from her seat. "That sounds like—"

Annabella Mitchell stormed through the office door. Her hair and make-up looked perfect, as if she'd just walked out of a beauty salon. But the ugly sneer on her face ruined anything good the makeover had hoped to achieve. "Is this some kind of joke?" Her voice was an ear-splitting screech as she waved a scrunched-up piece of paper in her hand.

Carmen stood, her heart pounding. "Annabella, please. Why don't you come in and sit down, and we'll—"

"And we'll what? Have a nice cup of tea while you tell me how I'm not good enough to be represented by you anymore?" Annabella marched forward, her hands now on her hips.

Out of the corner of her eye, Carmen saw Beverley hovering near the doorway, phone in one hand, the other clutched to her chest. Monica had moved away from her desk and also held her phone tightly in her hand.

Carmen surreptitiously waved them both back. "Annabella." She mustered her smoothest tone. "Please. If you'll just sit down, we can talk about this."

"What is there to talk about?" Annabella's shout echoed through the confined space of the office. "You've made it perfectly clear I'm being tossed out with the trash." Her mouth twisted into a cruel grin. "I only came here tonight to tell you how much this is going to ruin you. I'm going to make your name mud in this industry. When I'm finished, no one will want you as their agent. No one!"

"I'm calling the police." Beverley's voice quavered. "That's threatening behaviour."

"No, it's okay." Carmen had no idea how she sounded so calm and balanced. "Annabella's understandably upset. There's no need for us to involve anyone else." She took two tentative paces towards the actress. "I do get why you're upset. Believe me, this wasn't an easy decision. And you're not the only one we've let go."

"Oh, and that's supposed to make me feel better, is it?" Annabella threw her hands up. She stepped closer and pointed a finger in Carmen's face. "You'll pay for this. Just you wait and see. I know a lot of people. A *lot*."

Carmen recoiled at the bitterness and fury on the actress's face. Fear slithered down her spine. Annabella's threats were probably empty bluster, but what if they weren't? What if she *did* have that level of influence?

Jesus, she could ruin me. What had seemed so easy, so achievable before now hung like a wrecking ball above Carmen, just waiting to crash down and destroy everything she'd worked so hard for. *How did I underestimate her? And who else have I misread?* There were at least ten clients she'd yet to hear from after the final letters had gone out the week before. If they all took Annabella's stance…

Maybe I can retain her. And a few of the others who complain. It would mean she'd still have to work long hours, and she would have to carefully pick which new clients she took on, given that; however, surely that was better than the entire business going under. Of course, that would mean less time with Ash, but she'd understand. Wouldn't she?

"Annabella, I don't think there's a need for things to go that far. Can I suggest you come back tomorrow? We'll do lunch and talk this through."

A slight softening in Annabella's posture gave Carmen hope. "Lunch tomorrow?"

"Yes. Wait, let me just check my calendar." Carmen grabbed her phone and scrolled through her calendar. It would take a bit of shuffling, but if it headed off this danger, it was worth it. "One thirty?"

Annabella checked her own phone. "I suppose so." She pouted, then spun on her heel and shoved roughly past Beverley in the doorway, who had to clutch the doorframe to avoid falling over.

"Oh God, Beverley, are you okay?" Monica asked a millisecond before Carmen could.

They both rushed over to the older woman and took hold of an arm each.

"I'm…I'm okay." Beverley's eyes were wild. "That was scary."

"Come, sit down." Carmen led her over to the conference table and eased her into one of the chairs. "I'm so sorry that happened."

"Oh, it's not your fault." Beverley shook her head. "I never did like her. And she's rubbish in that soap."

Monica snorted, then full out laughed. "You're dead right. Jesus, what a drama queen."

Carmen turned back to Beverley. "I think we should all call it a day now, don't you? Are you okay to go home, or shall I call you a cab? You know what, I think I want to call you a cab anyway."

Beverley gazed up at her. "That's lovely. And I won't argue with you. That gave me quite a turn."

"Here, I'll take care of this. Get your stuff, and we'll leave together," Monica said. "I'll call for the cab while you pack up, then wait downstairs with you for it."

Carmen threw Monica a grateful smile. "Thank you." She took a step back to give them room. "Right, you two get going, and I'll lock up."

"Sure you'll be okay on your own?" Monica frowned. "What if she comes back?"

"She won't." Carmen rolled her shoulders, her muscles taut with tension. "She's said her piece. And I've cut her off with the offer of lunch tomorrow."

"You're not going to give in to her, are you?" Monica's voice was quiet.
"I…I don't know."

Monica opened her mouth, closed it again. With what looked like some effort not to say anything else, she turned to Beverley and helped her from the room.

Felicity opened the door and let Carmen into the house. "My God, you're as white as a sheet!" She pulled Carmen into a hug. "And you're shaking. Come and sit down."

Carmen, her mind numb, followed Felicity down the hall to the lounge. She waited there while Felicity quickly rustled up some sparkling water for them both.

"Here, drink this." Felicity handed her a glass.
"Thanks."

"I have to say, I'm with Beverley. I think you should have called the police."

Carmen rubbed at her face. "I think that would have made things considerably worse."

She'd filled Felicity in on the details as she'd ridden in the cab over. Carmen prided herself on respecting her clients' privacy, but after that scene, she'd needed someone to talk it through with, and Felicity was the obvious choice, given Ash was working.

"Hmm, maybe." Felicity sipped her water. "So, what now? I assume you're going to have your lawyer with you when you meet her for lunch tomorrow?"

Carmen blinked rapidly. That hadn't even occurred to her.

Felicity shook her head. "You must, darling. God knows what she'd say or do otherwise. I mean, it's not like you're going to take her back, is it?"

"Um…"

"What? Carmen, you can't be serious! She's a talentless hack who doesn't deserve you, especially after this evening's pathetic performance."

"But what if…what if she can do all that damage?"

"Then you'll find a way to deal with it. Have more faith in yourself. You didn't get this far without being brilliant, did you?"

Carmen's eyes pricked with tears. "I know, it's just…"

"What? Hard? Of course it's hard. Most of the important things in life are." Felicity leaned forward, pinning Carmen with an intense gaze. "You have every right to run that business how you choose. But the last few weeks you've been a different person, and it's been wonderful to see. And the reason is that you've allowed something other than work into your life. I don't just mean Ash. I mean the concept of free time, of going out without it being anything related to your job. Are you actually going to sit here and tell me you want to give all that up again just to keep Annabella bloody Mitchell happy?"

Carmen couldn't help her wry smile. "Well, when you put it that way."

"See? You know I'm right."

"Whatever."

They locked gazes and smiled at each other.

"So, how is the lovely Ash? Last time we talked, things had moved on from that silly 'let's just be casual' idea. Is everything still going well?"

"It is." Carmen swirled her drink, watching the ice cubes bump their way around the glass. "It's wonderful. It—she—really has grabbed me. Although I'm a little scared, if I'm honest."

"Of what?"

Carmen frowned as she tried to conjure the right words. "Of the way this seems to be consuming me already. Am I going to fall fast and deep and then get my heart broken?"

"Quite possibly." Felicity shrugged. "But that's absolutely no reason to back away from it. Sometimes we just have to do it. Be brave with our hearts. Dare to love, even though we're scared of how it might turn out. Because sometimes it turns out just fine."

Carmen took a deep breath and laid her hands on her knees, straightening her shoulders as she did so. "You're right. Again. Damn, I hate that."

Felicity laughed.

From somewhere in Carmen's bag her phone pinged with a text message notification. She pulled it out.

Still on for tonight? I have one more client and she'll be here any time now. Really looking forward to seeing you xx

Oh God. Ash. Dinner tonight. She'd forgotten all about it in the drama of the evening. Maybe she should cancel. She'd hate to do so because they couldn't see each other again until Sunday, but...

No, fuck that. I need to see Ash. But she also wanted to give Ash the chance to cancel—after all, Carmen knew she might not be able to shake this off and relax fully into the rest of the evening.

Only fair to tell you I'm not in the best of moods. Had a client turn up earlier and rip us to shreds for letting her go. It will be okay but I'm rather tired. Will totally understand if you'd prefer to cancel x

Definitely not! I want to hug you now.

Carmen's heart swelled, and she took a few moments to breathe before responding.

Then I'll see you at nine. Can't wait xx

Chapter 34

"HAVE YOU SPOKEN TO YOUR brother lately?" Ash sat back in her chair, willing her body to relax.

"Hmm." Carmen gazed into her espresso cup. "Last week."

"All good with him?"

"Yes."

Ash sighed. It was like trying to get blood out of a stone. Carmen was obviously exhausted after her intense day, and their conversation had been this stilted since they'd met an hour ago. "Look, do you want to call it a night? You're obviously tired, and that's okay, but—"

"No, I'm fine." Carmen's smile was forced. She took a sip from her drink. "How does your weekend look?"

"You, um, asked me that already." Ash kept her tone gentle. She wanted to support Carmen, of course she did, but right now it was difficult to know exactly how to do that. *Except, I guess, by just being here.*

"I did?" Carmen flushed and shook her head. "Sorry."

"It's okay." Ash saw the waitress approaching. "Shall we get the bill?"

"Sure."

Ash added her credit card to Carmen's on the small tray that held their bill.

As soon as they'd paid, Carmen stood and stretched. She walked around to Ash's side of the table and stepped in close. "I'm so sorry. I'm being crap company, aren't I?"

She looked contrite and sad, and it broke Ash's heart. Knowing from running her own business that reputation was everything, she could sympathise with how upset Carmen was at what that stupid actress had said.

"I know that was hard for you this evening. But please don't worry that you're not on top form. I understand."

"But it's such a waste of your time, isn't it? You deserve better company than I can offer."

Ash smiled and motioned for them to leave the restaurant. "Look, you are totally allowed to feel the way you do. Like I said earlier, I'm pretty sure I'd do the same in your position."

They stood outside the restaurant, the cool evening making both of them immediately pull on their jackets.

Carmen slipped her hand through the crook of Ash's arm and looked up at her. "I'm worried that, with all my drama, I'm too much for you to take on. That you'll run out of patience."

Ash pulled her closer. "I doubt that. You're an amazing person, and we're having a pretty amazing time together so far. So tonight isn't so good. Well, that happens. It wasn't anything to do with *us*. It was work-related, and anyone can have that happen to them. I don't see that as drama at all. Just normal life."

"Are you sure? I mean, with my whole new sexuality thing too, I don't want to—"

Ash slipped her arm free so that she could wrap both arms completely around Carmen, loving again just how incredible Carmen felt in her arms. "I'm sure. Trust me, okay?"

A smile, a real one, broke out on Carmen's face. "I do, you know. Completely."

Ash's heart beat a little faster at the conviction in Carmen's tone. "Good."

"I don't want to go home yet." Carmen exhaled loudly. "I'll understand if you don't want to, so please feel free to say no, but could we maybe find a pub or bar for another drink?"

Although she wasn't entirely sure it was the right idea, there was no way she was going to dampen Carmen's attempt to lift herself out of her mood. "I'm in. Come on. There's a place just up the road I know."

Carmen linked their arms once more. "Then lead on."

Five minutes later, they snagged a small table with two less-than-comfortable chairs in the centre of a pub that was busy but not heaving on this Thursday night. Ash politely pushed her way to the bar, ordered their drinks, and returned to their table with the two tall glasses carefully held out of harm's way as she weaved her way back.

"Here you go." She put the gin and tonic down in front of Carmen and gave her a warm smile before setting her own drink down.

Carmen's return smile was gorgeous, and Ash's heart thudded. *This woman...*

"Okay, before I sit back down I need to go to the loo," Ash said. "Be right back."

There was a queue for the toilets, but it was short. While she waited, Ash scrolled through the news on her phone and checked the notifications for the studio's page on Facebook. She was pleased to see she'd picked up another two five-star reviews, which was always good for business.

When she'd finished in the bathroom and washed her hands, she made her way back through the throngs towards their table.

She was perhaps twenty feet away, working her way around a big group of lads all drinking pints and talking loudly to each other, when she slowed her steps. There was a man sitting in her seat, chatting to Carmen. He was good-looking, with short, dark hair, a classically chiselled jaw, and, from what she could see of his upper body, totally fit.

Carmen laughed at something he said, nodded, then held out her hand as he offered her a card.

Is she taking his number? Ash's blood ran hot and cold; sweat broke out on the small of her back, and her stomach tightened to a sharp knot.

No, not Carmen. Not her. She's different. She's not like Vikki.

Is she?

Just as she managed to make her legs work again and pushed her way through the group, the man stood and threw Carmen a dazzling smile. Moments later, he walked out of the pub.

Carmen turned to Ash as she approached. "You were gone a while, is it busy back there?"

"Who was that?" Ash heard her own voice, heard the accusatory tone in it, but there was nothing she could have done to stop it.

Carmen flinched. "No one." Her tone was even, but a spark of fire flashed in her eyes. "Just some overeager man."

"You took his card." Ash's pulse pounded so loudly in her ears it almost drowned out the sounds of the pub around her.

"I think you should sit down." Carmen's voice was like cold steel.

Ash roughly pulled out her chair and sat, disgusted to feel the remnants of the body heat he'd left behind on the seat.

Carmen pinned Ash with a stare. "He came over to talk to me the minute you'd gone. Rather than cause a scene, I let him talk."

"You took his card," Ash repeated, her voice like gravel, her anger and fear making her shake.

"Yes. I did. Because it was by far the easiest way to get rid of him." Carmen sat back and shook her head. "Have you any idea how little some men understand the word *no*? I have learned over the years that with egos like that, it is far easier to assuage than argue. God knows they're stupid enough to think I *will* call them back." She shook her head again. "But I have to say, it's pretty upsetting that I'm having to explain myself this way. How on earth could you think that there was anything more to it than that?"

Ash swallowed. Was she jumping to the wrong conclusion, letting her fears take over? But Carmen had looked so relaxed with him…

"Oh my God." Carmen stared at her. "You still don't trust me, do you? Don't trust in what I've said I feel for you. Jesus, you're still waiting for me to walk away from this, from us." She blanched. "You can't get past this idea in your head that I'm only experimenting. When actually what I feel for you is stronger than anything I've felt in years."

Is that it? Do I trust her? I thought I did but… "No, it's…" She didn't know how to explain it, how to even explain her fears to herself, never mind Carmen. "This, us, has all happened so fast. I've been used to protecting myself, being cautious about who I get to know. Who I let in. Some things that happen to us have big consequences, you know? They affect us and—"

"I understand," Carmen said intently. "But tarring me with the same brush as that woman from your past is grossly unfair, isn't it?"

"On some level I do know that. Really I do."

"But you can't let it go?" Now Carmen's voice was quiet and sad, and Ash didn't know how to take that away, not when, deep down, Carmen might be right: Ash couldn't seem to let go of her fears. Not enough to make this work.

They stared at each other in silence for a few moments.

Carmen placed a hand on her forehead and let out a long breath. "This day has been awful. And I have literally no energy left tonight to prove myself to you." She shoved the man's card under her glass and stood. "I'm going to go. Please think about what I've said. I think we could have something special here. Something amazing." Her voice cracked. "But if you're always going to be looking over your shoulder for what could go wrong, what's the point of us continuing?"

Ash watched her pick up her bag. She should say something, make Carmen stay, but the words wouldn't come.

Carmen's eyes were wet, and she wiped quickly at them with a finger. "I... You mean so much to me, Ash. And I really wanted us to see what this could be. But I can't do that if you're not as committed to it as I am. If you come to the resolution that you can be, call me, okay? Please?"

Ash nodded, numb and unable to lift even a hand to wave goodbye. She watched Carmen walk out of the pub, her heart heavy.

Chapter 35

"ARE YOU OKAY?" MONICA FROWNED as she looked at Carmen. "You don't look very well. Are you sure everything went okay at lunch?"

"It did. The lawyer was great. Like I said, I don't think we need to worry about Annabella anymore. I'm just a little tired." She found a smile from somewhere. "Don't worry."

"Okay."

Carmen made herself a coffee and returned to her desk. She hadn't totally lied to Monica; she *was* tired. Exhausted, actually. But at least Annabella had been dealt with and wouldn't be heard from again. And Carmen had decided to stick to the plan and change the business around. It would be far too easy to use work as an excuse to escape from what had happened with Ash, but Carmen knew her tiredness today wasn't just about the argument—break-up?—with Ash. The last fifteen years had been one hell of a ride, and she did need to slow down a tad now.

Her phone pinged with a text message. Her hopes rose that it was Ash but dimmed when she saw it was Felicity.

Fancy a drink around 5? Short notice, I know, but I'm in the area for a dress fitting this afternoon x

She hadn't told Felicity about the evening before. While a part of her had wondered if getting it all off her chest with her best friend would help, she had simply been too tired when she'd finally returned home from the pub.

After packing up her desk just before five, she said her goodbyes to her rather surprised team and headed out. The bar Felicity suggested was only a five-minute walk from the office, which she was grateful for. She found her friend at a table near the window.

"Hello, darling." Felicity stood to greet her and held out her arms for their usual quick hug and cheek kissing.

To Carmen's horror, she found herself clinging to Felicity, fighting back tears.

"Carmen? What's happened? Are you okay?" Felicity eased back a little and looked at her. "My God, you look dreadful!"

"Thanks." Carmen chuckled, but it lacked mirth. "I feel it."

"Sit down." Felicity pulled out Carmen's chair and poured her a glass of wine from the bottle sitting in a cooler on the table. "Are you ill? Did something else awful happen?"

"The latter." Carmen sipped from her wine and composed herself before launching into the tale.

Once Carmen sank back in her chair, words exhausted, Felicity said, "I...I don't quite know what to say. You definitely said all the right things." She shook her head. "Imagine getting so stuck on one idea that you let it rule you all these years later. I mean, just because one woman did that to her. And don't get me wrong, I do sympathise with her; that must have been painful. But really."

"I know. That's the most frustrating thing about it. She's so level-headed about so many other things, so calm and understanding, yet this one thing she can't seem to leave behind."

"Will you contact her?"

"No." Carmen toyed with her glass. "As much as she means to me already, I won't run the risk of being put in that same situation again. She needs to work this through for herself and come to me when she has."

"What..." Felicity cleared her throat. "What if she doesn't?"

Carmen stared at her. It was an awful thought. If Ash couldn't work past this and gave up on them... "I would be devastated," she whispered. "She makes me so happy in so many ways, and I know we could only have more if she would give us a chance. If she can't..." She swallowed. "Then I suppose I have to respect her decision, as much as it would hurt me."

"Well, I think she would be an utter fool if she did walk away."

Carmen couldn't disagree. In only a few weeks, she and Ash had shared so much. Why would Ash want to throw that all away?

Ash's head still ached from a lack of sleep when she opened the studio at eleven on Saturday morning. The clanging of the shutters as they rolled up made her wince.

Coffee helped. A little. Thank God her first booked appointment wasn't until half past noon, and for the first time ever she prayed there'd be no walk-ins until then. When the door opened only ten minutes later, her heart sank, and it sank even further when she saw who'd stepped into the studio.

Felicity.

Oh, great.

"Good morning." Felicity spoke politely, but her posture was rigid, and the tightness around her mouth made Ash nervous.

"Hey." Ash's voice croaked, and she cleared her throat.

Felicity closed the door behind her and stepped further into the room. "Can we talk?"

Ash rubbed the back of her neck. "I'm kind of not really in the mood, so—"

"Excellent, I'll start." Felicity pinned her with a fierce look. "What on earth are you doing?"

"Felicity—"

"I can honestly say I've never seen Carmen so upset. She won't thank me for being here, but I care too much for her to let you do this to her." Felicity stalked closer. "Don't you realise what you're losing if you let your insecurity, however justified you feel it is, end things between you? Carmen is the most loyal, the most honest, and the most caring woman I've ever known. My God, her friendship has been everything to me these past twenty years or so, and I cannot imagine a better person to have by my side."

Ash folded her arms across her chest. "You don't understand."

"I understand all too well. You got scared; that much was obvious from the story Carmen told me last night." She tilted her head. "Fear is sometimes a good thing. It protects us, keeps us wary when we should be. But trust me on this, with Carmen you do not need to fear. Not in the slightest."

"This is very hard for me," Ash said after a moment. "I know you want to stick up for Carmen, and that's great. I'm genuinely happy she has you in her corner. But you don't seem prepared to take *my* feelings into account." She stared at the woman before her. "You've known Carmen over twenty years. Good for you. I've known her only a few months and—"

"And those few months should be more than long enough to show you her character. If you can't see it already by now, perhaps she *is* better off without you."

"She's an amazing woman; I know that!" Ash snapped. "Stop acting like I can't see how bloody wonderful she is. I do see that. Honestly, I do," she said in a quieter tone. "But this is all so new for her, and how are any of us to know if it's what she wants longer-term?"

"For God's sake, Ash, how do any of us know that with anyone?"

Ash's ire rose again. "This is different. It's her first time experiencing anything with a woman. That changes things."

"Actually, it doesn't." Felicity straightened. "But you unfortunately seem to think so. What a shame." She sighed. "I tried, at least. It was nice knowing you. I would have liked to get to know you better, as the partner of my best friend, but it seems that is not meant to be. Goodbye." She turned and seconds later was gone, marching past the studio window, not sparing a single glance back.

⁓

Ash woke up in a foul mood on Monday, and things didn't get any better as her day went on. She'd spent all of Sunday trying to avoid thinking about Carmen, and all that had been said, distracting herself with a trip to a travel exhibition out in Docklands. A part of her knew her stubbornness was not doing her any favours, but she was fed up with people telling her how she should feel and what she should do.

Oh sure, she knew, deep down, she ought to think about everything Carmen and, to a lesser extent, Felicity had said and work through this big barrier she'd put in front of what she and Carmen could be. And at least she'd made that much progress: She knew all of this was her own fault. But the fear of letting herself fall as deeply for Carmen as she expected to do, only for the rug to be pulled out from under her at some point, still held her back.

Shit, who was she kidding? She'd already fallen, hadn't she? She missed Carmen. She missed talking to her on the phone and spending time with her. Missed the laughs they shared and the kisses that consumed them.

At six, having a small gap in her schedule before her next client at six thirty, she attempted to rearrange the storeroom, only to drop two boxes of inks and scatter a box of latex gloves all over the floor. She gave up, slammed the storeroom door shut behind her, and stomped over to the chair. Her work with her clients, thankfully, had not suffered during this shitty day, even if the storage boxes had. She'd tidy up tomorrow, assuming she could somehow wake up as a whole new person.

The studio door opened.

"Surprise!" Sophie called, shutting the door carefully behind her.

A calm happiness descended on Ash, pushing back her grumpiness, as she took in her niece's beaming face. "Well, hello there."

Sophie bounded over and gave her an exuberant hug.

"Whoa, someone's happy." Ash held her at arm's length. "What's going on, monkey?"

Sophie blushed, flopped onto one of the sofas, and twirled her hair repeatedly until Ash joined her.

"Come on, spill. Something's up." Ash found a grin from somewhere.

"Maybe." Sophie chewed a lock of her hair. "Yeah, something good."

Ash pulled the hair from Sophie's mouth. "Spill!"

"Okay. God, pressure much?" Sophie paused, then squealed. "I've got a date!"

Ash's mouth dropped open. "You have?"

Sophie nodded. "With Keisha, in case that wasn't totally obvious." She laughed loudly.

"So Keisha's into girls too?" Ash's heart pounded, and she didn't know why.

"Maybe. I mean, I'm the first girl she's been interested in. She was totally honest with me about it, that she was only just realising she might like girls too. And we talked about it and how we were scared and all that. She hasn't told anyone yet, but that's okay." Sophie beamed at Ash. "I can't believe I did it! I actually asked her, yesterday after French. I thought I would die. I was so scared she'd, like, laugh at me or, worse, get angry. But she didn't!"

"Oh, wow. That is so great! I'm so happy for you." Ash gave her niece a quick hug, surprised at how Sophie's announcement made her feel. On the one hand, she was excited and pleased for her niece. On the other, she couldn't believe how blasé Sophie was being about the whole thing. Wasn't she remotely worried about Keisha's situation? What if Keisha changed her mind about liking girls? What if Sophie got invested in what they had and Keisha walked away?

Sophie leaped up. "Okay, gotta go! I'm meeting Trina at the cinema in ten minutes." She planted a big kiss on Ash's cheek. "See you at the weekend?"

"Sure." Ash was in a daze and barely lifted a hand to wave as Sophie sprinted out of the studio.

Two hours later, once her final client of the day had left, Ash sat back down on the sofa with a cup of tea and pondered Sophie's visit. Or, more accurately, pondered her own reaction to what Sophie had said. She'd been alarmed at Sophie's willingness to throw herself into whatever was happening between her and Keisha with, it seemed, zero thought for how it might play out. Was that the exuberance of youth? *Or am I just a scaredy-cat?*

She didn't used to be so fearful of committing to matters of the heart. Not until first Vikki, then Leesa had knocked her confidence. But she'd also worked through many of her issues through therapy, and a big part of her was concerned at how easily she'd forgotten all that good work the past few days. She thought she'd built up a good stock of self-confidence and the ability to take whatever life threw at her. The last few days it seemed she'd lost all of that. *But I was trying to protect myself from getting hurt, so that's okay, isn't it?* If she'd gone ahead with dating Carmen and then Carmen had realised being with a woman—or even just being with Ash—wasn't for her, where would that have left Ash? Heartbroken, surely.

Ah, said a small voice, *but what if Carmen hadn't done that? What if you were exactly what she wanted and nothing went wrong after all?*

This was always the trouble when getting involved with someone new. Trying to second-guess how things were going to turn out, always planning a few steps ahead to make sure you didn't get your heart ripped into tiny pieces.

But Sophie isn't trying to think ahead twenty-eight steps, so why are you? Sophie was just living for the moment, excited at what might happen between her and Keisha.

An uncomfortable feeling crept through her body, from her limbs inwards towards her belly. It wasn't fear. It wasn't even excitement.

It was regret, and it made her skin crawl.

I was just starting to have something amazing happen with Carmen—and I blew it because I forgot to live in the moment. Yes, of course there was a chance Carmen and she wouldn't work out, just as there was every chance Sophie and Keisha wouldn't work out. *But if you stop yourself from getting involved with someone just because it might go wrong in the future, you may as well spend the rest of your life alone.*

Ash's heart thumped painfully as she stood and exhaled a loud breath. "Fuck that," she said out loud to the empty studio.

Chapter 36

CARMEN FINISHED READING THE CONTRACT on her screen and closed it down. She sat back, rubbing at her aching eyes. It was only eleven in the morning, but her tiredness had stayed with her since the weekend. *Three more days to get through. Then I have a weekend to myself for once.*

Of course, the thought of having a whole two days to herself merely depressed her further. Last week, before everything had gone so wrong, if faced with a free weekend, she would have planned to see Ash at some point. Perhaps pop into her studio to take her some lunch. Maybe meet her for a late drink at the end of her Saturday. Maybe invite her back to her place…

But now none of those options were available to her. Having heard nothing at all from Ash since their disaster on Thursday, she was starting to believe they truly were over. Surely, if she meant anything to Ash at all, she'd have done that thinking already? *Maybe missed me a little?* Picked up the phone and told her what a mistake she'd made and how, of course, she did trust Carmen and wanted them to continue from where they'd left off?

Even if she said it, though, would I believe her?

Carmen stared morosely into her coffee cup, her gaze unseeing. *Maybe I could book myself into a spa for Saturday. Get pampered. Read a book. Something, anything, to take my mind off the hurt.*

She jumped as her intercom buzzed.

"Carmen," Beverley said, "I have a delivery person here for you. They're insisting you sign for the box personally."

"What? Who is it from?"

"I'm not sure, but the box is from Alma's."

Carmen leaned her chin on her free hand. Well, that was grossly unfair of life, wasn't it? As if she needed any more reminders of her time with Ash. Time that was now, it seemed, never going to be repeated.

"I'll be right out." There was no point in making a fuss about it—if the delivery person had been told to get her signature, that wasn't their fault.

When she walked out of her office into the reception area, Ash stood before her, the Alma's box in her hands.

Carmen's heart leaped into her throat.

"Hey," Ash said quietly.

Carmen stared, her mouth refusing to form words.

Ash held out the box; her hands were shaking. She looked terrified, as if she feared Carmen would throw her out. Or shout at her. Or perhaps both. "You know, Portuguese custard tarts fix everything. Remember?"

Carmen's stomach fluttered, and the corners of her mouth tugged up. "Oh yes, that's right. I remember."

Ash smiled tentatively, then threw a glance in Beverley's direction.

Carmen's receptionist tried very hard not to look as if she was eavesdropping, but given the drama playing out directly in front of her desk, Carmen couldn't fault her for being interested.

"Can we talk?" Ash asked.

Carmen nodded. "Let's go into my office." She turned and glanced back once to make sure Ash followed. She closed the door, thankful that Monica was out, and motioned for Ash to take a seat at the small meeting table in the far corner, underneath one of the skylight windows. After pulling out a chair for herself, she sat opposite Ash and waited. Her palms were damp, and her thoughts raced. She tried hard not to get her hopes up because she wasn't sure she could bear the heartbreak all over again.

Ash placed the box of pastries on the table and settled herself in her seat. She looked drained. As if she, too, hadn't slept at all these past few days. Her shirt, red with small white dots, was rumpled, and her hair looked lifeless and flat. The sight gave Carmen some small measure of satisfaction, even as a big part of her itched to wrap her arms around Ash and comfort her.

"I'm sorry." Ash's voice croaked, and she coughed to clear it. "God, I'm so sorry. I was an arsehole last week, and you didn't deserve that. I'm sorry for doubting you. I'm sorry for not being able to get past what happened before, with someone entirely different, and for using it against you. I know I totally overreacted in the pub, and I regret every bloody word I said."

Carmen's pulse slowed a notch at the words, and her breathing came a little easier.

Ash leaned forward. "So I'm here to ask you to forgive me." Her voice shook. "And I'm here to tell you I trust you. Completely. I trust you to always be honest with me. I trust you to care for me as much as I care for you. Because I care for you. So much. More than I ever did for Vikki. It… it scared me. How far and how quickly I was falling for you."

Carmen's breath caught, and she clutched at the hem of her shirt. Hearing those words, hearing the depth of emotion in Ash's voice, made her flash hot and cold and want to shout for joy all at the same time.

"And you're exploring all these new feelings, and together that just scared the crap out of me. I'm still scared, to be honest. I don't want my heart to get broken any more than anyone else does. But I can't fight what I feel for you. I tried, and it got me nowhere." Ash's hands twisted together on the table. "I'm not proud of trying to deny how I felt, but I honestly thought I was doing the right thing to protect myself from getting hurt. And instead, I hurt you."

Carmen nodded. "You did. I won't lie about that. But you being here now, that definitely helps." She managed a small smile but didn't rush to touch Ash or hold her. Ash's posture, rigid and tense, told her she still had more to say.

"I know this isn't easy for you. I know you've got a lot of things to still figure out. But I want you to know this—I am in this as far as it is humanly possible to get." Ash held her gaze, her eyes expressing such a depth of emotion that Carmen's heart began to pound. "I…I've missed you so much. Missed being with you and talking to you and knowing that you were a part of my life. Please, can you forgive me? Can we try again? Because I've honestly never wanted anything more in my life than a second chance with you." Ash swept a hand through her fringe as it flopped down her forehead, and Carmen's insides melted a little at the familiar gesture.

The sincerity of every word Ash had spoken shone like a beacon in the room. And the depth of feeling in Ash's expression—of genuine regret, tenderness, and want—told Carmen just as much as those words had. She knew Ash wouldn't be here now, saying everything she'd said, if she didn't truly want this. Want them and want them more than she wanted to protect herself. This, Carmen knew, was the biggest leap for Ash, and that more than anything told her what her response should be.

"Yes." Her voice struggled to work its way past the lump in her throat.

Ash shuddered as if she'd just dropped a great weight off her shoulders, and she reached out a hand.

Carmen took it and held it tightly. She smiled as Ash stared back at her. "Yes," Carmen said again. "Because I'm falling for you too, and I don't want to waste another minute not being with you." She stood, tugging Ash with her, and they stepped towards each other.

Then Ash's arms were around her, and Ash's lips pressed against her own. Everything fell back into place, right where it should be.

Chapter 37

THE NEXT EVENING ASH WAS a mix of nerves and excitement as she waited in her flat, lights turned down low, some classical music emanating from her laptop on the coffee table. It was past nine, and Carmen was on her way over for a late supper.

Turning up at Carmen's office and spilling her heart out had been nerve-wracking and thrilling all at the same time. Holding Carmen once more, tasting those sweet lips, had been like coming home; a contentment she'd never known had washed over her as she pulled Carmen tight against her body.

Today they were starting over, this time with no holding back. She was all in now. To hell with fear.

The doorbell chimed, and Ash leaped up to open the door to Carmen, who smiled shyly at her as she stepped into the flat.

"Hey." Ash didn't hesitate and didn't hold back. She stepped forward and wrapped her arms around Carmen.

Carmen moaned softly and pressed closer, slipping her arms behind Ash's neck and pulling her down to meet her lips.

They kissed for who knew how long. Long enough for Ash's heart to start a rapid racing and for her arousal to climb to new heights.

"Hi," Carmen said when she eventually pulled back.

Ash smiled. "Hi yourself." She stepped back. "Come on in."

Carmen dropped her bag by the door and kicked off her shoes.

The small gestures of comfort, at feeling at home enough to do so, made deliciously warm sensations squirm in Ash's belly.

"Quick tour?" Ash gestured with open arms.

"Yes, please." Carmen took her hand, and it felt so perfect, Ash had to swallow back the emotions that rose up.

She led Carmen around the small flat. "Main room, which, as you can see, is living room, dining area, and kitchen all in one."

"I love all the photos on the walls." Carmen gazed around her. "All the places you've been?"

"Pretty much. None from the Kruger trip yet. I've been a little distracted and haven't found time to print them." Ash grinned.

Carmen chuckled. "I can't think what you mean." She leaned up and kissed Ash softly.

Her heart full, Ash continued the tour. "That's the bathroom." She pointed to the relevant door. "And that, um, is the bedroom."

Carmen peeked around the door. "Lovely." When she turned back to Ash, she was blushing. "It's a cute place, and I like how it feels."

"Good. So, drink? I have wine, beer, juice—"

"Camomile tea?"

"It just so happens I did buy some." She tugged Carmen after her to the kitchen.

"Just for me?"

"Yes."

"That's very sweet."

Ash turned to look at Carmen.

Her face was flushed and her eyes misty.

"You okay?" Ash asked.

Carmen visibly swallowed. "Very. And so relieved."

Ash sighed and squeezed her hand. "I'm sorry I put you through all that."

"It's okay. You were scared. We all do things differently when we're scared. Trust me; I've still got some things to face up to in all of this too." Carmen grimaced. "For example, telling my mother about us."

"You'd really want to do that?"

Carmen stepped back. She ran her hands through her curls, a gesture that always mesmerised Ash, and puffed out a loud breath. "Not right now, if I'm honest. I'd prefer to leave that until I'm totally comfortable with all of this. I'd have more strength then, I think, to deal with any negative reaction."

Is she still not comfortable with this? Ash stopped herself from blurting out the words. *Wait a minute. She's forty-three and considering coming out. Of course she needs to be totally comfortable with all that's happening to her before she takes that big step.* "Anything I can do to help with that?"

Carmen came back to Ash and slid her arms around her waist. "Not right now. But thank you for asking. I just need to work through what this means for my perception of myself. For how others, as well as myself, have seen me all this time. And then decide who I want to tell and how to tell them." She paused, her eyes narrowed in thought. "I think what I really want is to understand and be happy in my new identity, whatever that is, before I come out to anyone else. And definitely before I speak to my less-than-tolerant mother."

"Okay, I get it." Ash kissed her softly. "Talk to me any time, okay?"

"I will." Carmen squeezed her.

"So how hungry are you? Because I have some soup in the fridge we could heat up, maybe with a salad on the side, or we could order in something more substantial."

"I'm not hugely hungry, to be honest." Carmen leaned up and kissed her. "Soup and a salad would be perfect."

Ash ran one hand lightly down Carmen's cheek. "Coming right up." She led Carmen over to the sofa. "You sit down, and I'll bring your tea over in a sec."

After she'd prepared the tea, then poured a juice for herself, she put the soup on a low heat and joined Carmen on the sofa.

Carmen immediately entwined their fingers, holding their joined hands on her thigh. "I love holding your hand. I love how our fingers fit together so well and how soft your skin is."

"Mm, it's one of my favourite things too."

They shared a sweet kiss, snuggling in close.

"God, it's nice to be somewhere quiet for once." Ash looked down at her. "No fighting for a table anywhere, no noisy people."

"Yes! Thank you for suggesting we meet at yours. I just couldn't face being out tonight."

"It was about time you saw my place." Ash kissed her. "But I do want to make one thing clear. Inviting you here doesn't, um, presume anything. You know, about sleeping together or anything like that."

Carmen blushed once more but smiled. "Thank you for saying that. I wasn't sure. But equally, I wasn't worried." She cupped Ash's chin. "I'll know when I'm ready for that, and trust me, you'll be the first to know."

Ash chuckled. "Good to know."

They looked into each other's eyes, soft smiles playing on their lips.

"I feel like we're almost back where we should be." Carmen's voice was soft.

Ash swallowed. "Yeah, I know what you mean." She paused. There was still one thing she'd never properly explained to Carmen, and she deserved to know it. And here in the safe space of her own flat, it felt like the perfect time to get it all out there. "Listen, I feel like I need to tell you all about Vikki. Not the abridged version, but the whole thing. I mean, if you don't want to hear it—"

"I do." Carmen's voice was quiet. "I want to understand. But only if you really are ready to tell me."

"I am." Ash twisted in her seat to face Carmen but didn't let go of her hand. Where to begin? "I was hooked on her from the minute she started working at the bank. I...I was such an idiot. I knew she was engaged, and I also knew that her fiancé, Dave, was as about as exciting as a trip to the dentist. She wasn't happy. I mean, she never said it outright, but the more time we spent together, the more we shared and laughed and talked, I knew she was doubting what she was doing."

"Did, um, did anything happen with her? I mean, you know, physically."

"No. Although it did seem as if Vikki was sometimes determined to push the boundaries of our friendship into something more. One night it all came to a head. After someone's birthday drinks after work, she kissed me. She was leaving, heading off home, and asked me to walk her to the Tube. She grabbed me in an alley behind the bar." Ash looked at Carmen. "I was so stunned, but of course I returned the kiss because by then I knew how much I felt for her."

Carmen said nothing, but her intent gaze held Ash's.

"After a couple of minutes she backed off, looking like she was about to have a heart attack, and sprinted off in the direction of the Tube before I could stop her." Ash paused. The memories hurt, but she wanted Carmen to know the whole story, so she ploughed on. "I went home and sent her about twenty text messages, begging her to call me. She never answered any of them. And the next morning in the office, she acted like nothing had happened."

"Oh no." Carmen clutched Ash's hand more tightly, and Ash's heart warmed at the sympathy and understanding in Carmen's expression.

"I felt as if I'd been slapped. No matter how many times I tried to get her to talk about us and about what had happened, she shut me down." She shook her head. "I'd fallen for her without even realising it, and she wouldn't even talk to me. And then there was her wedding. Everyone from work was invited, even me. I know I shouldn't have gone. But I suppose I wondered if she'd go through with it."

"That must have been very painful." Carmen's tone was careful.

Ash snorted. "It was a disaster. It was bad enough witnessing her say 'I do'. But later, after the dinner, when it was time for the bride and groom to have their first dance, she couldn't find Dave. Turns out he was in the hotel bar getting drunk with his mates. So she grabbed me instead."

"What?" Carmen's mouth fell open. "She got you to do the traditional first dance with her?"

"Yep. I was torn, wanting to humour her, because she was a bit drunk too, and not cause a scene. But at the same time it was a nightmare, trying not to hold her too close, not getting too caught up in the moment." She ran a hand through her hair. "I have no idea what anyone else thought of it all. Most people were just laughing, I guess thinking it was a bit of fun. When we were back at work, after she got back from her honeymoon, it was like we were strangers. Barely said a word to each other."

"Oh, Ash, I…I don't know what to say." Carmen cupped Ash's cheek in her warm hand. "What she did to you was very unfair. I don't know why she did it, played with you that way, but I can totally understand why it's impacted you so much."

"Yeah, it screwed me up, no doubt about that." Ash pressed closer, locking gazes with Carmen. "And I honestly thought I'd got past it all with my therapy sessions. It turns out that wasn't quite true. And again, I'm sorry about that."

"It's okay. Truly. Thank you for telling me." Carmen pursed her lips. "I know I've said it before—none of us can ever guarantee anything. And making false promises is not my thing. But what I can say is that I cannot imagine, in a million years, doing something like that to you. You mean far too much to me to play with your feelings."

Ash quivered at the strength of emotion in Carmen's voice.

Carmen trailed her thumb over the back of Ash's hand. "If this doesn't work out between us, it will be because we don't fit, don't make each other happy. There won't be any emotional games. That is absolutely not my style."

Relief coursed through Ash. She didn't want them pretending that life was perfect and nothing bad could happen. Knowing how strongly Carmen felt about doing this right, about treating each other with respect, was all she needed right now. "Good, because it isn't mine either."

She wrapped her arms around Carmen and held her tightly. When Carmen's lips found hers once more, she lost herself in the tender kiss, any thoughts of the past and previous hurts left far behind.

Chapter 38

"COME ON IN." CARMEN STEPPED aside to allow Ash to walk into her home. She closed the door behind Ash and turned to face her.

Ash looked delectable. The tight black jeans were back, this time paired with a plain, dark green shirt buttoned up to the collar. Her hair was swept back, the style that Carmen found irresistible.

"You look unbelievable." Ash's gaze roamed over every inch of Carmen until it felt like a physical caress.

Carmen sucked in a breath, astonished at how quickly her arousal could make itself known with just a look from Ash. "Thank you. You look wonderful yourself. That colour on you is spectacular."

"Why, thank you." Ash leaned in and dropped a soft kiss on Carmen's lips. "Am I the first one here?"

"Not quite. Felicity is in the kitchen."

"Ah." Ash shuffled her feet.

"Don't worry; she has just about forgiven you." Carmen smiled as Ash frowned. "Seriously, she has. It's okay."

Ash inhaled deeply, then nodded. "Okay. Lead on. Your turn to show me your house." She grinned.

It was so good to be back in the zone where they were comfortable with each other, where they could tease and smile and just…be.

Carmen gestured for Ash to follow her into the living room. The tour of the house lasted only a few minutes, long enough for them to steal a few more kisses along the way.

"I am still here, you know!" Felicity's voice boomed from the kitchen.

Carmen laughed. "All right, we're coming down."

She led Ash down the stairs and along the hallway to the kitchen.

When Carmen entered the room, Ash hovered in the doorway, clearly still unsure of the reception she would get from Felicity.

"Well, well. The prodigal girlfriend returns." Felicity stood with one hand resting on the breakfast bar, the other holding a glass of champagne.

Carmen blinked. Girlfriend? *Hmm, yes, I suppose she is.* She inhaled. *Wow, never had one of those before.*

"Hey, Felicity," Ash said. "How are you?" Her voice cracked a little.

Felicity circled the bar and strolled across the room, levelling a narrow-eyed stare at Ash.

Ash stood her ground, although her forefingers tapped rapidly against her thighs.

Carmen thought about stepping in to aid her, but she knew whatever Felicity threw at her, Ash was confident in where she and Carmen were now to throw it right back.

Felicity stopped about a yard away from Ash, her face still maintaining its stern expression. "I am very well, thank you." She broke into a wide smile. "And delighted to see you again. Here, this is for you." She handed Ash the glass of champagne.

"Should I be worried about it being poisoned?" Ash's mouth quirked.

Felicity guffawed. "No, you're safe. For now."

Ash grinned, but Carmen caught the hint of relief in her eyes. "All right. Cheers."

Felicity nodded, then turned and walked back to the bar. "One for you, Carmen?"

"Definitely." The doorbell rang. "And you may as well pour two more while you're there."

Ash leaned as casually as she could against the breakfast bar, grateful the glass of champagne didn't wobble in her hand. She was about to be introduced to famous actress Tamsyn Harris, and her nerves threatened to get the better of her.

Even though she and Carmen had come from very different backgrounds, Ash had never felt much disparity between them. Mainly because Carmen was, like her, a self-made businesswoman, which had them on a much more level playing field. But right now she became aware of the big difference in the circles they mixed in. It was a little overwhelming. However, Ash knew she just needed to roll with it. And hope like hell she didn't make a tit of herself.

"Don't be nervous," Felicity whispered close to her ear. Ash hadn't realised she'd walked round the bar to stand next to her. "Yes, she's world-famous, but she still sits down to pee, just like the rest of us."

Ash's laugh burst from her chest, and she threw Felicity a grateful look.

When Carmen came back into the room, all Ash could do was stare at her beautiful girlfriend. The dress she wore tonight, a shimmering creation of some kind of silky material in a deep bronze shade, showed off Carmen's shoulders—and legs and arms—to perfection. Ash throbbed with need once more; she knew tonight, if they had some proper time alone, she'd be struggling to contain her desire.

Carmen was closely followed by Tamsyn Harris and the honey-blonde woman who was presumably her fiancée. Ash knew her name was Maggie and that she was an author, but that was all as they'd mostly managed to keep details of Maggie's life out of the press.

A small, wiry brown dog wriggled past them and dashed straight over to Ash. It sat at her feet, gazing up at her.

"Ash, I'd like you to meet Tamsyn and Maggie. And Gizmo, of course."

Tamsyn strode over, her hand outstretched. "Lovely to meet you!" She pumped Ash's hand. "I've heard so much about you."

"Nice to meet you too. Obviously, I've heard a lot about you too."

Tamsyn laughed. "I can't think why." She winked conspiratorially.

"Hi, Ash, I'm Maggie." Ash went to shake her hand, but Maggie pulled her into a brief hug. "So glad you came back," Maggie whispered. "It's lovely to see her so happy."

When she pulled back, Ash stared at her, shocked—but also ridiculously pleased.

Maggie's mouth twitched.

While Ash petted Gizmo, smiling as he hopped up and down at her feet, Felicity greeted the newcomers with cheek kisses and quick hugs, then handed them their glasses of champagne. She raised hers and waited expectantly for everyone to look her way. "To love," she toasted.

Carmen turned bright pink; Ash was pretty sure her own face was the same colour. Tamsyn and Maggie gazed adoringly at each other, and Felicity simply laughed.

"Cheers!" she said, and everyone drank.

They sat down for the meal about twenty minutes later, by which time Ash's nerves had settled a little. After chatting to the group, Ash came to realise Tamsyn and Maggie were amazing, but not in a superstar way. They were far more down to earth than she would ever have imagined and both very funny.

When Tamsyn, Carmen, and Felicity began a conversation about a fashion show Tamsyn had been invited to, Ash turned to Maggie, who was seated on her left.

"So, Maggie, what do you write? I mean, I read somewhere that you write under two different pen names, but no one's ever said which names."

"Ah, yes, it's all top secret, you know." Maggie grinned. "But seriously, I wrote as Jessica Stewart for historical, mainstream fiction for many years. And now I focus solely on my other genre, lesbian fiction, where I write as Maddie Jones."

Ash's heart thumped. "*You're* Maddie Jones?"

"You've heard of me?"

"Um, just a little bit. You're one of my favourite lesfic authors!"

To Ash's surprise, Maggie blushed. "Really? Oh, that's lovely to hear."

"She's a fan?" Tamsyn smiled.

"Yes, I am. Big-time." Ash shook her head. "Okay, this officially just became too much. Favourite actress and favourite author both at the same table."

Everyone laughed, and Carmen wrapped an arm around her shoulders. "Can you cope?"

"Just about." Ash mimed wiping a fevered brow, and Carmen threw her a look filled with affection and…love? Whatever it was, it took Ash's breath away, and she had to swallow hard before she could speak again. "This is amazing. But more so because they're so…real. Ordinary."

"Don't let Tamsyn hear you say that," Maggie said in a stage whisper. "You'll ruin her."

"Oh, ha bloody ha." Tamsyn mock glared at her, then grinned.

After the meal, they had coffee in the living room before Felicity, Tamsyn, and Maggie—and Gizmo—left, sharing a cab home.

Once Carmen had closed the front door, she returned to the room and found Ash slouched comfortably on the sofa, a dazed look on her face.

"You okay?" Carmen asked.

Ash looked up at her. "I am. I'm in a very happy place right now."

"You look like it. Can I join you?"

Ash held one arm out to the side, and Carmen immediately sat next to her. When Ash wrapped an arm around her and pulled her in even closer, she sighed contentedly. "Ah, yes. Perfect."

She got a kiss on the top of her head for that.

"They're lovely," Ash said. "And I'm so happy I'm going to be at their wedding."

"I know! I'm so glad you were able to rearrange those three clients."

"I guess I'm lucky they like me so much."

"And why wouldn't they? You do amazing work. And I would imagine they know you wouldn't change their appointments lightly."

"Yeah, that's true. I've never done it to any of them before, so I guess the trust was there that it was something pretty important."

"I've read all the reviews of your studio on Google."

"You have?" Ash looked down at her, surprise clear on her face.

"Yes, of course! And I think trust is definitely at play. So many glowing testimonials from regular customers who are obviously coming back time after time. That's all down to you and the kind of person you are."

Ash twisted and tugged Carmen round to face her a little more. There was heat in her eyes, and Carmen's body responded instantly. When Ash kissed her, her lips moving so sweetly against hers, her arousal soared. And when Ash ran her fingers into Carmen's hair to tilt her head back, Carmen moaned.

She moved without thinking, without wondering where this would lead to and whether she was nervous about getting there or not. Slowly, carefully, so that she didn't snag her dress, she maintained their kiss but eased herself onto Ash's lap until she straddled her thighs.

Ash whimpered, a sound that pierced Carmen.

She wants me. It hadn't been in much doubt, not really, but Ash had held back, seemingly content with just the kisses they'd shared up until now. To hear her so obviously affected by Carmen's attempt to ramp things up boosted her confidence tenfold.

Ash ran her hands down from Carmen's hair to her shoulders and then to her hips. She deepened the kiss, her tongue pushing into Carmen's mouth, her hands firm on Carmen as she pulled.

Carmen surged against her, her blood singing with the desire to get close, then closer still. Their breasts pressed together, and Carmen gasped. The soft, pliant flesh moulding to hers was more arousing than she would ever have imagined. She slid her arms around Ash's back and increased the contact; the additional pressure against her nipples sent wonderful sensations straight to her clit.

Ash slid her hands lower and cupped Carmen's behind, and it was as if someone had turned on a furnace somewhere in the room.

Finally, Ash broke their kiss. "God, Carmen." Her breathing was laboured, her eyes glassy. "You're... Fuck." She groaned, then claimed Carmen's mouth once more and caressed Carmen's ass in slow, gentle circles.

Carmen moved her hips, seeking a firmer contact.

Ash obliged, grasping at her through the material of her dress, kneading her.

Carmen moaned once more, desperate for Ash to take this further, knowing she was more than ready for that now. She silently willed Ash to move under the dress but realised she'd have to ask. Ash wouldn't presume anything. Not just yet.

She lifted her head and gazed down at Ash. "I want you to—"

The doorbell rang.

They both jumped.

"Wait." Carmen held on to Ash a little more tightly. "They must have the wrong house. They'll go away in a min—"

The doorbell rang again. "Sorry, it's us," Tamsyn called, presumably through the letterbox. "I forgot my jacket."

"Shit." Carmen pressed her forehead to Ash's and groaned. "I suppose I'd better answer it."

Ash chuckled. "Yeah, something tells me she won't leave until you do."

Carmen eased off Ash's lap, straightened her dress, and walked to the hallway. She took a deep breath before she opened the door.

Tamsyn stood on her doorstep, grinning sheepishly.

"Tam, I am seriously going to kill you." Carmen glared at her.

"What? What did I—?" Tamsyn's gaze swept over Carmen. "Ohhhh. Sorry." Her smirk was evil.

"Never mind." Carmen rolled her eyes. "Did you say you'd left your jacket behind?"

"Yes, I think I left it just here in the hallway cupboard."

Carmen motioned her into the house. At the end of her path, the taxi waited on the side of the road, Maggie leaning from the window. Carmen threw her a wave and received a beaming smile in response.

"Got it!" Tamsyn trotted past her to the open door. "Sorry again for interrupting. Please, carry on." She winked. "See you next week!"

Carmen tutted and shut the door behind her without a word.

Tamsyn's laughter carried through the wood between them.

When Carmen returned to the living room, Ash was tapping furiously on her phone. She shot Carmen a rueful look. "Sorry, it's Sophie. Having a little crisis over her next date with Keisha." She ran a hand through her hair. "I kind of think I ought to call her, rather than texting, but…"

Carmen sat beside her. "It's fine. I understand." She pulled Ash into her arms. "I'm sorry for the interruption."

"Hey, not your fault. I'm sorry too. I feel a little torn between priorities right now."

Carmen kissed her but didn't linger, not wanting to restoke the fire when there would be no outlet for its flames. "It's fine. And don't worry; we are going to get back to what we were doing sometime very soon." She threw Ash her sultriest smile and revelled in the heat that smouldered in Ash's eyes.

"You'll get no argument from me for that." Ash kissed Carmen rather thoroughly. Then she pulled away and sighed. "Okay, I'm going to go, and I'll talk to my niece on the way to the Tube station."

"Want me to call you a cab?"

Ash stood. "No, it's fine. You know I like to walk."

"I do." Carmen kissed her once more. "Call me when you're home maybe?"

Ash's face lit up. "You're on."

Carmen showed her to the door, and they kissed again before Ash stepped out into the night.

"Thanks for a fantastic evening." Ash gazed down at her. "It was... You were wonderful."

"So were you." Carmen placed yet one more kiss on her lips. *Ugh, it is so hard to say goodbye!* She watched as Ash walked down the path, noting the way her jeans clung to her legs and backside, remembering how it felt to hold that body in her arms. Her temperature rocketed once more. *Jesus, how am I supposed to get to sleep now?*

Chapter 39

CARMEN SHOULD HAVE BEEN TIRED and resentful of the early start, but she was neither. And she couldn't seem to stop smiling. It had been a spectacularly good couple of weeks. Well, apart from not being able to see Ash much, of course. However now, after a full week apart due to clashing work commitments, Ash was beside her, driving them the last few miles to their hotel for the weekend of Tamsyn and Maggie's wedding.

"Are you going to stop grinning at all today?" Ash looked across at her as they waited at a traffic light.

"No, I don't think so." Carmen leaned across and kissed her cheek. "Sorry, you'll just have to get used to it."

"I can do that. It's brilliant. And I don't know what's better—the fact that you've cleared the last of the old clients from your books or that you've got a chance to sign Stefan Ward."

"I know! He thoroughly deserved that BAFTA last year, but I never imagined I'd be able to sign him. Then I hear on the grapevine that he's not happy with his agent, and I wasn't going to let that opportunity slide."

"Do you think he will sign with you?"

"I'm very confident."

"Life is pretty good for you right now, isn't it?"

Carmen stroked Ash's hand where it rested on the steering wheel. "It really is." She looked at the GPS. "Is that accurate, ten minutes until we get there?"

"Should be."

"Good. I'm rather desperate for the bathroom."

Ash laughed. "Want me to speed up?"

"No, don't get us arrested. I'll be fine."

They did indeed arrive ten minutes later and checked in quickly. They had separate rooms, as agreed, but a tingle of excitement ran through Carmen as she wondered if they'd actually use both later. Where they'd left things after the dinner party had held her on a lovely knife-edge of arousal all week. She knew it wouldn't take much to tip the balance.

"Want to meet for a quick drink before we have to leave?" Ash asked as they walked up the single flight of stairs to their rooms.

"Sounds good. Maybe around one? Tamsyn said the minibus that's collecting all the guests from here will arrive at one thirty."

"Perfect. Go make yourself beautiful." Ash winked.

"Are you saying I'm not already?" Carmen tried to give Ash an evil glare and failed miserably when her mouth twitched with mirth.

"Okay, let me rephrase: go make yourself even more beautiful."

"Sweet talker."

The weather forecast was good for the whole day, and Carmen knew the marquees would be warm inside, so she draped only a thin silk shawl over her shoulders. She made sure she had plenty of tissues in her handbag, plus her mascara. Her emotions were riding so high she was bound to be a blubbering mess when Tamsyn and Maggie finally said, "I do."

Ash waited for her in the bar, and Carmen barely resisted the urge to throw herself at her when she saw how she looked. The black dress trousers hugged Ash's hips and waist; the pale pink shirt highlighted her full breasts, with the buttons undone enough to show just a smidge of cleavage. It drew Carmen's gaze and made her breath hitch in her throat.

Ash smiled at her and opened her arms. "Will I do? You were kind of checking me out, so…"

Carmen leaned forward and kissed her lightly on the cheek. "Definitely," she murmured, keeping her hands firmly grasped on her handbag to avoid any unnecessary spectacle. "You're gorgeous."

Ash's cheeks pinked just a little. "Thanks. You, as ever, look stunning. Wow."

It was a new dress, bought especially for this wedding, and even Carmen could admit it suited her well. The one-shoulder style was not something she'd tried before, but the sales assistant had convinced her, and she didn't regret buying it. The material, soft and delicate, in a beautiful shade of teal, swished around her thighs as she moved, making her feel like a catwalk model. She saw Ash's gaze fall to the strappy heels she wore, higher than her usual style by far.

When Ash looked back at her, her eyes smouldered.

Carmen swallowed. "Like the shoes?"

Ash merely nodded.

They sat in the lounge bar of the hotel and talked quietly over a gin and tonic. Other wedding guests arrived over the next thirty minutes, and greetings were shared. Some people Carmen knew, some not.

"Carmen!" Tony, who did PR for Tamsyn, strode across the room towards her.

"Hi, Tony." They swapped air kisses.

"You remember Vanessa?" Tony gestured to the woman beside him, a statuesque blonde, who was at least twenty years younger than him.

"Of course." Carmen shook her hand. "Lovely to see you again." *And shocked actually, given that Tony usually goes through girlfriends at a vast rate of knots.* And now it was time for the return introduction. She was nervous, but determined. After all, if she couldn't be seen with a female partner at a same-sex wedding, where could she? "And this is my partner, Ash." It was the first time she'd said those words out loud to anyone, and a combination of excitement and trepidation shot through her veins.

Ash squeezed her hand, and Carmen glanced at her. A warm, supportive smile curled Ash's lips.

Carmen gripped Ash's hand a little more tightly and looked back at Tony. How would he react?

His expression went from shock to beaming smile in less than two seconds, and her shoulders eased out of their tensed position.

"Nice to meet you." Tony and Ash shook hands. "This is new, yes?" he asked Carmen.

"Yes, it is."

Tony leaned in. "Good for you." He kissed her cheek, then wandered off with Vanessa in tow.

"You okay?" Ash asked.

Carmen laid a hand on her own chest, aware of how hard her heart was beating, and took a couple of breaths. "Absolutely."

The luxury minibus transported them all to the cottage, where they stepped into a wedding fantasy land. The garden, perhaps half an acre in size, held two large marquees. One marquee was apparently set up for the ceremony, with rows of chairs facing a small dais visible through the open doorway. The other contained tables set up for dining, with a large bar area at one end. Off to the side, the catering staff were hard at work in two large but well-appointed caravans. All through the garden, wooden boardwalks led to and from the marquees to the temporary toilets and elsewhere, preventing the guests and staff from sinking into the lawn.

A waiter appeared with a tray of champagne, and Carmen and Ash each took a glass.

"This is amazing!" Ash shook her head. "But it's also pretty simple. No gold frills anywhere."

"Yes, that would absolutely not be their style. This is just them."

By the time an usher announced that everyone should take their seats, Carmen was on the edge of tears. The setting, the knowledge of what Tamsyn had gone through to get to this point, plus the fact that Carmen herself walked into the marquee with a woman on her own arm, all of it conspired to have her reaching for a tissue the moment she sat down.

"Still okay?" Ash looked concerned.

"Very emotional. But I'm fine. Honestly."

Ash kissed her, then sat back. She pressed her hand against Carmen's thigh, letting her know she was there if she needed her.

Carmen's tears fell as soon as she saw Tamsyn and Maggie walk down the aisle. Gizmo was on a lead between them, his head held high, a cream bow tie around his neck. Both women looked stunning in matching cream suits that had clearly been tailored for each of them. They carried a single orange rose each but handed those off to Maggie's nieces once they reached the front. The two young girls looked up at their auntie in awe, clutching the flowers in their small hands. Gizmo was placed in the care of Maggie's sister.

Tamsyn and Maggie stepped forward to stand before the official, a grey-haired woman in a flowing, deep blue smock dress, who smiled warmly at them.

Carmen's heart thumped wildly. She and Ash had front-row seats on Tamsyn's side of the aisle; Tamsyn's father was too ill to attend, and she had no siblings, so her side of the tent was filled with friends and colleagues from the industry. Maggie's side was filled with family and close friends, and a hush descended on everyone as the official raised her head to speak.

"Honoured guests, welcome." She smiled. "We're here today to witness and celebrate the marriage of Tamsyn and Maggie."

Oh shit, more bloody tears. Carmen thought she'd just about got them under control but no such luck. Another tissue was pressed into her hand from her right, and she turned to give Ash a grateful smile.

The official's melodious voice recited the few paragraphs that outlined, in lovely terms, the obligations Tamsyn and Maggie were committing to. The two women held hands tightly throughout, gazing into each other's eyes. Carmen was quite sure they had no awareness of any other person in the marquee.

The official inclined her head towards Tamsyn. "Do you, Tamsyn, take Maggie to be your lawfully wedded wife?"

Tamsyn nodded slowly. "I do." Her voice rang out loud and clear.

The official turned to Maggie. "And do you, Maggie, take Tamsyn to be your lawfully wedded wife?"

"I do." Maggie's voice wobbled, but her smile was huge.

"Then I now declare you married." The official beamed at them. "You may kiss the bride."

Tamsyn's smile lit up the room. She wrapped her arms around a tearful Maggie and kissed her, softly and slowly.

Ash also dabbed a tissue to her eyes, which made Carmen feel infinitely better, as she was a complete mess.

Everyone applauded and stood; some guests stepped forward to hug and kiss the brides. Tamsyn gently pushed past all of them and strode to the first row, where Carmen and Ash sat.

"You," Tamsyn said, her voice choked. "You helped make this come true. Thank you so much." She pulled Carmen into a hug and held her tightly.

"You are very welcome, my friend." Carmen looked at Tamsyn through watery eyes. "You deserve it."

Tamsyn ran her fingertips underneath her eyes. "Don't make me cry! This mascara's supposed to be waterproof, but I'm not so sure."

Carmen laughed and watched as Ash gave Tamsyn a quick hug of congratulations, her eyes wide as she probably realised just who she held in her arms.

Maggie walked over, also holding out her arms to Carmen. "Thank you. For everything."

"My pleasure."

"And now," Tamsyn said loudly, using all that acting training to project her voice to the far end of the marquee, "it's time to party!"

Chapter 40

CARMEN STUMBLED OFF THE DANCE floor and collapsed into her chair. "Oh, my poor feet!" She rubbed at her heels and sighed. She'd known it was a mistake the first time she stepped onto the dance floor, but dancing with Ash, to hold her close as they moved to the music, had been her paramount thought.

Ash chuckled. "I did try to warn you about those heels."

"I know, I know." She kissed Ash. "What time is it?"

"Just after eleven."

"Bloody hell, we've been here for hours!"

Laughing, Ash nodded. "I have no idea where the time has gone."

"Are you tired?"

"A little, to be honest. It was a pretty early start this morning."

"It was. How would you feel about calling it a night? The next shuttle bus must be leaving soon."

"Sounds like a good idea." Ash held out a hand. "Here, lean on me. In fact, you could take the shoes off. I'm sure these boardwalks would be okay with bare feet."

"No, it's fine. I've been in them all day, another fifteen minutes won't kill me."

They wandered through the marquee, the one that had originally been set up for the ceremony but now housed the dance floor, and found Tamsyn and Maggie. They sat quietly in a corner, arms around each other, watching everyone else enjoying themselves.

"Are you two off?" Maggie stood.

"We are." Carmen hugged her, then Tamsyn. "Too tired."

"So are we." Tamsyn frowned. "But apparently, we have to stay to the end. Something about this being where we live and having nowhere else to go."

"Nah, just sneak off into the house," Ash said. "No one will notice."

"This one is *so* good for my ego." Tamsyn thumbed in Ash's direction.

Ash made a choked sound. "Oh God, no! That's not what I meant. It's just that—"

"She's teasing, Ash." Maggie nudged Tamsyn in the arm. "Ignore her. But I do like your sneaking idea." She tapped her chin in thought.

"What's the point, though?" Tamsyn asked. "With this bunch partying in our back garden?"

"Ah. Yes." Maggie slumped. "Okay, I guess we have to stay."

"Thanks for a wonderful day," Carmen said.

"Thank you for being here."

All four of them shared hugs and cheek kisses goodbye.

Ash helped Carmen walk gingerly out to the lane where the shuttle bus stood waiting.

Twenty minutes later, they walked into the hotel and headed up the stairs. At the top, Carmen turned to Ash. "As much as we've spent the day together, I almost feel like we haven't had much time where it was just us two. I know we're tired, but could we perhaps get a nightcap? Maybe order something up to one of our rooms?"

Ash smiled and brushed her fingers down Carmen's cheek. "I'd love that. Give me a few minutes to freshen up, and I'll come to your room, okay?"

"Deal. What would you like to drink?"

"Gin and tonic would be great."

Carmen ordered the drinks as soon as she entered her room, then gratefully slid her feet out of the shoes and tossed them in a corner. She'd just used the bathroom and cleaned the make-up off her face when there was a knock on the door.

The hotel staff member carried in their drinks on a small tray and set it down on the table. Just as she left the room, Ash appeared in the corridor outside.

Carmen let her in. "Perfect timing."

"Nice." Ash looked down at Carmen's bare feet. "How are they?"

"Sore!"

"Hey, if you have any nice lotion or something, I can give you a foot rub. I've been told I'm good at them."

It was so tempting. "Um, that does sound lovely, but…" Carmen flushed. "Would it be okay if I washed my feet first? I mean, they've been in opened-toe shoes all day and—"

"Totally fine. I understand. You do that while I just sit down and have a sip of this." Ash picked up one of the drinks and moved to the armchair on the opposite side of the small table.

Carmen chuckled. "Okay, you just make yourself at home."

Ash raised her glass, and Carmen left her to it.

Washing her feet made them feel a hundred times better, although perching on the edge of the bathtub to do so and stop herself from sliding in, thanks to the silky nature of her dress, took a little concentration. Once she'd patted her feet dry, she retrieved the body lotion from her toiletry bag and headed back into the room.

"Better?" Ash asked.

"Much."

"Then let me see if I can make them even better still. Here, sit on the edge of the bed, and I'll pull the chair nearer."

They quickly arranged themselves, and Carmen handed over the lotion. In return she was given her drink, which she sipped with pleasure.

Ash carefully lifted one of Carmen's feet into her lap.

The first touch of the cool lotion on her tired foot was blissful. But when Ash started to firmly work the lotion into her skin, Carmen groaned aloud with unbridled pleasure.

"Good?" Ash asked quietly.

"Like you wouldn't believe." Carmen tipped her head back and closed her eyes.

Ash slowly massaged the lotion into every pore, from the ends of her toes all the way up to her ankles. She switched feet and repeated the process. It was heavenly, and it didn't take long for Carmen's mind to start thinking about how good it would feel to have Ash's hands working their magic on other parts of her body.

A few moments later, she wondered if they had developed some kind of telepathic link as Ash slowly began to caress her calves, then the backs of her knees. The latter area was, unbeknown to Carmen up to that point in time, an erogenous zone. The minute Ash's fingers began to stroke there, Carmen shuddered with arousal, her nipples hardening against her silk bra. She opened her eyes and lifted her head, meeting Ash's intense gaze.

Ash didn't stop moving her fingers. She caressed in slow figures of eight, from the middle of Carmen's calves to the backs of her knees. In the next moment, she lengthened her stroke and took the tips of her fingers up to the back of Carmen's thigh, teasing at the skin there before repeating the gesture with her other hand on the other thigh.

"Ash…" Carmen breathed, her heart thudding.

Somehow that one word seemed to be all Ash needed. She gently let go of Carmen's leg and lowered it from her lap. Then she stood and took the small step that brought her to the edge of the bed. Her legs touched Carmen's where they dangled over the bed.

"Sure?" Ash asked softly.

Carmen didn't hesitate. "Yes."

Ash's smile was molten. She placed her hands on either side of Carmen and kissed her.

When Carmen inhaled sharply, Ash's tongue immediately sought entrance, and Carmen gave it willingly. The touch of their tongues made her moan. She arched her torso upwards, needing to feel Ash against her.

Ash responded, pushing Carmen onto her back and climbing onto the bed with her. She held herself over Carmen as she gazed down at her. "I want you so badly," she whispered. "But stop me if you're not comfortable, okay?"

Carmen nodded but seriously doubted she'd tell Ash to stop anytime soon. Her entire body blazed with desire, with the need to know what it would feel like to make love with this gorgeous woman. Oh sure, a small part of her still worried about certain mechanics, but that was soon forgotten as Ash skimmed her fingers down Carmen's neck to the bare skin above her left breast revealed by the cut of her dress.

Ash caressed gently, teasingly, gazing into Carmen's eyes the entire time. When she drifted lower and cupped Carmen's breast through the dress, Carmen moaned and pushed up into her hand.

Ash leaned down and kissed her, massaging slowly, using her thumb to rub over Carmen's nipple, which stood so proud, even through the dress *and* her bra. Ash's mouth plundered hers, becoming more passionate, more powerful, by the second.

Carmen threw her arms around Ash's neck and let her fingertips play with the shaved area at the back of Ash's head. The hair there was incredibly soft.

Ash groaned, and the throbbing between Carmen's legs jumped into hyperdrive.

She shifted and fumbled for the side zipper of her dress, needing to be naked, to offer more of herself to Ash.

Ash's hand stilled her. "Let me," she said hoarsely.

Carmen nodded and watched as Ash pulled the zipper down and peeled away the front of the dress to reveal most of Carmen's torso and bra-clad breasts.

"I want to see you," Ash whispered. "All of you." She stood and held out her hand.

Carmen took it and let Ash pull her to her feet. The dress needed only to be eased off her shoulder for it to fall to the floor in a gentle swish.

Ash reached behind Carmen and managed to unhook her bra at the first attempt.

Carmen smiled at her. "You've done that before."

Ash waggled her eyebrows. "A few times."

"Something new I'll need to learn."

"Oh, I'm sure you'll be fine. And trust me, you'll get your first practice very soon."

As the bra fell away, Ash switched her gaze to Carmen's body and sucked in an audible breath. "God, perfect." She cupped both breasts.

Carmen arched once more; Ash's hands were so gentle. Almost too gentle. "Touch me. I won't break," Carmen managed to get out. "I want you. Please."

Ash crushed her mouth to Carmen's and increased the pressure of her hands on Carmen's breasts. It was exquisite. She kneaded and caressed, pinching Carmen's nipples between her thumb and forefinger before pressing her palms into the whole of her breasts.

Carmen clung to Ash, arms around her waist, and frantically pulled the shirt from Ash's trousers. Then she started to work on the buttons at the front of the shirt.

Ash broke their kiss and her concentration on Carmen's breasts to give her room to open them all.

Carmen pushed the shirt open and stared. Ash's breasts were bigger than her own—she'd pretty much figured that out already—and the curves of them, held snug by the white bra, were more enticing than she would have ever imagined. She leaned forward and kissed, softly, at the top of each curve, then licked a line all the way along the top of each bra cup.

Ash swayed and hissed out a breath.

"Okay?" Carmen asked.

"Very. Let me take this off." Ash pointed at her shirt.

"And these too." Carmen tugged at the waistband of her trousers.

Ash did as she was told and soon stood before Carmen in her bra and underwear.

"Now I get to try this too." Hesitantly, Carmen reached behind Ash and prayed she wouldn't fumble. It couldn't be that difficult, could it? *I mean, I've been putting on and taking off my own bra for about thirty years now.* She found the clasp with her fingertips, figured out it was three hooks, and *voila*, unsnapped it at the first attempt.

"Very good," Ash said.

Carmen grinned. "Piece of cake."

Then words deserted her as she peeled the bra down Ash's arms, revealing gorgeously shaped breasts that her hands—and, much to her shock, mouth—ached to touch. She moved back in and rubbed her thumbs carefully over Ash's nipples.

Once again Ash hissed out a breath, and Carmen, emboldened, this time swiped her tongue over one of the hard buds.

Dear God. She licked again before taking the nipple between her lips and pulling slightly. *Jesus, that's incredible.*

Everything south of her belly throbbed and ached with an intensity that was almost painful. She licked and sucked on Ash's nipples until Ash grabbed at her shoulders and growled, "I need to lie down if you're going to keep doing that."

Carmen sighed happily and stepped back. "Then let's lie down."

They stripped off their underwear, eased onto the bed together, and lay side by side, close but not quite touching.

"Still okay?" Ash asked.

Carmen shyly looked down Ash's body, taking in the way her breasts shaped themselves now she was on her side, the flatness of her abdomen, the small patch of curls between her legs. *This is her body. The woman I'm falling in love with. And I just want to touch her. Feel her. Love her.*

"Oh, yes." Carmen reached for her.

They took their time, but it wasn't necessarily gentle. They ebbed and flowed between moments of pure tenderness that made tears prick at Carmen's eyes and high passion that ripped long moans from her throat.

When Ash pushed her onto her back and covered her with her body, Carmen shuddered with how perfect it felt. Ash spent many minutes worshipping Carmen's breasts, laving them with her tongue until Carmen thought she might come from that alone.

Ash moved down her body, placing open-mouthed kisses over her ribs. Everywhere her lips touched sent more fire through Carmen's veins.

"I'd love to taste you." Ash gazed up at her, her eyes intense, her breathing heavy. "But it's okay if that's not something you'd like."

The thought of Ash's mouth on her had Carmen swooning. "Oh God, yes. Please."

Ash dipped her head and trailed her tongue along Carmen's belly, then moved down licking and nipping at the inside of Carmen's thighs.

Carmen thrust herself up towards her, not caring how wanton it might seem, merely desperate for Ash's mouth to find her, and soon. She was aching with need, desperate to know how it would feel to surrender to Ash this way.

The first touch of Ash's tongue in her wetness made her gasp. The second made her groan. Then Ash started a rhythm of long, slow strokes that made every nerve in Carmen's body stand at attention. When, a few moments later, her orgasm swept through her, Carmen clutched at Ash's arms where they held her hips down and cried out her pleasure.

"Still with me?" Ash traced a lazy pattern with her fingertips across Carmen's gently rounded belly. God, how she loved this belly, loved every curve of Carmen's body.

"Mhmm. Sorry, I'll be with you soon," Carmen mumbled.

"You take your time." Ash kissed her on the ribs, just below her heart. "I'm quite happy where I am."

God, was that an understatement. Making love to Carmen had been every bit as exciting as she'd expected. She'd tortured herself a few times the last couple of weeks with thoughts of how it might be, but it turned out she'd vastly underestimated.

Carmen was so sexy it took Ash's breath away. And *so* responsive. The way she moved her body into Ash's touches, the sounds she made. All of it had sent Ash extremely close to the edge of her own orgasm. She still throbbed. If Carmen wasn't ready to do anything in return, Ash might just have to deal with things herself to release the pressure.

"Do we have any water nearby?" Carmen lifted her head to look down her own body at Ash and smiled shyly. "Hi."

"Well, hello." Ash blew her a kiss. "Yes, I can get you some water." She eased away from Carmen's warmth and shimmied off the bed.

"Oh my God! Ash, your tattoo is fantastic."

Ash looked over her shoulder to see Carmen staring at her back. "Oh, yeah, of course! You've never seen it." She turned a little to look at her own back in the full-length mirror on the wall beside the bed. "You really like it?"

Carmen crawled to the edge of the bed and trailed her fingers over the phoenix's wings. "It's stunning." She met Ash's gaze in the mirror. "And it's so perfect for you."

Ash nodded and shivered as Carmen's fingers continued to trail over the design.

"It's also rather sexy." Carmen threw her a wink in the reflection.

"I'm glad you think so." Ash cleared her throat. "Let me get you that water." After finding a bottle in the minibar, she twisted the cap off and brought it back to the bed.

Carmen took the proffered bottle and gulped greedily before handing it back.

"Wow, you needed that." Ash took a few mouthfuls herself.

When she lowered the bottle back down, Carmen was staring at her, her gaze raking over Ash's naked body.

Ash swallowed hard. She put the bottle down on the bedside table.

"Come here." Carmen held out one hand. "Please."

Ash joined her on the bed. When Carmen pushed her swiftly onto her back, she let out a small yelp that turned into a moan as Carmen lay on top of her. The pleasing weight of her, pinning Ash to the bed, had her libido roaring back into top gear.

Carmen kissed her and pressed herself against Ash even more.

Ash wrapped her arms around Carmen's back, but they only got to stay there for a few moments since Carmen reached around and lifted Ash's arms above her head. "Leave them there? Please?" she asked huskily.

"Anything you want." Ash was on fire; Carmen taking charge like this was a delicious surprise.

Carmen smiled seductively at her, and Ash's heart almost stopped. Then Carmen was on the move, and Ash could only surrender. First stop was Ash's breasts, which Carmen seemed to revel in exploring. Ash's nipples ached from all the attention, but there was no way she would ask Carmen to stop.

When Carmen's mouth drifted further down her body, Ash tensed. "You don't have to; it's—"

"Shush." Carmen gazed up at her, over the swell of Ash's breasts. "I'm doing exactly what I want to do. Trust me."

Ash nodded slowly. "I do."

Carmen kissed Ash's belly before continuing on her way. Her first few touches, with both tongue and fingers, were tentative, but that was okay because Ash could barely breathe as it was. As Carmen's confidence grew, however, and her licks and caresses became firmer, Ash writhed beneath her, wondering if she would actually survive this. Carmen took her time, bringing Ash to the edge over and over again, whether by design or accident, and it was the perfect torture.

"Please, Carmen. Harder. There."

And Carmen gave her just what she needed, at just the right time, to send her over that delicious edge into pleasure-filled oblivion. Ash arched her hips off the bed, then collapsed back onto it with a loud exhale.

Carmen quickly crawled back up Ash's body and lay on top of her once more. Her eyes were wet as she gently cupped Ash's face. "My God, that was... You're so beautiful," Carmen whispered. "Sharing that with you was incredible."

"It…was." Ash sucked in a breath, needing to fill her lungs as well as push past the lump in her throat.

Carmen kissed her tenderly, and soft drops fell onto Ash's cheeks.

"Hey." Ash pulled back from the kiss. "Are you okay?"

Carmen nodded and wiped at her eyes. "I am. I'm just so happy. So incredibly happy." She inhaled deeply, then bit her bottom lip. "I'm in love with you, Ash. Completely and utterly in love with you." She looked a little afraid, as if unsure what Ash's response might be.

Ash's heart swelled with emotion. She'd dared to let go, to allow herself to love this woman, yet she'd still feared, deep down, that her feelings wouldn't be reciprocated. Hearing Carmen say those words and be the first to say them out loud meant everything. "It's true for me too. I love you. And I think I have for a while now."

"Oh, Ash." Carmen seemed to melt into her. She wrapped her arms around Ash and pressed their lips together in a tender kiss that rapidly became so much more. Soon they were perfectly entwined once again, skin hot and slick, mouths fused together as they explored each other's bodies. Their tiredness was set aside as their passion soared, and later—much, *much* later—they whispered their words of love once more and held each other close as sleep claimed them.

Epilogue

Ten months later

CARMEN GRIPPED ASH'S THIGHS AND couldn't help smiling as Ash swore softly above her. *Soon, darling, soon.* She focused back on her task and marvelled once again at how aroused making love to Ash could make *her*. Her own needs would have to wait, though; there wasn't even time for this, but Ash had looked so ridiculously sexy when Carmen had awoken, she hadn't been able to resist.

Moments later she upped her pace, rewarded by a long, wrenching groan and then, seconds after that, Ash's hips launching off the bed and her familiar guttural groan as she orgasmed. Carmen kissed her way back up Ash's body until she was wrapped in her arms. Their lips repeatedly met in soft kiss after soft kiss.

"You," Ash said in between kisses, "are so good at that."

"It helps that it's my absolute favourite thing to do to you."

Ash kissed her once more. "And yes, amazingly there *was* time for that. You were right. But now we really do have to get going, my love."

"I know. But thank you for indulging me." Carmen shot her a cheeky smile.

"Oh, trust me, the pleasure was all mine."

Two minutes later, they were rushing around the house, showering, packing the last items into their suitcases, and skipping coffee because there definitely wasn't time for that. Since moving in with Carmen, Ash had become the master of their morning routine, timing their coffee-making to perfection to fit with their leaving times—but not on days when Carmen ambushed her with morning sex. Carmen knew Ash wasn't ever going to complain, though, and she grinned at the thought.

Finally, they were out the door into the waiting cab. The ride out to Heathrow was relatively quick, and soon they were at the check-in desk.

"And you're flying to Vancouver today, yes?" the clerk asked as they handed over their passports.

"Yes!" Carmen said excitedly, and beside her Ash chuckled.

The check-in clerk, a young woman with flawless make-up and beautiful blonde hair, smiled at Carmen. She finished weighing and tagging their cases and handed back their passports. "Have a great time."

"Thank you!"

"You," Ash said as they walked away from the desk, "are being very cute right now."

"Am I?"

"You are. You're like a kid on Christmas Day."

Carmen laughed and hugged Ash to her. "Well, I can't help it. This is so exciting!"

Ash kissed her. "It is. I'm so happy we're doing this."

"Me too. Now, as you have left us plenty of time until boarding, of course"—Ash snorted with laughter—"that means I have time for a nice look in the shops once we're through security."

When Ash hung her head in her hands, Carmen guffawed.

They passed through security, then found a brasserie to have lunch. It wasn't until they sat down and arranged their hand luggage items near their feet that Ash asked the question Carmen had been anticipating ever since they'd left the house.

"Where's your laptop case?" Ash frowned deeply. "Have we left it somewhere?"

Before she could launch into full panic mode, Carmen placed a hand on her arm and gave her a warm smile. "Calm down. It's at home. Deliberately."

Ash stared at her. "Seriously?"

Although Carmen had done well to restructure her business, she still pulled some rather long hours two or three days a week. It was starting to ease, however, now that she'd hired not one but two more assistants, allowing her to enjoy her new home life a tad more. Ash had moved in about three months ago, and they were definitely still in their honeymoon phase. Although, Carmen thought, that hadn't worn off since Tamsyn and Maggie's wedding, and she honestly couldn't see it doing so for a long time yet. If ever.

"Yes, seriously." Carmen leaned forward and took Ash's hand. "This is our first big trip together. I didn't want any interruptions. So I had a long chat with myself and my three assistants and decided that this vacation is really going to be just that. A vacation."

"And how long did you hyperventilate after making that decision?" Ash's eyes twinkled.

"Oh, about three hours."

Ash laughed and tugged her closer for a quick kiss across the table. "You're amazing, and I love you."

"I love you too."

Their hotel in Vancouver was a delight. Only two blocks from the waterfront, it wasn't cheap, but they'd decided they could splurge for their three nights there.

Carmen rolled over to Ash's side of the huge bed and kissed her good morning.

"How did you sleep?"

Ash blinked a couple of times. "That is still being assessed. You?"

Carmen laughed and stretched. "I slept great. Want some coffee?"

The promise of coffee seemed to do wonders for Ash's state of consciousness, and she was quickly up and wrapped in one of the hotel's complimentary robes. While they sipped their coffees, they took the time to send some messages home, having promised a plethora of people that they would keep them up to date on their adventures. Given it was late afternoon in the UK and still school holidays, they weren't surprised when various responses pinged back almost instantly.

Carmen read hers and smiled, her heart expanding with every moment. "Felicity says hello and says that Peter is whisking her off to the south of France next week to celebrate their six-month anniversary."

"I like that man."

"I do too. He's good for her."

Ash snorted as she read something on her phone. "Message from Damian. He says you're not working hard enough to break me of my terrible travel habits if we had nearly three hours to kill at Heathrow before boarding."

Carmen laughed. "Did you tell him I engineered it that way so I could go shopping?"

Ash's expression brightened. "No! But I should. This. Time. Not. My. Fault," she mumbled as she tapped.

Carmen swallowed back a ball of emotion at her next message. "The next one's from Tristan."

Ash's looked up. "Yeah?"

Carmen took a breath before reading it aloud. "Mother's invited both of us to Christmas lunch this year! Says it's about time she got to know the man I love. I nearly died! Seems like you being with Ash has softened the old girl a bit. Thank you, thank you, thank you for deciding to come out to her too."

Ash stared at her. "She's invited Jean-Pierre? Seriously?"

Carmen sucked in a breath, her eyes dampening. "It appears so."

"Wow. That's amazing. She's really getting there, isn't she?"

"I think so. I know it's hard for her, but I'm so glad she's finally making the effort." She wiped at her eyes.

Coming out to her parents had been mildly scary. She'd briefly considered never doing so, thinking that perhaps it would make for an easier life. But she knew that would be unfair to Ash. When her mother had seemed sad that, once again, Tristan had declined Christmas lunch because he wanted to be with Jean-Pierre instead, Carmen had taken that as her cue. One Sunday she had told her parents about Ash, and her mother had taken the news calmly and matter-of-factly. Carmen didn't know if that was because her mother found it easier to think of two women together rather than two men or if she had softened her opinion. Her invite for Tristan's partner to be welcome at the next Christmas seemed to suggest the latter, which thrilled Carmen.

"Well." Ash leaned across the small table to give her a kiss. "I think it's great. Certainly, I'm happy—I never fancied heading into the lion's den alone this Christmas." Ash gave her a look of mock horror.

Carmen laughed. The next message was from Monica telling her everything was under control and not to worry, and she laughed some more.

"Sophie sends her love. She's all excited because Courtney is taking her shopping tomorrow for new sneakers." Ash grinned. "With rainbow laces. Apparently, Courtney's saying she might get some too."

"No! That's amazing."

Ash nodded, her smile wide. "It is."

They looked at each other for a moment, and Carmen knew Ash was thinking exactly the same thing: *We are so lucky*.

"So, um, before we head out to pick up the rental car, I have a surprise for you." Ash walked round to Carmen's chair and held out her hand.

Carmen allowed herself to be tugged upright. "What's going on?"

Ash blushed. "Well, I kind of wanted to treat you to something. Something special. Just because." She pulled Carmen into her arms. "I love you, and I always want to make you happy."

"Oh, you do, my love. Always." Carmen kissed the tip of Ash's nose.

"Good. But I figure it can't hurt to add a little extra in now and then." She waggled her eyebrows.

Carmen laughed.

"I upgraded our car. To a convertible. I know that was your dream, so…"

Carmen gazed at Ash, her love for this woman consuming her. *How did I get so lucky?* "You…you are incredible." Tears pricked at her eyes.

Ash held her close. "I think maybe we're just incredible together."

"We are. And I don't ever want that to stop." Carmen's heart thumped as Ash grabbed her and kissed her as if there was no tomorrow.

Other Books from Ylva Publishing

www.ylva-publishing.com

The Long Shot
A.L. Brooks

ISBN: 978-3-96324-247-2
Length: 266 pages (93,000 words)

Talented golfer Morgan has never won a major but she's so close—no thanks to her famous, sexist, golfing dad.

Career-focused TV producer Adrienne is making a documentary on rising-star Morgan. The only problem is that the irritatingly attractive golfer treats Adrienne's plan like an invasion of privacy.

A lesbian sport romance on fierce desires and risking careers to win the ultimate prize.

Changing the Script
Lee Winter

ISBN: 978-3-96324-296-0
Length: 317 pages (104,000 words)

LA-based indie filmmaker Alex Levitin finds herself in New Zealand to save the "worst movie ever". Things might go easier if she didn't almost run over the standoffish local cop, Sam Keegan, and if the film wasn't being sabotaged. As Alex and Sam reluctantly join forces to find the set saboteur, attraction flares.

A funny, small-town lesbian romance about clashing cultures and daring to dream.

The Roommate Arrangement
Jae

ISBN: 978-3-96324-279-3
Length: 333 pages (119,000 words)

Comedian Steph hopes to finally get her big break in LA. But to afford the rent, she needs a roommate. Enter Rae, a former cop guarding her wounded soul behind a tough exterior. At first, they clash horribly, but bit by bit, Steph breaks through the walls Rae has built around her.

Falling in love is no laughing matter in this opposites-attract lesbian romance with a bit of fake relationship.

The Words Shimmer
Jenn Matthews

ISBN: 978-3-96324-243-4
Length: 257 pages (80,000 words)

Anatomy lecturer Ruby has little in common with paramedic Mel, even though they've teamed up on a school garden project. Uptight, perfectionist Ruby would rather be anywhere else but in a garden full of children. Brash Mel loves kids and getting muddy, but struggles with her secret dyslexia. How can they ever connect?

A sweet, lesbian romance about growing something unexpected from the roots up.

About A.L. Brooks

A.L. Brooks was born in the UK but currently resides in Frankfurt, Germany, and over the years she has lived in places as far afield as Aberdeen and Australia. She works 9–5 in corporate financial systems and her dream is to take early retirement. Like, tomorrow, please. She loves her gym membership, and is very grateful for it as she also loves dark chocolate. She enjoys drinking good wine and craft beer, trying out new recipes to cook, and learning German. Travelling around the world and reading lots and lots (and lots) of books are also things that fight for time with her writing. Yep, she really needs that early retirement.

CONNECT WITH A.L. BROOKS
Website: www.albrookswriter.com
Facebook: www.facebook.com/albrookswriter
Twitter: @albrookswriter1
E-Mail: albrookswriter@gmail.com

Dare to Love
© 2020 by A.L. Brooks

ISBN: 978-3-96324-361-5

Also available as e-book.

Published by Ylva Publishing, legal entity of Ylva Verlag, e.Kfr.

Ylva Verlag, e.Kfr.
Owner: Astrid Ohletz
Am Kirschgarten 2
65830 Kriftel
Germany

www.ylva-publishing.com

First edition: 2020

No part of this book may be reproduced, scanned, or distributed in any printed or electronic form without permission. Please do not participate in or encourage piracy of copyrighted materials in violation of the author's rights. Thank you for respecting the hard work of this author.

This is a work of fiction. Names, characters, places, and incidents either are a product of the author's imagination or are used fictitiously, and any resemblance to locales, events, business establishments, or actual persons—living or dead—is entirely coincidental.

Credits
Edited by Sandra Gerth
Cover Design and Print Layout by Streetlight Graphics

Printed in Great Britain
by Amazon

58480784R00162